TEAM DE

TEAM DELTA

First edition. July 1, 2024.

ISBN: 979-8227518217

Written by Brian Leslie.

Table of Contents

INTRODUCTION

The relentless ticking of the clock echoed through the tense silence as four elite Special Forces teams raced against time to locate and rescue a highly valuable prisoner of war. Captain James Rodriguez of Team Alpha gripped the stock of his assault rifle, sweat beading on his brow as his squad hacked through the dense jungle undergrowth. Their target: an underground bunker where the POW was rumored to be held.

Miles away, Lieutenant Emily Thompson led Team Bravo up the treacherous mountain peaks, her ice axe biting into the frozen rock as they closed in on a remote enemy stronghold. Using advanced thermal imaging, they scouted for signs of the captive, the biting winds whipping their combat gear.

In the blistering desert expanse, Sergeant Miguel Ramirez rallied Team Charlie, their tan combat fatigues blending with the golden sands. Intelligence suggested the prisoner was inside a fortified compound, its walls lined with hostile forces ready to unleash hell.

And near the pounding surf, Major David Reynolds commanded Team Delta, expertly slipping past the perimeter guards of a coastal enemy camp. Their night vision goggles scanned the shadows as they searched building by building for the captured soldier.

The teams' radios crackled with encrypted updates - the POW was a high-value target, a Special Operations officer captured during a botched raid. He possessed critical intel that could shift the tides of the covert war they waged. Failure was not an option.

Adrenaline spiked as Team Alpha discovered a camouflaged entrance to the underground lair. With weapons raised, they descended into the blackness, following a maze of damp corridors to a heavy steel door. Explosive breaches blew it open, and they stormed the chamber - only to find it empty, save for bloodstains on the concrete floor.

Simultaneously, Team Bravo rappelled over the high walls of the mountain stronghold. Silenced gunfire and hand-to-hand combat ensued as they fought through the heavily guarded facility. But the prisoner had been moved, the cell empty and abandoned.

The desert sun seared as Team Charlie traded bullets with the enemy forces guarding the compound's entrance. Grenades detonated, shrapnel whizzing through the haze as they pushed forward with grim determination. Yet their target remained elusive.

It was Team Delta who finally struck gold. As they infiltrated the coastal encampment, night vision revealed a makeshift cell - and inside, the battered but alive POW. They swiftly cut him free and fought their way out under withering enemy fire.

As the smoke cleared, the daring rescue was an against-all-odds success. But it had come at a steep cost - two team members critically wounded, the others bearing scars of the brutal battle. The POW himself was in dire condition from weeks of torture and interrogation.

On the long flight back to base, the grim-faced operators remained on high alert, knowing the enemy would soon be in pursuit. Captain Rodriguez looked at the faces of his brothers and sisters in arms and saw the strength that had carried them through hell.

Once back on friendly soil, a grim debriefing followed as military intelligence hastily extracted the sensitive information from the liberated POW. The news was worse than anyone could have imagined - the enemy had a terrifying new bioweapon in development, one with the power to devastate the nation.

There was no time for rest as new orders came down. Using the intel gained, the Special Forces teams would be deployed once more, this time to infiltrate the enemy's most secure research facility and destroy the bioweapon by any means necessary.

As they prepared to depart on their next mission, Captain Rodriguez knew the stakes could not be higher. But he also knew his team had what it took to overcome any obstacle. They were the best of the best, forged from blood and fire. And they would fight to the last breath to keep their country safe from this terrifying new threat. No matter the cost, they would not fail.

CHAPTER 1

Deep in the dense jungle, Captain James Rodriguez led Team Alpha as they hacked through the undergrowth with military precision. The foliage hung heavy around them, damp with the humidity that seemed to press down on their shoulders like a living, breathing entity. Their mission objective was clear: locate and rescue the high-value POW before time ran out.

The tense silence was broken only by the relentless ticking of the clock, each second hammering home the urgency of their task. "Remember, we're on borrowed time," Captain Rodriguez said, his voice low and steady. "Stay sharp." The team members nodded in silent agreement, their eyes constantly scanning the surrounding area for any signs of danger or potential leads.

"Captain, I've got movement up ahead," whispered Sergeant Jackson, his gaze locked onto something just beyond the thick curtain of leaves. Captain Rodriguez motioned for the team to halt, his piercing brown eyes narrowing as he assessed the situation.

"Jackson, Diaz, flank left and right. The rest of you, hold your positions," he ordered, his voice barely audible above the rustling of the leaves. As the two soldiers moved into position, Captain Rodriguez couldn't help but think back to the countless missions he'd led before this one. They had faced numerous perils together, and each time they had emerged victorious. He knew they could do it again, but the weight of responsibility still pressed heavily upon him.

"Team, I want eyes on that target. If it's hostile, neutralize it. If not, let's keep moving," he said, gripping his assault rifle tightly. The team acknowledged the order with curt nods, their expressions betraying no hint of fear or uncertainty.

"Target acquired, sir. It's just a capybara," reported Diaz, easing the tension somewhat. Captain Rodriguez allowed himself a brief smile, acknowledging the soldier's observation before quickly refocusing on the mission at hand.

"Alright, let's keep moving," he said, his tone resolute. The team fell back into formation, their progress slow but steady through the oppressive jungle.

As they continued on their path, Captain Rodriguez couldn't help but feel the pressure mounting. Every tick of the clock was a reminder that the life of the high-value POW hung in the balance, and it was up to him and his team to bring them home safely. With each step, he pushed aside his own fears and doubts, focusing only on the mission and the unwavering trust he had in his team.

"Stay focused, Team Alpha," he reminded them, his voice firm yet reassuring. "We'll find our target, and we will bring them home. I have faith in each and every one of you."

"Thank you, sir," replied his team members in unison, their determination and loyalty shining through despite the oppressive atmosphere of the jungle. Together, they pressed on, the relentless ticking of the clock driving them forward as they closed in on their objective.

The sweat on Captain Rodriguez's brow glistened as it trickled down and merged with the jungle floor. Clutching his assault rifle, he scanned the dense foliage surrounding them, anticipating the unseen dangers lurking in the shadows. His team followed closely behind, their movements synchronized, and their senses sharpened like a predator stalking its prey.

"Watch your footing," Rodriguez warned, his voice barely above a whisper. "And keep an eye out for anything out of the ordinary."

"Copy that, sir," replied Diaz, stepping carefully over a tangle of roots while sweeping his weapon from side to side.

As Team Alpha advanced, they were met with challenges only seasoned soldiers could navigate. A sudden rustle in the bushes sent hearts pounding, but Martinez, quick on his feet, identified the source as a large iguana before it could cause alarm. The squad exchanged tense smiles, grateful for the reprieve, but remained vigilant.

"Damn, these vines are relentless," muttered Thompson, hacking through the undergrowth with his machete, opening up a narrow path for the others.

"Stay focused," Captain Rodriguez reminded himself, his thoughts racing alongside the ever-ticking clock. "One step at a time, and we'll get there."

"Sir, looks like we've got a steep incline coming up," reported Jenkins, squinting through the darkness at the formidable obstacle ahead.

"Alright, team, ropes out. We're going vertical." Rodriguez didn't miss a beat, his leadership shining through in even the most challenging situations. The squad quickly secured their gear and prepared to scale the treacherous slope.

"Cover me, I'll go first," ordered Rodriguez, knowing the risk involved in being the first to ascend. His muscles strained as he expertly climbed, setting anchors along the way to ensure his teammates' safety. One by one, they followed suit, their trust in each other evident in their swift and efficient movements.

"Good job, team," Rodriguez praised as they regrouped at the top of the incline, sweat pouring from their bodies but determination burning brightly in their eyes. "We're getting closer."

"Sir," interrupted Diaz, his voice low and urgent. "I've spotted an enemy patrol up ahead."

"Stay down, everyone," commanded Rodriguez, his mind racing through tactical options while he gripped his rifle even tighter. The weight of responsibility bore down on him – one wrong move could jeopardize the mission and the lives of his team.

"Let's wait for them to pass, then we'll continue. Stay alert and be ready for anything." Captain Rodriguez's heart pounded in his chest, but his exterior remained calm and composed.

"Copy that, sir," whispered his squad, their eyes locked on the lurking danger, their fingers poised on their triggers, and their unwavering trust in their leader guiding them through the perilous jungle.

The air hung heavy, suffocating Team Alpha as they pressed forward, the foliage closing in around them like a vice. Sunlight struggled to break through the dense canopy overhead, casting eerie shadows that seemed to dance and twist with every step they took. Captain Rodriguez's eyes scanned the murky gloom, his instincts razor-sharp and attuned to the smallest of movements.

"Keep moving, stay focused," he ordered, his voice barely more than a whisper in the oppressive silence. With each step, the humidity clung to their skin, their sweat-soaked uniforms offering no reprieve from the relentless jungle heat.

Rodriguez felt a bead of sweat trickle down his temple, but he didn't bother to wipe it away. There was no time for discomfort. His mind raced, analyzing every possible scenario, anticipating threats lurking behind each tree trunk and undergrowth.

"Sir, we've got a fork in the path ahead," Corporal Martinez reported, her voice betraying a hint of uncertainty.

"Take a moment to assess, then choose. Trust your instincts, Corporal," Rodriguez replied, his unwavering confidence in his team shining through.

Martinez nodded, taking a deep breath before scanning the diverging paths. "Left, sir. It seems less traveled and more concealed."

"Good call, Martinez. Stick to the shadows and keep the pace up," Rodriguez commanded, following her lead. He knew the importance of adaptability in this unpredictable environment, and he trusted his team implicitly.

"Thank you, sir," she responded, determination etched across her face as she led the way into the darker recesses of the jungle.

As they advanced, the encroaching vegetation threatened to choke their progress. Branches clawed at their faces, and vines twisted around their ankles like serpents waiting to strike. But Rodriguez moved with purpose, slicing through the undergrowth with his machete, determined to carve a path to their objective.

"Captain, we're making good progress," Sergeant Lewis reported, his voice strained from the physical exertion. "But we should be prepared for anything. This jungle holds many secrets."

"Agreed, Sergeant. We remain vigilant and adapt as needed," Rodriguez responded, his mind already strategizing for their next move. His determination to complete this mission and protect his team fueled his every step, driving him deeper into the heart of darkness that enveloped them.

"Copy that, sir," Lewis acknowledged, his eyes never leaving the treacherous terrain ahead.

With each passing moment, the weight of responsibility grew heavier on Rodriguez's shoulders, but he refused to let it break him. He was more than just a leader; he was a guardian, a mentor, and a protector. And he would stop at nothing to bring his team safely through this perilous jungle, no matter what challenges lay ahead.

The air hung heavy and damp, suffocating the team as they pressed forward. Captain Rodriguez's senses were on high alert, his eyes scanning for any signs of danger lurking in the shadows.

"Captain," Corporal Martinez whispered, her voice tense. "Movement, northeast, about fifty meters. Could be enemy patrol."

"Understood, Corporal. Team Alpha, prepare for contact. Proceed with caution," Rodriguez ordered, his voice low but firm, as he gripped his assault rifle tighter.

They moved silently, each member of Team Alpha communicating through hand signals, their trust in one another absolute. Rodriguez felt a surge of pride in his team; their professionalism and skill were unmatched.

As they crept closer to the potential threat, Specialist Thompson motioned to the others, his fingers forming the shape of a snake. Rodriguez understood immediately – venomous snakes, camouflaged within the undergrowth, blocked their path.

"Team, new plan," Rodriguez whispered into his headset. "Thompson, clear a safe route through those snakes. Lewis, keep your eyes on that potential patrol. We proceed with extreme care."

"Copy that, Captain," Thompson replied, pulling out his snake-handling equipment and expertly creating a safe path for the team.

"Captain," Lewis said, straining to see through the dense foliage. "Patrol confirmed. Four hostiles, armed."

"Thank you, Sergeant," Rodriguez acknowledged, his mind racing. "Let them pass. We'll continue once they're out of sight."

"Affirmative, sir," Lewis replied, his gaze locked on the enemy soldiers.

The team held their breath as the patrol passed, mere meters from their position. Rodriguez could feel the tension radiating off his teammates, their fingers itching to engage the enemy. But the mission came first, and they needed to stay focused.

"Alright, they're gone," Lewis reported quietly. "We're clear to move."

"Good. Team Alpha, let's keep moving," Rodriguez commanded, his heart pounding in his chest. "Stay vigilant, and remember: we leave no trace behind."

As they continued their treacherous journey, it was clear that the jungle had more surprises in store for them. But with Captain Rodriguez leading the way, Team Alpha knew they were in the best hands possible. Together, they would face whatever challenges lay ahead, determined to complete their mission and bring each other home safely.

Captain Rodriguez's boots sank into the damp jungle soil, his senses heightened as he guided Team Alpha deeper into the enemy's domain. His instincts were on high alert, feeling the weight of their mission bearing down on him. The POW's life hung in the balance, and every second mattered.

"Captain," whispered Sergeant Lewis, "I've got movement up ahead, 2 o'clock."

"Stay sharp, team," Rodriguez ordered, his grip tightening around his assault rifle. "Minimal noise. Let's see what we're dealing with."

As the team crept closer, Rodriguez could feel the tension growing within his squad. The jungle seemed to close in around them, its heavy foliage casting ominous shadows over their path. All around them, the sounds of the jungle had gone silent, as if holding its breath in anticipation.

"Sir, it's a sentry post," reported Private Thompson, peering through the leaves. "Two hostiles."

"Copy that," Rodriguez murmured, his mind racing. This close to their objective, stealth was paramount. "Thompson, take the one on the left. Lewis, you've got the right. Silenced weapons only. On my mark."

"Roger that, Captain," both soldiers acknowledged, their voices barely audible.

Rodriguez's heart pounded in his chest, his eyes locked on the enemy guards. He had to trust his team's abilities, and he knew they wouldn't let him down. With a quick nod, he gave the signal.

"Mark."

Two muffled shots rang out in unison, and the enemy sentries crumpled to the ground. Team Alpha moved forward, their focus unwavering.

"Good work," Rodriguez praised quietly. "We need to find that entrance. Keep your eyes peeled."

"Sir, I think I found something," Corporal Martinez called out, crouching beside a seemingly innocuous patch of vines and brush.

"Show me," Rodriguez ordered, joining Martinez at the site.

Martinez pulled back the foliage, revealing a concealed entrance to an underground lair. The hairs on the back of Rodriguez's neck stood up, as if electricity crackled in the air around him. This was it.

"Team Alpha," he whispered, his voice laced with anticipation, "prepare to breach. Our target is close. Watch each other's backs, and remember: we're bringing that POW home."

"Affirmative, Captain," the team responded in unison, their determination evident in their voices.

As Team Alpha readied themselves for the descent into darkness, Captain Rodriguez took one last moment to survey the jungle around them. They had come so far, faced countless dangers, and now their objective was within reach. He knew the challenges ahead would test every ounce of their skill and teamwork, but there was no turning back.

"Let's do this," he said, leading his team into the unknown.

The darkness of the underground lair loomed before them, swallowing any trace of light and leaving only a void. Captain Rodriguez's heart raced as the adrenaline coursed through his veins, but he remained composed, gripping his assault rifle tightly.

"Thompson, you've got point," Rodriguez ordered, his voice steady despite the trepidation he felt. "Ramirez, Reynolds, cover our six. We don't know what awaits us down there."

"Understood, Captain," replied Lieutenant Thompson, her calm authority barely betraying the weight of the responsibility she carried. She raised her weapon, took a deep breath, and stepped into the abyss, the rest of Team Alpha following close behind.

Descending into the pitch-black tunnel, they relied on their night vision goggles to navigate the seemingly endless path. Their footsteps echoed softly against the damp walls, amplifying the tension that filled each member of the team.

"Stay sharp, everyone," Rodriguez reminded them, his mind racing with thoughts of the dangers they could face at any moment. "Hayes is counting on us."

"Captain, I've got movement up ahead," Thompson whispered urgently, her tone alerting the others to prepare for whatever lay in wait.

"Everyone, hold position," Rodriguez commanded, raising his weapon and focusing on the area ahead. His senses were heightened, every sound echoing within the confines of the tunnel. Sweat beaded on his brow as he strained to identify the potential threat.

"Could be a patrol," Ramirez suggested, his voice low and controlled. "Or worse, another booby trap."

"Agreed," said Major Reynolds, his experience evident in his steady demeanor. "Proceed with caution."

"Copy that," Rodriguez replied, his instincts guiding their path. "On my mark... three, two, one, move!"

Team Alpha advanced cautiously, weapons raised and ready for whatever awaited them. As they turned a corner, they came face-to-face with a lone enemy soldier. In an instant, the soldier's lifeless body crumpled to the ground, expertly silenced by Lieutenant Thompson.

"Nice shot," Rodriguez commended her as they continued onward, his determination unwavering.

"Thanks, Captain," she replied, her focus already back on the mission at hand.

"Stay vigilant," he reminded them, knowing they were getting closer to their objective. He could almost feel the presence of Lieutenant Hayes, their captured comrade, just out of reach.

"Sir, I've got something," Ramirez called out, his voice barely above a whisper. "There's a door up ahead."

"Let's move," Rodriguez ordered, his heart pounding in anticipation. The team approached the door cautiously, weapons at the ready.

"Reynolds, check for any traps," the Captain instructed. Reynolds nodded and carefully examined the door, his practiced hands quickly determining it was safe.

"Clear, Captain," Reynolds confirmed, stepping aside to allow Rodriguez to make the call.

"Alright, Team Alpha," Rodriguez whispered, his voice laced with equal parts determination and apprehension. "On my count, we breach. Be prepared for anything."

"Affirmative, Captain," the team responded in unison.

"Three... two... one... breach!" And with that, Team Alpha stormed into the unknown, bracing themselves for whatever challenges lie ahead.

CHAPTER 2

The moonless night was pierced by the sudden burst of gunfire, illuminating the dense forest where Lieutenant Samuel Hayes had been silently moving. He had been on a covert operation, but now, it seemed, he was walking into a trap. General Viktor Kozlov and his forces had ambushed him, their cold blue eyes gleaming in the darkness as they closed in.

"Contact! Enemy fire!" Hayes shouted into his radio, immediately diving behind a fallen tree for cover. Bullets ripped through the foliage around him, leaves and branches falling like rain. His mind raced, trying to assess the situation. "Thompson, I'm pinned down. Kozlov's men have me surrounded."

"Copy that, Sam. Hold tight; we're coming for you," Lieutenant Emily Thompson replied, her calm voice a stark contrast to the chaos engulfing the forest.

Hayes peeked above his cover, quickly counting at least a dozen armed soldiers. They knew he was here, and they were closing in fast. He gritted his teeth, knowing he had to buy time for Thompson and the others to arrive. With a deep breath, he steadied his weapon and began to return fire.

As bullets whizzed past his head, Hayes' resourcefulness shone through. He fired in calculated bursts, taking out two assailants with well-placed shots. Despite the overwhelming odds, he remained focused and composed, his training keeping him alive in this deadly game of cat and mouse.

"Sam, we're en route. ETA three minutes," Thompson reported, her steady voice offering reassurance in the midst of chaos.

"Roger that," Hayes responded, sweat dripping down his brow as he expended the last of his ammunition. He glanced around, searching for something to use as a makeshift weapon. Spotting a large rock nearby, he grabbed it and hurled it towards an approaching soldier, striking him in the head and sending him tumbling to the ground.

"Nice shot, Sam," Thompson commended, her voice crackling through the radio. "Keep it up; we're almost there."

Hayes allowed himself a fleeting moment of satisfaction before refocusing on the task at hand. He knew he couldn't afford to let his guard down for even a second. In the shadows of the forest, Kozlov's forces continued their advance, determined to capture the elusive Lieutenant Hayes.

As the firefight raged on, only one thought consumed Hayes: survival. He had no intention of becoming a prisoner in the hands of General Viktor Kozlov, the ruthless commander known for his chilling disregard for human life. Hayes' loyalty to his comrades and country drove him to fight with every ounce of strength he possessed.

"Sam, we've got your back! Move!" Thompson's voice cut through the din of gunfire and explosions. Hayes seized the opportunity, darting from his cover and sprinting towards the rendezvous point. His heart pounded in his chest as he felt the bullets whizzing by, but he refused to give in to fear.

"Almost there, Emily!" he gasped, pushing his legs to carry him faster. As he neared the extraction point, he could see the faint outline of his comrades waiting for him. But still, Kozlov's forces pursued relentlessly, and as Hayes dove into the safety of his team's arms, he knew that this was far from over.

The shadows cast by the setting sun grew longer as Hayes scrambled through the underbrush, his breath ragged and heavy. Kozlov's forces were relentless in their pursuit, but he refused to give up without a fight.

"Delta team, flank left. Alpha team, cut off his escape route," General Kozlov's voice crackled over the radio with cold precision, betraying no sense of urgency or panic. He knew that victory was within his grasp, and all he needed to do was tighten the noose around his prey.

"Copy that, sir," responded the unit commanders, their words charged with determination. The soldiers moved swiftly and silently, executing Kozlov's orders with deadly efficiency.

"Sam, where are you?" Thompson's voice sounded in his earpiece, her tone laced with concern. "We need to regroup and get out of here."

"I'm trying, Emily!" Hayes gasped, his mind racing to conjure up a plan of escape. "But they're closing in on me from all sides."

"Stay focused, Sam. You can do this," she urged him, her unwavering confidence in him providing a much-needed boost to his morale.

As Hayes darted between trees and boulders, he could feel the enemy drawing nearer. Just when he thought he had found an opening, Kozlov's tactical brilliance shone through once more. A well-aimed shot caught Hayes in the leg, sending him tumbling to the ground, his vision blurring with pain.

"Got you," a soldier hissed triumphantly, standing over him with a rifle trained at his head. Hayes' heart sank as he realized that Kozlov had finally outmaneuvered him.

"Mission accomplished, General," the soldier reported, his voice devoid of emotion. "We have Lieutenant Hayes in custody."

"Excellent work," Kozlov replied, a sinister satisfaction creeping into his voice. "Bring him to me."

Hayes struggled to remain conscious as he was roughly hauled to his feet and dragged away by Kozlov's soldiers. As the darkness closed in around him, he whispered a silent prayer for strength and resilience in the face of the torturous ordeal that awaited him.

The sound of dripping water echoed through the cold, dimly lit chamber as Hayes stirred, disoriented and groggy from the drugs that had been administered during his extraction. He blinked, trying to bring his surroundings into focus, but his vision refused to clear.

"Where am I?" he wondered aloud, his voice hoarse and weak. Panic began to set in as he realized the gravity of his situation: captured by General Kozlov, alone, and at the mercy of a merciless enemy.

The sharp sting of ice-cold water on his face jolted Hayes back to full consciousness. He jerked involuntarily, only to find himself bound tightly to a metal chair. The cold seeped into his bones as his bare feet rested on the damp stone floor. His heart raced as he struggled to suppress his mounting fear and desperation.

"Ah, Lieutenant Hayes, so good of you to join us," Kozlov's voice cut through the air like a knife, his chilling presence sending shivers down Hayes' spine. The general stepped out of the shadows, his blue eyes boring into Hayes.

"Comfortable?" Kozlov asked mockingly, studying Hayes with an unnerving intensity. The lieutenant refused to respond, gritting his teeth in defiance.

"Very well," Kozlov continued, unfazed by Hayes' silence. "Let's get straight to the point. You will tell me everything you know about your operation and its intended targets."

Hayes clenched his jaw, struggling to maintain control over the panic that threatened to consume him. *Stay strong, remember your training,* he thought, trying to block out the pain that throbbed in his leg from the gunshot wound.

"Go to hell," Hayes spat through gritted teeth. Kozlov raised an eyebrow but remained eerily calm.

"Very well. I had hoped we could do this the easy way, but it appears you need some... persuading," Kozlov said, a cruel smile playing on his lips. He turned to one of his soldiers, who handed him a pair of pliers.

Hayes' blood ran cold as Kozlov approached him, the instrument of torture glinting ominously under the dim light. Despite every fiber of his being screaming at him to fight back, he knew there was no escape. He steeled himself for the agony that was sure to follow.

"Last chance, Lieutenant," Kozlov warned. Hayes swallowed hard, his eyes fixed on the pliers as he mentally prepared himself for what was to come.

"Never," he whispered, his voice barely audible but filled with determination.

"Suit yourself," Kozlov replied coldly, gripping one of Hayes' fingers tightly with the pliers. The pain that followed was indescribable; it ripped through Hayes, leaving him gasping for breath as his vision blurred and darkened at the edges.

"Ready to talk?" Kozlov asked, his voice dripping with sadistic pleasure. Hayes fought through the haze of pain, summoning every ounce of strength he possessed to meet Kozlov's gaze.

"Is that all you got?" he taunted, his voice wavering slightly. Kozlov's eyes flashed with rage, but he maintained his chilling composure.

"Very well," Kozlov responded, his voice colder than ever. "This is just the beginning."

As the torture continued, each passing moment felt like an eternity to Hayes. He clung to his resolve, knowing that giving in now would endanger not only his own life but also those of his comrades and countless innocent people. *Stay strong, Sam,* he told himself over and over again, refusing to let Kozlov break him.

With each blow, Lieutenant Samuel Hayes felt his consciousness slipping further away. Kozlov's relentless interrogation tactics had pushed him to the brink of collapse, but still he would not break. He focused on a single thought, repeating it like a mantra: *I will not betray my comrades or my country.*

"Tell me the location of your base," Kozlov demanded, his voice a low growl.

"Go to hell," Hayes spat, blood and defiance mingling in equal measure. Kozlov's fist collided with his jaw once more, sending searing pain radiating through his skull. But the lieutenant refused to succumb to the darkness that threatened to overtake him.

Just hold on, he told himself, gritting his teeth against the agony. *They'll come for you.*

"Kozlov's got Hayes," Captain Mitchell said grimly, looking up from the encrypted message he'd just decoded. Lieutenant Emily Thompson's heart dropped at the news, her hands tightening into fists as she fought to keep her emotions under control. She knew what Kozlov was capable of, and the thought of Sam enduring that monster's wrath made her blood run cold.

"Get the teams ready," she ordered, her voice steady despite the turmoil raging inside her. "We're going after him."

"Copy that, Lieutenant," Mitchell replied, springing into action as he relayed the orders to their fellow operatives.

Emily took a deep breath, steeling herself for the mission ahead. She knew they had little time to waste if they were to save Sam from Kozlov's clutches. As the Special Forces teams scrambled to mobilize, she couldn't help but think of the last time she'd seen Sam – his eyes grim, but determined, as they'd parted ways on their separate missions. *We'll get you out of there, Sam,* she promised silently, her resolve only growing stronger.

"Alpha Team, on me," she called out, watching as her squad of elite soldiers formed up around her. "We're going to get Hayes back, no matter what it takes."

"Oorah!" they chorused, their voices a united declaration of determination.

As the teams prepared for the mission ahead, Emily visualized the terrain they'd be facing; dense jungles and treacherous mountains stood between them and Sam's rescue. But no obstacle would deter them – they were relentless, driven by loyalty and a fierce sense of duty.

"Teams Alpha and Bravo, move out!" Emily commanded, leading her squad toward their transport. The roar of helicopter engines filled the air as they lifted off, each soldier focused on the task at hand: saving their captured comrade.

Through the pain and darkness, Sam clung to his unwavering belief in his fellow soldiers. He knew they would come for him – and when they did, Kozlov would finally face the full force of their wrath.

Emily Thompson's eyes darted across the array of satellite images, topographical maps, and intelligence reports laid out before her. The clock was ticking, and each second that passed brought Sam closer to a fate she refused to consider. She glanced over at Team Bravo, who were huddled around their own briefing table, tracing possible routes through treacherous mountain terrain.

"Intel suggests Hayes is being held in this compound," Emily said, circling the location on one of the maps. "Team Alpha will navigate the dense jungle surrounding the area, while Team Bravo scales these mountains to provide overwatch and sniper support."

"Copy that," responded Team Bravo's leader, Lieutenant Johnson, his eyes filled with steely determination.

"Time is not on our side, people," Emily continued, addressing both teams. "We need to move quickly and efficiently. Are there any concerns about the environment?"

"Jungle's always a mess," grumbled Sergeant Reynolds from Alpha Team. "But we've trained for this. We can handle it."

"Same goes for us," added Johnson, nodding toward his mountain-ready squad. "We're prepared for whatever these peaks throw at us."

"Good," Emily said, her voice steady but urgent. "Gather your gear and prep for extraction. This mission is time-sensitive; we can't afford any delays. Let's bring Hayes home."

"Oorah!" the teams chorused, their voices resolute and focused.

As they dispersed to gather their equipment, Emily couldn't help but feel the weight of the mission ahead. With each passing moment, Sam's situation grew more dire. She clenched her fists, steeling herself against the fear and doubt that threatened to creep in. *I won't let you down, Sam,* she thought fiercely. *We're coming for you.*

"Thompson, you good?" asked Reynolds, catching her eye as he hoisted a heavy rucksack onto his back.

"Of course," she replied, her voice firm and confident. "Just focused on the task at hand."

"Good," he said, nodding in approval. "We'll get him back. Count on it."

Emily's gaze returned to the maps, her mind already racing ahead to the challenges they would face. From navigating the treacherous jungle terrain to coordinating with Team Bravo on their mountain ascent, every aspect of the mission had to be executed flawlessly. She knew what was at stake, and failure was not an option.

"Alpha and Bravo, gear up and move out!" Emily commanded, watching as her fellow soldiers mobilized with practiced efficiency.

The two teams boarded separate helicopters, the downdraft from the rotor blades whipping up a frenzy of dust and debris. As the aircraft lifted off, Emily's thoughts were consumed by the mission – and the life hanging in the balance.

Hold on, Sam, she silently urged. *We're coming.*

Emily stood in the center of the makeshift training area, her eyes scanning the teams as they practiced their maneuvers. The raw determination etched on their faces was palpable, each movement precise and powerful. She could feel the camaraderie between them, forged by countless missions together and a shared desire to bring Sam home.

"Thompson, you're up!" called out Sergeant Davis from atop an obstacle. Emily, without hesitation, leaped onto the course and began navigating through it with agility and strength.

"Watch your footing on those rocks, Thompson!" shouted Reynolds from the sidelines, his brow furrowed with concern. "You slip up there, and we're one member down."

"Copy that," she replied, her voice steady as she carefully scaled the jagged wall before her. As she reached the top, she took a moment to look down at her teammates, their faces filled with trust and respect.

This mission was bigger than any individual – it was about loyalty to one another and to their country.

"Nice work, Lieutenant," praised Davis as Emily descended, her boots hitting the ground with a muted thud. "Alright, everyone, gather round for final debrief."

The soldiers huddled together, their breaths heavy from exertion but eyes unwaveringly focused on Emily as she relayed the latest intel.

"Time is of the essence, people," she stated firmly. "Kozlov won't hesitate to eliminate Sam if he thinks we're closing in. We need to be swift and silent."

"Alpha, you'll navigate the dense jungle terrain and rendezvous with Bravo at the base of the mountain," she continued, her gaze flicking between the teams. "Bravo, once we join forces, we'll ascend the treacherous peaks together. No room for error, understood?"

"Understood!" the teams chorused, their voices ringing out in unison.

"Then let's move out," Emily ordered, her heart pounding in her chest as the gravity of their mission settled upon her. Yet, she refused to let fear take hold, focusing instead on the trust she had in her comrades and their collective strength.

As they boarded their respective vehicles and prepared to embark on their dangerous journey, each soldier exchanged solemn nods, understanding the magnitude of what lay ahead. The engines roared to life, and with a final look at one another, they set off into the unknown – each determined to save their captured comrade, or die trying.

Emily stared ahead, her mind racing with thoughts of Sam and the challenges that awaited them. She knew the odds were stacked against them, but she also knew that together, they would face whatever lay ahead. *We won't fail you, Sam,* she vowed silently, as the horizon loomed closer. *We're coming for you.*

CHAPTER 3

Captain James Rodriguez stood at the head of a long steel table, his piercing brown eyes surveying the team leaders seated before him. Their faces were etched with lines of tension and focus, each one bearing the weight of responsibility for their respective teams. The secure briefing room was bathed in cold fluorescent light, casting sharp shadows across the maps and tactical equipment that littered the table.

"Remember, we're on the clock," Captain Rodriguez said, breaking the heavy silence. "As soon as the CO arrives, we need to be ready to receive our orders and move out."

His words hung in the air like a cloud of anticipatory smoke, thickening the already tense atmosphere. The room held its collective breath, waiting for the arrival of the man who would set their mission into motion.

The door swung open with a resounding creak, and a tall, imposing figure strode into the room. Commanding attention with every step, the commanding officer's presence filled the space, overshadowing the occupants with an aura of authority and urgency. His silver hair gleamed under the harsh lighting, framing a face chiseled from years of military service and steadfast determination.

"Listen up!" he barked, slamming a thick folder onto the table. The sound echoed through the room like a gunshot, alerting every muscle and nerve to snap to attention. "Our window is closing, and Lieutenant Hayes' life hangs in the balance. We've got intel suggesting he's being held in a mountainous region near the border. It's treacherous terrain, but if anyone can reach him, it's this team right here."

The CO's words cut through the air like a razor-sharp blade, slicing away any lingering doubt or hesitation. It was clear that time was of the essence, and there was no room for error. In the reflection of the commanding officer's unwavering gaze, Captain Rodriguez saw his own sense of duty and loyalty mirrored, a powerful reminder of what was at stake.

Captain Rodriguez's jaw tightened, his eyes narrowing as the gravity of the situation took hold. The flickering shadows in the room seemed to dance in time with the pulse pounding in his temples. He could almost feel the oppressive weight of the mountains bearing down on him, the cold wind biting at his exposed skin, a chilling reminder of what Lieutenant Hayes must be experiencing.

"Sir," Captain Rodriguez began, his voice low and steady despite the whirlwind of emotions churning within him. "We understand the urgency of this mission. What do we know about the enemy's defenses, their numbers? Any intel on potential weaknesses we can exploit?"

The commanding officer leaned forward, his hands gripping the edge of the table as he met Rodriguez's gaze with an intensity that matched his own. "Our sources indicate they're fortified deep within the mountain range, with patrols sweeping the surrounding area. It won't be easy getting in, but if there's a way, you'll find it."

"Understood, sir," Captain Rodriguez replied, his mind already racing through possible strategies and contingencies. This was more than just another mission; it was personal. He had trained with Lieutenant Hayes, fought alongside him, and would not rest until he brought him home safely. "We'll get him out of there, whatever it takes."

"Good. I expect nothing less from you and your team, Captain," the commanding officer said, his tone resolute. "Time is our greatest enemy now. You need to move quickly, and quietly. Make no mistake – this mission is as high-stakes as they come. Failure is not an option."

"Failure has never been an option for us, sir," Captain Rodriguez assured him, his words infused with the unmistakable conviction born from years of service and sacrifice. "We'll bring Lieutenant Hayes back, and the intel he carries with him."

"Very well," the commanding officer acknowledged, his expression softening ever so slightly. "I trust you and your team, Captain. You have your orders. Prepare your team and move out as soon as possible."

"Roger that, sir," Captain Rodriguez confirmed, offering a crisp salute before turning on his heel, his mind already focused on the task ahead. The stakes had never been higher, but he knew that with swift action and unwavering determination, they could – and would – succeed in their mission to rescue Lieutenant Hayes.

Captain Rodriguez's eyes scanned the faces of his team leaders as they gathered around a large, detailed map spread across a table in the secure briefing room. Their voices were low and determined, the weight of their mission evident in each word exchanged.

"Alright, let's go over our options," Captain Rodriguez said, his tone calm but firm. "We need to find the best way to extract Lieutenant Hayes without tipping off the enemy."

Lieutenant Emily Thompson, a fearless mountaineer with an uncanny ability to navigate through treacherous terrain, leaned closer to the map. Her keen intellect shone through her piercing blue eyes as she studied the mountainous region where Lieutenant Hayes was believed to be held.

"From what we know about the area, there are three potential extraction routes," she began, her voice steady and confident. She pointed to a jagged line on the map, indicating a steep ridge that cut through the mountains like a scar. "The first option is to traverse this ridge, which would allow us to move quickly while remaining concealed from view. However, it's also the most dangerous due to its sheer incline and risk of avalanches."

Captain Rodriguez nodded thoughtfully, considering the risks. He knew Emily's expertise in mountaineering was invaluable, but he couldn't shake the nagging feeling that any misstep could cost them dearly. "What about the other two options?"

Emily traced her finger along a second route, one that meandered through a series of valleys and narrow passes. "This path is less risky, but it'll take more time, and time isn't on our side. Knowing the enemy, they'll be expecting us to take the path of least resistance."

"True," Captain Rodriguez mused, rubbing his chin with a furrowed brow. "And the third option?"

"The third route is through a network of caves and tunnels," Emily explained, pointing to a series of small dots on the map. "It's a bit of a gamble since we don't have much intel on their layout, but if we can navigate through them successfully, it would give us the element of surprise."

Captain Rodriguez weighed each option carefully, his mind racing with the potential outcomes and consequences. He knew that a single misstep could jeopardize not only their mission but also the life of Lieutenant Hayes – a man who had endured unspeakable horrors at the hands of his captors.

"Emily," Captain Rodriguez said, looking her in the eyes, searching for any hint of doubt or uncertainty. "Which route do you believe gives us the best chance of success?"

"Sir, I recommend the ridge," she stated without hesitation. "While it is the most treacherous, it offers the quickest and most concealed approach. With my experience, I can guide the team through it safely."

Captain Rodriguez studied her face for a moment, recognizing the unwavering determination that had earned her the respect of her teammates. He trusted her judgment implicitly, and though the risks were high, he knew that their commitment to rescuing Lieutenant Hayes was absolute.

"Very well," he said, his voice firm and resolute. "We'll take the ridge. Prepare your gear and gather your teams. We move out at first light."

Sergeant Ramirez leaned over the table, a worn map of the desert terrain spread out before him. His dark brown eyes traced the contours and shadows with precision, his fingers hovering above the landscape as if sensing the heat and danger that lurked beneath.

"Captain," he said, his voice low and measured. "The enemy compound is surrounded by treacherous sand dunes and rocky outcrops. It's a hostile environment, but one that I am familiar with." He paused, glancing around at the faces of the team leaders gathered in the room. They were all tense, focused on the mission ahead.

"Based on my experience, I recommend we approach from the southeast," he continued. "There's a narrow canyon that will provide us cover during our advance. Once we reach the outskirts of the compound, we can use the natural camouflage of the terrain to our advantage."

Major Reynolds nodded thoughtfully, his piercing blue eyes fixed on the map. As the expert in covert operations, he knew that their success hinged on stealth and surprise. "I agree with Sergeant Ramirez," he said, his tone calm yet decisive. "We'll need to avoid detection for as long as possible. Our night vision capabilities will give us an edge, allowing us to navigate the darkness with ease."

Captain Rodriguez observed the exchange between his trusted team leaders, his thoughts racing. The stakes were high, but their determination was unwavering. He needed to trust their expertise and rely on their unique skills to bring Lieutenant Hayes home safely.

"Alright," he said, his voice steady. "Sergeant Ramirez, lead the way through the desert. Major Reynolds, have your team ready to move under cover of darkness. We must be swift and silent if we're to succeed."

"Understood, Captain," they replied in unison, their voices resolute.

As the team leaders dispersed to prepare their respective teams, Captain Rodriguez took a moment to gather his thoughts. He knew that the risks were great, and that every decision he made could mean the difference between life and death. But as he looked around at the determined faces of his team leaders, he felt a surge of confidence. They would do whatever it took to rescue Lieutenant Hayes and bring him home.

"Let's move out," he said, his voice filled with authority and conviction. And with that, the team set forth into the treacherous desert night, united in their mission to save one of their own.

Captain Rodriguez stood at the head of the table, his eyes scanning over the topographical maps and satellite images strewn across its surface. The team leaders huddled around him, their brows furrowed as they studied the terrain and enemy positions. In the dim glow of the briefing room, beads of sweat glistened on their foreheads, betraying the tension that hung in the air.

"Alright," Captain Rodriguez began, his voice steady and authoritative. "We've heard from Sergeant Ramirez and Major Reynolds. Now it's time to make some decisions."

Lieutenant Thompson, her fingertips tracing the mountainous region where Lieutenant Hayes was believed to be held, spoke up cautiously. "Captain, our extraction routes are limited due to the difficult terrain. It won't be easy getting him out of there."

"Understood, Lieutenant," Rodriguez replied, his jaw tightening. "But we must face these challenges head-on. We'll adapt and overcome, as we always do." His unwavering conviction resonated throughout the room, steeling the resolve of his team leaders.

"Captain," interjected Major Reynolds, "we'll need to find a way to neutralize their communication capabilities. If they manage to call for reinforcements during our infiltration, things could get ugly fast."

"Agreed," said Rodriguez, his brow furrowing as he contemplated their options. "I want you to work with Lieutenant Thompson on that. Find a way to cut them off before we go in."

While the team leaders continued to voice their concerns and suggestions, Captain Rodriguez listened intently, weighing each input against the risks and rewards it presented. The stakes were immense, but so was their determination to bring their comrade home.

"Remember, this is not just about rescuing Lieutenant Hayes," he reminded them. "It's about obtaining the critical intel he holds. We cannot afford any missteps."

As the moment of tension reached its peak, Captain Rodriguez's calm and authoritative presence seemed to fill the room. He took a deep breath, his eyes locked onto each of his team leaders in turn, instilling confidence and unity with his unwavering gaze.

"Final decisions," he declared, his voice firm and resolute. "Sergeant Ramirez, you lead us through the desert. Major Reynolds, your team infiltrates the enemy camp at night. Lieutenant Thompson, collaborate with Reynolds on disabling their communications."

"Understood, Captain," they replied in unison, their voices steady with newfound determination.

"Let's move out," he commanded, and with that, the team set forth into the treacherous unknown, united in their mission to save one of their own.

The sun dipped low on the horizon, casting long shadows across the barren landscape as Captain Rodriguez stood before his team leaders. The fierce determination in their eyes mirrored his own – they were prepared to face any challenge, overcome every obstacle, and risk everything for the sake of their comrade.

"Listen up," he began, his voice a perfect balance of command and encouragement. "I know we've faced our share of hardships in the past, but there's something different about this mission. We're not just fighting for Lieutenant Hayes; we're fighting for the information he holds."

Lieutenant Thompson nodded firmly, her steady gaze never leaving Captain Rodriguez. "We'll get him out, sir, and secure that intel. You can count on us."

Sergeant Ramirez clenched his fists, resolve etched into every line on his face. "We won't let you down, Captain. We're ready for anything."

"Good," replied Captain Rodriguez, allowing himself a brief smile. He knew the weight of the world rested upon their shoulders, but seeing their unwavering commitment bolstered his confidence in their ability to succeed.

"Let's go over the plan one more time," he instructed, his mind racing through each detail, every potential complication. His team leaders listened intently, their faces a picture of focus and determination.

As they finalized their strategies, Captain Rodriguez could sense the unity growing among them – a bond that would be their greatest strength in the trials to come. They were a well-oiled machine, each member an expert in their respective fields, and together they would rise to meet the challenges ahead.

"Remember," he said, his voice firm and resolute, "we'll face danger, we'll face uncertainty, but we will not falter. We will bring Lieutenant Hayes home and secure the intel he holds at all costs."

"Sir, yes, sir!" came the chorus of replies, as their voices echoed in unison, filled with an unwavering resolve.

"Dismissed," Captain Rodriguez ordered. He watched as his team leaders dispersed to prepare for the mission ahead, the bond between them stronger than ever. The sun slipped below the horizon, casting its final rays upon their silhouettes before they faded into the gathering darkness, ready to face whatever challenges lay ahead.

CHAPTER 4

The steel door to the secure briefing room swung open with a resounding clang, and Colonel Maria Vasquez strode in. Her polished boots echoed across the concrete floor as she made her way to the front of the room. The fluorescent lights overhead cast a harsh glare on her neatly tied back, black hair and reflected off the medals adorning her uniform. Her sharp brown eyes scanned the room, taking in the teams assembled before her.

"Attention!" barked a sergeant, and the room snapped into rigid formation. Shoulders squared, chests puffed out, and gazes locked forward – no one dared to breathe too loudly in the presence of Colonel Vasquez. The tension in the room was palpable, a live wire of anticipation that seemed to vibrate under the surface of each soldier's skin.

Colonel Vasquez's gaze lingered on each face for a moment, assessing their readiness. She could see the fire in their eyes: an unquenchable determination fueled by loyalty and duty. These were her soldiers, her responsibility, and she would not let them down.

"Listen up," she began, her voice steady and authoritative, cutting through the silence like a knife. "We have a high-priority mission, and I expect nothing less than your absolute best." As she spoke, her eyes continued to move from one soldier to the next, ensuring that her words penetrated deep into their souls.

"Failure is not an option," she stressed, pausing for effect. "We are all aware of the stakes – lives are on the line, and our national security hangs in the balance." Colonel Vasquez allowed herself a slight frown, the weight of the situation pressing down upon her. Despite the enormity of it all, she remained the picture of calm resolve.

"Each of you has been selected for this mission because of your unique skills and expertise," she continued, meeting the eyes of every soldier in the room. "I have no doubt that you are up to the task. But remember, this is a team effort – your success relies on your ability to work together and execute your individual assignments with precision."

Colonel Vasquez wasted no time. "Your mission is to locate and extract Lieutenant Samuel Hayes, who's been captured by enemy forces during a covert operation."

Lieutenant Emily Thompson's heart raced as Colonel Vasquez spoke, every beat fueling her determination to bring Sam back. She knew the challenges they faced, but she couldn't ignore the urgency in Colonel Vasquez's voice.

"Intel suggests that Hayes is being held in a heavily fortified compound," Colonel Vasquez continued. "We have very limited information on its location, so you'll be divided into teams to cover more ground."

Emily clenched her fists at the thought of Sam trapped within enemy walls. She had trained with him, shared victories and losses, and now his life hung in the balance.

"Time is of the essence," Colonel Vasquez emphasized, her eyes piercing the room. "With each passing hour, the risk to Lieutenant Hayes increases. We must act swiftly and decisively."

The gravity of their task weighed heavily on Emily, but she couldn't let doubt creep in. Failure was not an option. She looked around the room, seeing the same resolve mirrored in her comrades' faces.

"Each team will have specific objectives to achieve. Some of you will gather intel, some will create diversions, and others will secure our escape routes. But remember," Colonel Vasquez paused, driving home the point, "the ultimate goal is to bring Lieutenant Hayes home safely."

"Understood, Colonel!" The teams chorused, the sound reverberating through the room like a battle cry.

"Good. Now, I know this mission may push you to your limits, but I have faith in your abilities." Colonel Vasquez locked eyes with each soldier, reinforcing her confidence in them. "You are all here because you are the best of the best, and I expect nothing less than total commitment."

Emily felt a surge of adrenaline course through her veins, igniting a fire within. She knew they had to move as one cohesive unit, their fates intertwined in this dangerous undertaking. The stakes were high, but so was her determination.

"Let's bring our comrade home," Colonel Vasquez declared, her voice unwavering. "We leave at 0600 hours. Dismissed."

As the soldiers dispersed, Emily felt a renewed sense of purpose and resolve. Thoughts of Sam fueled her focus, propelling her towards the challenges that lay ahead. Her mind raced with strategies and contingencies, the gears turning as she prepared for the mission of a lifetime. There would be no room for error – they couldn't afford it.

And as she gathered her gear and made final preparations, Emily silently vowed to herself and her team: We will not fail.

The sun dipped below the horizon as Colonel Vasquez stood in front of a large holographic screen, her piercing eyes scanning the detailed schematics of enemy territory. With a flick of her wrist, she zoomed in on a fortified compound nestled within a dense forest. The soldiers leaned in, their faces a mix of determination and apprehension, as they absorbed the information before them.

"Listen closely," Colonel Vasquez commanded, her tone sharp yet steady. "This is where we believe Lieutenant Hayes is being held captive." Her fingers danced across the holographic interface, highlighting key points of interest. "We are up against an enemy force that is highly trained, heavily armed, and ruthless."

Emily's heart pounded in her chest, her mind racing with calculations and strategies to overcome the daunting odds they faced. She knew there was no room for error—failure would mean losing not only Hayes but potentially compromising national security.

"Intelligence reports indicate that the enemy has access to advanced weaponry, including anti-aircraft defenses and armored vehicles," Colonel Vasquez continued, her voice unwavering. "They have also employed skilled snipers and capable tacticians. We must be prepared for anything."

She paused, allowing the gravity of the situation to settle over the room. Then, with a steely glint in her eye, she pressed on. "But they are not invincible. Our intel has revealed several vulnerabilities we can exploit. Their perimeter defenses are weak on the southeastern side of the compound, and their communication network relies on a single central hub. This is our chance to strike swiftly and decisively."

"Precision and teamwork will be paramount," Colonel Vasquez stressed, her gaze flitting from one soldier to another. "If even one of us falters, the entire mission could fail. You must trust in your training, in each other, and in our objective. The risks are great, but so are the rewards."

"Understood, Colonel," Emily murmured, her jaw set with determination. She felt a surge of adrenaline course through her veins, igniting a fire within.

"Good," Colonel Vasquez replied, her eyes narrowing. "Now let's bring our comrade home."

As the team members dispersed to make final preparations for the mission ahead, Emily's mind raced with thoughts of potential obstacles and contingencies. She knew that the enemy was formidable, but she had faith in her team and their collective ability to overcome any challenge.

"Stay focused," she whispered to herself, clenching her fists tightly. "We cannot afford to fail."

The room crackled with an electric tension as Colonel Vasquez, her eyes fixed on the teams before her, began to outline their objectives in a voice that brooked no argument. The soldiers leaned forward, their expressions a mix of steely determination and focused concentration. Every word was absorbed, every detail committed to memory.

"Based on our intelligence, we believe Lieutenant Hayes is being held in one of three possible locations within the enemy compound," Colonel Vasquez said crisply, gesturing at the large map displayed on the screen behind her. "Our priority will be to sweep through each of these areas, neutralizing any resistance we encounter."

"Delta Team, you'll head for the barracks here," she pointed at the first potential location, her tone measured but urgent. "These buildings are likely to house their main fighting force. Be prepared for heavy resistance. Bravo Team, you will proceed to this underground bunker," her finger moved to another point on the map. "It's less accessible, but it's also the most secure location in the compound – a prime holding spot for high-value targets like Hayes."

"Finally, Alpha Team," Colonel Vasquez turned to Emily and her fellow operatives, her gaze unwavering. "You will infiltrate the command center, here. It's heavily fortified, but your objective is twofold: locate Hayes and disrupt their communication network by targeting their central hub. This will throw their forces into disarray, giving us the advantage we need."

Emily nodded sharply, her mind already racing with strategies and contingencies. Her blue eyes burned with a fierce resolve, and she could feel the weight of the mission settling on her shoulders. But it was not a burden she would bear alone; she glanced at her teammates, their own faces etched with determination, and drew strength from their shared purpose.

"Remember," Colonel Vasquez continued, her voice steady but charged with urgency, "time is of the essence. The longer Hayes remains in their hands, the greater the risk to his safety and our mission's success. We must be swift, precise, and relentless."

"Understood, Colonel," Emily replied, her voice firm and resolute. She knew that failure was not an option, and she would do everything in her power to ensure a successful outcome.

"Then let's move out," Colonel Vasquez commanded, her words ringing with authority. "Stay sharp, stay focused, and bring Lieutenant Hayes home."

As the teams prepared to embark on their respective tasks, the air was thick with purpose and conviction. They knew what was at stake, and the gravity of their mission only served to strengthen their resolve. With their eyes locked on the map one last time, they committed each detail to memory, readying themselves for the challenges to come.

The room seemed to shrink as the magnitude of the information swelled around them, pressing against their chests like a vise. Captain James Rodriguez felt sweat bead on his forehead, despite the chill in the air. He locked eyes with Colonel Vasquez for a brief moment, and the gravity of the situation became palpable.

"Alright, let's break this down," Colonel Vasquez said, her voice carrying the weight of national security in every syllable. "Each team will have specific assignments and targets. We cannot afford any mistakes."

"Team Alpha," she continued, directing her gaze towards James and his team, "your primary objective is to locate and extract Lieutenant Hayes. Based on our intel, he is likely being held in one of three locations." She pointed to a detailed map projected on the wall, her finger hovering over a cluster of buildings. "You'll have air support from Falcon One, and you'll be equipped with state-of-the-art surveillance gear to help identify potential threats."

"Understood, Colonel," James replied, his voice steady despite the mounting pressure. His mind raced, taking mental note of every detail and strategizing how best to utilize their resources. He knew the success of the mission hinged on their ability to adapt and overcome.

"Team Bravo," Colonel Vasquez addressed Lieutenant Emily Thompson and her team, "you're tasked with neutralizing the enemy's defensive capabilities. Our intelligence suggests they possess advanced anti-aircraft systems. Your job is to take them out before they pose a threat to Falcon One and our extraction plan."

"Copy that, Colonel," Emily responded, her face a mask of determination. She could feel the burden of responsibility settling on her shoulders, but she refused to let it crush her spirit. Instead, she channeled it into a laser-sharp focus, ready to guide her team through the treacherous task ahead.

"Finally, Team Charlie," Colonel Vasquez turned to Major David Reynolds and Sergeant Miguel Ramirez, "you'll be responsible for creating a diversion. We need to draw the enemy's attention away from Teams Alpha and Bravo long enough for them to accomplish their objectives. You'll have access to remote-controlled drones and other specialized equipment to assist in this endeavor."

"Roger that, Colonel," David replied, his voice firm and unyielding. He could feel the weight of the mission pressing down on him, but he refused to falter. The stakes were too high, and failure was simply not an option.

"Each team will report directly to me with any updates or changes in the situation," Colonel Vasquez instructed, her voice unwavering. "Remember, we're counting on you. The success of this mission has far-reaching implications for our nation's security, and Lieutenant Hayes's life hangs in the balance."

As the teams absorbed their individual assignments, they felt the gravity of their task settle deep within their bones. They knew the risks, understood the consequences, and were prepared to face the challenges ahead with unwavering determination. With a final nod from Colonel Vasquez, they dispersed, each member focused on their role in the mission and the lives that hung in the balance.

The door to the briefing room swung shut with a resounding thud, sealing away the weight of Colonel Vasquez's words. Captain James Rodriguez led his team down the dimly lit corridor, their boots echoing off the concrete walls. Their minds were focused on the mission ahead, and they moved with purpose, each step a testament to their unwavering determination.

"Alright, Alpha Team," James said, his voice steady and authoritative. "We've got our orders. Let's gear up and be ready to move out in thirty."

"Understood, sir," Lieutenant Emily Thompson replied, her blue eyes reflecting the gravity of their task as she matched her captain's stride. The rest of the team nodded in agreement, their expressions set with resolve.

As they walked, James couldn't help but feel a renewed sense of purpose swelling within him. His thoughts were consumed by the importance of their mission and the life of Lieutenant Hayes that hung in the balance. He knew the enemy was formidable and that they would need every ounce of skill and teamwork to succeed.

"Captain," Emily spoke up, her tone calm but laced with urgency. "I've been studying the layout of the compound. There's a weak point in their defenses we can exploit. It'll give us a fighting chance to get Hayes out."

"Good work, Thompson," James acknowledged, his mind working through the potential risks and rewards of this new information. "We'll discuss it further once we've suited up. Time is of the essence."

"Sir, I've reached out to our contacts in the area," Sergeant Miguel Ramirez chimed in, his voice measured and precise. "They'll provide us with real-time intel on enemy movements and any changes in their defenses."

"Excellent, Ramirez," James praised, knowing full well that such information could be the difference between success and failure. "Make sure to keep them on standby. We'll need their eyes and ears throughout this operation."

As they reached the armory, the team began to assemble their gear. The air was fraught with tension, but there was a palpable sense of determination among them, each member keenly aware of the lives at stake.

"Remember," James said, looking his team in the eyes as they readied themselves for the mission ahead. "We're not just fighting for Hayes. We're fighting for our country, our people, and our future. Let's make sure we bring him back alive and ensure our nation's security remains intact."

With that, the team finished gearing up and prepared to embark on their respective tasks, armed with a renewed sense of purpose and the knowledge that failure was not an option. They knew the challenges ahead would be great, but together, they were a formidable force, ready to face whatever lay in wait.

The secure briefing room door clicked shut behind them, leaving the teams to face the reality of the mission ahead. Captain James Rodriguez's eyes darted around, taking in the determined expressions of his comrades. Each team member was a reflection of strength, discipline, and commitment - qualities that would be put to the ultimate test in the hours to come.

"Alright, everyone," James said, breaking the silence. "Time to gear up and make your final preparations. We move out in thirty."

A chorus of acknowledgements sounded as the teams dispersed towards their respective stations. Emily Thompson, her blue eyes reflecting a steely resolve, headed straight for the communications center, ensuring they would have a reliable connection with headquarters throughout the operation.

Sergeant Miguel Ramirez, every bit the desert warfare specialist he was renowned to be, focused on calibrating the specialized equipment they would need to navigate the hostile terrain. His dark brown eyes were sharp and observant, aware that even the slightest error could jeopardize their chances for success.

Major David Reynolds checked and re-checked the ammunition supplies, his piercing blue eyes missing no detail. This mission required precision, and there would be no room for error or oversight.

As James gathered his own gear, his thoughts raced through the critical information Colonel Vasquez had shared during the briefing. The weight of responsibility bore down on him, but it also fueled his determination. Too much was at stake, and failure was simply not an option.

"Captain Rodriguez," Lieutenant Thompson called out from across the room, drawing James from his thoughts. "I've secured a satellite link with HQ. We'll have constant communication throughout the op."

"Good work, Thompson," James replied, nodding his approval before letting silence descend once more. Each team member knew their role and the importance of the tasks at hand. There was no need for further discussion; their focus was now entirely on the mission ahead.

As the teams made their final preparations, their thoughts were consumed by the upcoming challenges they would face. The risks were high, the danger ever-present, but they had been trained for this very moment - and they would not falter.

"Teams, fall in!" James commanded, his voice steady and resolute. The soldiers gathered around him, their faces reflecting a mix of determination and focus. "This mission will test us like never before, but we have faced adversity before and emerged victorious. Remember your training and trust in one another. We will succeed, and we will bring Lieutenant Hayes home."

With that, the teams dispersed to gather their gear, their minds focused on the trials ahead. As they left the room, it was clear that each soldier understood the gravity of the situation, and they were prepared to face whatever challenges lay in wait.

The deafening roar of helicopter blades cut through the air as Captain James Rodriguez stood at the edge of the landing zone. He watched with an unwavering gaze as the Blackhawk helicopters descended, their sleek silhouettes slicing through the twilight sky.

"Alright, team - this is it," he shouted over the din, his voice firm and focused. "Stick to your assignments and watch each other's backs. Let's move out!"

James led the charge toward the first helicopter, his muscular frame gliding effortlessly over the uneven terrain. The rest of his team followed closely behind, their eyes fixed on their leader as they boarded the aircraft.

"Two minutes to takeoff," the pilot announced through the headset, his words barely audible above the whirring of the engine.

As the helicopters ascended, James felt a surge of adrenaline course through his veins. It was a familiar sensation - one that had fueled him through countless missions. But there was something different about this operation; the stakes were higher than ever before.

"Stay sharp, everyone," James said, his piercing brown eyes scanning the faces of his team members. "We're heading into the lion's den, and we won't all make it out unscathed. But remember this: our success depends on our unity. We fight as one."

"Here's the plan," Lieutenant Emily Thompson interjected, her voice calm and authoritative. "We split into two teams. Alpha team will focus on securing the perimeter while Bravo team moves in to locate and extract Lieutenant Hayes."

"Roger that," Sergeant Miguel Ramirez replied, his dark eyes narrowing with determination. "Bravo team, gather your gear. Let's get ready to move on my signal."

James could sense the intensity radiating from his fellow soldiers, their expressions a blend of determination and steely resolve. As they prepared for the challenges ahead, he knew that their unwavering sense of duty would be their most powerful weapon.

"Stay focused and remember your training," Major David Reynolds advised, his reassuring voice cutting through the tension. "We've been through worse, and we'll come out on top."

James nodded in agreement, his mind racing with thoughts of the mission ahead. He knew that every second counted, and that any hesitation could prove fatal. But with his team by his side, he was ready to face whatever lay ahead.

"Approaching the drop zone," the pilot announced. "Prepare for landing."

"Let's do this," James said, determination etched across his face. "For Hayes, for our country, and for each other."

CHAPTER 5

The sweat on Emily's brow glistened as she hacked her way through the dense jungle undergrowth, the relentless sun casting dappled shadows through the vibrant green canopy. She could feel the oppressive humidity bearing down on her, making each breath a battle in itself. Team Alpha moved forward, expertly maneuvering around hostile wildlife as they searched for any signs of the underground bunker where Lieutenant Samuel Hayes was rumored to be held.

"Keep your eyes peeled, team," Emily breathed heavily into her radio, "we're getting closer."

A silent affirmative crackled through her headset from the other members of Team Alpha. They were veterans of countless missions like this, but the stakes felt higher than ever. The rescue of Lieutenant Hayes had become personal for everyone involved – his reputation preceded him and their responsibility weighed heavy.

"Captain," one of her men whispered into the comms, "I think I found something."

Meanwhile, Lieutenant Thompson led Team Bravo up treacherous mountain peaks, using their ice axes to scale the frozen rock and navigate the dangerous cliffs. Her piercing blue eyes scanned the landscape with focus and determination, all while keeping an eye out for any signs of the captive.

"Stay sharp, Bravo," Emily commanded, her words measured and precise, even as her breaths came out in small white puffs against the frigid air. "This terrain is unforgiving, but so are we."

"Copy that, Lieutenant," replied one of her mountaineer teammates, his gloved hands gripping the ice axe tighter.

Emily couldn't help but think about Sam, picturing the haunted look in his eyes that spoke volumes about his ordeal. A sense of urgency gripped her heart, willing her to push onward. It was a race against time, knowing that every moment spent searching could mean life or death for the captured soldier.

"Alpha, what's your status?" she asked over the radio, trying to keep her voice steady.

"Found a bunker entrance, Lieutenant. It's camouflaged, but it looks promising," came the reply through the static.

"Good work, Alpha. Be cautious and keep us updated," she responded, her heart racing at the news.

"Roger that," the voice on the other end affirmed before going silent.

With renewed determination, Emily and Team Bravo continued their ascent up the mountain, ice axes biting into the frozen rock with each heave. She couldn't shake the feeling that they were closing in on Sam, and his rescue was within their grasp. But there were still unknown dangers lurking ahead, and they had to remain vigilant.

"Bravo, let's pick up the pace," she urged, "we're not stopping until we find him."

A roiling sandstorm engulfed the barren landscape as Team Charlie pressed on, their tan combat fatigues blending seamlessly with the golden sands. The desert sun beat down mercilessly, and the swirling grit obscured their vision, but they were undeterred by the harsh conditions. The thought of Lieutenant Samuel Hayes, held captive somewhere in this desolate expanse, fueled their determination.

"Charlie, keep moving!" shouted Sergeant Miguel Ramirez, his voice muffled by the howling winds and his face half-covered by a scarf. "We're getting closer."

"Roger that, Sarge," replied one of his teammates, squinting against the stinging sand.

Miguel's mind raced with thoughts of Sam, the haunted look in his eyes after his capture. He knew they couldn't fail him; every second wasted was another moment of suffering for their comrade. As a seasoned desert warfare specialist, he understood the unforgiving terrain better than most, but even his considerable skills were put to the test here.

Meanwhile, under the cover of darkness, Team Delta expertly slipped past the perimeter guards of the coastal enemy camp. Major David Reynolds led the way, his night vision goggles scanning the shadows as they searched building by building for signs of the captured soldier.

"Delta, stay sharp and silent," whispered David into his headset, his voice measured and precise. "Keep an eye out for anything unusual."

"Copy that, Major," responded one of his teammates, his own goggles revealing a world of green-tinted shadows.

David felt a sense of responsibility not just for his team, but for Sam as well. They had all been trained to withstand torture, but there were limits to what any man could endure. He wondered what horrors Sam had faced at the hands of his captors, and it only strengthened his resolve to bring him home.

As Team Charlie pushed through the relentless sandstorm, Miguel caught sight of a looming structure in the distance. Could this be the fortified compound they were searching for?

"Charlie, I think we've found something," he reported into his headset, shielding his eyes from the relentless wind. "Stand by for confirmation."

"Be cautious, Charlie," came Captain Rodriguez's authoritative voice through the static. "We don't know what you're walking into."

"Understood, Captain," Miguel replied, signaling his team to approach the compound with caution.

Back at the coastal camp, Team Delta moved like shadows through the night, avoiding detection as they continued their search. David's heart pounded in his chest, knowing that Sam could be just around the corner, locked away and waiting for rescue.

"Major, I've got something!" whispered one of his teammates urgently.

"What is it?" David asked, his voice barely audible.

"Fresh bloodstains on the ground, leading towards that building over there," he pointed out, his voice trembling slightly.

"Delta, weapons ready," David ordered, trying to suppress the sinking feeling in his gut. "Let's find our man."

As both teams closed in on their targets, the tension was palpable. The fate of Lieutenant Samuel Hayes hung in the balance, and every member of the Special Forces was dedicated to bringing him home safely. It was a race against time, and failure was not an option.

"Stay focused, everyone," Captain Rodriguez urged through the radio. "We'll get him back."

The dense jungle closed in around Team Alpha as they moved cautiously, the sharp edge of Captain James Rodriguez's machete slicing through thick undergrowth. The humidity clung to their skin like a second layer of sweat-soaked clothing, and they marched on, the haunting calls of distant wildlife echoing through the foliage.

"Captain, I see something up ahead," whispered Sergeant Thompson, her eyes narrowing in concentration as she scanned the area.

"Let's take it slow—weapons raised," Rodriguez commanded, his voice low and measured. His piercing brown eyes locked onto the camouflaged entrance before them, and he sensed the unspoken agreement among his team: they were close.

They descended into the darkness, weapons poised, hearts pounding. The air grew heavy and damp as they navigated the maze of dimly lit corridors, their footsteps echoing eerily in the confined space. It felt as though the bunker itself was closing in on them, but Rodriguez knew that failure was not an option—they had to find Hayes.

"Keep your eyes peeled, team," he murmured, his voice barely audible above the sound of their boots splashing through shallow puddles. "We're looking for any sign of our man."

"Copy that, Captain," came the hushed response from his team.

As they turned a corner, Rodriguez's heart skipped a beat—the heavy steel door loomed before them, its imposing presence a sure sign that whatever lay behind it held vital importance. He motioned for his team to take cover as he prepared the explosive charge, the weight of their mission bearing down on him with each passing second.

"Charge set, Captain," one of his men reported, his voice tense with anticipation.

"Stand back," Rodriguez ordered, and they braced themselves for the deafening explosion. The door blew open with a thunderous boom, sending shards of metal flying through the air.

"Go, go, go!" Rodriguez shouted, leading his team into the chamber.

But their hearts sank as they found it empty, save for the bloodstains on the concrete floor. The room felt colder than the rest of the bunker, a chilling reminder of the torture that Hayes had likely endured within its walls.

"Damn it," Rodriguez muttered under his breath, running a hand through his cropped dark hair in frustration. "He's not here."

"Captain, what do we do now?" Thompson asked, her piercing blue eyes reflecting the determination that still burned within them all.

"Stay on the comms with the other teams," he replied, clenching his jaw in determination. "We don't leave until we find him."

"Understood, Captain," she said, her voice resolute.

As Team Alpha regrouped and continued their search, the weight of their mission hung heavier than ever. But they would not falter—failure was simply not an option. They were determined to bring Lieutenant Samuel Hayes home, no matter the cost.

"Three, two, one, go!" Lieutenant Emily Thompson's voice was steady as she and Team Bravo launched themselves off the edge of the mountain stronghold, their rappelling lines streaming out behind them like tendrils of steel.

Thompson's piercing blue eyes narrowed as she descended rapidly, the wind whipping her blonde hair across her face. Her mind raced with tactical calculations, but beneath it all simmered a fierce determination to rescue Lieutenant Hayes at any cost.

"Contact right!" Sergeant Johnson's urgent shout came through her earpiece just as she touched down on the icy ledge. Silenced gunfire echoed around them as they engaged the enemy guards patrolling the perimeter.

"Cover me!" Thompson ordered, gracefully taking down an approaching guard with a swift kick. She pressed her back against the cold stone wall of the fortress, heart pounding in her chest as she scanned the area for any sign of their captured comrade.

"Clear!" someone called out, signaling that the immediate threat had been neutralized.

"Move in," Thompson commanded, leading her team deeper into the heavily guarded facility. They moved with precision, their training evident in every step, every sweep of their weapons.

"Thompson, we've got something here," Corporal Davis reported, his voice tense over the comms.

"Show me," she demanded, quickly closing the distance between them. As she approached the cell, her heartbeat quickened with anticipation. But when she entered, her hope turned to ash.

"Empty," she muttered, staring at the abandoned cell with a mix of frustration and disappointment. "Damn it."

"Keep searching," Thompson ordered, her voice barely betraying her emotions. "We won't leave without him."

"Roger that, Lieutenant," came the reply, and the sound of boots on stone resumed as her team continued their search.

Meanwhile, Team Charlie was making their final approach on the fortified compound hidden deep within the desert expanse. Sergeant Miguel Ramirez, a seasoned desert warfare specialist, signaled his team to fan out as they neared the entrance.

"Steady," he whispered, his dark brown eyes scanning the area for any signs of movement. "On my mark."

The world erupted into chaos as Team Charlie traded bullets with enemy forces guarding the compound's entrance. Grenades detonated, sending shrapnel whizzing through the air and sandstorms kicked up by the commotion. Through it all, Ramirez remained steadfast, pushing forward with grim determination.

"Where is he?" he growled internally, frustration mounting as their target remained elusive. He glanced at his team, their tan combat fatigues blending with the golden sands, and knew they were all thinking the same thing – they had come too far to fail now.

"Charlie One to Bravo Lead, do you copy?" Ramirez called over the comms, his voice hoarse from the dry desert air.

"Bravo Lead here," Thompson's calm authority answered. "No sign of Hayes yet. You?"

"Negative," Ramirez replied, gritting his teeth. "Keep us updated. We'll find him, one way or another."

"Copy that, Charlie One," Thompson acknowledged before signing off.

As the gunfire continued to rage around them, Team Charlie pushed deeper into the compound, their unwavering resolve driving them onwards in their desperate search for Lieutenant Samuel Hayes. The stakes had never been higher, but their loyalty and camaraderie would not allow them to leave without their fellow soldier. They would fight until their last breath if need be – failure was simply not an option.

Captain James Rodriguez crouched in the inky darkness just outside the perimeter of the coastal encampment, his night vision goggles casting a green hue over the scene before him. The salty sea air stung his nostrils as he scanned the area, searching for an entry point.

"Delta One to all units," Rodriguez whispered into his headset. "We're at the target location. Stand by for confirmation."

"Copy that, Delta One," came the reply from Team Alpha's leader.

Rodriguez turned to face his teammates and signaled them to move forward. They crept through the shadows, evading the enemy guards patrolling the area with a stealth born from years of training. Each breath they took was measured, every movement calculated.

As they approached the heart of the camp, Rodriguez spotted what he had been searching for – a makeshift cell hidden between two dilapidated buildings. His heart began to race, not from fear, but anticipation. Was this finally it?

"Delta One to all units," he whispered urgently. "We have eyes on a possible holding cell. Proceeding to investigate."

"Be careful, Captain," Lieutenant Thompson warned from her position in the mountains. "We don't know what kind of resistance you might encounter."

"Understood, Bravo Lead," Rodriguez replied, his voice steady despite the weight of their mission.

The team moved closer to the cell, their weapons raised and ready for any surprises. As they reached the door, Rodriguez's night vision revealed a battered figure slumped against the wall, his bruised and bloodied face unmistakable – Lieutenant Samuel Hayes.

"Got him!" Rodriguez breathed in relief. "Delta One to all units, we've found Hayes!"

"Thank God," Ramirez's voice crackled through the comms. "Get him out of there, Captain."

"Roger that," Rodriguez responded, sheathing his weapon as he knelt beside Hayes, cutting the crude ropes binding him.

"Captain?" Hayes croaked, his voice weak but defiant. "You... you came for me."

"Damn right we did," Rodriguez replied, a fierce determination burning in his eyes. "We're getting you out of here, Lieutenant."

As he helped Hayes to his feet, the sound of gunfire erupted around them. The enemy had discovered their presence, and they were not going to let their prisoner go without a fight.

"Delta Team, weapons hot!" Rodriguez ordered, his authoritative tone rallying his teammates. "Protect Hayes at all costs!"

"Copy that, Delta One!" they responded in unison, forming a protective circle around Hayes as they fought their way through the encampment.

Bullets whizzed past them, each one a deadly reminder of the stakes they faced. But Rodriguez refused to entertain thoughts of failure. They had come too far, risked too much. He would see this mission through to the end, no matter the cost.

"Rodriguez, cover our six!" Thompson's voice cut through the chaos. "We'll rendezvous with you at the extraction point!"

"Understood, Bravo Lead," Rodriguez acknowledged, his heart pounding with adrenaline as they continued their desperate escape.

"Captain," Hayes rasped, leaning heavily on his rescuer. "I have... information. It's vital."

"Save it for later, Lieutenant," Rodriguez urged, his focus entirely on getting Hayes to safety. "Right now, our priority is getting you out alive."

The sound of helicopter blades slicing through the air filled Captain Rodriguez's ears as he surveyed the battlefield. The smoke from countless explosions had begun to dissipate, revealing the carnage left in its wake. Team Alpha and Team Bravo emerged from the jungle and mountain terrain, their expressions a mix of relief and fatigue. As they regrouped with Team Delta, they exchanged weary glances, knowing that their mission was far from over.

"Status report," Rodriguez demanded, his voice cracking with the strain of recent battles.

"Two KIA, sir," Sergeant Ramirez replied, his rugged face etched with sorrow. "Bravo Two and Charlie Three."

"Damn it." Rodriguez clenched his fist, anger and grief welling up inside him. He knew the risks associated with their mission, but the loss of comrades still weighed heavily on his heart. "Get them onboard for transport home."

"Copy that." Major Reynolds nodded solemnly, directing his team to retrieve their fallen brothers.

"Captain," Lieutenant Thompson approached, her blue eyes reflecting both concern and determination. "We need to get back to base ASAP. They'll be coming after us, and we need to debrief and plan our next move."

"Agreed," Rodriguez replied, casting one last glance at the battlefield before boarding the helicopter with Lieutenant Hayes, who was still leaning heavily on him for support.

"ETA to base is four hours," the pilot informed them as they strapped into their seats, the wounded receiving immediate medical attention.

"Stay sharp, everyone," Rodriguez warned, his piercing brown eyes scanning each member of the team. "We're not out of the woods yet."

As the helicopter lifted off, carrying them away from the danger zone, Rodriguez allowed himself a moment of reflection. The faces of their fallen teammates haunted him, but the knowledge that they had successfully rescued Hayes offered some solace.

"Captain..." Hayes' weak voice interrupted his thoughts. "I need to tell you... their plan... it's bigger than we thought."

"Focus on healing, Lieutenant," Rodriguez replied, his authoritative tone masking the concern he felt for his comrade. "We'll debrief when we're back at base."

"Understood, sir," Hayes nodded, his battered face a testament to his resilience and unbroken spirit.

Rodriguez exchanged worried glances with Thompson and Ramirez, knowing that the information Hayes possessed could change everything. As the helicopter sped toward their base, he couldn't shake the feeling that they were only at the beginning of a much larger battle. His resolve hardened, vowing to do whatever it took to protect his team and safeguard national security.

"Stay alert, stay alive," he whispered under his breath, his eyes never leaving the horizon, as the teams braced themselves for what was to come.

CHAPTER 6

A bead of sweat trickled down Captain Rodriguez's temple as he burst into the command center, his voice echoing through the cavernous room. "Team leaders, assemble! We need to find Lieutenant Hayes, and we need to do it now!" The urgency in his tone was palpable; there was no time to waste.

Captain Rodriguez radiated authority as he strode across the room, his piercing brown eyes scanning for the respective team leaders. His tall, muscular frame seemed to fill the space around him, commanding respect from the soldiers who quickly snapped to attention. As he moved, the weight of his past missions and the lives of his fallen comrades hung heavily on his shoulders, but Captain Rodriguez remained undeterred, fueled by an unwavering determination to protect his country.

"Thompson, Ramirez, Reynolds - gather 'round," he barked, waving them over with a practiced flick of his wrist. As each leader approached, they exchanged a brief nod of acknowledgement, their expressions grim and resolute. For a moment, their eyes locked, silently conveying both the gravity of the situation and the unspoken bond that united them in this crucial mission.

"Alright, listen up," Captain Rodriguez began, his voice steady and authoritative. "We have a limited window to locate and extract Lieutenant Hayes before it's too late. I want all teams working together, sharing intel, and supporting one another in any way possible. Understood?"

"Sir, yes sir," chorused the team leaders, their voices strong and unified.

"Good. Thompson, you'll take your team up into the mountains. They're treacherous terrain, but I know you can handle it." He paused, looking directly into Lieutenant Emily Thompson's piercing blue eyes, seeking reassurance in her steely resolve. Her expression remained calm and confident, a testament to her years of elite training.

"Thank you, sir," she replied, her voice steady and measured. "We won't let you down."

"Ramirez, your team will face the desert. It's hostile territory, but I trust you can navigate its challenges." Captain Rodriguez's gaze shifted to Sergeant Ramirez, whose squared shoulders and unflinching stare spoke volumes about his experience in the field.

"Understood, sir," Ramirez replied, his voice laden with determination. "We'll find Hayes and bring him home."

"Reynolds, your mission is coastal. Use stealth and precision to slip past the guards and locate any potential leads on Hayes' whereabouts." Major Reynolds met the Captain's gaze with unwavering focus, his commitment to the mission evident in every line of his face.

"Roger that, sir," Reynolds responded crisply. "We'll get it done."

Captain Rodriguez took a deep breath, allowing himself a moment to process the information shared by the team leaders. His mind raced, analyzing the puzzle before him and searching for patterns or connections that might lead them to Lieutenant Hayes. He knew the stakes were high, and the pressure was mounting, but he couldn't afford to falter now - not with Hayes' life hanging in the balance.

"Alright, everyone," he said finally, his voice filled with conviction. "Let's move out and bring our brother home. We've got this."

The dimly lit command center buzzed with anticipation, casting long shadows across the large table that seemed to groan under the weight of maps and intelligence reports. Team leaders huddled around it, their eyes darting from one document to another, brows furrowed in concentration. The tension in the room was palpable, each person acutely aware that every second wasted meant more danger for Lieutenant Hayes.

Captain Rodriguez stood at the head of the table, his hands clasped behind him as he surveyed the scene before him. His piercing brown eyes were alight with determination, reflecting both the urgency of the situation and the steely resolve that had carried him through countless missions. He took a deep breath, steeling himself for the discussion that lay ahead.

"Alright, let's get down to business," he began, his voice commanding and steady. "I want updates on your progress and any potential leads you've uncovered. We need to find Hayes, and we need to do it now."

As the team leaders exchanged tense glances, Captain Rodriguez could sense the unspoken concern that hung in the air – they all knew the odds were stacked against them, yet none dared articulate the fear that gnawed at their thoughts. But Rodriguez refused to give in to despair. Instead, he focused on the task at hand, mentally cataloging each piece of information as it was presented to him.

"Thompson, what can you tell me about your team's findings in the mountains?" he asked, turning to face Lieutenant Thompson. She straightened, her jaw set as she relayed the treacherous terrain they had encountered and the possible locations where Hayes might be held captive.

"Ramirez, how about your team's challenges in the desert?" Captain Rodriguez continued, shifting his gaze to Sergeant Ramirez. Sweat glistened on the sergeant's brow as he described the hostile forces guarding the compound and the scarcity of resources in the blistering heat.

"Reynolds, I need an update on the coastal mission." Major Reynolds didn't hesitate, emphasizing the stealth and precision required to slip past the perimeter guards and the discovery of the makeshift cell where Lieutenant Hayes was found.

As each team leader spoke, Rodriguez's mind raced, analyzing the information shared and searching for patterns or connections that might lead them to Hayes. He could feel the weight of responsibility bearing down on him, but he refused to let it crush his spirit.

"Thank you all for your reports," he said finally, his voice resolute. "We've got a lot of ground to cover, and we can't afford any missteps. We need to work together, pool our resources, and find Hayes – no matter the cost."

He looked around the table, meeting the gaze of each team leader in turn. In their eyes, he saw a reflection of his own determination – they were united in purpose, bonded by their shared commitment to rescue one of their own. And with that knowledge, Captain Rodriguez knew they stood a fighting chance.

"Let's get back to our teams and put these plans into action. Remember, we're in this together. We've already faced countless challenges, but we will not be defeated. We will find Hayes, and we will bring him home."

With renewed determination, the team leaders dispersed to relay the updated strategies to their respective teams. The tension in the room began to dissipate, replaced by an air of anticipation and readiness as they prepared to continue their search for Lieutenant Hayes, armed with new information and a united front against the enemy.

Captain Rodriguez's steely gaze fell upon Lieutenant Thompson, who stood straight-backed and attentive. Her piercing blue eyes met his, and she cleared her throat before beginning.

"Sir, my team has been scouting the mountainous regions to the north," Emily started, her voice firm with authority. "We've encountered steep cliffs, treacherous terrain, and harsh weather conditions. We have, however, managed to narrow down a few potential locations where Lieutenant Hayes could be held captive."

She traced her finger along the map, indicating the marked areas where the enemy might have hidden their prisoner. "These caves and abandoned outposts are our most likely options, considering the difficulty of access and their remote nature."

As Emily detailed the challenges her team faced, Captain Rodriguez couldn't help but admire her resilience and determination. He knew firsthand how unforgiving those mountains could be, yet she had successfully led her team through them in search of Hayes.

"Thank you, Lieutenant Thompson," he said, nodding his appreciation. "Your team's efforts are commendable, and your findings invaluable. Keep up the good work."

Turning his attention to Sergeant Ramirez, Captain Rodriguez raised an eyebrow, silently prompting him to share his team's progress. Miguel shifted his weight slightly and looked at the map, his dark brown eyes focused on the desert region to the south.

"Sir, we've concentrated our efforts on a compound deep within the desert," Miguel reported, his words concise and measured. "The hostile forces guarding it are heavily armed and well-coordinated, making infiltration particularly challenging."

He paused, the toll of their mission evident in the lines around his eyes. "Resources are scarce out there, sir - water, food, and even ammunition. The blistering heat has taken its toll on our equipment as well, but we're adapting and pushing forward."

Ramirez's stoic demeanor impressed Captain Rodriguez. Despite the hardship, he remained dedicated to the mission and refused to let the obstacles deter him.

"Your team is doing an exceptional job, Sergeant Ramirez," Captain Rodriguez said. "I know the desert can be unforgiving, but I have faith in your skills and perseverance."

As the information from both Emily and Miguel sunk in, Captain Rodriguez's mind raced with strategic possibilities. He knew that time was running out for Hayes, and he couldn't shake the gnawing feeling that they needed to act quickly or risk losing one of their own forever.

He mulled over the updates from each team leader, weighing the risks and potential rewards of each approach. The stakes were high, and his decision could mean the difference between life and death for Lieutenant Hayes.

"Alright," he finally spoke, determination hardening his voice. "Lieutenant Thompson, continue scouting those mountain locations and report back with any new developments. Sergeant Ramirez, maintain your focus on that compound – we need to know if Hayes is there. Keep me updated on your progress, and stay safe out there."

With a firm nod from each team leader, Captain Rodriguez knew they shared the same unwavering resolve to bring Hayes home.

The sound of the command center door creaking open cut through the tense air, and Major David Reynolds strode in with purpose. His piercing blue eyes surveyed the room as he approached the table, a sense of urgency emanating from his tall, imposing figure.

"Sorry for the delay," he said, laying down satellite images and notes on a coastal area. "Our intel just came in, and I wanted to bring it straight to you."

"Better late than never, Major," Captain Rodriguez replied, his eyes scrutinizing the new information. "What have you found?"

"Sir, our team managed to infiltrate the enemy's coastal base," Reynolds began, his voice measured and authoritative. "We had to use stealth and precision to slip past the perimeter guards. The slightest misstep would have compromised the mission, but my team performed admirably."

"Excellent work, Major," Captain Rodriguez praised. "Did you find anything that could help us locate Hayes?"

"Indeed we did, sir," Reynolds confirmed, pointing at one of the satellite images. "We discovered a makeshift cell hidden within a cave system. There were signs of recent occupation, and evidence suggests that Hayes might have been held there."

Captain Rodriguez studied the image intently, his mind racing to piece together the puzzle. He weighed the information from each team leader, searching for potential patterns or connections. Was Hayes being moved between these locations? If so, what was the purpose behind it?

"Reynolds, I need your team to go back and investigate that cell further," Captain Rodriguez ordered, determination lacing his words. "Look for any clues that might help us determine where they've taken Hayes next."

"Understood, sir," Reynolds nodded. "We'll leave immediately and report back as soon as we have more information."

"Thank you, Major," the captain acknowledged, his gaze not leaving the map before him. The gravity of the situation weighed heavily on him, and the burden of their comrade's life rested squarely on his shoulders.

As each team leader prepared to execute their orders, Captain Rodriguez couldn't help but feel a renewed sense of responsibility. He knew that it was up to him to guide these teams through the treacherous terrain, hostile forces, and hidden dangers that stood between them and Hayes. Time was running out, and any misstep could mean the difference between success and failure in their mission to bring one of their own home.

"Stay safe out there," he said softly, more to himself than anyone else. "We're coming for you, Hayes. Just hold on."

"Alright, everyone, listen up," Captain Rodriguez commanded, his voice echoing through the command center. The team leaders looked at him expectantly, their eyes reflecting a mix of tension and determination. "We need to work together if we're going to find Hayes in time."

"Thompson, your team's knowledge of the mountain terrain is unmatched," he continued, addressing Lieutenant Thompson directly. "I want you to take point on search and rescue operations there. Focus on the most likely areas where Hayes could be hidden."

"Understood, sir," Thompson replied, her face set with resolve.

"Ramirez, your team has experience in the desert. You'll continue searching for any signs of the enemy's compound and coordinate with Thompson's team to eliminate any hostiles you encounter," Captain Rodriguez ordered confidently.

"Roger that, Captain," Sergeant Ramirez responded, nodding firmly.

"Major Reynolds, as I mentioned earlier, your team will return to the coast and investigate the cell where Hayes was found," Captain

Rodriguez said, locking eyes with Reynolds. "Report back with any new findings."

"Affirmative, sir," Major Reynolds acknowledged, his expression serious.

"Excellent. Now, let's discuss resources." Captain Rodriguez shifted his focus to the map displayed on the table, tracing the routes each team would follow. "We need to pool our equipment and expertise to maximize our chances of success."

"Agreed," Lieutenant Thompson chimed in. "My team has specialized climbing gear and cold-weather supplies that we can share with the rest of you."

"Much appreciated, Thompson," Sergeant Ramirez interjected, his thoughts already racing ahead to how this collaboration would enhance their mission. "My team has acquired detailed satellite imagery of the desert region, which should help with navigation."

"Perfect," Captain Rodriguez nodded approvingly. "Reynolds, do you have anything to contribute?"

"Indeed, sir," Major Reynolds confirmed. "We've got advanced stealth technology on our side. We'd be happy to train the other teams in using it, so they can operate undetected."

"Excellent," Captain Rodriguez said, his eyes gleaming with anticipation. "This collaboration will give us the edge we need to bring Hayes home."

As the team leaders exchanged equipment, technology, and expertise, Captain Rodriguez couldn't help but feel a surge of pride at their unity. The enemy may have been formidable, but they were united by a shared purpose: rescuing Lieutenant Hayes and ensuring the safety of their country.

"Remember, teamwork and communication are key," Captain Rodriguez reminded them, his tone authoritative yet laced with camaraderie. "Stay focused, stay sharp, and stay alive. Let's bring our brother back."

With renewed determination and a strengthened bond between them, the team leaders dispersed to their respective missions, ready to face the challenges that lay ahead. They knew time was running out, but this collaborative approach had given them hope – and hope was a powerful weapon against any adversary.

Captain Rodriguez's eyes narrowed as he observed the team leaders locked in a heated debate. The large tactical map on the table was littered with scribbled notes, highlighted routes, and various markers indicating potential points of interest. Their voices overlapped, each trying to make their point heard over the others.

"Splitting up our forces is too risky!" Lieutenant Thompson argued, her hands gripping the edge of the table. "We need to concentrate our efforts on one location at a time!"

"Thompson's right," Sergeant Ramirez chimed in. "If we spread ourselves thin, we'll be vulnerable to enemy attacks."

"Enough," Captain Rodriguez's voice boomed, cutting through the cacophony of dissent. The room fell silent, all eyes turning to him. He took a deep breath, carefully considering their concerns before addressing them. "I understand your worries, but we cannot afford to waste time. We must cover ground quickly if we're to find Lieutenant Hayes alive." His piercing brown eyes bore into each of theirs, conveying his unwavering determination.

"However," he continued, acknowledging the valid points raised, "we must also ensure that we're working efficiently and minimizing risks. Each team should focus on their assigned areas, but remain in constant communication with the others. Should any team encounter significant resistance or require backup, we'll adjust our strategy accordingly."

The team leaders exchanged glances, mulling over Captain Rodriguez's proposal. Slowly, they nodded in agreement. With tensions diffused, they turned their attention back to the task at hand: planning the next phase of their daring rescue mission.

"Alright then, let's finalize our plans. Thompson, how soon can your team begin the mountain operation?" Captain Rodriguez asked, initiating the logistics discussion.

"Within the hour, sir," she replied confidently. "We're ready to move."

"Good. Ramirez, what about your desert team?"

"Same here, Captain. We can start as soon as we receive the satellite imagery from Thompson."

"Excellent," he said with a nod, making a mental note to ensure that the teams remained in constant contact and shared pertinent information swiftly.

"Reynolds, have your coastal team begin implementing the stealth technology training for the other teams. We need everyone to be proficient in its use before they set out on their missions."

"Understood, sir," Major Reynolds acknowledged, his expression focused and determined.

Captain Rodriguez surveyed the room, taking in the resolute faces of his fellow soldiers. Their confidence in his leadership was clear, and it only strengthened his resolve. "Remember, time is of the essence. Coordinate your movements, keep communication lines open, and follow the protocols we've established. We'll find Hayes and bring him home."

With renewed purpose, the team leaders dispersed to brief their respective squads on the updated plans. Though the mission ahead was fraught with danger and uncertainty, Captain Rodriguez knew one thing for certain: the unity and determination of his team were their strongest weapons against the enemy. And those weapons would not waver.

Captain Rodriguez stood before the team leaders, his piercing brown eyes locked onto each of them in turn. The weight of responsibility hung heavy in the air, but it was clear that he would not let it crush their spirits or determination.

"Listen up," he began, his voice steady and commanding. "I know we've faced challenges in our search for Lieutenant Hayes, but I have no doubt that we possess the skills and resources necessary to overcome them. Our enemy may be formidable, but they've underestimated us. They've underestimated our resolve, our ingenuity, and our commitment to this mission."

His gaze swept across the room, meeting the focused eyes of Lieutenant Thompson, Sergeant Ramirez, and Major Reynolds. Each of them held themselves with an unwavering sense of purpose – a testament to the strength of their bond and the trust they placed in one another.

"Every one of you has demonstrated time and time again your ability to adapt and excel under pressure," he continued, his words ringing with conviction. "And now, we must channel that same tenacity and drive into rescuing Lieutenant Hayes and putting an end to the enemy's plans once and for all."

He paused for a moment, allowing the magnitude of their task to settle upon them. It was a sobering reminder of the stakes involved, but one that only served to steel their resolve further.

"Each team will face its own unique set of challenges," Captain Rodriguez said, addressing each leader in turn. "But I am confident that by pooling our knowledge and resources, by standing united, there is no obstacle we cannot overcome."

As he spoke, the captain could feel the energy in the room shift, the atmosphere charged with renewed determination. He looked into the eyes of his fellow soldiers, seeing the fire of conviction burning within them. They were ready to take on whatever the world threw at them – together.

"Let's move out," he ordered, his tone firm and resolute.

With a synchronized nod, the team leaders dispersed from the command center, each heading to their respective teams to implement the strategies they had discussed. As they strode away from the table, their steps brimming with confidence, it was clear that their bond had only been strengthened by the challenges they faced.

Captain Rodriguez watched them go, his chest swelling with pride. The road ahead would be treacherous, but he knew that together, they would prevail. For Lieutenant Hayes, for their country, and for each other – they would leave no stone unturned in their quest for justice.

And as he turned to join his own team, Captain Rodriguez couldn't help but feel a deep sense of gratitude. It was an honor to lead such a dedicated group of soldiers, and he wouldn't trade it for anything in the world.

The sun dipped low on the horizon, casting long shadows across the makeshift base as the teams assembled, ready to embark on their mission. Captain Rodriguez stood at the head of his own team, watching as the others prepared themselves with quiet determination.

"Alright, everyone," he called out, his voice steady and commanding. "We know what we're up against, and we know what we have to do. Let's stay focused and work together. We'll find Lieutenant Hayes and bring him home."

Lieutenant Thompson approached Captain Rodriguez, her piercing blue eyes reflecting her resolve. "My team is geared up for the mountains, Captain. We'll search every inch of that terrain until we find Sam."

"Good," he nodded, appreciating her tenacity. "And remember to keep an open line of communication. We need to be in sync if anything unexpected arises."

"Understood, sir," she replied, saluting before turning back to her team.

Sergeant Ramirez crossed paths with Rodriguez, wiping sweat from his brow. "Desert team is ready, Captain. We've got extra supplies and intel on the compound. We'll do whatever it takes to locate Lieutenant Hayes."

"Thank you, Sergeant," said Rodriguez, offering a firm nod. *We're going to need every bit of strength we can muster,* he thought.

As the teams moved into position, a palpable sense of anticipation hung in the air. Years of training, experience, and trust between them would now be tested like never before. Yet, amidst the tension, there was also a feeling of unity – knowing they were part of something greater than themselves, bound by a common purpose.

"Stay sharp, everyone," he reminded them as they began to mobilize. The weight of responsibility weighed heavy on his shoulders, but he knew he could rely on the people around him. *We're coming for you, Sam,* he promised inwardly, his thoughts filled with images of the captured lieutenant. *We won't let you down.*

"Captain," a voice called out from behind him, pulling Rodriguez from his reverie. It was Major Reynolds, her gaze unwavering and resolute.

"Major," he acknowledged, turning to face her.

"Coastal team is prepared for infiltration. We'll scour that area until we find where they're holding Lieutenant Hayes."

"Excellent," he replied, clasping her shoulder in gratitude. "I have every confidence in your team's abilities. Stay safe out there."

"Likewise, Captain," she said, offering a small smile before rejoining her team.

As the sun dipped below the horizon and darkness began to envelop the landscape, the teams set off on their respective missions, united in their pursuit of one goal – rescuing Lieutenant Samuel Hayes and bringing him home.

"Godspeed," Captain Rodriguez whispered as he watched them disperse, the words carried away by the wind. And with a deep breath, he turned and led his own team forward, stepping into the unknown with courage and determination.

CHAPTER 7

The jungle loomed ominously around Captain Rodriguez and his team, the dense foliage casting eerie shadows as they moved cautiously through the undergrowth. Rodriguez scanned the area, his piercing brown eyes taking in every detail of their surroundings, his muscular frame tense with anticipation.

"Alright, Team Alpha, we're splitting up to cover more ground," he said authoritatively, his voice cutting through the stifling silence of the jungle. "Jackson, Martinez, you're with me. We'll head deeper into this hellhole. The rest of you, fan out in different directions. Keep your comms open and report any findings immediately."

"Copy that, Captain," came the chorus of responses from his tightly-knit group, their faces a mix of determination and apprehension.

As Rodriguez led Jackson and Martinez further into the green abyss, the sounds of the other team members faded into the distance. The three men moved silently, their combat boots barely making a sound on the damp, leaf-covered jungle floor.

"Stay sharp and watch your step," Rodriguez warned, his voice barely above a whisper. He knew all too well that the enemy was cunning and resourceful, capable of turning even the most innocuous-looking stretch of land into a death trap.

His instincts were soon proven right. As they rounded a bend in the narrow path they followed, Rodriguez spotted a nearly-invisible tripwire stretched between two trees. He halted abruptly, holding up a hand to signal the others to stop.

"Booby traps," he muttered, nodding toward the thin wire. "Looks like we're on the right track. But we need to proceed with extreme caution from here on out."

"Understood, sir," Jackson replied, his eyes wide with alarm. Martinez simply nodded, his expression grim.

With painstaking precision, Rodriguez bent down and carefully disarmed the trap, his hands steady and practiced. Each movement was deliberate and calculated, a testament to his years of experience in the field.

"Jackson, take point," he ordered once the trap was rendered harmless. "Keep your eyes peeled for more of these. Martinez, cover our six."

The three men resumed their cautious trek, now acutely aware of the potential danger lurking around every corner. Rodriguez's mind raced with thoughts of what lay ahead, but also with concern for the other teams and the challenges they faced. His heart ached for Lieutenant Hayes, the man they were all here to find and rescue.

"Captain, I've got another one," Jackson whispered urgently, having spotted yet another tripwire. Rodriguez nodded, moving forward to disarm it as he had done moments before.

"Good catch," he praised Jackson quietly, his mind already calculating their next move. The traps they had encountered so far were rudimentary, but he knew better than to underestimate their enemy. Just one misstep could cost them everything.

As they pressed on, navigating the treacherous jungle terrain and the increasingly elaborate traps laid out by the enemy, Captain James Rodriguez steeled his resolve. He would not let his team down, nor would he allow Lieutenant Hayes to remain a captive. With each step, they drew closer to the truth, inching ever nearer to the showdown that loomed on the horizon.

Ice crunched beneath Lieutenant Emily Thompson's boots as she dug her crampons into the frozen surface, her breath a misty fog in the frigid air. The towering mountain peak loomed above them, a formidable challenge that dared Team Bravo to conquer its heights. Emily's gloved fingers tightened around her ice axe, the cold metal biting through the fabric and numbing her fingertips. Determination burned within her, fueled by the knowledge that somewhere out there, Lieutenant Hayes was depending on them.

"Keep moving, team!" Emily barked, her voice barely audible over the howling wind that whipped around them, threatening to send them hurtling from the cliff face. "Hayes is counting on us!"

"Roger that, Lieutenant," came the muffled reply of one of her teammates, his words lost amidst the gale-force winds.

One by one, they ascended the icy cliffs, their bodies straining against gravity and the elements, a testament to their resolve and specialized training. For hours, they clawed their way upward, refusing to let the mountain defeat them.

"Almost there," Emily murmured to herself, willing her exhausted limbs to push on. The wind roared in her ears, as if mocking her determination.

At last, they reached a relatively flat vantage point, their frost-covered faces revealing the toll of their arduous climb. With haste, Emily unhooked the thermal imaging device from her belt, her numb fingers fumbling with the buttons.

"Let's see what you're hiding," she whispered, scanning the landscape below for any sign of warmth amidst the freezing wasteland. Her heart raced with anticipation, hoping for the breakthrough they so desperately needed.

"Got something," she announced, her voice laced with excitement. "Looks like a heat signature coming from that cave system to the west."

"Good job, Lieutenant. We'll gear up and head there immediately," one of her teammates replied, his voice muffled by the layers of clothing protecting him from the biting cold.

"Stay sharp, everyone," Emily warned, her piercing blue eyes scanning the horizon for any signs of danger. "We don't know what's waiting for us down there."

"Understood, Lieutenant," came the chorus of replies as they prepared to descend and investigate the potential hideout.

As they rappelled down the mountain, Emily couldn't help but think of Lieutenant Hayes, a fellow soldier and friend who had endured unimaginable suffering at the hands of their enemies. She knew that each moment they wasted could mean the difference between life and death for him. Failure was not an option.

"Stay focused, stay alive," she repeated to herself like a mantra, the words echoing in her mind against the howling wind. For Lieutenant Hayes, and for all those who relied on them, Team Bravo would not falter. They would prevail.

The sun beat down mercilessly on Team Charlie as they moved like ghosts through the desert landscape, their tan combat fatigues blending seamlessly with the golden sands. Sergeant Miguel Ramirez led his team with quiet determination, his dark brown eyes scanning the horizon for any signs of movement or danger.

"Stay low and keep moving," Ramirez instructed in a hushed tone, his words barely audible above the wind that whipped sand into tiny tornadoes around them. "We don't want to draw any unnecessary attention."

"Copy that," replied a team member, his voice muffled by the cloth wrapped around his face to protect against the relentless sand and heat.

As they continued their trek, Ramirez couldn't help but think about Lieutenant Hayes. They had trained together as young soldiers and had developed a bond that went beyond military duty. He knew he could not afford to let his emotions cloud his judgment, but the thought of his comrade in enemy hands spurred him on with renewed vigor.

"Spread out and search this area," Ramirez ordered when they reached the base of a rocky outcropping. "Hayes could be anywhere."

"Sir, I think you should see this," called a soldier moments later, his voice tinged with excitement.

Ramirez hurried over, his boots sinking into the soft sands as he navigated the dunes. The soldier pointed out a hidden entrance partially obscured by rocks and sand.

"Looks like an underground tunnel system," Ramirez observed, his heart pounding with anticipation. "This could be our ticket to finding Hayes."

"Should we call it in?" asked another team member, his hand hovering over the radio transmitter clipped to his vest.

"Negative," Ramirez replied, his voice firm. "We don't know what we're dealing with yet. We go in quietly and assess the situation first."

"Understood, Sergeant."

With practiced precision, Ramirez's team donned their night vision goggles and cautiously entered the tunnels, the darkness swallowing them whole. The air was cool and damp, a stark contrast to the blazing heat above ground.

"Stay sharp," Ramirez whispered as they moved forward, their weapons at the ready. "We don't know what's lurking in these shadows."

The team crept through the labyrinthine passageways, alert for any sign of danger or clue that could lead them to Hayes. Ramirez could feel the weight of responsibility bearing down on him, but he refused to let it break his concentration. He owed it to Hayes – and his team – to see this mission through.

"Think I found something, Sarge," a soldier suddenly announced, his voice echoing through the tunnel.

"Show me," Ramirez demanded, his heart quickening at the prospect of a breakthrough.

"Footprints, heading deeper into the tunnels," the soldier explained, shining his headlamp at the dusty floor. "Could be our guy, or it could be the enemy."

"Only one way to find out," Ramirez replied, his determination unwavering. "Follow the trail, but stay vigilant. We're getting closer, I can feel it."

"Copy that, Sergeant."

As Team Charlie pressed on, Ramirez couldn't help but wonder what fate had befallen Lieutenant Hayes in the clutches of their enemies. He steeled his resolve, vowing that no matter what challenges awaited them in the dark depths of the tunnels, they would not stop until they found their comrade and brought him home.

"Three... two... one... execute," Major David Reynolds whispered into his earpiece, his intense blue eyes focused on the coastal enemy camp below. The moonless night provided perfect cover as Team Delta infiltrated under a veil of darkness.

In synchronized precision, the team silently took out the unsuspecting perimeter guards, their bodies crumpling to the ground without a sound. David's heart pounded in his chest as adrenaline surged through him, but he maintained his composure, leading his team from building to building while scanning for any clues or signs of Lieutenant Hayes' presence.

"Major, we've got something," Corporal Martinez called over the radio, his voice hushed yet urgent. "Building six, third room on the left."

"Copy that, en route," David replied, moving swiftly and silently across the compound with his team following closely behind. They slipped into the dimly lit room, where Martinez pointed at a nondescript bookshelf.

"Found a hidden switch," he explained, pressing a small button camouflaged among the bindings.

The bookshelf swung open, revealing a concealed chamber filled with maps and documents. David's eyes widened as they scanned the details – intricate plans for a devastating bioweapon signed by General Kozlov himself.

"Photograph everything," David ordered, his mind racing with the implications of this discovery. "Relay the intel to the other teams. This could be the break we need to find Hayes and put a stop to Kozlov's plans."

"Roger that, Major," Private Jenkins responded, snapping pictures with his high-resolution camera. As the team documented the evidence, David couldn't shake the feeling that time was running out for Hayes.

"Stay sharp," he warned his team, knowing the enemy could discover their presence at any moment. "We're not out of the woods yet."

"Understood, sir," came the chorus of replies, each voice laced with determination.

As they continued their search, David's thoughts raced with the weight of their mission. The stakes were higher than ever – not just for Hayes, but for countless innocent lives at risk from Kozlov's bioweapon. Failure was not an option, and David would do whatever it took to ensure the success of their operation.

"Let's move out," he commanded, his voice steady and resolute. "We've got a comrade to find and a world to save."

Captain Rodriguez's piercing brown eyes scanned the dense jungle around him as he led his team deeper into the treacherous terrain. The humidity weighed on them like an oppressive force, but they pressed on, knowing that each step could bring them closer to finding Lieutenant Hayes.

"Stay sharp, and keep your eyes peeled for any signs of enemy patrols," Rodriguez instructed his team in a hushed tone, fully aware that danger could be lurking behind every tree.

"Copy that, Captain," replied Corporal Adams, her voice steady despite the tension in the air. She wiped her brow with the back of her hand, sweat dripping from her forehead.

As Team Alpha pushed forward, the already dim light filtering through the foliage became even scarcer, casting eerie shadows on the jungle floor. Each soldier kept their weapon raised, ready to react at a moment's notice.

Suddenly, a twig snapped nearby, followed by the rustling of leaves. Rodriguez gestured for his team to take cover, his heart pounding in his chest as an enemy patrol emerged from the undergrowth.

"Engage only if necessary," Rodriguez thought, hoping they could avoid detection and a firefight. But fate had other plans.

"Contact!" whispered Private Wilson, his voice barely audible as he opened fire on the unsuspecting enemy soldiers, neutralizing two of them with well-placed shots.

"Move in!" Rodriguez ordered, rushing from his hiding spot and engaging the remaining hostiles with expert precision. Within moments, the skirmish was over, and the enemy patrol lay motionless on the jungle floor.

"Good work, Team Alpha," Rodriguez praised them, knowing that swift efficiency was crucial to their mission's success. "Let's keep moving."

As they continued their search, Corporal Adams stumbled upon something unexpected – a hidden underground bunker concealed beneath thick foliage.

"Captain, I've found something," she called out, her voice betraying a mix of excitement and caution.

"Let's take a look," Rodriguez responded, his curiosity piqued. He approached the entrance, running his hand along the edges of the concealed door, impressed by the enemy's ingenuity.

"Stay alert," he warned, pushing the bunker door open with one hand while keeping his weapon at the ready in the other. The team cautiously descended into the darkness below, their weapons raised and senses heightened, prepared for any potential threats lurking within.

The air inside the bunker was cool and damp, a stark contrast to the sweltering jungle above. Rodriguez couldn't help but wonder if this hidden refuge held the key to finding Hayes – or perhaps something even more sinister.

"Search every inch of this place," he commanded, his voice echoing off the concrete walls. "And remember, we're not alone out here."

"Understood, Captain," his team replied in unison, their voices filled with determination as they began scouring the bunker for clues.

As they delved deeper into the underground labyrinth, Rodriguez couldn't shake the feeling that they were closing in on something monumental – something that could change the course of their mission and, possibly, the fate of the world.

High above the treacherous mountain peak, the wind howled and whipped around Lieutenant Emily Thompson as she expertly scaled the icy cliffside. Her gloved fingers gripped her ice axe with practiced precision, finding purchase in the frozen surface. She could feel the cold seeping into her bones, but she refused to let it slow her down.

"Almost there, team," she called out to her fellow climbers, her voice full of determination despite the biting chill. "Keep pushing!"

"Roger that, Lieutenant," came a chorus of replies from Team Bravo, their breaths misting in the frigid air as they followed their fearless leader.

As they neared the summit, Emily spotted something unusual – a barely visible seam in the rock face. Inching closer, she realized it was a concealed entrance to a cave system, the perfect place for an enemy hideout or a captive lieutenant.

"Found something!" she announced, her heart pounding with anticipation. "Let's check it out."

"Copy that," her team confirmed, securing their climbing gear and preparing to venture into the darkness below.

The moment they crossed the threshold, Emily was struck by the eerie silence of the caves, her headlamp casting long shadows on the walls. Her instincts told her something important lay hidden within these tunnels, and she resolved to leave no stone unturned in her search for Hayes.

"Stay sharp, everyone," she warned, her voice echoing through the caverns. "No telling what we might find in here."

"Understood, Lieutenant," her team responded, their voices tense but resolute.

Meanwhile, in the sweltering desert heat, Sergeant Ramirez led Team Charlie toward a fortified compound shimmering like a mirage on the horizon. The sun beat mercilessly on their backs, but they refused to waver, driven by the knowledge that every minute counted.

"Looks heavily guarded," Ramirez observed, studying the compound through his binoculars. "We need a plan to get inside."

"Let's hit 'em hard and fast," came a suggestion from one of his men, eager for action.

"Negative," Ramirez replied, his mind racing with strategies. "We need a diversion. Split into two groups – one to create a distraction, the other to infiltrate the compound."

"Copy that, Sergeant." The team divided, ready to put their plan into motion.

"Remember, we're here to find Hayes," Ramirez reminded them. "Stay focused on the mission, and watch each other's backs."

"Roger that," came the unified response as Team Charlie sprang into action.

As Emily navigated the labyrinthine caves, her thoughts remained firmly on Hayes, praying she would find him alive and unharmed. Simultaneously, Ramirez executed their daring plan to breach the enemy compound, the tension mounting with every passing moment.

"Please let us be in time," Emily whispered under her breath, her resolve unwavering as she pushed further into the darkness, a growing sense of urgency driving her forward.

"Let's make this count," Ramirez thought, taking a deep breath as the first explosion erupted, signaling the beginning of their assault.

Both teams knew the stakes were high, and they were prepared to face any challenge to accomplish their mission and bring Lieutenant Hayes home.

The moonlit waves lapped against the shore as Team Delta emerged from the shadows, their silhouettes barely perceptible against the coastal landscape. Major Reynolds signaled his team to fan out, their eyes scanning for the entrance to the underground facility they believed held Lieutenant Hayes.

"Keep it tight and quiet," Reynolds whispered into his headset, his voice barely audible above the sound of the crashing waves. "Hayes is depending on us."

As they silently approached a rocky outcrop, a hidden door revealed itself, blending seamlessly with the surrounding terrain. With a nod from Reynolds, Team Delta infiltrated the secret entrance, their suppressed weapons at the ready.

"Stay sharp, people," Reynolds cautioned as they descended into the dimly lit corridors of the enemy stronghold.

"Copy that, Major," came the hushed replies, each member of the team acutely aware of the risks involved in their operation.

The further they ventured into the bowels of the facility, the more intense the atmosphere became. The stifling air seemed to press down on them, heavy with anticipation and the unknown dangers that lay ahead. It was nothing new to these seasoned soldiers, but the knowledge that one of their own was trapped somewhere within these walls added another layer of urgency to their mission.

"Contact!" hissed one of the operatives, spotting a pair of enemy guards rounding a corner. In an instant, two suppressed shots rang out, and the guards crumpled to the ground.

"Keep moving," Reynolds ordered, leading his team deeper into the labyrinthine complex.

Meanwhile, Emily Thompson clung to the icy cliff face, her mind focused solely on finding Hayes. She could feel the cold seeping into her bones, but she pushed through the pain and fatigue, knowing that time was running out.

"Stay strong, Sam," she thought, her determination solidifying with each upward movement. "We're coming for you."

Back in the underground facility, Reynolds and his team pressed on, their senses heightened as they encountered sporadic enemy resistance. They dispatched each threat with lethal efficiency, their unwavering commitment to rescuing Hayes driving them forward despite the mounting challenges.

"Major, we've got something," a team member whispered, gesturing to a set of double doors that seemed out of place amidst the stark concrete walls.

"Let's check it out," Reynolds instructed, positioning his team to breach the room.

"Ready?" he asked, receiving silent nods in return. With a swift kick, the doors burst open, revealing a dimly lit chamber filled with the hum of machinery.

"Stay alert," Reynolds warned as they entered, aware that this could be where Hayes was being held captive.

As they searched through the facility, Emily continued her treacherous ascent, Ramirez and his team breached the desert compound, and Rodriguez navigated the booby-trapped jungle. Each team faced unique challenges, but their focus remained unshakable – to rescue Lieutenant Hayes and ensure the safety of their comrades.

"Time is running out," Reynolds thought, his heart pounding as he scanned the room for any sign of Hayes. "We have to find him."

The sun dipped below the horizon, bathing the landscape in a crimson hue as Emily's ice axe struck the frozen mountain face with a resounding crack. Her breath formed clouds of vapor that dissipated into the frigid air, her mind focused solely on the mission at hand. She glanced down at her teammates, their faces etched with determination.

"Keep pushing," she called out, her voice unwavering despite the biting wind. "We're getting closer."

"Copy that, Lieutenant," one of her team members shouted back, his grip tightening on his ice axe.

Far below, in the treacherous labyrinth of the underground facility, Reynolds and his team discovered a hidden chamber containing vital information about Kozlov's bioweapon plans. The documents, hastily photographed and sent to the other teams, fueled their resolve to find Hayes before it was too late.

"Guys, we're onto something here," Reynolds said, his eyes scanning the pages with a sense of urgency. "We need to find Hayes now. Keep moving."

In the sweltering desert heat, Ramirez and his team navigated the network of tunnels beneath the enemy compound, relying on their training and instincts to avoid detection. Sweat dripped from their brows, their hearts pounding as they moved deeper into the enemy's lair.

"Stay sharp, everyone," Ramirez whispered, wiping his brow as he led the team through the dark passages. "Hayes has to be close."

"Understood, Sergeant," replied a team member, the green glow of night vision illuminating his face.

As Rodriguez's team crept through the booby-trapped jungle, sweat mixed with mud painted their faces, disguising them further among the foliage. Their movements were calculated and precise, each step taken with cautious determination.

"Captain, we found an entrance to a bunker over here," whispered one of Rodriguez's men, pointing to a hidden door beneath a tangled mass of vines.

"Good work. Let's check it out, but be careful," Rodriguez commanded, his eyes narrowing as they approached the entrance.

Back on the mountain, Emily's team reached a ledge that provided a panoramic view of the surrounding area. As they caught their breath, she pulled out her binoculars and scanned the region, searching for any sign of Hayes or Kozlov's forces. "I've got a heat signature two clicks east," she reported, her heart racing at the thought of finding her comrade.

"Copy, Lieutenant," a teammate replied, already securing his gear to resume the climb. "Let's get moving."

"Remember, stay focused," Emily urged them, her blue eyes reflecting both determination and the toll of past missions. "We're going to find him."

"Roger that, Lieutenant," the team chorused, their resolve unwavering.

As night fell, each team pressed forward, inching closer to finding Lieutenant Hayes and unraveling General Kozlov's sinister plans for the bioweapon. The tension mounted with every passing moment, their hearts pounding in unison as they prepared for the next phase of their mission – the most critical yet. Failure was not an option; the lives of countless innocents, and one of their own, depended on their success.

CHAPTER 8

Captain James Rodriguez crouched behind a stack of rusted barrels, the stagnant smell of decay permeating the secluded corner of the enemy stronghold. Beside him, Lieutenant Emily Thompson's chest heaved as she caught her breath, the adrenaline from their recent skirmish still coursing through her veins. They had managed to slip away from the chaos momentarily, seizing the opportunity for a brief respite.

"Nice work with the guards back there," Captain Rodriguez commended, his voice low and steady.

"Thanks, sir," Emily replied, wiping the sweat from her brow. "You weren't too shabby yourself."

In that moment, their eyes locked, each taking in the other's battle-worn features. The unspoken connection between them had been growing stronger throughout the mission, forged by shared danger and unwavering mutual trust. Rodriguez couldn't help but admire Emily's resilience and determination; it reminded him of the fire that had once burned within himself early in his career.

Emily's piercing blue eyes seemed to search Rodriguez's soul, communicating without words her gratitude for his leadership and support. She recognized the weight he carried on his shoulders, the responsibility for his team's safety, and the nightmares of fallen comrades that undoubtedly haunted him. And yet, here he stood—undaunted, ready to risk everything for the sake of their mission.

"Captain," she finally spoke, her voice calm and measured, "I want you to know that I've got your back, no matter what happens."

"Likewise, Lieutenant," Rodriguez responded, his brown eyes unwavering. Deep down, he knew that they were two sides of the same coin, both driven by an unyielding sense of duty and loyalty. This mission was more than just another operation; it was a testament to the bonds they had formed as a team.

As they allowed themselves this rare moment of vulnerability, Rodriguez felt a renewed surge of determination. The mission was far from over, and he knew that they would need every ounce of strength and courage to see it through. He allowed himself a small nod before steeling his gaze once more.

"Alright, Lieutenant," he ordered, the authority returning to his voice. "We've got a job to do. Let's move out."

With their unspoken promise hanging in the air, Captain Rodriguez and Lieutenant Thompson prepared themselves for the challenges ahead, their connection only growing stronger in the face of adversity.

Gunfire shattered the momentary stillness, its cacophony echoing through the air like the crack of a whip. Captain Rodriguez's instincts kicked in as he grabbed Lieutenant Thompson by the arm, pulling her down behind a stack of wooden crates. They moved with practiced precision, their bodies angled to minimize any exposure to enemy fire.

"Contact, three o'clock!" Rodriguez called out, his voice steady despite the chaos around them.

Thompson peered around the edge of the crates, quickly assessing the threat. Her piercing blue eyes narrowed as she spotted a group of enemy combatants advancing on their position. "Four tangos, armed and closing in," she confirmed.

Rodriguez could feel the adrenaline coursing through his veins, sharpening his senses and honing his focus. He had been in countless firefights before, but this one felt different—more personal. Protecting his team was always his top priority, but now it felt as though there was even more at stake.

"Stay low," he ordered, his brown eyes meeting Thompson's gaze for a brief second. In that instant, they exchanged a silent understanding—their plan to flank the enemy and neutralize the threat. Rodriguez gave a curt nod, and Thompson returned it, her expression resolute.

"Copy that, Captain," she replied, her voice calm and confident despite the hail of bullets ricocheting mere inches from their cover.

As they prepared to move, Rodriguez couldn't help but marvel at Thompson's unwavering resolve. Despite the harrowing ordeals they had faced together, she remained an impenetrable force, determined to see their mission through to the end. It was clear that whatever connection they had forged during their brief respite had only served to strengthen their resolve.

"Cover me," Rodriguez said, his voice barely audible over the din of gunfire.

"Roger that," Thompson acknowledged, steeling herself for the task ahead.

With their plan set, Captain Rodriguez and Lieutenant Thompson readied themselves to confront the enemy head-on. They knew that they couldn't afford any missteps; the stakes were simply too high. But as they moved into action, their determination was unwavering, fueled by the unspoken bond that had been forged in the heat of battle.

A hailstorm of bullets tore through the air like a swarm of deadly hornets, their stings vicious and unforgiving. Captain Rodriguez kept his body low, muscles tense, as he moved in perfect sync with Lieutenant Thompson. Their synchronized movements were akin to a lethal ballet, a testament to their seamless teamwork.

"Stay close," Rodriguez whispered, his voice taut with urgency as they navigated the treacherous battleground. His mind raced with tactical calculations, each thought carefully balanced against the risks they faced.

"Roger that," Thompson replied, her breaths measured and controlled. She trusted Rodriguez implicitly, her instincts telling her that this was the man who would lead them to victory or die trying.

Rodriguez's heart pounded in his chest, adrenaline surging through his veins as they closed in on the enemy. He could feel the intensity of the firefight building, the oppressive weight of danger bearing down on them. But there was no room for fear, not when their very lives depended on their actions.

"Three... two... one... Go!" Rodriguez commanded, and they sprang into action.

As they engaged the enemy, Captain Rodriguez took up position behind a crumbling wall, providing suppressing fire while Thompson maneuvered to a better vantage point. His weapon roared in his hands like a beast unleashed, each shot a desperate plea for survival.

"Almost there, Captain," Thompson called out, her voice strained but steady. "Just a few more seconds."

"Make it count," Rodriguez replied grimly, his thoughts turning to the wounded teammate they'd left behind. If they didn't succeed now, all their sacrifices would be for naught.

As he continued to lay down cover fire, Rodriguez couldn't help but think of how far they'd come together. From the moment they'd first met during training, he'd known Thompson was something special. She had a fire within her that refused to be extinguished, a determination that shone like a beacon in even the darkest moments.

"Ready," Thompson announced, her voice barely audible over the cacophony of gunfire.

"Give 'em hell," Rodriguez said, his own resolve steeling as they prepared to make their move.

"Copy that, Captain."

With a final surge of effort, they pressed forward, their combined strength a force to be reckoned with. They knew that the battle was far from over, but as long as they fought together, there was nothing they couldn't overcome.

Thompson's finger tightened around the trigger, her breath held steady as she zeroed in on her targets. The metallic scent of spent ammunition filled her nostrils, and the roar of gunfire echoed in her ears. With methodical precision, she eliminated one enemy combatant after another, their bodies crumpling to the ground like discarded marionettes.

"Nice shooting," Rodriguez praised, his voice a welcome anchor amidst the chaos. "Keep it up, Thompson. We're making progress."

"Thanks, Captain," she replied, her focus unwavering. She could feel the weight of their mission bearing down on her, but she refused to let it crush her spirit.

As they continued their advance, Rodriguez's keen eyes scanned the battlefield, ever vigilant for threats or potential opportunities. It was then that he spotted him – a wounded teammate, struggling to crawl to safety, blood staining the dusty ground beneath him.

"Thompson!" Rodriguez barked, urgency lacing his tone. "I've got eyes on Hayes. He needs immediate medical attention."

"Copy that, Captain," she replied, her eyes narrowing with renewed determination. "Where is he?"

"Ten meters to your right, behind that broken pillar." His gaze met hers, conveying unspoken trust and a shared resolve to save their comrade.

"Understood. Cover me." Thompson sprinted towards Hayes, her movements lithe and swift, each step fuelled by a fierce refusal to lose another member of their team. Her heart raced, but she pushed the fear to the recesses of her mind, focusing instead on the task at hand.

"Always," Rodriguez assured her, shifting his position to provide better cover fire. As he watched her tend to their injured teammate, he felt a surge of pride and gratitude. Thompson was more than just an exceptional soldier; she was the embodiment of all they fought for – loyalty, courage, and an unyielding commitment to their cause.

"Stay with me, Sam," Thompson urged, her voice gentle but firm as she began administering life-saving medical aid. "You're going to be okay."

"Thompson's got him, Rodriguez," Sam whispered weakly. "I'm not going anywhere."

"Damn right," Rodriguez muttered under his breath, a fierce determination taking hold of him. They would see this mission through, and they would do it together – as a team, bound by more than just duty.

Bullets whizzed through the air like deadly hornets, their stinging impact muffled by the relentless gunfire. Captain Rodriguez gritted his teeth, beads of sweat trickling down his temple as he squeezed off rounds at the approaching enemy.

"Thompson, status?" he shouted, his voice barely audible above the cacophony of battle.

"Almost done!" Thompson's response was punctuated by the ripping sound of medical tape being torn from its roll. She wrapped it tightly around Lieutenant Hayes' midsection, her hands steady despite the adrenaline coursing through her veins. "Just need to secure this dressing."

"Copy that," Rodriguez replied, his gaze never leaving the encroaching enemy. He fired off a few more shots, forcing them to take cover behind a crumbling wall. Their retreat, however brief, gave him some respite, but he knew it wouldn't last.

His thoughts raced, analyzing their situation with the precision and focus that had seen him through countless perilous missions. They were cornered, low on ammunition, and with an injured teammate – not ideal, but not impossible either. It would take all their skill and determination to get out of this alive. And they would, he silently vowed. No soldier left behind.

"Rodriguez, I've stabilized Hayes. We need to move now!" Thompson's urgent cry snapped him back to the present, just as the enemy began to regroup for another assault.

"Right," he muttered, his heart pounding in his chest. The time for silent contemplation was over; now was the time for action. "Cover me, I'll grab Hayes."

"Understood." Thompson took up a defensive position, her rifle aimed at the enemy's makeshift cover as Rodriguez hoisted their battered comrade onto his broad shoulders.

"Go!" Rodriguez commanded, and together they sprinted towards the nearest exit, their movements synchronized and fluid like a well-oiled machine. Every step was fueled by a potent mix of desperation, loyalty, and unspoken camaraderie.

As they crossed the threshold into relative safety, Rodriguez glanced back at Thompson, their eyes locking for a brief moment. No words were needed; their shared gaze spoke volumes.

"Nice work out there," he said breathlessly, setting Hayes down gently against a wall.

"Couldn't have done it without you," she replied, her voice tinged with gratitude. "Now let's finish this mission and get everyone home."

"Agreed." With a mutual nod, Captain Rodriguez and Lieutenant Thompson steeled themselves for the next challenge that awaited them, bound by a silent understanding forged in the crucible of battle.

The dim glow of emergency lights flickered along the narrow corridor, casting disjointed shadows that danced in a macabre rhythm. Between ragged breaths and the muted echo of distant gunfire, a palpable tension filled the air as Captain Rodriguez and Lieutenant Thompson pressed on.

"Stay sharp, Emily. We're close now," Rodriguez cautioned, his voice low and deliberate. Thompson's eyes met his with steely resolve, her grip tightening on her weapon.

"Whatever it takes, James. We've come too far to fail now," she replied, her gaze never wavering. The unspoken bond between them had only deepened throughout the mission, a silent understanding that they would lay down their lives for one another without hesitation.

As they rounded a corner, the pair came face-to-face with a heavily fortified door, the last barrier standing between them and their objective. The harsh glare from its security lights starkly illuminated the sweat-streaked faces of two battle-hardened soldiers who had been through hell and back together.

"Looks like we've got company," Thompson noted, nodding towards the armed guards flanking the entrance. "Ready to make some noise?"

"Always," Rodriguez replied, the ghost of a smile playing at the corner of his mouth. He locked eyes with Thompson, and in that instant, a silent plan formed between them.

With adrenaline coursing through their veins, they leaped into action. Rodriguez unleashed a hail of suppressing fire, forcing the guards to take cover as Thompson deftly sprinted closer. Her movements were fluid and precise, a deadly dance honed by years of training and experience.

In the chaos, Rodriguez allowed himself a momentary pause, his thoughts racing. *We've made it this far, but the real test is just beginning. We'll need to rely on each other more than ever if we're going to succeed.*

As if sensing his thoughts, Thompson glanced back at him, her eyes burning with determination. He nodded in return, his resolve further steeling itself. They were a team, bound by duty and loyalty, and they would see this mission through to the bitter end.

"Let's go," Rodriguez whispered, reloading his weapon and preparing for the next stage of their assault. Together, they pushed forward, ready to face whatever challenges lay ahead.

The smell of gunpowder still hung heavy in the air as Captain Rodriguez and Lieutenant Thompson stared down the dimly lit corridor, their eyes locked on the heavily guarded door that stood between them and their objective.

"Thompson, cover me," Rodriguez said, his voice low and steady. He reached into his tactical vest and withdrew a small explosive device, the smooth casing reflecting the flickering light above.

"Copy that, Captain," Thompson replied, her piercing blue eyes scanning the surroundings for any potential threats. She raised her rifle, prepared to engage any enemy that dared to cross their path.

In the silence of the moment, Rodriguez felt the weight of the mission bearing down on him. *One wrong move, and it all ends here*, he thought. But there was no room for doubt, not with so much at stake.

Expertly, Rodriguez attached the explosive device to the door, setting the timer with practiced precision. The LED display blinked red, counting down the seconds to detonation. He caught Thompson's gaze, the unspoken understanding between them stronger than ever.

"Three... two... one..." Rodriguez whispered under his breath, and then the world exploded into chaos.

The explosion tore through the door like a predator's jaws, sending splinters of wood and shards of metal flying through the air like deadly shrapnel. The force of the blast reverberated through the entire structure, shaking the ground beneath their feet.

"Move!" Rodriguez shouted, his voice barely audible over the ringing in his ears. He charged forward, Thompson hot on his heels. The disoriented guards were picking themselves up from the rubble, but they didn't stand a chance against the duo's relentless assault.

Captain Rodriguez fired off a volley of rounds, cutting down the first wave of enemies before they could even raise their weapons.

Thompson moved like a shadow, taking out the remaining guards with lethal efficiency.

As the last enemy crumpled to the floor, Rodriguez took a moment to survey the carnage. *We did it. But at what cost?* He couldn't help but wonder how many more lives would be lost before this mission was over.

"Captain," Thompson said, her voice snapping him back to the present. "We need to keep moving."

"Right," Rodriguez agreed, taking one last look at the remains of the door, now nothing more than a memory in the wake of their explosive entrance. He reloaded his weapon and turned to face his lieutenant, determination etched into every line of his expression. "Let's finish this."

Smoke still lingered in the air as Captain Rodriguez and Lieutenant Thompson crossed the threshold, stepping into the dimly lit room beyond. The sharp scent of burnt metal and gunpowder permeated their senses, a stark reminder of the destruction they had just wrought.

"Captain, what do you think we'll find in here?" Thompson asked, her voice hushed, as if to avoid drawing unwanted attention. She scanned the room with her piercing blue eyes, her posture tense and ready for action.

"Whatever it is, it's important enough for them to post those guards," Rodriguez replied, his gaze never leaving the shadows that seemed to be closing in around them. His heart pounded in his chest, anticipation mingling with anxiety as he considered what challenges might lie ahead.

"Watch my six," he commanded, moving forward with practiced caution. Thompson nodded, covering his back as they ventured deeper into the unknown.

A sudden noise, like the crackle of broken glass underfoot, echoed through the space. Thompson tensed, her weapon at the ready. Rodriguez held up a hand, signaling her to wait.

"Who's there?" he called out, his voice authoritative yet tinged with concern. He knew that even in the heat of battle, hesitation could cost lives, but something about this situation felt different.

"Captain Rodriguez," a familiar voice emerged from the darkness, causing both soldiers to lower their weapons slightly. Sergeant Ramirez stepped into the faint glow of a flickering light fixture, his dark brown eyes filled with relief.

"Ramirez! What happened to you?" Thompson asked, her tone laced with worry. "We thought you were..."

"Captured? I managed to slip away, but not before gathering some intel," Ramirez replied, cutting her off. "I found out where they're keeping Major Reynolds."

Rodriguez's eyes narrowed, his mind racing with the implications of this revelation. *So, Reynolds is still alive. We have to rescue him and complete the mission.* He knew time was of the essence.

"Lead the way, Sergeant," Rodriguez ordered, his voice firm with resolve. "We're getting the Major out of here."

As they followed Ramirez deeper into the enemy stronghold, Rodriguez couldn't help but feel a renewed sense of purpose. Despite the odds, they had made it this far, and he was determined not to let his team down.

"Stay sharp, everyone," he thought, his grip tightening on his weapon. "This is far from over."

CHAPTER 9

Agent Smith sat hunched over his laptop, his fingers hovering above the keyboard as he stared at the encrypted message on the screen. Beads of sweat trickled down his forehead, his heart pounding in his chest. The dimly lit room around him seemed to close in as he read the words again, struggling to comprehend their meaning.

"Smith," the message began, "you have been chosen to provide false intel to General Kozlov. This decision is not up for debate. For your own safety and that of your family, you must comply immediately."

He leaned back in his chair, a heavy sigh escaping his lips. He knew all too well about General Viktor Kozlov's brutal reputation, the countless lives he had destroyed in the name of power and control. Yet, here he was, presented with an opportunity to strike a blow against the man who had haunted his nightmares for years. The weight of the decision bore down on him, crushing his spirit with each passing moment.

"Can I really do this?" he whispered to himself, his voice barely audible even in the quiet room. "What if it fails? What if he finds out?"

"Damn it," he muttered, clenching his fists. With renewed determination, Agent Smith set to work crafting a report filled with lies, hoping they would be enough to mislead Kozlov and protect those he cared for.

As his fingers danced across the keyboard, he carefully detailed a fabricated rendezvous point deep within an abandoned industrial complex. He described how Team Alpha was planning to meet with another resistance group there to exchange vital intelligence about the enemy's movements and supply lines.

"Perfect," he thought, "Kozlov will never pass up an opportunity like that."

To make the deception even more believable, he added a diversionary tactic that Team Alpha would supposedly use to mislead any pursuers: a series of false radio transmissions mimicking the chatter of several other teams. This would hopefully draw Kozlov's forces away from the real resistance groups and into the trap Smith was setting.

"God help us all," he prayed silently as he hit send, sealing their fates with a single click.

General Viktor Kozlov sat in the dimly lit room, his cold blue eyes scanning the words on the screen before him. The message from Agent Smith had arrived, and with every line that he read, his confidence grew. A thin smile formed on his lips as he considered the possibilities that this intelligence presented.

"Finally, a chance to crush them once and for all," he muttered under his breath, his voice low and menacing.

He leaned back in his chair, fingers steepled in thought. "Sergeant Petrov, gather the men. We have some traps to set."

"Of course, General," replied Sergeant Petrov, a hint of nervousness in his voice.

As they prepared their forces, Kozlov studied the false intel meticulously, ensuring every detail was accounted for. He knew that even the smallest of errors could ruin his plan. But deep down, he believed wholeheartedly in the effectiveness of the information he had been given.

"Team Alpha will never know what hit them," he thought, an icy determination taking hold inside him.

Meanwhile, Team Alpha, following the false intel provided by Agent Smith, trekked through the dense jungle, their boots sinking into the muddy ground with each step. The stifling heat and humidity clung to their skin like a second layer, making every movement a struggle.

"Stay sharp, everyone," whispered Captain Stone, the team's leader, as they neared the designated rendezvous point. "We don't know what we'll find here."

The team members exchanged nervous glances, the tension palpable as they gripped their weapons tightly. They moved cautiously, their senses heightened, as they scanned the shadows for any signs of danger.

"Captain, are we sure about this intel?" asked Lieutenant Taylor, sweat trickling down her face as she swatted away an insect buzzing around her ear.

"Agent Smith has never let us down before," replied Captain Stone, his eyes scanning the dense foliage surrounding them. "We have to trust him."

"Understood, sir," said Taylor, her doubts momentarily assuaged.

As they reached the abandoned industrial complex, Team Alpha paused, taking in the eerie silence that hung over the area like a shroud.

"Something doesn't feel right," murmured Sergeant Diaz, his brow furrowed as he stared at the rusted metal structures around them.

"Stay focused," Captain Stone ordered, pushing aside his own unease. "No matter what happens, we stick together and see this mission through."

"Copy that, sir," the team members responded in unison, their determination resolute despite the uncertainty that lay ahead.

Unbeknownst to them, General Kozlov watched from a distance, his cold blue eyes filled with satisfaction as his plan began to unfold. The trap was set, and now it was only a matter of time before Team Alpha would be caught in its deadly embrace.

The sudden cacophony of gunfire shattered the tense silence, and Captain Stone barely had time to react before bullets tore through the thick foliage around Team Alpha. Instinct took over as he dove for cover behind a fallen tree, shouting orders to his team.

"Take cover! Return fire!"

Lieutenant Taylor scrambled to find shelter behind an overturned metal drum, her heart pounding as she fired back at the unseen enemy. She could hear the whizzing of bullets flying past her ears, each one feeling like it was just inches away from claiming her life.

"Captain, we're surrounded!" yelled Sergeant Diaz, sweat pouring down his face as he unleashed a barrage of suppressing fire towards the enemy positions.

"Keep your heads down and maintain your fire!" barked Captain Stone, his mind racing to devise a plan amidst the chaos. "We'll fight our way out of this!"

As explosions echoed through the dense jungle, Captain Stone couldn't help but wonder how they had fallen into such a deadly trap. The intel had been precise – or so they thought. But now, with their lives hanging in the balance, doubt gnawed at his gut, threatening to consume him.

"Focus," he told himself, shaking off the uncertainty. "You've led your team through worse."

Meanwhile, high up in the treacherous mountain peaks, Team Bravo battled against the biting winds and icy conditions as they made their way toward a suspected enemy stronghold. Lieutenant Emily Thompson, her face reddened and chapped from the cold, gritted her teeth against the gale that threatened to sweep her off her feet.

"Stay close, people! We don't want to lose anyone in this storm!" she shouted into the wind, her eyes scanning the snowy terrain for any signs of danger.

"Copy that, Lieutenant!" came the muffled response from Major Reynolds, his voice barely audible above the howling wind. He and the rest of the team trudged on, their determination unwavering despite the brutal conditions.

"Captain Rodriguez," Emily muttered under her breath, pulling her scarf tighter around her face. "We'll find you. We won't let Kozlov win."

As they pushed onward, navigating treacherous cliffs and icy slopes, Team Bravo's resilience and determination burned brightly like a beacon in the frozen wilderness. Though the wind sought to extinguish their hope, they pressed on, fueled by the knowledge that their comrades were counting on them.

A deafening boom echoed through the mountains, shaking the very ground beneath Team Bravo's feet. Emily Thompson instinctively glanced upward, her eyes widening in horror as she saw the massive avalanche hurtling toward them.

"Move! Move!" she screamed, her voice barely audible over the thunderous roar of cascading snow and debris. "Get to cover, now!"

The team sprang into action, their survival instincts kicking in as they scrambled for whatever shelter they could find. Major Reynolds grabbed Sergeant Ramirez by the arm, hauling him toward a small crevasse just ahead.

"Thompson, this way!" he shouted, his words punctuated by the sound of cracking ice and the relentless approach of the avalanche.

Emily followed, her heart hammering in her chest as she darted across the treacherous terrain. Snow sprayed around her like shrapnel, but she refused to let fear slow her down. She couldn't afford to; lives were on the line.

"Go, go, go!" she urged, diving into the crevasse just as the avalanche's icy fury crashed down upon them. The world went dark for a moment, the air thick with powder and the tortured screams of the mountain itself.

"Is everyone alive?" Emily called out, her breath ragged as she tried to steady her racing pulse.

"Affirmative," replied Reynolds, pulling himself to his feet. "Ramirez? Vasquez?"

"Still here, sir," Ramirez grunted, rising from a crouch. "Vasquez is okay too."

"Good," Emily said, relief flooding through her. "But we can't stay here. We need to regroup and figure out our next move."

"Agreed," Reynolds nodded. "Let's get moving."

Meanwhile, in the blistering heat of the desert, Team Charlie approached the fortified compound that housed General Kozlov's forces. Sweat dripped down Sergeant Miguel Ramirez's face as he wiped his brow with the back of his hand, trying to ignore the scorching sun overhead.

"Two hundred meters," Colonel Maria Vasquez whispered into her radio, her voice strained with tension. "Enemy forces guarding the entrance heavily."

"Copy that, Colonel," Captain Rodriguez replied from his position on Team Alpha. "Proceed with caution and await further instructions."

Miguel squinted at the compound through the heat haze, taking in the imposing walls and armed guards. He felt a knot tighten in his stomach as they prepared for the direct confrontation ahead. They'd faced tough odds before, but this was something else entirely.

"Ready?" Maria asked, her brown eyes meeting each of her team members' gazes in turn.

"Ready," Miguel affirmed, his jaw set with determination.

"Let's move," Maria ordered, leading the charge toward the enemy lines.

With a thunderous crash, the compound walls crumbled under the barrage of Team Charlie's explosives. Dust and debris filled the air as they charged through the breach, their eyes locked on the enemy forces ahead.

"Cover me!" Maria shouted, her voice barely audible over the cacophony of gunfire and explosions.

Miguel nodded and fired a burst from his rifle, providing cover while Maria dashed forward. She hurled a grenade at an enemy machine gun nest, ducking behind a pile of rubble as the explosion shook the ground.

"Didn't expect this much resistance," Miguel muttered under his breath, gritting his teeth as he reloaded his weapon. This was supposed to be a quick operation, but it seemed General Kozlov had other plans.

"Focus, Ramirez!" Maria shouted, her gaze fixed on the enemies pouring in from all directions. "We need to push through!"

"Copy that, Colonel!" Miguel replied, determination surging within him.

As Team Charlie fought tooth and nail against the overwhelming odds, their thoughts were clouded by the knowledge that every second counted. Lieutenant Hayes' life hung in the balance, and they couldn't fail him now.

Meanwhile, on a moonlit beach far from the desert compound, Team Delta moved silently through the darkness. Waves lapped gently at the shore as they infiltrated the coastal enemy camp, their movements fluid and stealthy.

Captain James Rodriguez scanned the area with his night vision goggles, searching for any sign of Lieutenant Hayes. The tension in the air was palpable, each team member acutely aware of the high stakes of their mission.

"Building three clear," Lieutenant Emily Thompson whispered into her radio, her voice low and urgent. "Moving on to building four."

"Copy that, Thompson," Rodriguez replied, his own voice barely more than a breath. "Stay sharp."

As they navigated the enemy camp, staying hidden in the shadows, Rodriguez couldn't help but feel a weight on his chest. This mission had to succeed – they'd lost too many good soldiers already. But he couldn't let his emotions cloud his judgment; focus was crucial now more than ever.

"Captain, I've found him," Emily's voice crackled into his earpiece, her tone tense with relief and urgency. "Hayes is in building six. He's alive, but we need to move fast."

"Understood," Rodriguez responded, his heart racing. "Team Delta, regroup at building six. We're getting Hayes out of here."

With renewed determination, Team Delta moved as one, their resolve unwavering despite the odds stacked against them. They would rescue Lieutenant Hayes and bring him home – no matter the cost.

The sound of rumbling engines echoed through the coastal camp, raising a sense of panic among Team Delta. Captain Rodriguez watched as enemy trucks rolled in, offloading reinforcements that now swarmed the area, searching for any sign of intruders.

"Damn it," he hissed under his breath. "Emily, we've got company. Keep Hayes hidden and stay out of sight."

"Copy that, Captain," Emily replied, her tone tense but focused as she secured Hayes in a dark corner of the building.

Rodriguez signaled to his team, their eyes conveying a shared understanding: they needed to outmaneuver these new threats without alerting them to their presence. Each member moved with stealthy precision, darting between the shadows of buildings and staying low to avoid detection.

"Captain, I've spotted a patrol coming our way," one of the soldiers whispered into his radio, his voice barely audible. "They're armed and ready, sweeping every building."

"Divert their attention," Rodriguez ordered, his mind racing as he formulated a plan. "Create a distraction – but make sure it's not traceable back to us."

"Roger that," came the reply. Moments later, a small explosion erupted in the distance, drawing the enemy soldiers away from Team Delta's position.

"Nice work," Rodriguez commended, allowing himself a brief moment of satisfaction before refocusing on their mission. "Now let's move. We don't want to be here when they come back."

Meanwhile, the other teams faced their own challenges, each narrowly escaping General Kozlov's traps. Team Alpha fought their way out of the jungle ambush, relying on their instincts and camaraderie to survive. Team Bravo outran the avalanche, using their mountaineering expertise to find shelter and regroup. And Team Charlie, battered but unbroken, pushed through the heavy resistance at the compound, determined to complete their mission.

As each team overcame their respective obstacles, a collective sense of relief washed over them. They had survived – for now. But there was still work to be done. Regrouping and continuing their mission, they were united by a single goal: the rescue of Lieutenant Hayes.

"Captain, we've managed to slip past the reinforcements," Emily reported, her voice hushed as she and Hayes rejoined Team Delta. "Are we clear to proceed?"

"Affirmative, Thompson," Rodriguez replied, his eyes scanning the area for any lingering threats. "But stay sharp. I don't trust Kozlov to give up that easily."

"Understood, Captain," she acknowledged, her determination unwavering. "We'll get Hayes out of here – together."

With renewed vigor and a fierce commitment to their mission, the teams pressed on, each step bringing them closer to rescuing Lieutenant Hayes. But even as they navigated the dangers set by General Kozlov, a new challenge loomed on the horizon – one that would test their resilience and resolve like never before.

Emily's piercing blue eyes darted from shadow to shadow, her breaths measured and controlled as the teams regrouped. The moonlit beach stretched before them, the waves crashing against the shore providing a rhythm for their synchronized movements. They were on the cusp of something big – she could feel it in every fiber of her being.

"Captain Rodriguez," Emily whispered into her earpiece, her voice steady despite the anticipation coursing through her veins. "All teams are present and accounted for. What's our next move?"

"Stand by, Thompson," he replied, his tone betraying an undercurrent of tension. "We're waiting for intel on Hayes' location."

As they awaited further instructions, the members of each team exchanged tense glances, their fingers twitching near their weapons. They had faced the worst General Kozlov could throw at them, but there was no telling what lay ahead. Emily couldn't help but feel a sense of pride in her comrades – together, they had defied the odds and escaped certain death. But they couldn't afford to rest on their laurels – not with Lieutenant Hayes still in enemy hands.

"Command, this is Captain Rodriguez. Any update on Hayes' whereabouts?" Rodriguez pressed, breaking the silence that had settled over the group.

"Receiving new transmission now, Captain," came the terse response, followed by a momentary pause. "Intel confirms Hayes is being held in a heavily fortified bunker located five clicks south of your current position. Surveillance images indicate increased enemy activity surrounding the area. Proceed with extreme caution."

"Copy that, Command," Rodriguez acknowledged, his voice firm. "We'll get Hayes out – no matter the cost."

"Good luck, Captain," the voice on the other end concluded, leaving the team with a stark reminder of the danger they faced.

"Alright, everyone," Rodriguez addressed the teams, his resolve unwavering. "We know where Hayes is, and we're going in to get him. This won't be easy, but I have faith in each and every one of you. Let's move out."

As they set off towards the bunker, Emily allowed herself a brief moment of introspection. She knew the risks, understood the stakes – but she couldn't suppress the flicker of hope that burned within her. They had come this far, defied all odds, and she was determined to see this mission through to the end.

"Sam," she thought, her heart aching for her captured comrade. "Hold on just a little longer. We're coming for you."

The team's footsteps echoed in unison as they ventured deeper into enemy territory, the weight of their mission bearing down upon them. Yet with each step, their resolve only grew stronger, fueled by an unshakeable determination to rescue Hayes and bring him home.

But unbeknownst to them, General Kozlov was already preparing for their arrival – setting a trap that threatened to ensnare them all in a deadly game of cat and mouse from which there would be no escape.

CHAPTER 10

The secure briefing room was cast in an eerie blue glow from the large, holographic map projected in the center. Captain James Rodriguez leaned forward, his piercing brown eyes studying every detail of the enemy's research facility, as his team leaders gathered around him. Colonel Maria Vasquez stood at the head of the table, her voice steady and authoritative.

"Listen up. This mission is of the utmost importance. We have reason to believe that General Kozlov's forces are on the verge of completing a devastating bioweapon. If we fail to retrieve the intel and neutralize the threat, the consequences will be catastrophic."

Captain Rodriguez felt the weight of his responsibility settle on his broad shoulders, but he remained unflinching. He had faced countless dangers in his career, and this mission was no different. His duty to protect his country and his team drove him forward, even in the face of such peril.

"Alright, teams," Rodriguez said, his voice carrying through the room with natural authority. "We need to coordinate our efforts and move in quickly. Time is not on our side."

As the team leaders began discussing their plan of action, the professionalism and teamwork evident in their strategizing, Rodriguez couldn't help but feel a sense of pride. Each member of the elite squad knew their role and understood the gravity of their task. They were prepared to risk everything for the success of the mission.

"Team Alpha, you'll infiltrate the outer perimeter and disable any security systems," Rodriguez directed, his gaze never leaving the holographic map. "Stealth is key. We can't afford to alert the enemy to our presence."

"Understood, Captain," replied the Team Alpha leader, his expression a mixture of determination and focus.

"Team Bravo, once inside, you'll navigate the facility's corridors, eliminating any enemy guards along the way. Remember, every second counts."

"Copy that, sir," the Team Bravo leader acknowledged, her eyes narrowing with resolve.

"Team Charlie, we're counting on your technical expertise to bypass any locked doors or security measures we encounter."

"Roger that, Captain. We won't let you down," came the confident reply from the Team Charlie leader.

"Finally, Team Delta, your primary objective is to locate and secure the bioweapon intel. Stay alert for unexpected resistance."

"Affirmative, Captain," said the Team Delta leader, his jaw set in determination.

As the teams continued to iron out the specifics of their plan, Rodriguez's thoughts turned inward. He knew that each member of his squad was highly skilled and well-prepared, but he also understood that the enemy they faced was a formidable one. The specter of General Kozlov loomed over them all, a reminder of the high stakes at play.

"Alright, everyone," Rodriguez finally said, breaking the silence that had fallen over the room. "We move out in twenty minutes. Gear up and synchronize your comms. This mission is critical, and we must succeed. Failure is simply not an option."

The team leaders exchanged solemn nods before dispersing to prepare their respective teams. As the room emptied, Captain Rodriguez took one last look at the holographic map, steeling himself for the challenges that lay ahead. The fate of their nation rested on their shoulders, and they would stop at nothing to ensure its safety.

Under the cover of night, Captain Rodriguez led Team Alpha along the edge of the enemy's research facility. The moonlight cast eerie shadows on the grim, concrete walls as they moved with stealth and precision. Rodriguez scanned the perimeter, his brown eyes alert and vigilant.

"Ramirez, disable those security cameras," he whispered into his comms.

"Copy that, Captain," Sergeant Miguel Ramirez replied, his fingers deftly manipulating the advanced technology in his hands. Moments later, the red lights of the security cameras flickered and went dark, leaving the team undetected.

"Nice work," Rodriguez commended him, tension evident in his voice. "Reynolds, take point. Let's move."

Major David Reynolds nodded, his piercing blue eyes reflecting determination as he guided the team through the shadows, expertly avoiding detection. Every movement was calculated, every step taken with utmost care. Time was running out, and failure was not an option.

"Remember, we need to reach the central control room without raising any alarms," Rodriguez reminded his team, his voice low and steady. "Stay focused."

Meanwhile, Lieutenant Emily Thompson led Team Bravo through the dimly lit corridors of the facility. Her heart pounded against her chest, but she remained composed, her years of elite training serving her well in this high-pressure situation.

"Guards up ahead – two of them," she whispered, signaling her team to take cover. She watched as the guards approached, their voices low and unintelligible. In a split second, she launched herself forward, engaging one guard while another member of her team took down the other.

The sound of bones breaking echoed through the hall as she swiftly and silently incapacitated her opponent, keeping him from calling for reinforcements. Adrenaline coursed through her veins, fueling her focus and determination.

"Move forward, stay sharp," she ordered her team, scanning the corridor for any signs of danger. "We need to reach the bioweapon intel before it's too late."

"Roger that, Lieutenant," her team replied in unison, their voices hushed and disciplined.

As Team Bravo continued through the maze-like corridors, a sense of urgency hung heavy in the air. The lives of countless people rested on their shoulders, and they could not – would not – let them down. With each step, they moved closer to preventing a catastrophic disaster, driven by their unwavering loyalty to their country and comrades.

As Team Charlie approached a heavily fortified door, Sergeant Miguel Ramirez studied the intricate security measures in place. The dimly lit hallway cast eerie shadows on the team's faces, emphasizing their unwavering determination.

"Damn, this is one sophisticated lock," muttered Ramirez, his fingers deftly maneuvering a set of specialized tools to bypass the security system. He glanced at Major David Reynolds, who stood guard nearby, his piercing blue eyes scanning for any signs of enemy movement.

"Time's running out, Ramirez. We need to get through this door and secure the intel," Reynolds said, his voice measured but urgent. "What's the plan?"

"Working on it, Major," Ramirez replied, sweat beading on his forehead as he focused on the complex task. "Just need a few more seconds."

The tense silence was suddenly shattered by the sound of distant gunfire – Team Delta must have encountered unexpected resistance.

Captain James Rodriguez's voice crackled over the comms, his concern evident even through the static: "Team Delta under fire! They've run into a heavily armed enemy squad!"

"Ramirez, we need that door open now!" barked Reynolds, his heart racing with the knowledge that every second counted.

"Got it!" Ramirez triumphantly announced as the lock clicked open, granting them access to the secured area. The team rushed inside, their senses heightened as they prepared for whatever awaited them beyond the door.

Meanwhile, Team Delta found themselves pinned down by enemy gunfire in a narrow corridor. Bullets ricocheted off the walls, sparks illuminating the faces of soldiers fighting for their lives. Lieutenant Emily Thompson gritted her teeth, her mind racing to formulate a plan amidst the chaos.

"Cover me!" she yelled, dashing towards a nearby barricade under a hail of bullets. As she arrived, she caught sight of an enemy soldier attempting to flank her position. With lightning-fast reflexes, she took aim and fired, dropping him before he could get a shot off.

"Thompson, we need to push forward!" Captain Rodriguez called out over the gunfire, urgency lacing his voice.

"Understood, Captain," she replied, her mind racing with tactical calculations. "We'll find a way through this!"

As Team Charlie worked tirelessly to extract crucial intel, Team Delta continued their desperate struggle against overwhelming odds. Time was running out, and the stakes had never been higher. Each soldier fought on, driven by loyalty, duty, and an unwavering commitment to their comrades and their nation – they would not fail.

Emily Thompson's heart pounded in her ears, drowning out the cacophony of gunfire as she assessed the situation. Team Delta was pinned down, taking heavy fire from enemy soldiers in fortified positions. She knew that if they didn't act fast, the mission would be compromised.

"Captain Rodriguez, we need to create a diversion!" Emily shouted over their comms, her voice steady despite the adrenaline coursing through her veins. "Team Bravo will flank the enemy from the left side – we'll draw their fire and give Team Delta a chance to push forward."

"Copy that, Thompson. Good luck," Captain Rodriguez responded, his voice tense with concern.

"Alright, Bravo, you heard the captain. Let's move out!" Emily commanded, gesturing for her team to follow as she sprinted toward the enemy's blind spot. The soldiers moved like shadows, their movements precise and coordinated as they advanced through the dimly lit corridor.

As they neared the enemy's position, Emily signaled for her team to take cover. "On my mark," she whispered into her comms. "Three...two...one...now!"

The members of Team Bravo burst from cover, their weapons blazing as they unleashed a hail of bullets on the unsuspecting enemy soldiers. The diversion worked – the enemy's attention shifted to Bravo, giving Team Delta the opportunity they needed to advance.

"Delta, go! We've got their attention!" Emily called out, her eyes scanning the area for any threats. As Team Delta surged forward, she couldn't help but feel a rush of pride at their teamwork and determination.

Meanwhile, Team Alpha had infiltrated the central control room of the research facility. Their skilled hacker, Corporal Davis, was hard at work cracking the complex security system guarding the crucial intel about the bioweapon.

"Come on, come on..." Davis muttered under his breath, his fingers flying across the keyboard as he navigated the labyrinthine network of firewalls and encryption. The rest of Team Alpha stood guard, their eyes darting to every entrance as they braced for the inevitable arrival of enemy reinforcements.

"Got it!" Davis exclaimed, his face breaking into a grin as the final security barrier fell away, revealing the data they needed.

"Great work, Corporal," Lieutenant Samuel Hayes said, his voice tight with tension but still carrying the weight of authority despite his weakened state. "Now let's get that intel and get out of here before we're overrun."

As Team Alpha raced against time to secure the vital information, Emily Thompson continued to lead Team Bravo in their diversionary assault, her resilience and quick thinking proving invaluable in the heat of battle. With each passing second, the stakes grew higher, and the soldiers knew that failure was not an option. They fought on, fueled by loyalty, duty, and the knowledge that the fate of their country hung in the balance.

The deafening sound of an alarm echoed through the research facility, accompanied by the sudden blaring of red emergency lights. Lieutenant Emily Thompson's pulse quickened as she realized that their cover had been blown. "Bravo Team, we've got company!" she barked into her earpiece.

"Copy that," came the terse response from Captain Rodriguez, who was leading Team Delta towards their objective. "Stay sharp and hold your ground."

As Team Bravo braced themselves for the inevitable onslaught, a chilling voice crackled over the facility's PA system. "I commend your efforts, but you have underestimated my determination," it said, revealing the formidable presence of General Viktor Kozlov himself.

"Kozlov's here?" whispered one of Bravo Team's soldiers, his eyes widening in disbelief. "We're in deep trouble."

"Focus! We can't afford to lose our cool now," Thompson commanded, her steely blue eyes scanning the surroundings for signs of movement. "He's not the only one determined to protect what's at stake."

No sooner had she spoken these words than a heavily armed squad of elite guards appeared, bearing down on them with merciless precision. Bullets flew and punches were exchanged as both sides fought for supremacy in a desperate struggle.

"Sam, any idea where the bioweapon is located?" Emily urgently asked Lieutenant Samuel Hayes over the comm line, knowing that his recent ordeal must have left him weakened.

"Working on it," he replied, his voice strained but unwavering. "Give me a moment to cross-reference the intel we just retrieved."

"Make it fast," she implored, ducking behind a pillar as an enemy guard opened fire in her direction. She could hear the mounting chaos around her as more of Kozlov's forces converged on their position. Every second counted, and they couldn't afford any missteps.

"Got it!" Hayes finally exclaimed, his tone triumphant despite his weakened state. "The bioweapon is in Lab 12B, near the facility's core."

"Copy that, Sam. Stay strong," Thompson responded, her voice a mixture of gratitude and concern. She relayed the information to her team, determination flooding her veins as they prepared to move forward. "Bravo Team, new target: Lab 12B. Let's move!"

As they fought their way through Kozlov's elite guards, each member of Bravo Team knew that the stakes had never been higher. But with Lieutenant Hayes' resilience providing crucial information and Lieutenant Thompson's steadfast leadership guiding them, they refused to back down from the challenge.

"Stay focused and watch each other's backs," Thompson ordered, her eyes blazing with fierce resolve. "We're not leaving this place without destroying that bioweapon."

Sweat dripped down Captain Rodriguez's forehead as he led his team through the labyrinthian corridors of the research facility, their boots pounding against the cold metal floors. Time was running out, and he could feel the weight of their mission pressing down on him like a crushing vise.

"Bravo Team reports they're nearing Lab 12B," Sergeant Ramirez reported, his voice tense with anticipation.

"Good," Rodriguez replied, his eyes scanning the corridor ahead for any signs of enemy resistance. "Keep pushing forward, Alpha Team. We need to rendezvous with them before they reach the bioweapon."

As they raced through the complex, each twist and turn seemed to present a new obstacle, as if the facility itself was conspiring against them. Booby traps lay hidden in the shadows: tripwires, pressure-sensitive floor panels, and motion-activated turrets all threatened to halt their advance with lethal force.

"Watch your step!" Lieutenant Thompson warned, narrowly avoiding a concealed pitfall in the floor. "These bastards aren't making it easy for us."

"Neither will we," Captain Rodriguez muttered, his jaw set with determination. He turned to his team, adrenaline coursing through his veins. "Fan out and disarm what you can. Stay sharp."

"Copy that, Captain," Ramirez answered, expertly disabling a nearby tripwire as the team moved cautiously forward.

As they pressed on, the sporadic sound of gunfire echoed through the facility, a grim reminder of the fierce battles still raging between Kozlov's forces and the other teams. The knowledge that their comrades were fighting for their lives only fueled their resolve.

"Captain, we've got company!" Thompson called out, her keen senses detecting the approach of enemy reinforcements.

"Take them out, but keep moving," Rodriguez ordered, returning fire with his own weapon as they continued their relentless advance. "We can't afford to slow down."

"Understood," Ramirez acknowledged, a steely glint in his eyes as he eliminated an enemy soldier with ruthless precision.

As they neared the bioweapon's chamber, Captain Rodriguez could feel his heart pounding in his chest. They were so close now - the fate of their nation hanging in the balance. The thought sent a shiver down his spine.

"Alpha Team, Bravo Team has breached Lab 12B," Ramirez reported, his voice tense. "They're preparing to set the charges now."

"Copy that," Rodriguez replied, his voice taut with anticipation. "We'll be there in no time."

Finally, they reached the chamber, its reinforced doors standing like a final barrier between them and their objective. Inside, they found Bravo Team hard at work, expertly placing explosives around the large, cylindrical container housing the deadly bioweapon.

"Nice work, Thompson," Rodriguez praised, clapping her on the shoulder. "Let's finish this."

"Roger that, Captain," she responded, her blue eyes flashing with determination as the teams worked together to secure the last of the explosives.

As the final charge was set, Rodriguez couldn't help but think of what was at stake - and of Lieutenant Hayes' incredible resilience that had brought them this far. He clenched his fists, determined to see this mission through to the end.

"Explosives armed and ready, Captain," Thompson confirmed, her voice steady despite the gravity of the moment.

"Good," Rodriguez answered, taking a deep breath and meeting the gaze of each member of the combined teams. "Let's get clear and blow this thing to hell."

"Sir, yes, sir!" came the unanimous response, each soldier filled with a renewed sense of purpose.

The countdown to detonation began, and as they retreated from the chamber, Captain Rodriguez knew that there was no turning back. They had come too far, fought too hard, to fail now. The safety of their nation depended on it.

"Let's move, soldiers!" he shouted, leading his team through the facility with renewed urgency. "We're not done yet!"

"Sir, yes, sir!" they echoed, their voices resolute as they followed him into the fray.

With the explosives set and the countdown ticking, Captain Rodriguez's heart pounded in his chest as he led his team through the twisting corridors of the research facility. The hum of machinery echoed through the dimly lit halls, each step bringing them closer to their escape and the impending destruction of the bioweapon.

"Stay sharp," Rodriguez whispered into his headset, eyeing every shadow for signs of enemy movement. "We're still not out of this hellhole."

"Roger that, Captain," responded Thompson, her voice steady over the comm link. "Keep an eye out for any surprises."

As they neared the exit, a sudden crash echoed down the corridor towards them. The sound made Rodriguez instinctively reach for his sidearm, his senses on high alert. He knew better than to assume they were home free.

"Move!" he barked, urging the team forward. "We don't have much time left!"

"Captain!" shouted Ramirez, pointing at a figure emerging from the shadows ahead. It was General Kozlov, flanked by a squad of heavily armed soldiers. Their weapons were trained on the team like a pack of wolves ready to pounce.

"Damn it! Keep moving!" Rodriguez ordered, his thoughts racing for a plan. He couldn't let the lives of his team and the success of the mission be jeopardized now.

"Split up!" Thompson suggested, sliding behind a nearby pillar for cover. "We'll draw their fire and give the others a chance to get clear!"

"Agreed," Rodriguez replied, his mind calculating the odds as bullets whizzed past him. "Ramirez, Reynolds, take Bravo and Charlie teams with you and make your way to the extraction point."

"Copy that, Captain," Ramirez acknowledged, his voice resolute. He and Reynolds led their respective teams down a separate corridor, hoping to avoid the worst of the enemy's forces.

"Thompson, Hayes, you're with me," Rodriguez called out, exchanging fire with Kozlov's soldiers. "We'll give them hell."

"Sir, yes, sir!" they responded in unison, their determination unwavering.

Rodriguez took a deep breath, his thoughts briefly turning to the families and lives that depended on their success. He couldn't let them down. They wouldn't fail.

"Move on my mark... three, two, one – go!"

As Rodriguez and his teammates sprinted into action, a hailstorm of bullets chased them through the corridor. The deafening sound of gunfire filled the air, drowning out the relentless ticking of the countdown in their ears.

"Captain!" shouted Thompson, her voice strained as she fired back at the enemy. "We need to get out of here now!"

"Almost there!" Rodriguez yelled, desperately trying to focus on their escape route despite the chaos surrounding them. "Just a little further!"

Suddenly, an explosion shook the facility, causing dust and debris to rain down all around them. The ground beneath their feet trembled violently, threatening to throw them off balance.

"Damn it!" Rodriguez cursed, realizing that the detonation had come too soon. With Kozlov and his forces still hot on their heels, the team found themselves trapped between the impending destruction of the bioweapon and the ruthless enemy soldiers determined to make sure they didn't survive.

"Captain! What do we do?!" Hayes shouted over the noise, his eyes wide with terror.

"Stay focused, Lieutenant!" Rodriguez commanded, his heart racing as he searched for options. "There has to be another way out!"

And with that, they plunged deeper into the collapsing facility, racing against time and fate itself. As the walls crumbled around them and the roar of destruction grew louder, Captain James Rodriguez knew that their only hope was to find a way out – or die trying.

CHAPTER 11

The humid air hung heavy as Captain James Rodriguez sliced through the dense undergrowth, leading Team Alpha deeper into the jungle. Sweat dripped down his forehead, stinging his eyes, but he didn't dare slow down.

"Intel says Lieutenant Hayes might be in this area," he said, scanning the treacherous terrain with his piercing brown eyes. "Stay sharp and keep an eye out for any signs of him or enemy activity."

His team members nodded, their faces tense with anticipation. Emily Thompson, her blonde hair matted with sweat, raised a hand to shield her eyes from the dappled sunlight filtering through the canopy above. "Captain, there's something moving up ahead," she whispered, her voice steady despite the urgency in her words.

The team froze, muscles coiled like springs, ready to react to any potential threat. A low growl echoed through the trees, followed by the rustling of leaves. A jaguar emerged from the shadows, its tawny coat blending seamlessly with the foliage. It locked eyes with Rodriguez, a primal challenge in its gaze.

"Easy, now," Rodriguez murmured, his hand hovering over his sidearm. His heart pounded in his chest, but his face remained a mask of calm determination. The jaguar hesitated, then retreated back into the underbrush with a final, defiant snarl.

"Let's keep moving," Rodriguez commanded, his voice betraying no hint of the adrenaline coursing through his veins. He knew they couldn't afford to waste time; every moment they spent in this hostile environment brought them closer to exhaustion and increased the risk that Hayes would slip further from their grasp.

As they pressed onward, the terrain grew increasingly treacherous - glistening vines threatening to trip them at every step, thorny branches reaching out to snag their uniforms. Rodriguez's mind raced, considering every possible outcome of their mission. What if they were too late? What if Hayes had already been moved to another location? He shook off the doubts, focusing instead on the task at hand.

"Intel has never let us down before," he muttered under his breath, as much to reassure himself as his team. They had to find Hayes; too much was at stake for them to fail now.

"Sir, we've got a clearing up ahead," Thompson reported, her voice a beacon of hope amid the oppressive jungle.

"Good. We'll regroup there and reassess our approach," Rodriguez replied, allowing himself a glimmer of optimism. The possibility that they were close to finding Hayes renewed his determination, stoking the fire within him that had carried him through countless missions.

As Team Alpha pushed towards the clearing, each member acutely aware of the dangers surrounding them, Captain James Rodriguez knew that failure was not an option. They would find Lieutenant Samuel Hayes, no matter the cost - it was a promise he had made to himself, his team, and his country. And he intended to keep it.

The wind howled like a vengeful spirit as Team Bravo rappelled down the sheer face of the mountain stronghold. Lieutenant Emily Thompson surveyed the scene below, her blue eyes focused and unyielding despite the biting cold that threatened to seep into her bones. She knew that every second mattered in their mission to find Lieutenant Hayes.

"Keep it tight!" she shouted over the roar of the wind, her voice steady and commanding. Each member of her team moved with practiced precision, their feet finding purchase on the rocky surface as they descended.

As they reached the bottom, they fanned out into formation, their silenced weapons at the ready. Shadows danced along the walls, hinting at enemy forces lurking around every corner. Thompson's mind raced with strategies, her instincts sharpened by years of elite training guiding her through the darkness.

"Thermal imaging shows a cluster of heat signatures near the eastern tower," she relayed to her team, her words crisp and clear despite the chaos surrounding them. "Stay alert and engage with extreme caution."

As they pressed forward, the unmistakable sound of muffled gunfire filled the air. Thompson's heart pounded in her chest, each beat fueling her determination to rescue Hayes. Her team followed suit, engaging in both hand-to-hand combat and precise shooting, taking down enemy soldiers with ruthless efficiency.

Scaling the treacherous mountain peaks with expert agility, Thompson led her team higher, their objective growing closer with every step. As they climbed, her thoughts turned to Hayes, a fellow soldier taken captive by an enemy who knew no mercy. She couldn't allow herself to entertain the thought of leaving him behind.

"Push forward!" she urged her team, her breath visible in the frosty air. "We're close!"

Utilizing advanced thermal imaging, Thompson scanned the area for any sign of their captured comrade. She knew the stakes had never been higher – not just for Hayes, but for the world that hung in the balance. They had to find him before General Kozlov could execute his terrifying plans.

"Sir, I've got something!" one of her teammates called out, his voice tense with anticipation. "There's a heat signature coming from that building!"

"Go!" Thompson ordered, the weight of responsibility heavy on her shoulders. As they stormed the building, she knew that every moment counted; the fate of countless lives hinged on their success.

As Team Bravo fought their way through the stronghold, their resolve and skill were tested at every turn. But Lieutenant Emily Thompson refused to waver – she was determined to bring Lieutenant Samuel Hayes home, no matter the cost. And as they drew closer to their objective, she couldn't shake the feeling that time was running out.

The scorching sun beat down on Sergeant Miguel Ramirez as he crouched behind a crumbling sandstone wall, his eyes narrowed against the onslaught of the blistering desert winds. The stinging sands whipped around him, each grain a tiny needle piercing through his fatigues. Sweat poured from his brow, but his grip on his rifle remained steady.

"Ramirez, we've got company!" shouted Private Davis, her voice barely audible over the howling wind. A flurry of bullets whizzed past them, kicking up miniature sandstorms as they struck the ground.

"Return fire!" Ramirez commanded, his voice low and powerful. He rose from his cover, squeezing off several rounds at the enemy forces guarding the compound's entrance. Around him, Team Charlie sprang into action, their shots echoing in the vast emptiness of the desert.

"Jones, flank left! Harris, give me cover fire!" Ramirez barked out orders while remaining vigilant to any changes in the battlefield. He could feel the oppressive heat sapping his strength, but he refused to let it break him – not when the fate of Lieutenant Hayes hung in the balance.

As the intense firefight continued, Ramirez couldn't help but reflect on his harsh upbringing in the unforgiving desert. It had shaped him into the man he was today – a seasoned desert warfare specialist who would stop at nothing to protect his comrades. But despite his years of experience, the desert never ceased to challenge him with its relentless heat and scarcity of resources.

"Water!" gasped Private Thompson, collapsing behind a nearby dune. His face was gaunt, his lips cracked and parched from dehydration.

"Stay focused, Thompson. We'll find water soon," Ramirez reassured him, though he knew that in this barren wasteland, such a promise was difficult to keep. As he turned back to the battle at hand, he saw the enemy forces begin to retreat, the compound's entrance now exposed.

"Team Charlie, move up!" Ramirez yelled, leading his team through the swirling sandstorm. The sun bore down on them like a merciless hammer, but Miguel Ramirez was unyielding in his pursuit of victory. For Lieutenant Hayes and the countless lives at stake, he would push himself and his team to their limits – and beyond.

A relentless wave crashed against the rocky shoreline, spraying white foam into the air and momentarily blinding Major David Reynolds. He blinked away the saltwater, his night vision goggles bringing the darkened coastal enemy camp into sharp relief. The pounding surf was a constant reminder of the unforgiving environment they'd been thrust into.

"Delta Two, stay on course. We need to find Hayes," Reynolds whispered into his radio, his voice measured but insistent. The team moved stealthily along the beach, their shadows barely visible against the moonlit sand.

"Copy that, Delta One," Sergeant Mercer replied, taking point as they slipped past the perimeter guards with practiced ease. Reynolds could see the tension in his comrade's movements, a testament to the high stakes of their mission.

As they approached the first building, Reynolds signaled for his team to fan out. Each member knew their role – time was of the essence, and they couldn't afford any mistakes. Reynolds took a deep breath, pushing aside thoughts of his wife and children back home. He needed to focus; lives were at stake.

"Clear," whispered Private Daniels after a thorough search of the first building. Reynolds nodded, motioning for them to move on to the next one. His heart pounded in his chest, each beat echoing the urgency of their task.

"Major, I've got movement in the third building," Lieutenant Cooper reported, her voice tight. Reynolds tensed, anticipation building within him as he quickly assessed the situation.

"Proceed with caution, Cooper. Keep your eyes open for any sign of Lieutenant Hayes," Reynolds instructed. The weight of responsibility rested heavily on his shoulders, but he refused to let it break him.

"Affirmative, sir," she acknowledged, moving silently towards the building. Reynolds watched through the night vision goggles as she expertly neutralized a guard, her movements swift and precise.

"Building three clear, sir. Still no sign of Hayes," Cooper reported, her voice betraying a hint of frustration. Reynolds clenched his fists, the frustration gnawing at him too.

"Stay focused, Delta Team. We'll find him," Reynolds said firmly, though doubt began to creep into his thoughts. What if they were too late? What if all their efforts were in vain?

"Delta One, we've got company!" Sergeant Mercer's warning snapped Reynolds back to the present. He saw a group of enemy soldiers moving towards their position, weapons at the ready.

"Engage only if necessary. Keep searching for Hayes," Reynolds ordered, his mind racing with possible scenarios and outcomes. They couldn't afford to lose any more time.

"Roger that, sir," Mercer replied, disappearing into the shadows as Reynolds continued his search. Each building held the potential to yield the prize they so desperately sought - Lieutenant Samuel Hayes, alive and unbroken.

As Reynolds moved from one building to another, his determination never waned. The fate of his comrade and countless lives hung in the balance, and he refused to let them down. Even in the face of overwhelming odds, Major David Reynolds would fight on.

The jungle's oppressive heat seemed to close in around Captain Rodriguez as he watched a venomous snake slither past his boots. He could feel the sweat dripping down his back, but he couldn't afford to let his discomfort distract him. The intel indicated that Lieutenant

Hayes might be held somewhere in this dense foliage, and time was of the essence.

"Alpha Team, stay sharp," Rodriguez ordered while scanning the area with his rifle at the ready. "Hayes could be anywhere."

"Captain, we got movement up ahead," Private Johnson whispered urgently, his eyes locked on something in the distance. Moments later, three heavily armed enemy soldiers emerged from the undergrowth, clearly guarding something important.

"Standby," Rodriguez murmured into his comms. His heart pounded in his chest as he considered their options. They had to get past these guards without raising an alarm. "Thompson, can you take out the one on the left?"

"Affirmative, Captain," Lieutenant Thompson replied, her voice steady despite the pressure of the situation. She steadied her rifle, took aim, and fired a single, silenced shot. The guard dropped to the ground, unnoticed by his comrades.

"Nice shot," Rodriguez praised, before turning to Sergeant Jackson. "You're up, Sarge. Distract the other two so we can move in."

"Copy that," Jackson said, grabbing a small rock and hurling it into the bushes off to the side. As the guards turned towards the noise, Alpha Team rushed forward, swiftly dispatching them with precision.

"Area secured," Rodriguez breathed, noting the entrance to a hidden bunker nearby. This had to be where they were keeping Hayes. "Stay alert, team. We're going in."

Meanwhile, high above on the mountain, Lieutenant Thompson led Bravo Team with unerring skill, navigating treacherous cliffs and using her advanced thermal imaging to scan for any sign of their captive comrade.

"Thompson to Delta One," she said, her voice crackling through the radio. "We've got a possible heat signature in a cave system on the northern face. Moving to investigate now."

"Copy that, Thompson. Good luck," Reynolds replied from his position on the coastal enemy camp, where his own team was engaged in a tense search for Hayes.

"Alright, Bravo Team. Let's move," Thompson commanded, rappelling down the sheer rock face with her team following suit. They knew they had to work fast if they were going to rescue Hayes and put a stop to General Kozlov's plans.

Back in the desert, Sergeant Ramirez barked orders as bullets whizzed past them, kicking up clouds of sand around Team Charlie. "Cover fire! Mason, flank left!" he yelled, his eyes scanning the compound's entrance for any sign of weakness.

"Ramirez, I think I found something," Corporal Evans called out over the deafening sound of gunfire. "There's a weak point in the wall just west of the gate. We can breach it and get inside."

Beneath the sweltering jungle canopy, Captain Rodriguez wiped the sweat from his brow as Team Alpha hacked their way through the dense foliage. The intel they'd received about Lieutenant Hayes' possible location had led them to this treacherous terrain, and every nerve in his body was on high alert.

"Captain," Specialist Carter called out, her voice tense, "I've intercepted a transmission from Kozlov's men. They're talking about moving Hayes and some kind of... bioweapon."

"Bioweapon?" Rodriguez's eyes narrowed, his jaw clenching. "What do we know about it?"

"Nothing yet, sir," Carter replied, her fingers flying over her portable decryption device. "Just that it's something big. Something dangerous."

Rodriguez gritted his teeth. Not only were they racing against the clock to save Hayes, but now they had to stop a potentially catastrophic weapon from falling into the wrong hands. Taking a deep breath, he barked orders at his team. "Alright, we need to move faster. Pick up the pace!"

"Roger that, Captain!" his team responded in unison, their determination renewed by the heightened stakes.

The tense atmosphere intensified as each team engaged in fierce battles with the enemy forces. In the mountain stronghold, Team Bravo rappelled down the rock face, guns blazing, while Lieutenant Thompson expertly dodged bullets and returned fire.

"Bravo Two, cover my six!" she yelled, weaving through the hailstorm of gunfire. Her heart raced as adrenaline coursed through her veins. She knew there was no room for error.

In the blistering desert expanse, Team Charlie traded bullets with the enemy guarding the compound's entrance. Ramirez and his team charged toward the weak point in the wall, using their training and expertise to outmaneuver and overpower their adversaries.

"Charlie Four, on my signal, breach the wall!" Ramirez commanded, his eyes never leaving the enemy's position. The fate of their mission and the lives of countless people hinged on their success.

"Three... two... one... breach!" With a thunderous explosion, Team Charlie broke through the compound's defenses, opening the way for their assault.

At the coastal enemy camp, Team Delta moved stealthily from building to building, searching for Hayes amidst the chaos of battle. Reynolds' mind raced as he considered each new piece of intel, anticipating General Kozlov's next move.

"Delta One to all teams," he said into his radio, his voice calm but urgent. "We have confirmation that Kozlov's men are moving Hayes and the bioweapon. We cannot let them escape. Every second counts."

"Copy that, Delta One," the other team leaders replied, their voices filled with resolve.

The stakes had never been higher, and each team knew that failure was not an option. As gunfire echoed through the air and danger lurked around every corner, they pressed forward, determined to stop General Kozlov and save their comrade, no matter the cost.

An explosion erupted in the distance, ripping through the air like a malevolent force. Captain Rodriguez's heart hammered in his chest as he plunged forward, his team following closely behind him. The dense jungle foliage seemed to close in around them, but they charged ahead, driven by their mission.

"Alpha Two, cover our six!" Captain Rodriguez barked into his radio, sweat pouring down his face. Every second counted, and the sense of danger was palpable. Bullets whizzed past them, cutting through leaves and branches, a deadly reminder of the enemy's relentless pursuit.

"Copy that, Alpha One," Lieutenant Thompson replied, her voice calm yet determined. She positioned herself to provide cover for the team, her eyes scanning the treacherous terrain for any sign of movement. The tension was suffocating, but they couldn't afford to let fear take over; too much was at stake.

"Bravo Three, we need a distraction – now!" Major Reynolds called out, his focus unwavering as he led Team Bravo in their ascent of the mountain stronghold. Muffled gunshots punctuated the air, and the smell of cordite filled their nostrils as they engaged in hand-to-hand combat with the enemy forces. Each member of the team knew the odds were stacked against them, but they fought on, fueled by their determination to find Hayes and neutralize the bioweapon.

"Charlie Four, set charges along the eastern wall. We need an exit strategy!" Sergeant Ramirez commanded, his dark eyes narrowed as he assessed the situation. Sand whipped around them, stinging their skin and obscuring their vision, but Team Charlie pressed on, their resolve unwavering.

Beneath the pounding surf, Team Delta moved like shadows, their night vision goggles illuminating the darkness as they slipped past the perimeter guards. "Delta Two, clear the next building," Reynolds ordered, his voice barely audible above the crashing waves.

"I've got your back, Major," came the whispered response.

"Alpha One, we have eyes on Hayes!" Thompson's voice came through the radio, her excitement barely contained. "He's being moved toward the helipad, but there's a heavily armed team guarding him!"

"Stay focused, Lieutenant," Rodriguez warned, his mind racing. They were so close, yet the odds seemed insurmountable. But failure wasn't an option – not now, not ever.

"Bravo, Charlie, Delta – converge on Alpha's position. We need to move fast!" Rodriguez commanded, his voice laced with urgency. As gunfire echoed through the air and explosions rocked the surrounding area, the teams fought their way through the enemy positions, inching closer to their ultimate goal.

"Captain, I see them," Thompson said, her breath ragged as she took aim. "I can take out the guards, but we need to move – now!"

"Make it count, Lieutenant," Rodriguez replied, his heart pounding in his ears.

Thompson exhaled slowly, steadying her aim, and squeezed the trigger. The shot rang out, echoing through the chaos. Suddenly, an explosion unlike any they had encountered before erupted, consuming the helicopter in a blaze of fire and sending a shockwave rippling through the air.

"NO!" Rodriguez yelled, his voice drowned out by the roar of the flames. The world went silent for a moment, time seemingly suspended, as the realization of what had just happened settled over them like a shroud.

"Alpha One! Was Hayes aboard that helicopter?!" Reynolds' voice crackled through the radio, the fear evident in his tone.

"Unknown, Delta One... unknown."

CHAPTER 12

The shadows clung to the team like a second skin as they slithered through the underbrush. Waves lapped against the shore, muffling the sound of their footsteps on the sand. Emily scanned the darkness, her eyes picking out the shapes of the enemy encampment. The adrenaline coursing through her veins reminded her why she had joined the Special Forces in the first place – the challenge, the thrill, and the camaraderie.

"Delta Team, proceed with caution," Emily whispered into her headset, her voice steady despite her racing heart. "Stick to the plan, and we'll have Hayes back with us in no time."

A chorus of affirmations echoed through the comms, a testament to the unwavering trust her teammates placed in her leadership. Their resolve only fueled Emily's determination to rescue Lieutenant Hayes.

As they crept closer to their target, the silhouettes of enemy guards emerged from the gloom. Their patrol route took them dangerously close to the entrance of the makeshift cell that held Hayes captive.

"Three hostiles, twelve o'clock," Emily reported, her piercing blue eyes locked onto the enemy's movements. She gauged their patrol pattern, calculating the best way to avoid detection. "Hold your positions. Wait for my signal."

Her heart thudded in her chest, but her mind was clear and focused. She knew each member of her team, their strengths and weaknesses, and how to utilize them most effectively. The lives of her comrades rested in her hands, and she refused to let them down.

"Ready," came the whispered responses from her team, their voices a mixture of steely resolve and quiet intensity.

Emily watched the guards carefully, noting the precise moment when their backs were turned. "Now," she commanded, leading her team forward in a swift, silent advance.

As they closed in on the entrance to the cell, she wondered what horrors awaited them inside. Lieutenant Hayes was a strong man, but weeks of torture could break even the most resilient of souls. She just hoped they weren't too late.

"Stay sharp, everyone," she reminded her team as they prepared to breach the cell. "We're almost there."

Her thoughts turned briefly to her own past – the grueling training sessions, the life-threatening climbs up some of the world's most treacherous peaks – and she knew that all those experiences had led her to this moment. There was no turning back now, and she wouldn't have it any other way.

"Let's bring Hayes home."

The moon's light glinted off the blade of Captain Rodriguez's knife as he crept up on the nearest guard, his muscles tensing in anticipation. He signaled to Sergeant Ramirez and Lieutenant Thompson to take down the other two guards patrolling the vicinity.

"Go," he whispered, his voice barely audible even to himself.

With swift, calculated movements, Team Delta sprang into action. Rodriguez's knife found its mark, slicing through the air before plunging into the guard's neck, severing his carotid artery. The man collapsed without a sound.

"Two down," Ramirez reported quietly, his own target dispatched with lethal efficiency.

"Third one's out," Emily confirmed, her hands already wiping clean her bloodied blade.

"Good work, team," Rodriguez praised, scanning the area for any signs of detection. "Reynolds, keep watch. We're breaching the cell."

Major Reynolds nodded, eyes sharp as he took a defensive position near the entrance. Meanwhile, Rodriguez, Thompson, and Ramirez approached the cell door, their specialized tools at the ready.

"Emily, you're on lock duty," Rodriguez said, knowing her steady hands and technical expertise would make short work of the task.

"Roger that," she responded, focusing intently on the lock, her fingers deftly maneuvering the lock-picking tools.

As she worked, Rodriguez couldn't help but recall the countless missions they had completed together, each one a testament to their unwavering dedication and unbreakable bond. But this mission was different; it was personal. They were rescuing one of their own, and failure was not an option.

"Got it," Emily announced, her voice tinged with satisfaction as the lock clicked open. "Door's unlocked, Captain."

"Nice job, Lieutenant," Rodriguez commended, his hand on the door handle. "Stay alert, everyone. No telling what's waiting for us inside."

"Always am, Captain," Ramirez replied, his voice as steady as ever.

"Let's do this," Rodriguez declared, pushing the door open and leading his team inside the cell.

The dim light of the cell cast eerie shadows on the walls, revealing the figure of Lieutenant Samuel Hayes slumped against the far corner. His once-pristine uniform was now tattered and covered in dried blood, his body bearing the marks of unimaginable cruelty.

"Sam!" Emily's voice caught in her throat as she rushed to his side, her heart aching at the sight of her fellow soldier – a man she had trusted with her life countless times before.

"Thompson," Hayes rasped, managing a weak smile despite his battered state. "Took you long enough."

"Check his vitals, Ramirez," Rodriguez ordered, his voice laced with concern as he watched Emily gently cradle Hayes' head in her lap.

"Copy that, Captain," Ramirez replied, kneeling beside them and swiftly assessing Hayes' injuries. His fingers moved with practiced precision, checking for any broken bones or signs of internal bleeding.

As Emily's piercing blue eyes scanned the bruised and battered face of her comrade, she fought back the anger welling up inside her. The monsters who had done this to him would pay dearly, she vowed silently. But for now, caring for Hayes took precedence over vengeance.

"His pulse is steady, Captain," Ramirez reported. "He's dehydrated and malnourished, but I don't think there are any life-threatening injuries."

"Can he move?" Rodriguez asked, clenching his fists in anticipation of their imminent escape.

"I can manage," Hayes interjected, determination flashing in his eyes. "Just give me a hand."

"Sounds like our guy," Emily thought, pride swelling in her chest. She knew that if anyone could withstand such torture and still have the strength to fight, it was Sam Hayes.

Rodriguez nodded, satisfied with the assessment. "Alright, team. We need to move fast. Help Hayes up and let's get the hell out of here."

"Captain, I'm picking up movement outside," Reynolds warned through the team's earpieces. "We've got company."

"Understood, Major," Rodriguez replied, urgency creeping into his voice. "Emily, Ramirez, help Hayes up. We're extracting him now."

"Roger that, Captain," Emily said, taking one of Hayes' arms and draping it over her shoulder while Ramirez took the other. They carefully lifted him to his feet, mindful of his injuries.

"Stay close, Sam," Emily whispered as they began their slow, cautious journey towards the exit. "We'll get you out of here in one piece."

"Wouldn't have it any other way, Thompson," Hayes managed a weak chuckle, his resilience shining through the pain.

As they moved through the encampment, the shadows danced around them, mirroring the intensity of their determination and unwavering loyalty. Together, Team Delta would face whatever dangers lay ahead and emerge victorious – for the sake of their fallen comrade and the mission at hand.

With Lieutenant Hayes' eyes locked onto Emily's, a flicker of hope began to shine through the haze of pain and exhaustion clouding his gaze. The dim light from the moon cast eerie shadows across the cell, accentuating the deep bruises adorning his battered body.

"Sam, it's us – Team Delta," Emily said softly, her voice steady and reassuring as she knelt beside him. "We're here to get you out."

His lips curved into a weak smile, and he nodded slowly, his eyes never leaving hers. "Knew...knew you'd come, Thompson."

Emily's heart swelled at his unwavering trust in their team. It was their unbreakable bond that had carried them through countless missions, and now it would guide them out of this hellish nightmare.

"Of course, we wouldn't leave you behind," she murmured, gently squeezing his hand before turning her attention to his restraints. "Ramirez, I need your help with these cuffs."

"Copy that, Lieutenant," Ramirez replied, swiftly moving to assist her. Together, they worked meticulously to cut through the metal bindings, careful not to cause any further harm to Hayes' already injured wrists.

As the cuffs fell away, Hayes let out a sigh of relief, flexing his fingers and testing his mobility. "Thanks, guys," he mumbled, his words laced with gratitude and determination.

"Any time, Sam," Ramirez replied with a grin, patting him on the shoulder. "Now let's get you home."

"Stay close, Sam," Emily whispered, her mind racing with plans to navigate their escape. She knew the layout of the encampment like the back of her hand, but the risk of detection loomed over them like a dark, ominous cloud. "We'll get you out of here in one piece."

"Wouldn't have it any other way, Thompson," Hayes managed a weak chuckle, his resilience shining through the pain.

"Alright, team, let's move out," commanded Captain Rodriguez, his voice low and firm in their earpieces. "Stay sharp and keep communication lines open."

"Roger that, Captain," Emily replied, her mind shifting seamlessly into mission mode. As they began their slow, cautious journey towards the exit, she couldn't help but marvel at the strength of her team. No matter the odds stacked against them, they would face whatever dangers lay ahead and emerge victorious – for the sake of their fallen comrade and the mission at hand.

The faint echo of boots on concrete reached Emily's ears, her heart thudding in her chest as the sound grew steadily closer. She signaled to her team, eyes wide with urgency. "We've got company," she hissed into her comms, the adrenaline coursing through her veins.

"Perimeter formation, now!" Captain Rodriguez barked. The team sprang into action, encircling Hayes as they prepared for the enemy forces' arrival.

"Stay low, Sam," Emily urged, her hand resting protectively on his shoulder. He nodded and hunkered down beside her, his breaths shallow but steady.

"Thompson, you take point," ordered Captain Rodriguez, his voice calm but firm. "Ramirez, watch our six."

"Copy that, Captain" - both Emily and Ramirez responded in unison, their voices echoing each other's determination.

Emily peered around the corner of the makeshift cell, her blue eyes scanning the shadows for any sign of movement. Her mind raced with tactical calculations and possible scenarios, assessing every threat and planning for contingencies. *We can do this,* she thought, steeling herself for the battle ahead.

"Movement, northeast corner" - Ramirez's voice crackled through the comms, his tone low and tense. "Three guards, armed."

"Roger that," Emily replied, her grip tightening on her weapon. "On my mark... three, two, one, engage!"

The flurry of gunfire filled the air as Team Delta dispatched the enemy forces with ruthless efficiency. As the last guard fell, Emily glanced over at Hayes, relief flooding her when she saw he was unharmed.

"Keep moving," she urged, her voice a mix of authority and concern. "We're not out of the woods yet."

"Understood," Hayes responded, his voice strained but resolute, gritting his teeth against the pain. "Lead the way, Thompson."

"Stay on me," Emily said, her voice steady and reassuring. As they moved cautiously through the encampment, she couldn't help but feel a surge of pride in her team. Together, they were an unstoppable force - one that would see them all safely through even the darkest night.

"Captain, we've got more hostiles incoming" - Ramirez's voice was tense as he relayed the information. "Two o'clock, approximately ten meters out."

"Stay frosty, team" - Captain Rodriguez commanded. "We'll fight our way through. Hayes is our priority."

"Copy that" - Emily responded, her mind already racing with strategies to keep their path clear. She glanced at Hayes, his face a mask of pain but determination etched in every line. "We're gonna get you home, Sam" - she promised, her eyes unwavering.

"Counting on it" - Hayes managed a strained smile, his words filled with gratitude and trust. Their bond, forged in fire and tested on countless missions, was unbreakable - and together, they would triumph against any odds.

The darkness of the encampment was shattered by sudden bursts of gunfire, illuminating the grim faces of Team Delta as they moved like shadows through the chaos. Captain Rodriguez kept his focus sharp, leading his team and Lieutenant Hayes safely away from danger.

"Ramirez, take point," he ordered, his voice low but authoritative. "Thompson, stay close to Hayes."

"Roger that, Captain," Ramirez replied, expertly maneuvering between the makeshift buildings and debris, keenly aware of the potential threats lurking behind every corner.

"Captain, I think we can cut through this alley," Emily suggested, her blue eyes scanning their surroundings for any signs of enemy movement.

"Good call," Rodriguez agreed, nodding to Major Reynolds who swiftly moved to cover their flank.

With hearts pounding, the team advanced cautiously through the narrow passage, their footsteps barely making a sound as they navigated the labyrinth of the encampment. The air was tense with anticipation, each member keenly aware that one wrong move could be their last.

"Contact!" Reynolds suddenly whispered, his voice tight with adrenaline. "Three hostiles approaching from the east."

"Got it," Rodriguez replied, his mind racing as he weighed their options. "Ramirez, Thompson, engage. Hayes and I will stay back."

"Copy that," Emily and Ramirez responded in unison, readying their weapons and slipping stealthily into position.

As the enemy guards drew closer, Team Delta sprang into action. Emily and Ramirez took out two of the hostiles with swift, lethal efficiency, while Reynolds dispatched the third with a well-aimed shot.

"Clear," Reynolds announced, his expression remaining focused on the task at hand. "Let's keep moving."

"Captain," Hayes murmured, his voice weak but determined, "I don't want to slow you down. If I'm putting you all at risk—"

"Sam," Rodriguez interrupted, his voice firm yet compassionate, "we're not leaving you behind. We're a team. You'd do the same for any of us."

Hayes nodded, his eyes reflecting gratitude and trust as he leaned heavily on Emily for support, drawing strength from her unwavering presence.

"Captain," Ramirez warned, his gaze locked onto their surroundings, "we've got more enemies closing in. We need to move fast."

"Understood," Rodriguez replied, his mind calculating the best route to ensure Hayes' safety. "We'll take that path to the west. It's our best option."

"Let's go," Emily urged, her determination to see them all through this ordeal evident in every step.

As Team Delta pressed onwards, they encountered pockets of resistance, engaging in intense firefights and close-quarters combat. Despite the escalating intensity of the battle, each member remained focused on their mission – securing Lieutenant Hayes' safe extraction. Their teamwork and expertise were unmatched, and their resolve unshakable.

"Almost there," Rodriguez assured his team, his eyes scanning the area for the quickest and safest escape route.

"Then let's finish this," Reynolds declared, his voice steely with resolve.

Focused and unyielding, Team Delta continued to navigate the encampment, knowing that they had come too far to fail now. Together, they would see this mission through to the end – and bring their comrade home.

Emily's pulse thrummed in her ears as she scanned the battlefield, her keen eyes taking in every detail. The moonlight cast eerie shadows over the encampment, turning the makeshift structures into grotesque silhouettes. Gunfire echoed through the night, punctuating the tense silence that enveloped Team Delta.

"Stay close, Hayes," Emily instructed, her voice low and steady. "We've got your back."

"Thank you," he replied, his gratitude evident despite his weakened state. He leaned on her for support, but there was a resolute fire in his eyes that spoke of his determination to see this through.

"Captain, we need to move quickly," Ramirez warned, his gaze locked onto their surroundings. "Enemy forces are closing in."

"Understood," Rodriguez replied, his mind calculating the best route to ensure Hayes' safety. "Follow me, and stay sharp."

As they pressed on, Team Delta encountered pockets of resistance. But even under fire, Emily's mind worked like a well-oiled machine, processing information and formulating strategies with astonishing speed. She directed her comrades with precision, ensuring that they utilized their tactical expertise and teamwork to neutralize the enemy forces efficiently.

"Cover that flank!" she ordered, her piercing blue eyes assessing the situation. "Ramirez, Reynolds, take those two out!"

"Copy that!" Reynolds shouted, moving swiftly to obey her command. With each exchange of gunfire, the team's trust in one another grew stronger, their synchronized movements a testament to their unwavering bond.

"Stay focused," Emily reminded herself, knowing that they had come too far to fail now. Her thoughts were a whirlwind of tactics and calculations, but at their core was an iron resolve to see this mission through to the end – and bring their comrade home.

"Three hostiles up ahead," Rodriguez reported, his voice tense but controlled. "Thompson, Hayes, stay behind us. We'll clear a path."

"Stay behind me, Sam," Emily murmured softly, her hand gripping his arm protectively. "You're going to make it out of here."

"Emily, I—" Hayes began, but she silenced him with a firm look.

"Save your strength," she insisted, her blue eyes blazing with determination. "We've got this."

As if on cue, Team Delta moved as one, engaging the enemy with unrelenting focus. Despite the escalating intensity of the battle, each member remained committed to their mission – securing Lieutenant Hayes' safe extraction. And as they fought, side by side, there was not a shred of doubt in their minds that they would succeed.

"Almost there," Rodriguez assured them, his voice steady and resolute. "Just a little further, and we'll have our ticket out of here."

"Let's finish this," Reynolds announced, his voice equally unwavering. And with that final declaration, Team Delta surged forward, propelled by their dedication to saving one of their own.

The cool coastal breeze whipped across Emily's face, stinging her eyes as she stared down the barrel of her rifle. The distant sounds of gunfire and explosions echoed in her ears, a cacophony that only served to fuel her determination.

"Reynolds, take point," Emily ordered, her voice steady despite the adrenaline pumping through her veins. "Rodriguez, cover our six. Hayes, stay close."

"Copy that," came the terse replies from her team members, their voices tinged with the same resolve that coursed through her own heart.

As they advanced through the wreckage of the encampment, shattered glass and debris crunching underfoot, Emily allowed herself a brief moment of introspection. They've come so far, but the thought of losing anyone now - especially Hayes - was unbearable. She shook off the grim thoughts and focused on the task at hand, her mind racing with tactical calculations and contingency plans.

"Contact!" Reynolds shouted, his rifle erupting with a burst of gunfire as he engaged the enemy forces blocking their escape route.

Emily moved swiftly towards a fallen wall, providing cover for Hayes as Rodriguez and Reynolds eliminated the remaining threats. Their teamwork was a well-oiled machine, each member instinctively knowing their role in this life-or-death dance.

"Clear!" Rodriguez called out, signaling the end of the skirmish. Emily could sense the relief washing over Hayes, even if he didn't show it outwardly.

"Good work, everyone," she praised, her eyes scanning the horizon for any more potential dangers. "Let's keep moving. We're almost there."

"Thanks, Emily," Hayes whispered, his voice hoarse from exhaustion and pain. "I wouldn't have made it without you and the team."

"Never leave a man behind," Emily responded, her blue eyes locking onto his for a brief moment before turning back to the treacherous path ahead.

"Reynolds, scout ahead and secure our exfil," she commanded, her mind refusing to accept anything less than success. "We'll cover you."

"Roger that," Reynolds replied, already disappearing into the shadows with practiced stealth.

Emily took a deep breath, steadying herself for the final push. With every step, they moved closer to freedom - and to the promise of safety for one of their own.

"Stay sharp, everyone," she warned, her voice barely audible above the howling wind. "We're not out of this yet."

But as the extraction point came into view, a sense of triumph swelled within Emily's chest. They had done it - against all odds, they had prevailed. And as Team Delta made their way towards the waiting helicopter, Lieutenant Hayes in tow, Emily knew that their unbreakable bond and unwavering determination had been the key to their success.

"Welcome home, Sam," she whispered, allowing herself a small smile as the helicopter blades roared to life.

CHAPTER 13

In the depths of Lieutenant Hayes' memories, the haunting echoes of his capture resurfaced.

"Who are you?" Sam struggled to make out the shadowy figures encircling him. A rough hand grabbed his jaw, forcing him to meet the cold blue gaze of General Kozlov.

"Your worst nightmare," Kozlov sneered, striking Sam's face with a clenched fist. The sickening crack of bone reverberated through the small, dank room. Blood filled Sam's mouth, the taste of iron stinging his senses.

"Where are you keeping Emily?" His voice was a pained rasp, desperate for information about his comrade.

"Your concern is touching, Lieutenant," Kozlov chuckled darkly. "But she is not your immediate problem."

Sam's heart rate quickened. Emily, if you're alive, stay strong. I won't let them break me. He gritted his teeth as two soldiers dragged him across the cold concrete floor, chains rattling around his wrists and ankles. They threw him into a crude metal chair, securing him tightly.

"Tell us what we want to know, or the pain will only get worse," Kozlov warned, his voice low and menacing.

"Go to hell." Sam spat blood at the General's feet, defiance burning in his eyes. He braced himself for the inevitable retaliation.

In response, Kozlov nodded to a soldier wielding a long, twisted rod, its end glowing red-hot. The searing heat approached Sam's exposed flesh, and he gasped involuntarily, fear twisting his gut. I have to endure this. For Emily. For my team.

"Last chance, Lieutenant," Kozlov said, almost casually. "Give us the intel, or suffer."

"Never." Sam's voice was barely audible, but there was no mistaking the determination behind it.

The white-hot pain tore through him as the rod made contact, his screams echoing off the damp stone walls. The smell of charred skin filled the air, and Sam fought to maintain consciousness, every nerve ending aflame.

"Very well," Kozlov said coldly, watching as the soldier continued his sadistic work. "We have plenty of time."

Sam's vision blurred, but he focused on a single thought – Emily, alive and free, her piercing blue eyes filled with hope. He clung to that image, even as darkness threatened to claim him.

"Sleep is a luxury you won't have, Lieutenant," Kozlov's voice ripped through the darkness, shattering the thin veil of respite Sam had found in unconsciousness.

His body jolted awake, muscles seizing in protest as he fought to regain his bearings. The cold, damp cell seemed to close in on him, but Sam's mind raced with thoughts of escape. He would not give in; he could not let his comrades down.

"Tell me about your team," Kozlov demanded, pacing the room like a predator stalking its prey. "Their weaknesses, their plans..."

"Go to hell," Sam growled through clenched teeth, every fiber of his being focused on resisting the urge to divulge anything that could endanger his fellow soldiers.

A wicked smile spread across Kozlov's face, and he nodded to one of his men. "Water, I think."

Sam steeled himself as a bucket of ice-cold water was thrown over him, his breath catching in his throat as the shock hit his system. He suppressed a shiver, refusing to show any sign of weakness.

"Your silence will only prolong your suffering, Lieutenant," Kozlov warned, a cruel glint in his eyes. "But we can be patient."

"Your patience doesn't scare me," Sam spat back, summoning the strength to meet Kozlov's gaze. "I've been through worse than this."

"Have you?" Kozlov asked, an edge of curiosity creeping into his voice. "We shall see about that."

As Kozlov's men moved to inflict a new round of torment upon Sam, he drew upon the deepest reserves of his training and determination. Every ounce of pain they inflicted only fueled his resolve to resist, to protect his comrades at all costs.

"Remember, Lieutenant," Kozlov taunted, relishing the sight of Sam's battered body. "There's no rescue coming for you. No one even knows you're alive."

"Emily does," Sam thought to himself, his heart swelling with a mixture of love and pride. He knew she would never give up on him, just as he would never betray her or their team.

"Enough!" Kozlov barked suddenly, displeased by Sam's continued defiance. "If physical pain won't break you, let's see how well you handle the isolation."

Sam could hear the footsteps receding, leaving him alone in the cold darkness of his cell. The door slammed shut, sealing him off from the world.

"Stay strong, Emily," Sam whispered into the void, clinging to the thought of her courage and determination. "I'll find a way out."

Bound by chains and bathed in sweat, Lieutenant Samuel Hayes hung from the wall of his cold, dank cell. Beads of blood trickled down his arms, staining the jagged scars that marked his battered body. Every breath felt like a razor slicing through his lungs, yet he refused to succumb to the pain.

"Think of Emily," he whispered to himself, recalling the image of her fierce blue eyes and unwavering determination. "She's out there, fighting for me."

"Ah, Lieutenant Hayes," General Kozlov sneered as he entered the cell, his icy voice sending shivers down Sam's spine. "I see you're still with us."

"Go to hell," Sam gritted out between clenched teeth. The words were weak, but his spirit remained unbroken.

"Such defiance," Kozlov chuckled, circling Sam like a predator sizing up its prey. "But I wonder how much longer you can keep it up."

Sam's mind raced, searching for any memory of his team and their mission that could anchor him to the world beyond this nightmare. He remembered the sound of Emily's laughter, the feel of her hand grasping his during a harrowing climb, the way she had looked at him when they'd received their orders - fierce and resolute. It was those memories that tethered him to his resolve, fueling his will to survive.

"Your friends are long gone, Lieutenant," Kozlov taunted, sensing the vulnerability hidden beneath Sam's stoic facade. "And soon, so will you be."

"Never," Sam hissed, his gaze locked on Kozlov's soulless eyes. "I won't give you the satisfaction."

"Very well," Kozlov said, nodding to one of his men who approached Sam with a wicked-looking blade. "Let's see how you fare against a fresh round of agony."

As the blade sliced into Sam's flesh, he screamed, but his mind retreated to memories of his team - their camaraderie, their strength, their unwavering loyalty. He saw Emily scaling a treacherous cliff, fearless and unyielding, and knew that her determination mirrored his own.

"Your pain is your weakness," Kozlov whispered, leaning in close as the blade continued its brutal dance across Sam's skin. "And it will be your downfall."

"Wrong," Sam choked out, locking eyes with the merciless general. "It's my strength."

With each new cut, each fresh wave of agony, Sam clung tighter to the memories of Emily and his team. They were his lifeline, the key to enduring this hellish torment. And in the face of unimaginable pain, Lieutenant Samuel Hayes refused to let go.

The cold steel of the chains dug into Sam's wrists as he hung from the ceiling, sweat trickling down his brow and mingling with the blood from his countless wounds. He gritted his teeth, focusing on the distant sound of dripping water to momentarily escape the searing pain that permeated every inch of his body.

"Tell us what you know, Lieutenant," Kozlov demanded, his voice calm and controlled, a stark contrast to the fury in his eyes. "Your resistance is futile."

Sam glared at the general, the flickering light of the dimly lit room casting shadows across his bruised face. "I have nothing to say to you," he spat, knowing full well that his defiance would be met with more pain.

"Very well," Kozlov replied, nodding to one of his men who stepped forward with a set of pliers. As the cold metal clamped around Sam's fingernail, he steeled himself for the agony that was to come.

In that moment of excruciating pain, Sam retreated within his mind, recalling his team's last mission together before their fates diverged. He remembered Emily's steady hand as she guided them through treacherous terrain, her unwavering determination driving them forward. Her strength was a beacon of hope amidst the darkness, and Sam latched onto it now, using it to fortify his resolve.

"Where are your comrades?" Kozlov asked, watching intently as Sam's face contorted with pain. "Surely they're looking for you."

"Even if they were," Sam gasped, his voice barely audible, "I wouldn't betray them to the likes of you."

Kozlov narrowed his eyes, his icy gaze boring into Sam's very soul. "We'll see about that."

The door to the chamber slammed open, revealing a figure silhouetted against the harsh light of the hallway. Kozlov's men tensed, their weapons raised and ready to fire at any moment. Sam's heart raced, his mind reeling with the thought that his team might have discovered his location.

"Stand down," Kozlov ordered, noticing the newcomer's uniform. "This is one of our own."

The figure stepped forward, revealing a high-ranking officer who looked upon Sam with a mixture of curiosity and disgust. "General, I've come to inform you that we've intercepted communications from the enemy. Our security has been compromised – they're closing in on this location."

Kozlov's eyes narrowed, his grip on the pliers tightening. "Then we must make haste. Double the guards and prepare for our departure."

"Understood, General," the officer replied, swiftly exiting the room.

As the realization of their impending discovery settled in, Sam's resolve strengthened. He refused to succumb to Kozlov's brutal techniques, even as the pain intensified. He would not betray his team; he would not give Kozlov the satisfaction of breaking him.

"Your time is running out, Lieutenant," Kozlov snarled, his voice dripping with venom. "Choose wisely: cooperate or suffer."

"Either way," Sam whispered, his voice hoarse but unwavering, "I won't break."

With a furious scowl, Kozlov tightened the pliers once more, and Sam braced himself for the agony that was sure to follow. But no matter the pain, no matter the cost, he would hold onto the memories of his comrades, their unbreakable bond fueling his determination to resist until the very end.

Kozlov's pliers dug into Sam's flesh. Agony seared through him, but he refused to scream.

"Tell me the plans," Kozlov hissed, but Sam only glared back.

"Go to hell," he spat, blood dripping from his lips.

Kozlov twisted the pliers, and Sam clenched his teeth, forcing himself to focus on anything but the pain. He needed information – their weaknesses, their plans.

"Your defiance is futile, Lieutenant," Kozlov snarled, pausing for a moment before continuing his torment.

Sam's eyes darted around the room, searching for any clues. A map on the wall, hastily scribbled notes – anything.

"Who else was involved?" Kozlov demanded, but Sam remained silent.

The door creaked open, and an officer entered, whispering urgently in Kozlov's ear. Their lowered voices made it difficult to hear, but Sam strained to listen, catching fragments of their conversation.

"...change of plans...tonight..."

"...moving to the secondary location..."

"...security breach..."

"Enough!" Kozlov barked, shoving the officer out of the room. "I will deal with you later."

He turned back to Sam, cold fury in his eyes. "You really are stubborn, aren't you? But you'll break, eventually."

"Never," Sam thought, steeling himself for the next round of torture. His mind raced, piecing together the fragments of information he'd heard. He would endure, he would survive, and he would use this knowledge against them.

"Let's continue," Kozlov said, gripping the pliers once more.

Sam braced himself, but his resolve never wavered. Every strike, every cruel twist of the pliers, only fueled his determination. He would not give in, not when his comrades were counting on him.

"Your friends won't save you," Kozlov sneered, but Sam ignored the taunt.

"Keep talking, General," Sam thought, gritting his teeth against the pain. "The more you say, the more I'll have to use against you."

With every question, every torment, Sam stored away the information he gathered – their plans, their weaknesses. And as the hours dragged on and the pain intensified, he clung to that knowledge like a lifeline.

For when the time came, he would be ready.

Days bled into nights, each indistinguishable from the last. Sam's body bore the marks of his prolonged ordeal – bruises darkened to an angry purple, fresh cuts crisscrossing old scars, and a dull ache that seemed to seep into his bones.

"Tell me," Kozlov demanded, his voice dripping with cold malice. "The access codes."

"Go to hell," Sam spat through gritted teeth, his eyes blazing with defiance.

"Very well." The general signaled for his henchman to begin another round of torment.

Sam tensed, bracing for the inevitable blow. It came swift and brutal, but he had learned to anticipate their movements somewhat, allowing him to steel himself against the worst of the pain. He hid a grim smile as he catalogued each of their tactics, filing them away for future use.

"Still nothing?" Kozlov sneered, his patience clearly wearing thin. "You are quite resilient, Lieutenant Hayes, but even you have limits."

"Maybe," Sam thought, refusing to give the general the satisfaction of hearing his doubts. "But I won't break, not today."

"Again," Kozlov ordered, his voice like ice.

As the blows rained down, Sam carried his mind elsewhere, summoning images of Emily's fierce determination and the unwavering loyalty of his comrades. These memories fueled him, lending him strength in his darkest moments.

"Once more," Kozlov said, a hint of frustration creeping into his voice.

"Your men are getting sloppy," Sam taunted between gasps, his voice wavering but defiant. "Guess they're getting tired, too."

"Silence!" Kozlov roared, striking Sam hard across the face.

"Got under your skin, didn't I?" Sam thought, tasting blood on his lips. In that moment, he drew strength from the knowledge that he was still a threat to them, even in his weakened state.

"Enough!" Kozlov bellowed, storming out of the room. "I will return tomorrow, and you will talk."

"Good luck with that," Sam muttered under his breath, resisting the urge to laugh despite the pain. As his captors filed out of the room, he let himself sink into the darkness that threatened to envelop him.

"Stay strong," he whispered, clinging to the glimmer of hope that shimmered in the distance. "Just a little longer."

With each passing day, Sam's determination only grew stronger. He would survive this torture, he vowed, and when the time came, he would make them pay for what they had done – not just to him, but to his comrades and country.

"Never give up," he repeated like a mantra, the words echoing through the cold, dark cell. "Never surrender."

"Never surrender," Sam whispered, the words echoing in his mind as he floated through the haze of memory.

The door to the cell slammed shut with a deafening bang, jolting Lieutenant Hayes back into the present. Disoriented, he blinked rapidly, forcing himself to focus on his surroundings. The cold concrete floor beneath him, the dim light filtering through the narrow window – all reminders that he was no longer trapped in the nightmare of his past.

"Sam!" Emily's voice cut through the fog, urgent and concerned. "Are you with me?"

He turned to face her, his eyes locking onto hers – those piercing blue eyes that had seen him through so many missions before. For a moment, the scars of his past seemed to fade away, replaced by a newfound determination.

"Emily," he said, his voice steady but low. "I'm here."

"Good." She nodded, her face etched with worry. "We need to move. The enemy's closing in, and we can't afford to wait any longer."

As they scrambled to their feet, Sam's thoughts raced, a flurry of memories and plans. He knew that their escape would be a treacherous one, but he also knew that he couldn't let his past define him any longer. Each step forward was a testament to the strength that had carried him through, a constant reminder that he would not be broken.

"Let's go," he ordered, his voice firm and resolute. Together, they sprinted down the hallway, their footsteps echoing in the empty space.

"Left," Emily called out, guiding them towards a narrow staircase. They descended quickly, ignoring the ache in their legs and the pounding in their chests. Every second counted, and they could not afford to slow down.

"Remember the plan," Sam thought, his mind racing alongside his body. "Stay focused."

"Almost there," Emily panted, her breath ragged but determined. "Just a few more levels."

"Keep pushing," Sam urged himself, the pain in his body dull compared to the memories that had tormented him. "You've survived worse."

Finally, they burst through the exit door and into the night, their hearts pounding with adrenaline and fear. The darkness enveloped them, offering a momentary reprieve from the danger that pursued them.

"Over here!" Emily whispered, motioning towards a nearby vehicle. They climbed inside, their bodies shaking from exertion and anticipation.

"Drive," Sam commanded, his voice steady despite the storm of emotion raging within him. As the engine roared to life, he allowed himself a brief glance in the rearview mirror, taking in the scars that adorned his face – a constant reminder of the strength that had carried him through.

As the memories faded, Lieutenant Hayes tightened his grip on the steering wheel, resolute in his mission. With Emily by his side and the fire of determination burning within him, he would face whatever challenges lay ahead – for himself, his comrades, and his country.

CHAPTER 14

The air hung heavy with the stench of sweat and fear as Team Delta crouched in the shadows, their breaths shallow and measured. The dim glow of a single bulb illuminated the battered figure of Lieutenant Samuel Hayes, suspended from the ceiling by crude chains. His chest heaved with labored breaths, exhaustion etched into every bruise that marred his once-handsome face.

"Sam," Emily whispered, her heart clenching at the sight of her comrade. "Hold on. We're getting you out of here."

She signaled to her team, their night vision goggles reflecting the determination in her piercing blue eyes. They moved with an almost preternatural silence, their years of elite training driving them forward like well-oiled machines. As they closed in on the makeshift cell, Emily's mountaineering instincts kicked in, her agile muscles ready to respond to any obstacle.

"Delta Two, cut him down," she ordered, her voice steady and calm despite the urgency of their mission.

"Yes, ma'am." Delta Two stepped up and, within moments, the gleaming edge of a combat knife sliced through the restraints that bound Sam. He crumpled to the ground, hissing in pain but managing to stay conscious.

"Thanks," he rasped, meeting Emily's gaze with gratitude that only deepened her resolve to see him safely extracted. She nodded, helping him to his feet as the rest of the team formed a protective circle around them.

"Thompson, we've got company!" Delta Four called out suddenly, just as the distant wail of alarms pierced the oppressive silence. Emily swore under her breath, knowing that time was no longer on their side.

"Everyone, defensive positions! We need to create some distance between us and the enemy," she commanded, her mind racing to formulate a strategy that would give them the upper hand. "Delta One, lay down suppressing fire. Delta Three, prep smoke grenades."

"Copy that, Lieutenant!" came the simultaneous replies, each team member moving with practiced efficiency to execute their tasks.

As the first shots rang out and enemy forces began pouring into the area, Emily's thoughts turned to Sam. She knew he was in no condition for a prolonged firefight, but she also recognized the fierce determination that burned within him. He wouldn't let his weakened state hold him back, not when his comrades were risking their lives for him.

"Sam, you're with me," she said, her voice carrying the weight of her trust in him. "You know these bastards better than any of us. Help us find an opening."

"Understood," he replied, his eyes scanning the chaos unfolding before them. He tucked himself behind a crumbling wall, gripping his weapon tightly as adrenaline coursed through his veins.

"Delta Team, stay close and keep your heads down!" Emily ordered, leading the charge as they advanced through the hail of gunfire, their tactical maneuvers honed by years of relentless training. They moved like wraiths through the smoke and confusion, their singular goal to protect Sam and bring him home alive.

"Bravo Team, on me!" Lieutenant Thompson's voice cut through the cacophony of gunfire and explosions as she sprinted, her blonde hair whipping behind her. She slid into position behind a ruined pillar, her ice blue eyes scanning the battlefield for optimal vantage points.

"Thompson, we need to create an escape route," Captain Rodriguez's gruff voice crackled over the comms. "Coordinate with Alpha and Charlie. Keep Hayes safe."

"Copy that, Captain," she replied, her mind already racing with potential strategies. She barked orders to her team, their well-honed instincts kicking in as they took up positions along the perimeter.

"Alpha, Charlie, this is Bravo Leader. We're providing cover fire. Make us a path out of here."

"Understood, Bravo Leader," came the responses from both teams, their voices tense but determined.

"Ramirez, I need you to reinforce our defensive line," Thompson said, nodding towards the approaching Sergeant, his face streaked with dirt and sweat.

"Got it, Lieutenant," he replied, his dark eyes focused as he directed his men to fortify their position.

With the perimeter secure, Thompson allowed herself a moment to assess the situation. The enemy was relentless, but so were they. Every man and woman under her command was a force to be reckoned with, forged by years of training and bound by loyalty. And they would not fail.

"Captain, we're holding them off, but we need that exit now," she reported, turning her attention back to Rodriguez.

"Roger that, Lieutenant. It's coming. Be ready to move on my mark," he replied, his voice unwavering despite the chaos surrounding them.

Thompson leaned against the pillar, her chest heaving as she caught her breath. Her thoughts lingered on Hayes, weakened but still fighting alongside Delta Team. His determination was inspiring, but she couldn't shake the nagging worry that he wouldn't make it out of this alive.

"Focus, Emily," she chided herself, her eyes narrowing as she spotted an enemy combatant attempting to flank them. She squeezed off a round, watching as the man crumpled to the ground. There would be time for doubt later; right now, they had a mission to complete.

"Bravo Team, stand by," Thompson ordered, locking eyes with each member of her team, their nods and grim expressions confirming their readiness. "When the Captain gives the order, we move. And we don't stop until we're all out of here."

"Oorah!" came the chorus of replies, their voices resolute and strong.

"Mark!" Captain Rodriguez's voice roared over the comms, signaling their moment of escape.

"Move, Bravo! Go, go, go!" Thompson shouted, leading her team forward as Alpha and Charlie blew a hole in the compound wall, creating a path to freedom.

And though the way was fraught with danger, they knew they were not alone. They were a united front, ready to face whatever challenges awaited them. Together, they would bring Hayes home.

Smoke and gunfire filled the air as Captain Rodriguez stood at the center of the chaos, his eyes locked onto Team Delta. Their night vision goggles glinted in the firelight, a stark green against the haze, as they took point and led the way through the destruction.

"Delta, on me," he barked, his voice steady despite the cacophony around him. "Charlie, prepare to detonate."

As if on cue, explosions rocked the compound, shaking the ground beneath their boots. The charges that Team Charlie had strategically placed sent shockwaves through the enemy forces, buying them precious moments to push forward.

"Keep moving!" Rodriguez shouted, his heart pounding in his chest, adrenaline coursing through his veins. He knew that every second counted, and their window for escape was rapidly closing.

"Captain," Major Reynolds called out from behind, his voice strained with effort. "We've got more hostiles incoming. We need to pick up the pace!"

Rodriguez nodded, acknowledging the urgency. He glanced back at Hayes, who, despite his weakened state, fought alongside them with unwavering determination. A surge of protectiveness washed over him, fueling his resolve to see this mission through.

"Thompson, Ramirez – provide suppressing fire. We need to break through their lines!" Rodriguez ordered, his fingers tightening around his rifle. He could feel the weight of responsibility bearing down on him, but now was not the time for doubt or hesitation.

"Copy that, Captain," Lieutenant Thompson responded, her calm demeanor a testament to her training and experience. She exchanged a quick nod with Sergeant Ramirez before they both unleashed a hail of bullets, pinning down the enemy combatants and giving Team Delta an opening to advance.

"Go, go, go!" Rodriguez urged, following closely behind Delta as they charged forward, their night vision goggles guiding them unerringly through the smoke and gunfire. He allowed himself a brief moment of hope, a glimmer of light in the darkness that surrounded them.

"Almost there," he whispered to himself, steeling his resolve. They had come too far to fail now. And with each step they took, their goal – freedom for Lieutenant Hayes and ensuring the safety of his team – grew nearer.

An explosion shook the ground beneath them, and in that moment, Lieutenant Emily Thompson wielded her ice axe with deadly precision. The enemy combatant lunged toward her, but she anticipated his movements, parrying his strike and delivering a swift, powerful blow with the sharp end of her axe. He crumpled to the ground, lifeless.

"Captain, two more coming from the east!" Thompson shouted, her voice steady despite the adrenaline coursing through her veins.

"Got it. I'll take the one on the left, you handle the right," Captain Rodriguez replied, his authoritative tone a familiar comfort amidst the chaos.

"Roger that," she acknowledged, her heartbeat thundering in her ears as she prepared for her next adversary.

In this high-stakes game of life and death, each breath could be their last. But together, they were a force to be reckoned with – their trust forged in the fires of countless missions. They moved in tandem, a seamless dance of violence and survival.

As the two enemies charged, Thompson sprang into action, her mountaineering skills translating into agile movements that allowed her to dodge a hail of bullets. She closed the distance between her and the enemy, swinging her ice axe with lethal accuracy. A spray of crimson stained the air as the enemy fell, defeated.

Captain Rodriguez's shots rang out, expertly taking down his target. As the body hit the ground, he scanned their surroundings, searching for any additional threats.

"Area clear. We need to keep moving," he said, his thoughts racing to formulate their next move. "Thompson, can you lead us through the labyrinth of this compound?"

"Affirmative, Captain," she responded, her piercing blue eyes filled with determination. "I've studied the layout extensively. Follow me."

Their confidence in one another was unshakable, a bond tempered by shared experiences on and off the battlefield. As they navigated the treacherous terrain, their minds were in sync – each movement calculated, each decision made with a singular goal: protect Lieutenant Hayes and ensure the safety of their team.

"Stay alert," Rodriguez warned, his voice barely audible over the cacophony of gunfire and explosions. "This isn't over yet."

"Understood," Thompson replied, her grip tightening on her ice axe. "We'll get through this together."

And with that, they pressed onward, their unwavering trust in one another a beacon of hope in the midst of the storm.

The smoke hung low in the air, its acrid taste a reminder of the chaos around them. Emily Thompson focused on her breathing, her chest rising and falling beneath the weight of her gear. The battle raged on, gunfire and explosions threatening to drown out her thoughts. She gripped her ice axe tightly, ready for what was to come.

"Alpha Team, we need cover fire!" Captain Rodriguez shouted into his radio, his voice taut with urgency.

"Copy that, Captain," came the response. "Suppressing fire inbound."

With a deafening roar, a hail of bullets erupted from Team Alpha's position, momentarily silencing the enemy's onslaught. Emily glanced over at Lieutenant Hayes, still weak from his captivity but determined to fight alongside his rescuers.

"Stay close, Sam," she said, her voice steady despite the relentless gunfire. "We'll get you out of here."

"Thanks, Thompson," he replied, a grim smile playing on his lips. "I've got some intel on their tactics – we can use it to our advantage."

"Let's hear it," she said, her eyes narrowing as she assessed their surroundings.

"Two things," he began, his words measured despite his weakened state. "First, they tend to favor ambushes in tight spaces. Second, they rely heavily on their communication network. If we can disrupt that, we'll have a better chance of making it out alive."

"Understood," she nodded, her mind racing to formulate a plan. "Delta Team, on me!"

As Team Delta moved swiftly through the compound, Emily kept her eyes peeled for any signs of an ambush. Her mountaineering skills, honed through years of scaling treacherous peaks, lent her an agility that proved invaluable in this war-ravaged terrain.

"Thompson, I've got an idea," Hayes whispered, gesturing towards a nearby communications tower. "If we can take that out, it'll throw them off balance."

"Good thinking," she replied, her jaw set with determination. "Let's do this."

With Team Alpha's suppressing fire covering their advance, they sprinted towards the tower. Emily could hear her heart pounding in her ears, a steady rhythm amidst the cacophony of battle.

"Cover me!" Hayes shouted as he dashed forward, his knowledge of enemy tactics giving him the edge he needed to dodge bullets and avoid traps.

"Got your back, Sam!" she called, her ice axe at the ready for any close-quarters combat.

As they neared the tower, their objective within reach, Emily marveled at Lieutenant Hayes' resilience. Despite the harrowing ordeal he'd endured, he remained unshakable – a testament to his unwavering sense of duty.

"Almost there," she thought, her muscles screaming for relief. "We'll make it through this. Together."

"Thompson, now!" Hayes yelled, drawing her attention back to the task at hand. With a nod, she sprang into action, determined to see their mission through to the end.

A hail of gunfire echoed through the night, briefly illuminating the dark mountainside as Team Bravo descended on ropes from the jagged peaks above. Emily's heart raced with a mixture of relief and renewed determination at the sight of their comrades joining the fray.

"Bravo's here to back us up!" she shouted over the din of battle, her voice steady and authoritative.

"About time!" Hayes replied, his eyes scanning for threats amidst the chaos. "Let's keep moving!"

As Team Bravo closed in, they unleashed a torrent of bullets upon the enemy forces, allowing Emily and the others to advance with calculated speed. They moved as one, their years of elite training evident in every step, every bullet fired. With each passing second, their objective grew closer – and so too did the possibility of escape.

"Stay close, Sam," Emily urged, her piercing blue eyes locked onto Hayes' bruised face. "We'll get you out of here."

"Lead the way, Thompson," he nodded, his expression betraying a hint of gratitude beneath the pain.

Together, they pressed forward, weaving through the smoke-filled battlefield with unerring precision. As they encountered pockets of resistance, they neutralized each threat with ruthless efficiency, always ensuring that Hayes remained protected at all costs.

"Watch your six!" Emily warned, quickly dispatching an enemy combatant who'd attempted to flank them. "They're getting desperate."

"Desperate or not, we're getting out of this hellhole," Hayes vowed, his voice firm despite his weakened state. "Thanks to you and the teams."

"Couldn't have done it without you, Sam," Emily replied, her thoughts turning to the countless lives that would be saved by the vital intelligence Hayes carried. The weight of their mission bore down on her, but she refused to let it break her resolve. They were almost there – they just had to hold on a little longer.

"Bravo's got our back, Alpha and Charlie are making progress on the other side," she said, her mind racing as she strategized their next move. "Delta, let's push forward and clear a path!"

"Copy that, Lieutenant Thompson!" Team Delta responded in unison, their night vision goggles granting them an edge in the darkness.

With a renewed sense of urgency, they surged ahead, Emily's ice axe gleaming menacingly as she cleared a path for Hayes and the others. The end was in sight; failure was not an option.

"Stay focused, stay alive," she reminded herself, every muscle tensed, every instinct sharpened. "We're almost there."

Smoke billowed around Captain Rodriguez as he scanned the battlefield, his piercing brown eyes darting from one point to another, assessing their situation. His tall, muscular frame was tensed and ready for action, a living embodiment of strength and determination.

"Team Delta, status report!" he barked out, his voice cutting through the cacophony of gunfire and explosions.

"Captain, we've found an escape route!" replied a member of Team Delta, her voice filled with urgency. "It leads through a series of underground tunnels – should allow us to avoid enemy reinforcements!"

"Excellent work," Rodriguez said, nodding in approval. "Everyone, prepare to move out!"

"Captain, we've got pockets of resistance along the way," Lieutenant Thompson warned, her calm authority evident even amidst the chaos. "We'll have to engage them in close-quarters combat."

"Understood, Lieutenant. Let's make this quick and efficient. Hayes, you good to go?"

"Ready as I'll ever be, sir," Lieutenant Hayes replied, his voice strained but determined. Despite his injuries, he was eager to put his knowledge of the enemy's tactics to use, helping to ensure their safe escape.

"Alright, teams! On me!" Captain Rodriguez ordered, leading the charge into the underground tunnels, the rest of the units following closely behind. The air was thick with tension as they descended into the darkness, night vision goggles casting an eerie green glow on their surroundings.

"Contact left!" Sergeant Ramirez shouted, alerting the others to the presence of enemy combatants. He moved with swift precision, his lean build allowing him to navigate the tight confines of the tunnel with ease as he eliminated the first threat.

"Stay sharp, everyone," Major Reynolds advised, his imposing figure offering reassurance to those around him. "Keep moving, and watch each other's backs."

"Copy that, Major," Emily responded, her piercing blue eyes never straying from the path ahead. "We've got this."

As they pressed on, their expert training and coordination were evident in every action, their movements a seamless blend of speed and precision. For every enemy that emerged from the shadows, there was a quick, decisive response – a well-aimed shot, a perfectly timed strike.

"Almost there," Emily thought to herself, her ice axe cleaving through the darkness as she eliminated another foe. "Just a little further."

"Keep pushing, we're nearly at the exit!" Captain Rodriguez shouted, his authoritative tone spurring them onward. "Stay focused, stay alive!"

"Roger that, sir!" Team Delta replied, their night vision goggles guiding them through the last stretch of the tunnel.

"Captain, I can see the light up ahead!" Hayes called out, hope flaring in his voice. They had made it through the resistance, but they knew the battle wasn't over yet. Still, they had come so far, and they would not let anything stand in their way.

"Let's move, teams!" Rodriguez commanded, his determination unwavering. "We're bringing Hayes home, no matter what it takes!"

The flickering light of the tunnel exit grew larger with each stride, casting an eerie glow on Lieutenant Emily Thompson's face as she sprinted forward. Her heart pounded in her ears, drowning out the cacophony of explosions and gunfire echoing from behind them. She could feel the weight of responsibility bearing down on her, every fiber of her being focused solely on ensuring the safety of her team and Hayes.

"Push harder! We're almost there!" Emily shouted, her voice a mix of urgency and determination. She glanced back over her shoulder to see her teammates following suit, faces taut with concentration and adrenaline.

"Thompson, hold up!" Lieutenant Hayes called out, his breath ragged but resolute. "I've got something that might help."

Emily slowed her pace, watching as Hayes fumbled with a device he had retrieved from one of their fallen enemies. She allowed herself a moment of curiosity, wondering what advantage this could possibly give them.

"Keep moving!" Captain Rodriguez barked, snapping her focus back to the task at hand. "Hayes, whatever you've got, make it quick!"

"Got it," Hayes replied, activating the device with a triumphant smirk. A series of deafening blasts echoed through the tunnel, followed by the distant sound of collapsing earth. "That should slow them down a bit."

"Good work, Hayes!" Emily praised, her thoughts turning to the extraction point just beyond the tunnel. She knew they were running out of time, and every second counted. "Alright, teams – let's move!"

As they burst through the tunnel exit, the scent of fresh air filled their lungs, momentarily overwhelming their senses before the reality of their situation came crashing back. The extraction point was just ahead, yet still painfully out of reach.

"Cover fire!" Captain Rodriguez ordered, his voice cutting through the chaos as enemy forces closed in around them. "Thompson, Hayes – lead us to the extraction point!"

"Roger that, sir!" Emily responded, her ice axe at the ready and her mountaineering instincts guiding her movements. With each swift, agile step, she felt a renewed sense of purpose, her eyes locked on their destination.

"Stay close, everyone!" Hayes shouted, his knowledge of enemy tactics providing invaluable insight as they navigated the treacherous terrain. "We're almost there!"

"Thompson, watch your six!" Sergeant Ramirez warned, his voice strained with effort as he dispatched another enemy combatant. "I've got your back!"

"Thanks, Ramirez!" Emily called out, her heart swelling with gratitude for her team's unwavering support.

"Extraction point in sight!" Captain Rodriguez announced, the sound of approaching helicopters filling the air. "Let's finish this!"

"Copy that, sir," Emily thought, her muscles screaming in protest as she pushed herself to the limit. They had come so far, fought so hard, and she refused to let anything stand in their way now. "Just a little further."

With one final burst of speed, the teams sprinted towards the extraction point, the promise of safety and success within their grasp. The roar of the helicopters grew louder, drowning out the sounds of battle behind them, as Lieutenant Thompson led her team to victory.

CHAPTER 15

Beneath the cold, unforgiving sky, Captain James Rodriguez and Team Alpha pressed against the jagged rock face as bullets whizzed overhead. The entrance to the underground lair loomed before them, guarded by enemy forces that swarmed like hornets defending their nest.

"Move! Move!" Captain Rodriguez shouted, his voice a mixture of urgency and determination. He fired round after round at their assailants, providing cover for his team as they inched closer to their objective.

"Almost there, Cap!" Lieutenant Emily Thompson called out, her blue eyes reflecting the chaos unfolding around them. She vaulted over a boulder, diving into a shallow trench with Ramirez and Reynolds close behind.

Explosions rocked the area, the ground trembling beneath their feet. Rodriguez gritted his teeth as he felt the concussive force rattle his bones. But there was no time to dwell on the physical discomfort. Their mission – to rescue Lieutenant Hayes – relied on their ability to breach the underground fortress.

The deafening sound of gunfire echoed through the underground corridors, ricocheting off the walls and creating a cacophony of noise that threatened to consume them. Amidst this chaos, Rodriguez's mind raced as he strategized, knowing that each second they spent under fire put Hayes at greater risk.

"Reynolds, we need a hole in that wall," he ordered, pointing at a weak point in the enemy's defenses.

"Copy that, Cap," Major David Reynolds replied, swiftly loading an anti-armor rocket into his launcher. The graying soldier took aim, his piercing blue eyes locked on the target, and pulled the trigger. A trail of smoke and fire streaked across the battlefield as the rocket found its mark, blowing a gaping hole in the concrete barrier.

"Go, go, go!" Rodriguez urged, leading the charge as they surged forward, their boots pounding against the dusty ground.

"Covering fire!" Thompson yelled, unleashing a hail of bullets that held the enemy at bay, if only for a moment. Her calm authority was infectious, inspiring confidence in her teammates despite the overwhelming odds they faced.

"Almost there," Ramirez muttered under his breath, eyes narrowed with intensity as he fired off several well-placed shots that felled two of Kozlov's men.

As they neared the entrance to the underground lair, Rodriguez couldn't help but feel a surge of pride in his team. Their unwavering determination and skill had carried them this far, and he knew that together, they could overcome any obstacle. But deep down, a nagging doubt threatened to surface – would it be enough to save Lieutenant Hayes?

The ground trembled beneath Captain Rodriguez's boots as an explosion tore through the air, deafening him momentarily. Shrapnel whistled past his head, and he glanced to his left just in time to see two of his team members – Ramirez and Thompson – caught in the blast radius.

"Medic!" he roared above the cacophony, his heart pounding in his chest. "Ramirez and Thompson are hit! I need a medic now!"

"Copy that, Cap!" Reynolds shouted back, scrambling to reach the wounded soldiers. The grizzled veteran moved with surprising agility for his age, dodging enemy fire as he made his way to Ramirez and Thompson's side.

"Stay with me," Rodriguez told himself, forcing his attention back to the battle. He couldn't afford to let his emotions take over – not when so many lives were on the line. As he fired off a spray of bullets, he caught sight of the growing pool of blood surrounding his fallen comrades, and his gut clenched with dread.

"Captain, we've got multiple tangos advancing on our position!" cried out Jenkins, his voice strained with urgency as he unloaded round after round into the approaching horde.

"Damn it!" Rodriguez cursed under his breath. He knew he couldn't abandon his wounded team members, but they were sitting ducks in their current position. His mind raced, searching for a solution amidst the chaos.

"Jenkins, Martinez, lay down some suppressing fire!" he ordered, hoping to buy some time. "Reynolds, how are they?"

"Thompson's stable, but Ramirez is in bad shape, Cap!" Reynolds shouted back, his hands slick with blood as he worked tirelessly to stem the bleeding. "We need to get them both out of here ASAP!"

"Understood." Rodriguez gritted his teeth, his eyes scanning the battlefield for any advantage they could exploit. "We need to fall back and regroup. Martinez, help Reynolds carry our wounded. Jenkins, keep those tangos at bay!"

"Roger that, Cap!" they responded in unison, springing into action.

As Rodriguez provided cover fire, his thoughts churned with a mix of fear and determination. His team was hurting, their morale faltering – but he knew he couldn't allow them to give in to despair. Lieutenant Hayes's life depended on it. And so, as the weight of his responsibility bore down upon him, Captain Rodriguez steeled himself for the battle ahead, vowing to do whatever it took to bring his entire team home.

With each step forward, an explosion shook the walls around them, sending dust and debris raining down like a hailstorm. Emily Thompson gritted her teeth as she pressed herself against the cold, damp stone, her pulse pounding in her ears. The narrow underground corridor provided little cover from the onslaught of enemy fire, and Team Alpha found themselves fighting for every inch of ground.

"Cover me!" she shouted, darting out into the open to return fire at the shadowy figures ahead. Their enemies were relentless, clearly unwilling to let them advance any further into their stronghold. As she squeezed off several rounds, a bullet grazed her arm, slicing through the fabric of her uniform and leaving a stinging trail of blood in its wake.

"Damn it!" she hissed, ducking back behind cover as her teammates laid down a barrage of suppressing fire. Her body ached with fatigue, her mind clouded by a growing sense of dread. Every minute they spent battling their way through these tunnels was another minute Lieutenant Hayes remained in the clutches of General Kozlov's ruthless forces. The weight of that knowledge threatened to crush her resolve, but she refused to let it break her.

"Thompson, are you okay?" Captain Rodriguez called out, concern lacing his voice as he continued to fire at the enemy.

"Nothing I can't handle, Cap," she replied, gritting her teeth as she ripped a piece of fabric from her sleeve and hastily wrapped it around her wound. "But we need to find another way. We're not getting through this gauntlet."

"Agreed," Rodriguez said, his voice heavy with frustration. "We're running out of time. We need to move faster if we want to save Hayes."

"Cap, I think I see a side passage up ahead!" Jenkins shouted, pointing towards a dimly lit opening in the wall. "It might be our only option!"

"Alright, Team Alpha, let's make a break for it!" Rodriguez ordered, rallying his team with a determined glare. "On my mark...now!"

As one, the team surged forward, bullets and debris flying all around them as they sprinted for the side passage. Their lungs burned and their muscles screamed in protest, but they couldn't afford to slow down – not when Lieutenant Hayes's life hung in the balance.

"Move, move, move!" Emily shouted, her voice hoarse from the strain, as she provided cover fire for the rest of the team. She could feel the exhaustion settling into her bones, the weight of their mission dragging her down like an anchor. But she refused to give in to despair. There had to be a way to save Hayes – and she was determined to find it, no matter what the cost.

Captain Rodriguez's boots skidded on the damp floor as he led Team Alpha into the side passage, narrowly avoiding a hail of bullets that ricocheted off the walls. The dimly lit tunnel seemed to stretch endlessly before them, its shadows mocking their desperate flight. It was as if they were being swallowed by darkness itself, and Rodriguez couldn't shake the ominous feeling that fate had turned against them.

"Keep moving!" he barked, pushing his exhausted team forward. Their breaths came in ragged gasps as they stumbled through the narrow passageway, each step taking them further from the deafening chaos of the battle. But with every heartbeat that passed, Rodriguez felt the weight of failure settling over him like a shroud.

"Cap, we can't go on like this," wheezed Jenkins, clutching his side as he limped alongside Rodriguez. "We're losing ground, and we haven't even caught a glimpse of Hayes."

"Damn it all," muttered Emily, her face pale beneath a layer of sweat and grime. "We're not gonna make it in time, are we?"

The hopelessness in her voice cut Rodriguez to the core, and for a moment, he faltered. As Captain, it was his job to keep his team focused and motivated, but the crushing reality of their situation threatened to drag him under. He could feel the ghosts of past failures clawing at his mind, whispering doubts about his ability to lead this mission.

"Get a grip, James," he told himself, gritting his teeth as he fought to suppress the turmoil within him. "This isn't about you – it's about saving Hayes and getting your team out alive."

"Listen up, everyone," Rodriguez shouted, forcing conviction into his voice. "I know it looks bad, but we've faced worse odds before. We're not giving up on Hayes, understand? We'll find him – or die trying."

"Right behind you, Cap," Jenkins replied, nodding grimly as he wiped the sweat from his brow. The others echoed his sentiment with weary nods and murmured affirmations, their resolve momentarily strengthened by Rodriguez's words.

But as they pressed on through the treacherous maze of tunnels, Rodriguez couldn't escape the gnawing doubt that plagued him. General Kozlov had always been a formidable adversary, but this time, it felt as if the odds were insurmountable. The enemy forces seemed to be everywhere, and the labyrinthine corridors only served to confuse and disorient them further.

"Damn you, Kozlov," Rodriguez muttered under his breath, slamming his fist against the cold stone wall. "What have you done with Hayes?"

"Cap, we've got company!" Emily shouted, her voice tense as she alerted the team to an approaching group of enemy soldiers. Instinctively, Rodriguez raised his weapon, his heart pounding in his chest as he prepared for another brutal firefight.

"Stay sharp, Team Alpha," he ordered, trying to ignore the sinking feeling in his gut as his finger tightened on the trigger. He knew that every second counted – that with each passing moment, they were losing precious time to save Lieutenant Hayes.

But as the bullets began to fly once more, Captain James Rodriguez couldn't help but wonder if they were already too late.

Amidst the cacophony of gunfire and the acrid scent of burning metal, Captain Rodriguez caught a glimpse of Thompson shielding Ramirez with her own body as they took cover behind a crumbling wall. Her fierce determination broke through the haze of exhaustion and doubt that had settled over him.

"Thompson, Ramirez, fall back!" Rodriguez barked, laying down covering fire as he moved to join them. He could see the pain etched on Ramirez's face as he tried to suppress a groan from his injured shoulder.

"Sir, we can't go on like this," Thompson said, her voice strained but steady. "We need to find another way."

"Agreed," Rodriguez replied, scanning the area for an alternative route. "Reynolds, any ideas?"

"Cap, there's a side tunnel about twenty meters ahead," Reynolds shouted, pointing towards a narrow opening barely visible amidst the chaos. "It might lead us around the main force."

"Alright, let's move. Thompson, help Ramirez. Reynolds, you're on point." As the team began to push forward, Rodriguez felt a surge of pride at their unwavering commitment, despite the odds stacked against them.

"Captain," Ramirez said between gritted teeth, his eyes meeting Rodriguez's. "I'm sorry. I should've been more careful."

"None of that now, Sergeant," Rodriguez said firmly, clapping him on the back. "You've got nothing to be sorry for. We're in this together, and we'll get out of it together."

"Damn right, Cap," Thompson chimed in, offering a weak smile. "We've come too far to give up now."

Just then, a sudden lull in the battle engulfed them, as if the very air had been sucked from the underground lair. The eerie quiet was punctuated only by the harsh sound of their labored breathing and the distant echo of footsteps.

"Stay sharp," Rodriguez whispered, his senses on high alert. "This could be a trap."

"Or it could be our chance to make a move," Reynolds countered, his eyes locked on the side tunnel. "We can't afford to waste any more time, Cap."

"Alright," Rodriguez nodded, his heart pounding in anticipation. "Let's do this. But stay close and watch each other's backs. We're not leaving anyone behind."

"Understood, Captain," they responded in unison, their voices low but filled with determination.

As Team Alpha advanced cautiously into the darkness, Rodriguez couldn't escape the nagging fear that they were running out of time. The odds seemed insurmountable, but he refused to let doubt consume him. He knew that Lieutenant Hayes was depending on them – and he would do everything in his power to ensure that they didn't let him down.

With the acrid smell of smoke and gunpowder still hanging heavy in the air, Captain Rodriguez's eyes scanned the dimly lit corridor as he assessed their situation. The lull in battle was a brief respite, but the urgency gnawed at him like a relentless beast. Lieutenant Hayes was still out there, and Rodriguez knew every passing second brought them closer to losing him for good.

"Alright, team," Rodriguez barked, his voice steady despite the turmoil churning inside him. "We've faced worse odds before. We can do this. But we need a new plan."

"Captain, I think I noticed a pattern in the enemy's movements," Thompson said, her piercing blue eyes locked on the shadows ahead. "It seems they're heavily guarding a specific area. Maybe that's where they're holding Hayes."

"Good observation, Thompson," Rodriguez commended her. "Let's exploit that."

As they huddled together, the team brainstormed ideas, their minds racing against time. Rodriguez could sense their exhaustion and frustration, but he admired their determination to push forward.

"Here's what we'll do," Rodriguez began, laying out a new strategy. "Thompson, you and Jackson will create a diversion near that heavily guarded area. Draw their attention while the rest of us slip through and find Hayes."

"Understood, Captain," Thompson nodded, a spark of confidence in her eyes.

"Reynolds, you and Martinez provide cover fire for Thompson and Jackson. Keep the enemy pinned down as much as possible," Rodriguez continued, his voice firm and authoritative.

"Copy that, Cap." Reynolds acknowledged, gripping his weapon tightly.

"Meanwhile, Johnson and I will sneak around the other side of their defenses," Rodriguez concluded, his gaze fixed on each of his team members, ensuring they understood their roles. "We'll locate Hayes and bring him back to safety."

"Let's get our brother back," Johnson said, his voice barely above a whisper but carrying the weight of conviction.

"Damn right," Rodriguez agreed, clenching his fist. "Remember, we're Team Alpha – and nothing can stop us when we work together."

"Captain, are you sure about this?" Thompson asked, concern etched on her face. "We're all banged up pretty bad, and it's going to be tough."

"Listen," Rodriguez replied, his eyes locking onto hers as he spoke with unwavering sincerity. "We've been through hell together, and we'll keep pushing forward until we bring Hayes home. We don't let our own down."

"Roger that, Captain," Thompson said, her resolve strengthened by his determination.

"Then let's move. Time's running out," Rodriguez ordered, leading the way as they split into their assigned groups.

As the team moved forward, Rodriguez couldn't help but wonder if they'd find Lieutenant Hayes in time or if they were walking into yet another deadly trap. But he refused to let doubt cloud his mind; he owed it to his team and to Hayes to have faith in their abilities and their mission. They would conquer the odds, no matter how insurmountable they seemed.

Captain Rodriguez's heart raced as he signaled the assault, his finger poised on the trigger of his rifle. The adrenaline coursing through his veins drowned out the pain from his injuries, and for a moment, he felt invincible. "Team Alpha, let's move!" he barked, his voice filled with determination.

"Roger that, Captain," Thompson replied, her eyes locked onto their target - a heavily fortified enemy position. She knew they had to be quick and precise if they wanted any chance at success.

"Reynolds, Ramirez, you're with me," Rodriguez ordered as he charged forward, taking cover behind a crumbling wall. Bullets ricocheted off the concrete, showering them with dust and debris, but they pressed on.

"Suppressive fire!" Reynolds shouted, his experienced hands steady on his weapon as he unleashed a torrent of bullets to keep the enemy at bay. Ramirez followed suit, his sharpshooting skills evident in the way he effortlessly picked off targets while maintaining constant cover fire.

"Thompson, Johnson, flank left and try to find an opening," Rodriguez commanded, his mind racing with potential scenarios and strategies. They couldn't afford to lose this battle. Lieutenant Hayes's life depended on it.

"Copy that, Captain," Thompson acknowledged, her agility and mountaineering skills shining as she scaled a nearby ledge, evading enemy fire with ease. Johnson moved in tandem with her, their teamwork seamless despite their exhaustion and injuries.

"Push forward, Alpha!" Rodriguez urged, his fierce determination driving him as he led the charge deeper into enemy territory. His team fought with renewed vigor, refusing to let their setbacks hold them back.

"Captain, we've got a breach on the left!" Thompson called out, her breath ragged as she vaulted over a barricade and slid into cover. "We can make a move now!"

"Go, go, go!" Rodriguez shouted, his heart pounding in his chest as he and the others seized the opportunity. As they advanced, a hail of bullets tore through the air, narrowly missing them.

"Keep pushing!" Reynolds yelled, his voice strained with effort as he continued to provide cover fire. "We're almost there!"

Rodriguez couldn't help but be amazed by his team's tenacity and skill, even in the face of adversity. They were battered and bruised, but their spirit remained unbroken. He silently vowed not to let their efforts be in vain, focusing on the task at hand with unwavering determination.

"Captain, we've got more hostiles coming in from the right!" Ramirez warned, his voice tense as he spotted the approaching threat. "We need to move fast."

"Understood," Rodriguez replied, gritting his teeth as he formulated a new plan on the fly. "Reynolds, get ready to breach that door. Thompson, Johnson, keep those hostiles at bay. Ramirez, cover our six."

"Roger that, Captain," they all responded in unison, their voices resolute despite the chaos surrounding them.

As the Team Alpha fought tooth and nail against General Kozlov's forces, Rodriguez knew they were making progress, inching closer to their goal of rescuing Lieutenant Hayes. But with each step forward, they faced new challenges and risks, and the outcome of this battle was far from certain. Rodriguez couldn't shake the feeling that something bigger awaited them - an ultimate test of their skills, their resolve, and their loyalty to one another.

With bullets whizzing past his head, Captain Rodriguez watched as Reynolds expertly set an explosive charge on the door leading to the heart of General Kozlov's underground lair. The sound of enemy gunfire grew louder, and he could feel the heavy breaths of his teammates as they fought through pain and exhaustion.

"Charge set, Captain!" Reynolds shouted over the deafening cacophony of the firefight.

"Everyone, get back!" Rodriguez ordered, pulling Thompson away from the doorway just as the explosion blew it open, sending dust and debris flying into the air. He could barely see through the thick haze, but he knew they had to push forward before the enemy regrouped.

"Move in! Go, go, go!" he barked, leading the charge into the now-exposed chamber, his weapon ready for any hostiles that awaited them inside.

"Captain, something's not right," Ramirez warned, his voice tense as he scanned the room. "It's too quiet."

"Stay sharp," Rodriguez replied, feeling the hairs on the back of his neck stand up. This was it – their final push to save Lieutenant Hayes. But he couldn't shake the nagging sensation that they were walking into a trap.

Suddenly, a hail of gunfire erupted from the shadows, catching Team Alpha off guard. The team dove for cover, returning fire with fierce determination.

"Thompson, can you make out their positions?" Rodriguez shouted amidst the chaos, trying to pinpoint the source of the enemy fire.

"Negative, Captain. They're concealed by the darkness," she replied, her voice strained as she fired off another round.

"Damn it!" Rodriguez thought to himself, frustration mounting as he realized their disadvantage. They were running out of time, ammo, and energy, and he knew they couldn't afford any more casualties.

"Ramirez! Reynolds! On me!" Rodriguez called out, hatching a desperate plan in his mind. "We're going to create a diversion while Thompson and Johnson flank them. Ready?"

"Ready, Captain," they both replied, reloading their weapons as they prepared for the risky maneuver.

Rodriguez took a deep breath, steeling himself for what was about to come. "On my mark... Now!"

The three of them burst from cover, guns blazing, drawing the enemy fire away from Thompson and Johnson. As the bullets whizzed by, Rodriguez felt an unsettling mix of fear and adrenaline surge through him. He couldn't help but question if this would be their last stand and if he had led his team into a fatal situation.

"Captain! We're in position!" Thompson's voice crackled over the radio, snapping Rodriguez back to reality.

"Hit them hard!" Rodriguez commanded, pushing aside his doubts as he continued to lay down suppressive fire.

"Roger that," Thompson replied, and with that, she and Johnson unleashed a torrent of gunfire onto the unsuspecting enemy forces.

"Captain! We've got them on the ropes! But there's still no sign of Lieutenant Hayes!" Johnson called out, his voice filled with equal parts relief and concern.

"Keep pushing forward!" Rodriguez shouted back, his resolve unwavering as he led his team deeper into the heart of the enemy stronghold. He knew they had come too far to give up now, even in the face of seemingly insurmountable odds.

As they advanced, the sounds of gunfire and explosions gave way to an eerie silence, which only heightened Rodriguez's unease. The darkness seemed to close in around them, suffocating any hope that remained.

"Captain, I've found something," Reynolds whispered, shining his flashlight on a door at the end of the corridor. It was marked with an ominous symbol – an indication that they had just stumbled upon General Kozlov's inner sanctum.

"Be ready for anything," Rodriguez warned his team, his hand gripping his weapon tightly as he approached the door. He knew that whatever awaited them on the other side would be the culmination of their mission – and potentially their final test.

"Ready when you are, Captain," Thompson said, her voice determined even as fear threatened to consume them all.

Rodriguez took a deep breath and nodded, signaling Reynolds to breach the door. As the explosive charge detonated, the door flew open, revealing...

"Captain! Look out!" Ramirez shouted, but it was too late. A merciless hail of gunfire tore through the smoke-filled room, as Team Alpha dove for cover, the outcome of the battle uncertain, and their fates hanging in the balance.

CHAPTER 16

The flickering glow of the holographic map cast ominous shadows on Captain James Rodriguez's face as he stood alone in the dimly lit room, his back pressed against the cold wall. His piercing brown eyes studied every inch of the enemy's research facility layout before him, searching for vulnerabilities, weaknesses in their defenses.

"Damn it," he muttered under his breath, clenching his jaw.

As he stared at the intricate web of the facility's structure, ghostly images of fallen comrades began to materialize in his mind. Their faces haunted him, each one a painful reminder of the sacrifices made in the name of duty and country. He could hear their final cries, see the life draining from their eyes as they fought bravely by his side.

"Was it worth it?" The question ricocheted through his thoughts, leaving a trail of doubt and uncertainty in its wake.

Captain Rodriguez shook his head, trying to dispel the memories, but they clung to him like a shroud. His hands trembled slightly, and he balled them into fists, nails digging into his palms. The weight of those lives lost bore down on him, threatening to crush him beneath the burden of responsibility.

"Focus, James," he whispered to himself, forcing his gaze back to the flickering map. "You can't afford to let them down again."

He knew his team relied on him, depended on his strength and tactical brilliance to guide them through the most treacherous of missions. But as the faces of his fallen friends continued to emerge from the recesses of his memory, Captain Rodriguez couldn't help but wonder if he was truly worthy of their trust and loyalty.

"Get it together, Captain," he admonished himself, taking a deep, steadying breath. He had a mission to complete, lives to save, and a ruthless enemy to bring down. There was no room for doubt or hesitation.

But even as he tried to summon the unyielding resolve that had carried him through countless previous missions, the shadows of his past still clung to him, a constant reminder of the fine line between life and death, victory and defeat. And as Captain Rodriguez stood there, locked in an internal battle against his own demons, the flickering light of the holographic map seemed to taunt him, daring him to face the darkness within and emerge victorious.

The sound of ticking from an old military-issue clock filled the dimly lit room, each tick echoing like a gunshot in Captain Rodriguez's mind. Holographic images danced before him, casting eerie shadows on the cold steel walls, as he studied the intricate layout of General Kozlov's research facility. His fists clenched at his sides, knuckles turning white with the intensity of his grip.

"Can we really do this?" he muttered under his breath, his jaw tightening as he tried to suppress the rising tide of doubt within him. Kozlov was a formidable adversary, cunning and ruthless, surrounded by an army that seemed unstoppable. How could his small, elite team hope to triumph against such overwhelming odds?

"Failure is not an option," he whispered fiercely, forcing himself to focus on the task at hand. But even as he tried to banish his fears, they clung to him like shadows, impossible to escape.

"Captain, you've got this," he told himself, but the words rang hollow in his ears, drowned out by the ghosts of his past. In a desperate attempt to silence them, he looked away from the flickering map and caught sight of a framed photograph on the nearby table. The smiling faces of his wife and children stared back at him, their eyes full of love and trust.

"Everything I do, I do for you," he murmured, his voice cracking with the weight of emotion. For a moment, he allowed himself to be vulnerable, to remember what truly mattered in this world - the people he loved, the ones who gave him strength when all else seemed lost.

"Focus on the mission, Captain," he reminded himself, blinking back tears as he returned his gaze to the holographic map. He couldn't afford to let his emotions cloud his judgment, not when so much was at stake. With renewed determination, he began to strategize, his mind racing through countless possibilities and potential pitfalls.

"Alright team, listen up," he called out, his voice firm and authoritative as his squad gathered around the flickering map. "We've got a hell of a mission ahead of us, and the odds might not be in our favor. But we've faced worse and come out on top. We're going to take down Kozlov's research facility, and we're going to do it together."

He could see the trust in his team's eyes, their unwavering belief in him as their leader. And though doubt still lurked in the corners of his mind, Captain Rodriguez knew he couldn't afford to let them down. Not now, when everything - his country, his family, his fallen comrades - depended on their success.

"Let's get to work," he said, his eyes filled with determination as he turned back to the holographic map. Together, they would face the darkness and emerge victorious, no matter the cost.

Captain Rodriguez's boots thudded against the cold, concrete floor as he paced back and forth in the dimly lit room. The sound echoed off the walls, a relentless rhythm that mirrored the turmoil brewing within him.

"Damn it," he muttered under his breath, his fists clenching at his sides. "How can I lead them into this?"

"Cap, you've got to stop beating yourself up," a voice said from the doorway. It was Lieutenant Davis, his second-in-command and trusted confidant. Rodriguez stopped pacing and looked at Davis, his expression a mix of desperation and determination.

"Easy for you to say, Lieutenant," he replied, his voice tense. "You're not the one with the lives of your entire team resting on your shoulders."

"None of us are here because we were forced to be, Captain," Davis countered, stepping into the room. "We trust you with our lives because you've always brought us home."

Rodriguez closed his eyes, his jaw clenched tightly as he took a deep breath. He knew Davis was right, but the weight of their mission seemed to crush him from all sides, making it hard to breathe, let alone think clearly.

"Alright," he responded, exhaling slowly. "But what if this time is different? What if this time, I can't bring us all back?"

"Then we go down fighting together," Davis said firmly, his eyes locked on Rodriguez's. "That's what we signed up for."

The Captain held Davis's gaze for a moment before nodding, the strength of his team's loyalty and faith in him empowering. It was time to put his doubts aside and focus on the task at hand.

"Thank you, Davis," he managed, his voice steadier than before. "I needed that reminder."

"Anytime, Cap," Davis replied with a grin. "Now, let's go brief the team. We've got a job to do."

"Right," Rodriguez said, his eyes burning with renewed determination. He took one last deep breath, pushing down any lingering uncertainties as he strode out of the room, Davis at his side.

The pressure was still immense, but Captain Rodriguez knew he couldn't afford to waver. With his team behind him, their unwavering trust in his leadership, and the memory of his family driving him forward, he would face this mission head-on - no matter the odds.

Captain Rodriguez's eyes snapped open as a sudden flashback filled his mind. He was back in the sweltering jungle, the humidity clinging to his skin like an unwanted second layer. The distant crackle of gunfire and the acrid smell of smoke hung heavy in the air. It had been a do-or-die mission - infiltrate the enemy camp, neutralize their commander, and get out alive. And just like now, the odds had been stacked against them.

"Captain, are we really going through with this?" Private Harper had asked, wiping sweat from his brow. "I mean, we're outnumbered three-to-one."

"Harper's right," Sergeant Thompson chimed in, concern etched on his face. "We've never faced anything like this before."

Captain Rodriguez remembered how suffocated he had felt by the weight of his team's doubts. The ghosts of fallen comrades loomed over him, whispering their fears into his ear. But deep within himself, he had found his resolve.

"Listen up," he had said, his voice steady and authoritative. "I know the odds don't look good. I know you're scared. Hell, I'm scared too. But if we don't take this chance, countless more lives will be lost. We don't have a choice. Either we stand together and fight, or we watch our world crumble around us. I need your trust. I need your unwavering commitment. Can you give me that?"

His team had looked at each other, their fear replaced by determination. One by one, they had nodded, signaling their allegiance to their Captain.

"Let's do this, Captain," Sergeant Thompson had said, clapping him on the shoulder. "We've got your back."

With the memory still fresh in his mind, Captain Rodriguez could feel the strength of his past self surging through him. They had faced insurmountable odds before and emerged victorious. He had led them through hell and back, and every time they had trusted him to bring them home.

"Captain, we're ready when you are," Lieutenant Davis's voice brought him back to the present, his team gathered around him in silent support.

"Thank you, all of you," Captain Rodriguez said, his voice heavy with emotion. "I won't let you down."

He could see the unwavering trust in their eyes, the camaraderie that bound them together like a well-forged chain. They were more than just a unit; they were a family. And he would do everything in his power to protect them, no matter the cost.

Captain Rodriguez took one last deep breath, filled with the resilience and determination that had seen them through countless battles. It was time to face this new challenge head-on, armed with the knowledge that his team believed in him just as much as he believed in them. Together, they would defy the odds once more – and emerge triumphant.

With newfound determination coursing through his veins, Captain Rodriguez clenched his fists once more. The faces of fallen comrades flashed before his eyes, each one a testament to the sacrifices made in the name of their mission. He would not let their deaths be in vain. His eyes, filled with a fierce resolve, seemed to burn as he made a silent vow to himself and those who had gone before him – he would not let them down.

"Alright, time to gear up," he announced to the team, his voice authoritative yet laced with an underlying encouragement. They responded with affirmative nods, each one preparing themselves for the battle ahead.

Captain Rodriguez reached out towards a nearby table, his hand closing around the familiar grip of his assault rifle. With practiced efficiency, he checked its ammunition, ensuring that it was properly loaded and ready for the fight. His fingers moved over the weapon with the precision of someone who had devoted years to mastering its intricacies, leaving no room for doubt or hesitation.

As he did so, his thoughts were a swirl of strategic calculations and memories of past victories. The stakes had never been higher, but with every click of the rifle's mechanisms, his confidence grew. This was a battle they could win, he told himself. And they would do so together, as a team.

"Captain, we've got the intel we need on General Kozlov's forces," Lieutenant Davis reported, approaching him with a tablet in hand. "It won't be easy, but we've faced worse odds before."

Captain Rodriguez nodded, taking the tablet from Davis and scanning the information on the screen. His mind raced with potential tactics and countermeasures, weighing the risks and rewards of each option. As he pondered their next move, his inner thoughts were a blend of determination and cautious optimism.

"Alright, here's the plan," he began, addressing his team. "We know their defenses are formidable, but we also have the element of surprise on our side. We'll split into two teams – Alpha and Bravo. Alpha will focus on creating a diversion while Bravo infiltrates the facility."

"Remember," he continued, his gaze sweeping across the faces of his comrades. "We're not just fighting for ourselves, but for everyone who has made the ultimate sacrifice. We owe it to them to see this mission through to the end."

With a chorus of affirmations, the team set about their final preparations, each one ready and willing to follow their captain into the fray. Captain Rodriguez could feel the weight of their trust in him, the camaraderie that bound them together like steel.

"Let's move out," he commanded, his voice steady and resolute. They had faced insurmountable odds before, and they would do so again, with the unyielding determination that had brought them victory time and time again.

Captain Rodriguez's eyes locked with his own reflection in a tarnished mirror, the flickering light casting shadows that danced across his battle-hardened features. In the depths of those piercing brown eyes, he saw not only a seasoned warrior but also the weight of responsibility he bore for the lives of his comrades – both living and dead.

"Never again," he whispered, the words barely audible over the distant rumble of machinery and the pounding of his heart. "I will not fail you."

With one final, lingering glance, Captain Rodriguez tore his gaze away from the mirror. Though the doubts still gnawed at the corners of his mind, they were no match for the fierce determination that now surged through him like a wildfire. He could feel it in every fiber of his being, as tangible as the cold steel of the assault rifle gripped tightly in his hands.

As he strode towards the door, each step fueled by unwavering resolve, he replayed the plan in his head. "Alpha Team, you'll create a diversion," he murmured to himself, visualizing the sequence of events that would follow. "Bravo Team, we'll infiltrate the facility, find General Kozlov, and put an end to this nightmare once and for all."

With a deep, steady breath, Captain Rodriguez pushed open the heavy door and stepped into the dimly lit hallway beyond. The air was thick with tension, anticipation crackling like static electricity as he made his way towards the briefing room.

"Captain!" A voice called out from behind him, momentarily halting his determined march. It was Lieutenant Johnson, one of the few remaining members of their original squad. His face was etched with concern, but also a glimmer of hope that brightened his eyes.

"Are you ready for this, sir?" Johnson asked, his voice a mix of worry and admiration. He had seen Captain Rodriguez at his lowest, but also witnessed firsthand the indomitable spirit that had carried them through countless battles.

"More than ever, Lieutenant," Captain Rodriguez replied, a steely edge to his voice. "We've come too far to turn back now."

Together, they continued down the corridor, their footsteps echoing with purpose as they approached the briefing room. The door loomed before them like a gateway to destiny, and Captain Rodriguez knew it was finally time to face the challenge head-on.

"Let's do this," he declared, his gaze unwavering and his voice filled with the thunder of a thousand storms. With a nod from Johnson, the door flew open, revealing the expectant faces of their team – the last hope against General Kozlov's tyranny.

"Listen up!" Captain Rodriguez barked, commanding the attention of every soldier in the room. "This is it. This is our moment. We have trained, we have fought, and we have sacrificed for this very day."

As his speech flowed, so did his confidence. He could feel the energy in the room rising, buoyed by the fierce determination that radiated from each member of his team. And as he looked into their eyes, he knew, without a doubt, that they were ready.

"Let's make history," he concluded, his voice resolute. "For our fallen comrades, for our families, and for freedom."

With that, Captain James Rodriguez led his team out of the briefing room and into the heart of battle, steadfast in his renewed resolve to triumph against all odds.

CHAPTER 17

The safe house's dimly lit basement buzzed with the uneasy hum of whispered conversations. Soldiers huddled in tight circles, their faces etched with tension and disbelief as they processed the revelation of the double agent's identity. The atmosphere was thick with uncertainty, each person second-guessing who they could truly trust.

Colonel Maria Vasquez stood apart from the rest, her sharp brown eyes scanning the room. Her posture remained impeccable despite the weight of the situation, reflecting years of rigorous training and discipline. She took a deep breath, steeling herself for what was to come. It was time to take control of the chaos.

"Silence!" she barked, her authoritative voice cutting through the air like a razor-sharp blade. Instantly, the murmurs ceased, and all eyes turned to her. "Gather around. We have new intel provided by the double agent."

The soldiers, still reeling from the shock, obeyed without question. They formed a semicircle around the colonel, their eyes filled with a mix of distrust and anticipation. Colonel Vasquez pulled out a tablet, swiping through the contents before addressing the teams again.

"Listen up," she began, her voice calm yet commanding. "Our double agent has uncovered vital information about enemy installations and troop movements. This is our chance to strike back."

As she relayed the information, Colonel Vasquez made a point to maintain eye contact with each member of her team, projecting an aura of confidence. She knew that in times like these, her unwavering resolve would be contagious.

"Alpha Team, you'll target the enemy's communication center," she continued, pointing at the map displayed on the tablet. "Bravo Team, your objective is the munitions depot. And Charlie Team – you're tasked with taking out their fuel reserves."

Each team nodded in understanding, their determination slowly rising to the surface as they received their orders. They knew that now, more than ever, they had to focus on the mission at hand and put their faith in Colonel Vasquez's leadership.

"Remember," she said, her gaze sweeping over the assembled soldiers. "Our enemy is cunning and ruthless – but so are we. We'll use this new intel to our advantage, striking where they least expect it. Trust in your training, trust in your team, and most importantly, trust yourselves."

As her speech came to an end, she could see a flicker of renewed determination in the eyes of her team members. It wouldn't be easy, but they would rise above the betrayal and press forward to achieve their objectives.

"Dismissed!" she ordered, watching as the teams dispersed to prepare for their mission. Colonel Vasquez allowed herself a brief moment to exhale, her thoughts weighed down by the responsibility resting on her shoulders. But there was no time for doubt – the fate of the operation and the lives of her soldiers depended on her unwavering commitment to success.

Captain James Rodriguez clenched his fists, his knuckles turning white as he struggled to process the identity of the double agent. Around him, his team members – including Lieutenant Emily Thompson, Sergeant Miguel Ramirez, and Major David Reynolds – shared a mixture of anger, betrayal, and determination etched on their faces. The air was thick with tension as they grappled with the implications of this revelation on their mission.

"Damn it!" Sergeant Ramirez cursed under his breath, slamming his fist against the wall. "How could we have been so blind?"

"Focus, Ramirez," Captain Rodriguez ordered, his authoritative tone betraying a hint of his own frustration. "We can't change the past, but we can use this intel to our advantage."

"Captain's right," Lieutenant Thompson chimed in, her voice calm and measured despite the turmoil she was feeling. "We've got new targets and objectives now. Let's focus on how we're going to bring the fight to the enemy."

The team gathered around the table, poring over maps and documents detailing the enemy's movements and key installations. Their voices were filled with urgency and determination as they discussed potential strategies to capitalize on the new information.

"Based on this intel, their main communication hub is vulnerable," Major Reynolds pointed out, tracing a finger along the map. "If we can take it out, we'll disrupt their entire command structure."

"Agreed," Captain Rodriguez said, his piercing brown eyes scanning the room for input. "But we need to make sure we're not leaving ourselves exposed. Ramirez, what are your thoughts on the best approach?"

"Coordinated strikes, sir," Ramirez replied, his dark brown eyes locked onto the map. "Hit them from multiple angles simultaneously. Divide their attention and create chaos."

"Excellent idea," Rodriguez nodded, allowing himself a brief smile. "Alright, people, let's get to work. We've got a mission to plan and execute."

As the team continued brainstorming, Captain Rodriguez couldn't help but feel a sense of pride in their resilience. Despite the shock of the betrayal, they were determined to see this mission through and bring justice to the traitor.

"Remember," he said, his voice firm yet encouraging, "we're not just fighting for ourselves – we're fighting for our country and everyone who's counting on us. We will overcome this betrayal and complete our mission."

With renewed determination, the team dove back into their planning, each member focused on the task at hand, ready to strike back against the enemy with everything they had.

Captain Rodriguez's gaze locked onto the satellite images displayed on the screen, the enemy bases and movements laid bare before them. The room was filled with quiet intensity as each member of the team studied the intel, searching for vulnerabilities they could exploit.

"Look here," Lieutenant Thompson said, pointing at a section of the screen where a convoy of vehicles seemed to be leaving one of the enemy's fortified positions. "If we can intercept them en route, it might cause enough confusion to weaken their defenses."

"Good eye, Thompson," Rodriguez acknowledged, his mind racing with the tactical possibilities. He turned to face the rest of the team, determination burning in his eyes. "We'll need to divide into smaller units to maximize our impact and keep the enemy off-balance. Reynolds, I want you to lead Bravo Team and focus on taking out that convoy. Ramirez, you'll head up Charlie Team and target their communications infrastructure."

"Roger that, Captain," both men replied in unison, their faces etched with steely resolve.

"Thompson, you're with me on Alpha Team. Our primary objective will be taking out their command center. If we can disrupt their leadership, we'll throw the entire enemy operation into disarray."

"Understood, Captain," Emily responded, her blue eyes reflecting the weight of responsibility she carried.

As the teams moved quickly to gather their gear, Captain Rodriguez felt his heart pounding in his chest. They were about to embark on an incredibly dangerous mission, but he had faith in the abilities of every single person in the room. Their enemy may have struck first, but it was time to show them just what they were up against.

"Time is of the essence," he reminded them all, his voice steady and commanding. "We strike fast, and we strike hard. Remember, we're not only fighting for ourselves – we're fighting for our country. Let's make sure we give them hell."

"Oorah!" the teams chorused, their voices a unified blend of anger and determination.

As they filed out of the room, Captain Rodriguez allowed himself a moment to take a deep breath, steadying his nerves. This operation would test not only their skills but also their trust in one another – trust that had been shaken by the revelation of the double agent among them.

But as he looked into the eyes of his comrades, Rodriguez saw only unwavering loyalty and commitment. They were ready to face this challenge head-on, united in their determination to complete their mission and strike back against the enemy. And with that thought bolstering his resolve, he followed his team into the night, prepared for the battle ahead.

The moon cast a pale glow on the ruined buildings surrounding them, casting eerie shadows as the teams moved stealthily through enemy territory. Captain Rodriguez led his team down a narrow alleyway, his breathing measured and controlled despite the adrenaline coursing through him.

"Keep your eyes peeled," he whispered into his headset, every muscle in his body tensed for action. "Remember, they're watching."

"Roger that, Captain," Lieutenant Thompson responded from somewhere behind him, her voice barely audible. The teams had spread out to cover more ground, but they were never far from each other – a fact that provided some small comfort in this hostile environment.

Rodriguez's gaze flickered over the broken windows and crumbling facades of the deserted buildings, searching for any sign of movement or danger. He knew that beneath the apparent stillness, their enemy was waiting, poised to strike at the slightest misstep. It was like navigating a minefield, where one wrong move could prove fatal.

"Alpha Team, this is Bravo. We've reached our target point," Sergeant Ramirez's voice crackled through the headset, breaking the silence.

"Copy that, Bravo. Proceed with caution," Major Reynolds instructed, his tone both authoritative and reassuring.

As Rodriguez rounded a corner, he spotted a small door partially hidden by debris. His heart raced in anticipation; this was their entry point, according to the intel. He signaled to his team to approach, and within seconds they were gathered around the entrance, weapons at the ready.

"Thompson, you're up," he murmured, barely loud enough for her to hear. She nodded and moved forward, deftly picking the lock with practiced ease. As the door swung open, revealing a dimly lit corridor, the team exchanged tense glances before slipping inside.

Once they were all in position, Rodriguez gave the signal to advance, his brown eyes scanning the darkness for threats. They moved with the precision and efficiency of a well-oiled machine, each member of the team acutely aware of their role and responsibilities.

"Captain, I've got eyes on the target," Thompson whispered into her headset as they reached the end of the corridor. "Looks like we caught them off guard."

"Good work, Lieutenant. Secure the area and prepare for extraction," Rodriguez instructed, his voice betraying none of the relief he felt at this small victory.

As they executed their assigned tasks, Rodriguez couldn't help but think about the double agent who had risked everything to provide them with this invaluable intel. He wondered what motivated someone to betray their own people, even if it was for a greater cause. Was it fear? Guilt? Or something else entirely?

"Captain, we're all set here," Reynolds reported, snapping Rodriguez out of his thoughts.

"Roger that, Major. Let's get moving – we're not out of the woods yet," Rodriguez replied, knowing that the real test was yet to come.

With renewed urgency, the teams retraced their steps, making their way back through the treacherous terrain. Though they had accomplished their immediate objectives, the mission was far from over – and with trust shattered among them, they would have to rely on more than just skill and training to see this battle through.

"Stay sharp," Rodriguez warned as they approached the extraction point. "We can't afford any mistakes now."

"Understood, Captain," came the chorus of determined voices, each one echoing the unwavering commitment they shared to bring down the enemy – no matter the cost.

With a sudden explosion of gunfire, the night air tore alive around them. Rodriguez instinctively dropped to a crouch, scanning the terrain for any sign of the enemy's position. In the darkness, he spotted muzzle flashes in the distance, and his pulse quickened.

"Contact! Twelve o'clock!" he barked into his comm unit. "Reynolds, Thompson, flank left. Ramirez, you're with me."

"Roger that, Captain," came the responses, as the teams sprang into action.

Bullets whizzed past Rodriguez's head, but he paid them no mind. All that mattered now was the mission – and making sure his people made it out alive. As they advanced, he felt a surge of pride at their well-coordinated movements, each member seamlessly executing their role with precision honed by years of training.

"Thompson, give me a status update," he demanded, his voice steady despite the chaos unfolding around him.

"Enemy positions identified, Captain," she replied, her calm authority unmistakable even amid the deafening roar of gunfire. "We're moving in to neutralize."

"Good work. Give 'em hell," Rodriguez said, allowing himself a grim smile as he and Ramirez pressed forward.

As they closed in on the enemy's makeshift bunker, Miguel lobbed a grenade through the narrow window, its explosion silencing the barrage of bullets for a moment. They used the brief reprieve to storm the entrance, guns blazing.

"Captain, we've secured the bunker," Rodriguez reported, his voice tinged with adrenaline-fueled triumph. "But there's still heavy resistance outside."

"Understood. We're on our way," Reynolds replied, his own voice strained with exertion.

As Rodriguez and Ramirez fought their way back outside, they found themselves in the midst of an all-out firefight. The scene was one of sheer chaos, with bullets flying in all directions and the stench of gunpowder thick in the air. But amidst the bedlam, Rodriguez could see his team's expertise shining through – each member moving with purpose, their actions precise and calculated.

Still, he knew they couldn't afford to get complacent. The enemy was desperate, their tactics increasingly reckless as they tried to regain control of the situation. It would only take one mistake for everything to unravel.

"Stay focused, people," Rodriguez urged them, his voice carrying over the din of battle. "We're not out of this yet."

He could feel the weight of his responsibility pressing down on him, the knowledge that the lives of his team rested squarely on his shoulders. But it was a burden he'd carried before, and he would do so again – because that's what leaders did.

"Reynolds, Thompson, Ramirez – regroup on me!" he shouted, knowing that their best chance at victory lay in their unity. As they converged on his position, he felt a renewed sense of determination coursing through him. Together, they would turn the tide of this battle – no matter the cost.

"Let's finish this," he declared, his words met with a chorus of grim resolve from his comrades.

As they charged forward, Rodriguez knew it wouldn't be easy. But with each step, he reminded himself of the stakes – the lives that depended on their success, the mission that had brought them here. And with that thought burning in his mind, he led his team onward, ever closer to the heart of the enemy's stronghold.

As Captain Rodriguez led his team through the enemy's stronghold, the sight of a burning tank ablaze in the distance seared itself into his memory. The sound of shattering glass joined the cacophony of gunfire and explosions, echoing like a symphony of destruction through the war-torn streets.

"Captain, we've got incoming!" Lieutenant Thompson yelled, her voice strained with urgency. "Enemy reinforcements from the east!"

Rodriguez peered down the street, noting the approaching troop transports and armored vehicles. His mind raced, calculating their options as adrenaline coursed through his veins.

"Change of plans, people," he barked, his tone focused and determined. "Thompson, Ramirez – intercept those transports before they unload! Reynolds, Hayes – take out those armored vehicles with me. We'll rendezvous at the extraction point."

"Copy that, Captain," Reynolds replied, his calm demeanor a stark contrast to the chaos around them.

The teams split off, each group moving with purpose and efficiency as they adapted to the new threats. As Rodriguez, Reynolds, and Hayes approached the armored vehicles, they took cover behind a pile of rubble, surveying the situation.

"Alright," Rodriguez muttered to himself, his eyes darting between the enemies and potential weak spots. "We hit them fast and hard, then fall back. Use your grenades for maximum impact."

"Understood, Captain," Hayes responded, still bearing the marks of his recent ordeal but unwavering in his determination.

In a single coordinated strike, the three soldiers launched their grenades, creating a deafening explosion that tore through the enemy vehicles. The element of surprise worked in their favor, leaving the enemy disoriented and vulnerable.

"Move, move, move!" Rodriguez shouted, leading his teammates through the smoke and debris, evading the surviving enemy forces.

Meanwhile, Thompson and Ramirez moved with catlike agility, quickly closing the distance between them and the enemy transports. As they neared, Thompson took aim with her rifle, firing precise shots at the drivers, while Ramirez provided suppressing fire.

"Last one, Em," Ramirez called out, his voice tense but steady.

"Got it," Thompson responded, and with a final well-placed shot, the last transport screeched to a halt, its driver lifeless.

"Let's link up with the others," Ramirez suggested, his eyes scanning for any signs of additional threats.

Back at the extraction point, Rodriguez's heart pounded in his chest as he watched his team reassemble, knowing that each successful objective brought them closer to victory. As they exchanged relieved glances, their camaraderie fortified by the trials they had faced together, he knew that they had delivered a crushing blow to the enemy's forces. But there was still work to be done.

"Captain, we've cleared the area," Thompson reported, her breaths coming in short gasps as she maintained her composure. "What's our next move?"

"Excellent work, everyone. We've gained a crucial advantage, but we can't afford to let our guard down," Rodriguez replied, his voice tinged with both pride and caution. "We need to press forward and maintain the momentum. The mission isn't over yet."

With renewed determination, the team moved out, ready to face whatever challenges awaited them in the ongoing conflict.

As the dust settled around them, Captain Rodriguez surveyed his team, their faces etched with a mixture of relief and tension. The revelation of the double agent's identity had shaken them to their core, and Rodriguez could see the seeds of doubt beginning to sprout in their eyes. He clenched his fists, anger boiling beneath the surface at the betrayal that threatened to fracture the unity they had worked so hard to build.

"Listen up," he commanded, his voice resonating with authority. "I know this is tough. We've been stabbed in the back by one of our own, but we can't let that divide us now. We need to pull together if we're going to complete this mission."

"Captain, how can we trust anyone now?" Lieutenant Thompson asked, her blue eyes hardened by the recent events. "Who's to say there aren't more traitors among us?"

"Emily's right," Sergeant Ramirez chimed in, his gaze flickering between his comrades. "We can't afford to be blind to the possibility of more betrayals."

Rodriguez gritted his teeth, knowing that the fear and suspicion gnawing at his team were valid concerns. But he also knew they couldn't let it consume them.

"Look, I understand your fears," he admitted, meeting each of their gazes with unwavering resolve. "But we've trained together, fought together, and bled together. I refuse to believe that any of you would turn on your brothers and sisters in arms. We've come too far and sacrificed too much to let anything break us apart now."

"Captain's right," Major Reynolds interjected, his calm demeanor lending weight to his words. "We have a job to do, and we're not going to let one traitor's actions derail us from our objective."

"Agreed," Lieutenant Hayes added, the haunted look in his eyes momentarily giving way to determination. "We can't change what's happened, but we can choose how we move forward."

The team fell silent, their minds grappling with the gravity of the situation. Rodriguez could see them processing the betrayal, the anger and hurt mingling with a fierce desire to complete the mission. He knew they needed to channel that energy into action.

"Alright then," he declared, his voice filled with conviction. "We're going to push through this and finish what we started. We'll deal with the traitor when the time comes, but for now, our focus needs to be on taking down the enemy and completing our objectives."

Nods of agreement rippled through the group, their faces hardening with resolve as they acknowledged the path laid before them.

"Let's do it," Thompson said, her voice steely with determination. "For those who've fallen, and for all the lies we were fed. Let's make sure their sacrifices weren't in vain."

"Damn right," Ramirez echoed, his expression resolute. "We're still standing, and we'll keep standing until we've won."

"Then let's get moving," Rodriguez ordered, his heart swelling with pride at the unwavering determination displayed by his team. "We have a job to finish, and we're going to see it through together."

As they set off, Rodriguez couldn't help but marvel at the resilience and tenacity of his comrades. Despite the weight of betrayal bearing down on their shoulders, they refused to be crushed. And he knew, without a doubt, that they would emerge victorious – not just against the enemy, but against the shadows of doubt that had threatened to consume them.

The sun dipped below the horizon, casting long shadows across the desolate landscape as the teams moved stealthily through enemy territory. Rodriguez led the way, his senses on high alert, his eyes scanning every inch of their surroundings for threats. The weight of responsibility pressed down on him, the knowledge that the lives of his comrades were in his hands.

"Movement ahead," Reynolds whispered, his voice barely audible even to those nearest to him. He gestured subtly, indicating the direction from which the disturbance had come.

"Stay sharp," Rodriguez murmured, his fingers tightening around the grip of his weapon. "We knew this wouldn't be easy, but we have to keep moving forward."

"Roger that, sir," Hayes replied, his voice steady despite the physical and emotional toll extracted by recent events. In his eyes burned a fierce determination to see this mission through to its conclusion, no matter the cost.

As they crept closer, the sounds of enemy forces grew more distinct – the low murmur of voices, the clanking of weaponry. They were close now, perhaps closer than they'd ever been, and Rodriguez could feel the adrenaline surging through his veins, coiled like a spring ready to burst into action.

"Thompson, Ramirez, you two flank left," Rodriguez ordered, his voice hushed and authoritative. "Reynolds, Hayes, you're with me. We'll circle around and hit them from the right. Remember, we've got the element of surprise on our side. Let's make it count."

"Got it, Captain," Thompson acknowledged, her gaze focused and resolute as she and Ramirez broke away from the group, vanishing into the shadows cast by the rapidly darkening sky.

Rodriguez took a deep breath, steeling himself for the battle ahead. He knew there would be casualties – there always were – but he refused to let his mind linger on the possibility of loss. Instead, he focused on the task at hand, the mission they'd sworn to complete together.

"Ready?" he asked Reynolds and Hayes, his voice steady but laced with urgency.

"Always," Reynolds replied, his eyes focused and unyielding, while Hayes merely nodded, his expression etched with equal parts determination and apprehension.

To Rodriguez's left, he heard the faintest rustle of movement – Thompson and Ramirez, initiating their part of the assault. He exchanged a quick glance with Reynolds and Hayes, then gave the signal to move.

As they burst forth from the cover of shadows, gunfire erupted around them, the sharp crack of bullets piercing the air as the enemy scrambled to respond to the sudden onslaught. Rodriguez moved with calculated precision, each shot finding its mark as he cut a path through the enemy ranks.

"Push forward!" he shouted over the din of battle, his heart pounding in his chest. "We're almost there!"

Just as the tide of battle seemed to be turning in their favor, a shrill, piercing sound cut through the night – an alarm, signaling the approach of enemy reinforcements. The teams froze, their faces etched with a mix of surprise and dread.

"Damn it," Reynolds muttered, his gaze darting between the rapidly approaching foes and the still vulnerable objective. "We're running out of time."

"Stay focused," Rodriguez insisted, his voice tight with tension. "We'll handle the reinforcements. The mission is all that matters now."

"Captain!" Thompson's voice crackled over the comm, her words punctuated by the sound of gunfire. "We've got more incoming from the east! We're pinned down and can't reach the objective!"

Rodriguez's heart clenched with fear for his teammates, the urgency of the situation weighing heavily upon him. With enemies closing in from all sides, their window of opportunity was quickly closing, and the cost of failure loomed large in his mind.

"Thompson, hold your position," he ordered, his voice unwavering despite the overwhelming odds they faced. "We'll find a way through."

"Copy that," Thompson acknowledged, her tone resigned but determined.

As Rodriguez exchanged a grim glance with Reynolds and Hayes, he knew that their mission hung in the balance, teetering on the brink of disaster. Failure was not an option – not for them, not for their fallen comrades, not for the countless lives at stake.

"We'll get through this," he vowed, his words laced with equal parts determination and desperation. "Together."

The gunfire intensified around them, the enemy closing in like a vice, as Rodriguez and his team prepared to face the seemingly insurmountable challenge before them. The stakes had never been higher, nor the odds more daunting, but they would fight to the bitter end – together, as a team. And as the final push began, one thing was certain: the outcome of this battle would forever change the course of their lives.

CHAPTER 18

Captain Rodriguez surveyed the dimly lit briefing room, his team arrayed before him—each member an embodiment of determination. The air was thick with anticipation; their breaths hung like mist in the hushed stillness. He stepped forward, his boots echoing softly against the concrete floor, the sound a somber drumbeat to the gravity of their task.

"Listen up," he began, his voice carrying the weight of command, resonant and clear. "We're not just soldiers tonight; we are the thin line between order and chaos." He paused, locking eyes with each of his team members in turn, ensuring his words left indelible marks upon their resolve.

"The bioweapon we're tasked to destroy," he continued, punctuating each word with steely intent, "it's not just a threat to our nation—it's a death knell to global stability." His hands clenched into fists at his sides, betraying the surge of adrenaline that coursed through him. "I will not sugarcoat this: failure is not an option. We dismantle their plans, or we pay the price in innocent lives."

A collective breath was drawn as the team absorbed the gravity of Rodriguez's words. The silence was soon broken by the shuffle of movement, the clinking of metal, as they transitioned into action.

"Gear up," Rodriguez ordered, his tone shifting from inspirational to operational. He strode among them, each step purposeful, as his team equipped themselves with the precision of seasoned warriors. Kevlar vests were secured, combat boots laced tight, firearms checked and loaded with the intimate familiarity of a craftsman's tools.

"Martinez, you're on point," he said, nodding to the sharpshooter whose eyes flickered with acknowledgment. "Hanley, I need your eyes on our six." The communications specialist gave a curt nod, her fingers deftly adjusting the dials on her radio set.

"Jackson, Taylor, breach and clear," he continued, assigning roles with the ease of a maestro conducting an orchestra. Each member fell into their assigned duty, moving with the fluid choreography of those who had trained for this moment countless times.

Rodriguez watched his team, his gaze lingering momentarily on the patches adorning their uniforms—the insignia of their unity and shared purpose. He strapped his own tactical belt tightly around his waist, feeling the familiar weight of his sidearm against his thigh.

"Check your gear, check your buddy," he instructed, his eyes sweeping over the scene of quiet efficiency. The sound of Velcro straps and safety checks filled the room, a symphony of preparedness.

"Comms check," he called out, pressing the earpiece snugly into place. One by one, the affirmations crackled through the static, each voice a testament to readiness.

"Good," Rodriguez affirmed, his brown eyes reflecting the soft glow of the tactical maps that lined the walls. "Remember your training, trust in your team, and keep your focus sharp. We move as one unit, one force, one unstoppable tide. Let's bring that weapon down."

With a final nod, Captain Rodriguez signaled the end of the briefing. His team rose, a singular entity of lethal capability, ready to step into the night where destiny awaited.

Under a cloak of darkness, the silhouettes of Captain Rodriguez and his team glided through the dense underbrush, their boots barely whispering against the forest floor. The moon, a thin crescent in the ink-black sky, offered scant illumination, but their night-vision goggles painted the world in shades of green and gray, revealing a landscape fraught with danger.

Rodriguez moved with the confident stealth of a predator, his hand signals crisp and clear, each one directing his team's silent advance. They were ghosts among the trees, a breath away from the enemy's lair, every muscle tensed for action. His focus was absolute, the mission parameters etched into his mind as they closed in on the research facility—a monolith of steel and secrecy that hunched ominously against the night.

The captain paused, his piercing gaze scanning the perimeter. A flicker of movement ahead caught his attention; he crouched lower, signaling his team to do the same. Through the tangled branches, he spotted them—patrolling guards, their shadows stretching long and ominous across the ground. He counted four, their rifles slung casually, unsuspecting of the threat that lurked just beyond their line of sight.

With a series of subtle gestures, Captain Rodriguez communicated his plan. Two fingers pointed at his eyes, then at two of his team members, assigning targets. They nodded imperceptibly, each understanding the gravity of silence in this precarious dance with death.

The team split like water flowing around rocks, moving into position with fluid precision. Rodriguez's heart pounded, not with fear, but with the adrenalized clarity that came with countless missions. This was where he thrived, where every decision shaped the line between success and catastrophe.

In synchronized perfection, they struck. There was no sound save for the dull thud of bodies hitting the ground, the soft rustle of leaves beneath their weight. The guards crumpled, neutralized by expert hands in a choreography of incapacitation. No alarms shattered the peace of the night; the facility remained ignorant of its breached defenses.

Rodriguez allowed himself a brief moment to survey the downed guards, ensuring each was secure and silent. His team regrouped, eyes on him for the next command. With an almost imperceptible nod, he signaled the advance. They had breached the first barrier, but the night was far from over. Ahead lay the heart of darkness, the vessel of a threat that could change the world. It was theirs to destroy.

Rodriguez signaled a halt with an upraised fist, the team freezing amidst the labyrinthine sprawl of sterile hallways. Ahead, a door loomed, its electronic keypad glowing ominously in the gloom. He shot a glance at the tech expert, his eyes conveying urgency beneath the steady thrum of mission tempo.

"Jones," he whispered, the name slicing through the silence like a blade. "We're up."

The wiry technician stepped forward, fingers already dancing across the touchscreen device strapped to his wrist. With deft movements born of countless rehearsals, Jones interfaced with the security panel, his screen casting a pale light on focused features. Moments stretched like taut wire as code cascaded down the display.

"Almost there, Cap," Jones murmured, the words barely audible. Rodriguez's gaze didn't waver from the corridor behind them; every shadow could conceal a threat, every whisper of sound a harbinger of discovery.

A soft beep cut through the tension, and the door's lock disengaged with a click that sounded like victory. Rodriguez nodded, satisfaction a fleeting ghost across his stern visage. They slipped through the gap, the door sealing shut with a hiss, erasing their presence from the enemy's eyes.

Beyond lay a warren of corridors, angles and intersections branching off like veins. Rodriguez's mind mapped each turn, a mental blueprint overlaying reality. He had studied this place, dreamed it, every corner and dead end etched into his memory alongside the faces of those who depended on him.

"Echo formation," he ordered, voice a low growl. The team fanned out, flowing through the complex with predatory grace. Rodriguez took point, rifle at the ready, senses hyper-alert to any disturbance in the oppressive stillness.

They passed doorways sealed with warnings, the very air heavy with unspoken threats. Rodriguez's pulse thumped in his ears, yet his breathing remained even, controlled—a calm amidst the storm of anticipation. Each step they took was a step closer to oblivion or salvation.

He halted before an intersection, peering around the edge. A camera swiveled lazily in the distance. His hand signals were crisp, clear—three fingers, then a sweep of his hand. The team responded instantly, disappearing into alcoves, blending with shadows until they were nothing but whispers in the dark.

Rodriguez counted heartbeats, waited for the lens to point away, and crossed the open space in a silent sprint. The others followed, a seamless relay of motion and discipline. This was no mere infiltration; it was a testament to their unity, their purpose.

Corridor by corridor, they drew closer to the venom nested within the facility's core. Rodriguez felt it in his bones—the weight of responsibility, the echo of stakes higher than any they'd faced. Yet doubt had no place here, not in his mind, not in his team.

This was what they were trained for. This was what they lived for.

And they would not fail.

Bullets ricocheted off the concrete, sending chips of debris into the air. Captain Rodriguez dropped to one knee behind an overturned lab bench, his team fanning out beside him with tactical precision. The sudden burst of gunfire from enemy patrols had erupted without warning, a violent greeting in the sterile halls of the research facility.

"Bravo team, flank left! Echo, lay down suppressing fire!" Rodriguez's voice was a fierce command, slicing through the chaos. His finger squeezed the trigger in controlled bursts, providing cover for his teammates as they moved to execute his orders.

Muzzle flashes strobed in the dim corridor, casting elongated shadows that danced on the walls like specters of war. Rodriguez watched as his team advanced, each member moving with lethal intent—a dance of death choreographed by years of rigorous training.

The enemy fell back, their numbers dwindling under the relentless assault. Rodriguez could sense the shift in momentum, the predatory focus of his team as they cleared the area with disciplined shots. This wasn't just a firefight; it was a statement, a refusal to be halted by any force.

"Area clear," came a curt report over the comms.

Rodriguez rose, signaling the all-clear with a clenched fist. "Move out. Stay sharp."

They advanced deeper into the bowels of the facility, the tension winding tighter with every step toward the epicenter of their mission. Finally, they stood before the heavily fortified section housing the bioweapon—a sinister heart pumping poison through unseen veins.

"Delta and Foxtrot, you're on security detail. Gamma, with me—breach and clear," Rodriguez ordered, his eyes scanning the formidable defenses. The team split seamlessly, each group peeling away with nods of understanding.

He watched as Delta set to work on a panel, fingers dancing across the interface with a deftness born of necessity. Foxtrot deployed a series of compact jammers, the soft beeps confirming the dulling of electronic eyes that might give them away.

Rodriguez joined Gamma at the door. They exchanged a look, no words needed—their resolve said enough. With a silent countdown, they breached the barrier, slipping into the heart of danger with only their trust in each other as armor against the unknown perils that lay beyond.

Silhouettes melded with shadows, the team moved with a silence that belied their lethal intent. Delta's hands stilled—the panel blinked off; security feeds severed like vital arteries cut. Foxtrot's jammers hummed a silent lullaby to the surveillance systems, cradling them into obliviousness. The path was clear, a trail of darkness weaving straight to the malignancy within.

"Gamma, stack up," Rodriguez whispered, his voice barely audible above the thrum of adrenaline coursing through him.

The door loomed, an imposing barrier between them and the objective—one final obstacle. He took a moment, checking his weapon one last time, ensuring there would be no hesitation when the moment called for action. Beside him, his squad mirrored the motion, a choreography of readiness and resolve.

"Three... two..." Rodriguez counted down with his fingers, feeling each number tick away in his chest like a heartbeat.

On zero, the breach charge erupted, the door buckling under the controlled fury. They poured through the gap, a flood of precision and purpose. Inside, the chamber opened up—a cavern of steel and sinister intentions. At its center stood canisters, grotesque in their potential for devastation.

"Contact front!" The call snapped Rodriguez back to the present, where a phalanx of elite guards had formed, their weapons trained with deadly focus.

Instinct guided him now, muscle memory born from countless drills and live-fire engagements. He dropped to a knee, returning fire, the rapport of his rifle punctuating the chaos. Gamma flanked left and right, their movements synchronized, a unit honed through trials of fire and blood.

"Suppressing fire!" he commanded, shifting position to gain a better vantage point.

Bullets ricocheted off metal surfaces, sparks dancing wildly in the dimly lit expanse. The enemy was skilled, but Rodriguez knew his team was better. They had to be. Everything hinged on this moment, on the eradication of the threat before them. As he exchanged fire with the enemy, Rodriguez felt the weight of his duty anchoring him, fueling his determination to see this mission through to its explosive end.

Captain Rodriguez locked eyes with the enemy's ringleader, a silent challenge hanging between them. With a sudden burst, he charged, his unit at his back. They clashed amidst a cacophony of gunfire and shouted commands, the chamber echoing with the sounds of battle.

Rodriguez ducked a wild swing, countering with a precise jab to his assailant's throat. He spun, catching another guard with a sharp kick, feeling the crunch of bone. His team was a whirlwind of lethal grace around him, each member playing their role with deadly efficiency.

"Delta, secure that flank!" he barked, dodging a spray of bullets. The designated marksmen found their perches, sighting down their scopes with an almost serene focus. Shots rang out, each one finding its mark in the chaos.

"Bravo, I need a path!" Rodriguez shouted over the fray. Explosive specialists moved forward, planting charges with practiced hands before falling back to safety. The subsequent blasts tore through the enemy's ranks, sowing confusion and fear.

Through the smoke and debris, Rodriguez spotted the bioweapon - a monstrous edifice of metal and malevolence. His boots pounded against the cold floor as he closed the distance, every sense alert for the ambush he knew would come.

"Cover me!" His voice cut through the din, commanding and clear. His team rallied, forming a protective ring as he knelt by the canisters. Their gunfire was a relentless drumbeat, holding the line against the surge of reinforcements.

With steady hands, Rodriguez set the charges, the digital readouts a stark contrast to the primitive violence erupting around him. He glanced up, meeting the unwavering gaze of his comrades, their trust in him absolute. This was more than a mission; it was a pact sealed in blood and honor.

"Charge is set!" He rose, checking the connections one final time, ensuring nothing was left to chance. The red lights blinked in unison, a morbid countdown to oblivion.

"Fall back!" he commanded, and together, they retreated, their movements fluid even under the weight of impending destruction. Behind them, the chamber housing death incarnate awaited its fiery demise, the first victory in a war fought in shadows.

Rodriguez's hand shot up, slicing through the thickening air with a swift gesture. "Move out!" The words were a trigger, releasing his team from their momentary stillness into a symphony of motion.

Alarms clawed at their ears, a shrill cacophony that echoed off the sterile walls of the facility, urging haste. Red lights strobed in frenzied beats, painting their retreat in urgent shades as they pivoted and darted down the labyrinthine corridors.

Bullets hailed after them, a metallic storm unleashed by the enemy's desperate bid to reclaim control. Rodriguez felt the percussion of gunfire rattle his bones, the close shaves of near misses that sang past his ear.

"Delta formation," he barked, the order barely audible over the roar of combat. In seamless accord, his team fanned out, a living bulwark against the tide of adversaries that surged from every shadow.

A door ahead splintered under the assault of relentless gunfire. Rodriguez lunged forward, his movements a blend of instinct and strategy honed on countless battlefields. He slammed a fresh magazine into his rifle, the click a reassuring note amid the discord.

"Bravo team, flank left. Echo, hold the rear." His commands cut through the chaos, a lifeline for his team as they navigated the onslaught. They responded in kind, their actions precise, a testament to the trust threaded through their ranks.

An enemy soldier lunged from a side passage, weapon raised in a grim dance of death. Rodriguez twisted, his response etched in muscle memory. A sharp crack, and the threat crumbled, a silent testimony to his lethal accuracy.

"Keep moving!" he urged, propelling his team forward with the force of his will. They were a machine of flesh and fury, every member integral to the whole, every action a step towards survival.

The bioweapon chamber loomed behind them, a tomb awaiting its final tenant. Rodriguez dared a glance back, noting the digital timer's unwavering march towards zero. This was the fulcrum upon which fate would tilt.

"Stairwell, twenty meters," he called, signaling the path to salvation. The stairway mouth gaped open, an abyssal maw ready to swallow them whole. They plunged into its depths, boots thundering against metal as they descended into uncertainty.

At each landing, resistance flared like a blight. But Rodriguez's tactics were water on fire, quenching each outbreak with ruthless efficiency. They wove a pattern of survival with lead and resolve, leaving echoes of defiance in their wake.

"Almost there. Stay sharp," Rodriguez ground out between clenched teeth. Adrenaline coursed through him, a river raging against the banks of exhaustion. Each step was a victory, each breath a rebellion against the encroaching night.

Finally, the exit loomed, a rectangle of faint hope amidst the pressing gloom. Rodriguez emerged first, his silhouette a beacon for his team as they spilled out into the cool embrace of pre-dawn air.

"Rally point, three clicks west. Double time it!" The command spurred them on, lungs burning with effort, legs pumping with the last reserves of strength. They left behind the groans of the wounded facility, its lifeblood spilling in sparks and flame.

As they breached the treeline, a concussive wave roared behind them, the earth shuddering in protest. Rodriguez didn't need to look back to know the bioweapon was no more. Their mission, this harrowing gauntlet of fire and ferocity, had been fulfilled.

But there was no pause for triumph, no respite for the weary. They pressed on, Rodriguez's keen eyes scouting the path ahead, ever the sentinel for his team, his nation, his world. Ahead lay the promise of extraction and the burden of survival, carried on the shoulders of those who dare to walk through hell for the sake of humanity.

Sprinting through the underbrush, Captain Rodriguez's boots pounded the earth with the rhythm of escape. The extraction point was a beacon in the distance, the throb of helicopter blades cutting through the air like a siren call to salvation. His lungs seared with each inhalation, but his focus remained unyielding—on the safety of his team and the completion of their mission.

"Move, move!" he barked, his voice a gravelly command that propelled his team forward. They were shadows flitting through the forest, specters driven by purpose, leaving behind the chaos that had been their battleground mere moments ago.

The clearing opened up before them, bathed in the pale glow of dawn's first light. The helicopter, a hulking silhouette against the awakening sky, churned the air into a frenzy. Rodriguez scanned the perimeter with the precision of a hawk as his team converged on the bird.

"Check in," Rodriguez snapped, his eyes never ceasing their vigil. One by one, they reported, voices terse with fatigue but edged with victory. He counted them off in his head, paired each voice with a face, a life entrusted to his leadership.

"Last man, Captain!" The final confirmation came through, a statement punctuated by the slamming of the helicopter door.

"Go, go, go!" The pilot needed no further urging, the craft lifting from the ground as if eager to divorce itself from the tainted soil below.

Rodriguez secured himself last, his hand gripping the cold metal for a moment longer than necessary. Then he allowed himself to be pulled into the belly of the machine, the roar of the engines swallowing the sound of his heartbeat.

As they ascended, Rodriguez stationed himself by the window, his gaze magnetically drawn to the ruin they left in their wake. Below, fire consumed the facility, a pyre for the demonic creation it once housed. Smoke clawed at the sky, desperate fingers trying to obscure the stars, but failing. It was done; the threat neutralized, the world a breath safer.

"Good work, team," he said, though he had to raise his voice to be heard over the din. The words were simple, but they carried the weight of their shared ordeal. Nods and weary smiles were exchanged, silent acknowledgments of the bond forged in the crucible of combat.

Rodriguez's brown eyes reflected the flames below, mirrors to the inferno they had wrought for peace. But even as the fires raged, there was a glimmer of something else within those depths—relief, perhaps, or the hint of pride. Not for the destruction, but for what it represented: a battle won in the war that never seemed to end.

The helicopter banked sharply, angling towards the horizon where the sun cast the sky in hues of blood and gold. Rodriguez watched the landscape shift beneath them, the dark blanket of night surrendering to the dawn.

"Rest up," he said, more to himself than the others. "We'll need it." The road ahead was uncertain, fraught with perils yet unseen. But for now, in this fleeting moment of ascent, they were untouchable, soaring on the wings of their triumph.

And Captain James Rodriguez knew, as the cool wind whispered past, that they were ready for whatever lay ahead.

CHAPTER 19

Shadows clung to the walls of the dim corridor as Captain Rodriguez led his team with silent precision, the light from their tactical goggles casting an ethereal glow. Muscles tensed like coiled springs, they advanced, boots whispering against concrete. The air was cool and sterile, carrying the faint hum of distant machinery at work within the bowels of the research facility.

"Alpha in position," Rodriguez murmured into his comms, the sound barely above a breath.

A sudden flicker of movement ahead snapped his piercing brown eyes to attention. A patrol of armed guards rounded the corner, rifles at the ready, unaware of the predators that lay in wait. The team froze, melding into the darkness as if part of the infrastructure itself.

"Engage on my mark," he whispered, every word laced with lethal intent.

Time slowed, the world reduced to heartbeats and the soft exhale of controlled breathing. Rodriguez raised his hand, fingers poised for the takedown signal. He could see Lieutenant Thompson's blue eyes beside him, steady and calculating. Three... Two... One—his hand dropped.

Silencers whispered death as Alpha Team sprang into action. Confusion etched on the guards' faces was rapidly replaced by the finality of silence. A series of precise, muted thuds echoed softly, bodies crumpling to the floor in synchronized collapse.

"Clear," Thompson confirmed, her voice a ghost in the dark.

"Move out," Rodriguez commanded, stepping over the neutralized threat with the ease of long practice. They pressed on, the fallen guards now mere shadows in their wake, as they delved deeper into the heart of danger.

"Bravo, we divide and conquer," Lieutenant Emily Thompson whispered, her breath fogging the cold metal of her rifle's scope. With calculated precision, she gestured to half the squad, her hand signals crisp under the flickering lights. "Upstairs is ours; the rest of you, sweep the lower levels. Sync watches—ten minutes, no more."

Her piercing blue eyes met each of her team members', instilling them with a silent confidence before she led her group in a swift ascent up the narrow stairwell. The rhythmic tap of their boots melded with the distant hum of machinery. They emerged onto the upper floor, a labyrinth of sterile hallways stretched out before them.

"Stay sharp," Thompson breathed, leading the way. Her shadow danced against the walls as she moved, blonde hair a stark contrast to the darkness enveloping them.

Meanwhile, Sergeant Miguel Ramirez stood before the obstinate steel door that barred Team Charlie's advance. His fingers worked deftly, a set of lock picks glinting faintly in the dim light. The click of tumblers falling into place was music to his ears—a symphony of impending entry. With a subtle twist, the lock yielded, and he eased the door open, signaling his team forward.

"Like clockwork," he muttered under his breath, a wry smile fleeting across his tanned features. The corridor beyond lay bathed in shadows, promising secrets and peril intertwined. Ramirez took point, his dark eyes scanning for threats in the stillness, the ghost of his desert upbringing whispering caution with every step.

Team Bravo's boots whispered against the tile as they prowled the corridors above. Lieutenant Thompson's mind raced, mapping routes and formulating strategies with the precision of a grandmaster. Every corner turned was a potential ambush, every closed door a mystery holding its breath.

"Echo Three, status?" she radioed, her voice a controlled murmur.

"Lower level clear," came the terse reply, almost drowned by the white noise of static.

"Copy that. Eyes up—we're not alone here." Thompson's instincts screamed at her, a sixth sense honed on windswept peaks and in frozen crevasses.

The upper level sprawled out like a puzzle, each piece methodically investigated under Thompson's watchful command. She paused, gaze narrowing on a ventilation grate—too high for most, but not for her. In another life, it could have been a climb in the Alps, but tonight, it was just another path to victory.

"Here," she motioned, reaching up to grip the metal edges. Her muscles flexed, a testament to grueling climbs and relentless training. With a quiet pop, the grate came free, revealing the dark maw within. "Hayes, you're with me. We take the vent."

Below them, Ramirez and his team advanced through the newly opened passageway, the air thick with anticipation. The soft glow of infrared illuminated their path, casting an otherworldly pallor over their faces as they inched closer to the heart of the facility.

"Anything?" Ramirez asked, the urgency of their mission thrumming through his veins.

"Negative," came the hushed response, the silence stretching taut between them.

"Keep moving," he ordered, his voice barely a whisper. His finger rested against the trigger, ready to unleash hell should the shadow ahead prove more than just a trick of the light.

Twenty chapters of tension had brought them here—to this dance with danger in the bowroot of treachery. The teams converged toward their singular goal, united by resolve and guided by the silent vows they'd made: to protect, to serve, and to emerge from the darkness triumphant.

Major David Reynolds crouched behind a stack of crates, his team's presence reduced to the shallow breaths and the soft rustle of fabric against metal. The security checkpoint ahead bristled with sentries, their weapons a silent promise of violence. Reynolds surveyed the scene—his mind a whirlwind of strategy and calculation.

"Echo Two, you're up," Reynolds whispered into his comms, his voice an undercurrent in the still air. A faint nod from across the corridor was the only acknowledgment before a small object—a distraction device—rolled silently toward the checkpoint. Its innocuous appearance belied its impending impact.

The seconds stretched thin as Reynolds counted down. Three... two...

A sudden clatter erupted to the left, far from their hidden position, as the device unleashed a barrage of sound and light. The guards snapped to attention, weapons drawn, their formation breaking as they moved to investigate the source of the commotion.

"Move," Reynolds commanded, his figure slicing through the darkness like a specter. Team Delta flowed forward, a shadow within shadows, past the distracted guards and beyond the checkpoint. No shots fired; no alarms raised. They were ghosts in a fortress of steel and suspicion.

Meanwhile, in the bowels of the facility, Team Alpha's mission was reaching its crescendo. Corporal Jensen's fingers danced over the keyboard in the control room, bypassing firewalls with the grace of a virtuoso. His screen flickered, lines of code cascading down as he hunted for the digital heart of the facility's defenses.

"Almost there," Jensen muttered, the tension coiling in his shoulders. Captain Martinez stood watch, her eyes scanning the space for any hint of interruption while the rest of Alpha held their perimeter—a ring of steel and resolve.

"Got it!" Jensen exclaimed, a surge of triumph lancing through the static-charged air. Alarms fell silent, lights dimmed, and doors unlocked with a symphony of clicks that sang of newfound vulnerability.

"Alpha to all units," Martinez's voice crackled over the comms, "you have a green light. Security systems are down."

In the distance, the unmistakable echo of boots on concrete signaled the approach of reinforcements. But it was too late—their window was open, and opportunity beckoned with a siren's call. Each team, each soldier, pressed onward, driven by the knowledge that tonight, the fate of nations rested in their hands.

Lieutenant Emily Thompson's boots made no sound on the polished floor as she led her team through the labyrinth of the research facility. Her breaths were even, measured, and her blue eyes flickered with a sharp focus beneath the rim of her night-vision goggles. They had breached the heart of the enemy's operations, and every step drew them closer to the poison they sought to contain.

"Stack up," she ordered in a whisper that barely reached her team's ears. The command was unnecessary; they were already moving with the flawless coordination of a well-oiled machine. Sam Hayes, his face still etched with the shadows of captivity, nodded from her six, his rifle at the ready.

The door before them was unassuming, but the sign beside it read 'Restricted Access: Authorized Personnel Only' in stark, red letters. Emily motioned for two of her teammates to take position. She counted down with her fingers. Three... Two... One.

The door burst open, hinges protesting, as the team stormed the room. Inside, a sterile scent filled the air, mingling with the tang of chemicals. Long benches cluttered with petri dishes, microscopes, and centrifuges stretched out beneath white fluorescent lights. Here, in this sanitized tomb, death was crafted with cold precision.

"Clear!" one of the operatives called out, sweeping the room with his weapon. Emily strode in, her movements quick and decisive. "Document everything. We need evidence for the eggheads back home."

As her team set to work, taking photos and collecting samples, Emily scanned the lab for any sign of the bioweapon. Her gut clenched; it had to be here somewhere.

"Thompson, movement!" Hayes's voice snapped her to attention, and she swiveled just as a concealed door at the far end of the lab swung open. A group of figures spilled out—lab coats over body armor, desperation etched into their faces. Enemy scientists, armed and frantic, their intentions clear as they leveled their weapons.

"Contact!" Emily barked, diving behind a steel cabinet as gunfire erupted. Bullets pinged off metal surfaces, sending shards of glass and splinters of plastic flying.

"Bravo, engage!" she commanded, popping out from her cover to return fire. Her team responded with disciplined bursts, the report of their silenced weapons a staccato rhythm against the chaos. Emily felt the familiar surge of adrenaline, the dance of danger that she had come to know so intimately on mountain cliffs and in war zones. She moved like a tempest, her training guiding each shot.

Sam Hayes was a force unto himself, his shots finding their marks with lethal efficiency. The enemy scientists fell one by one, their gambit crumbling under Bravo's onslaught.

"Area secure," Emily announced, scanning the room for any further threats. No more doors opened; no more enemies came. The silence returned, save for the labored breathing of her team and the distant echoes of other skirmishes unfolding elsewhere in the facility.

"Good work, Bravo," she said, her voice steady despite the pounding of her heart. "Let's continue the search. This isn't over yet."

Her team acknowledged with grim nods, reloading and preparing to move out. The laboratory, once a cradle of destruction, was now just another waypoint on their path to justice. Emily Thompson knew that the stakes were higher than any peak she had ever summited. But she was ready. They all were.

The dim glow of Sergeant Ramirez's flashlight swept across the room, cutting through the darkness to reveal stacks upon stacks of unmarked crates. The air was stale and heavy with anticipation as Team Charlie moved in, their boots quiet against the cold concrete floor.

"Fan out," Ramirez whispered, his eyes never leaving the ominous containers. He could feel the weight of his responsibility; somewhere within this labyrinth of wood and nails lay a threat to countless lives.

Each member of Team Charlie approached their task with practiced precision. They pried open lids, rifled through packing material, felt along the inner walls for any irregularities. Time was an enemy almost as formidable as those that lurked in the shadows beyond.

"Nothing here," Corporal Jensen reported, closing yet another empty crate with frustration simmering in his voice. But Ramirez knew better than to let impatience dictate their mission. Diligence was their ally, thoroughness their weapon.

"Keep looking," he instructed, his own fingers probing the corners of a crate for the faintest hint of a false bottom. Then, there it was –

a subtle discrepancy beneath his touch. With a nod to Jensen, they worked together to reveal a hidden compartment.

"Got something," Ramirez announced, a mix of triumph and trepidation in his tone. Inside the secret space lay vials of a sinister, amber liquid – the bioweapon, no doubt.

"Document it. Let's make sure this nightmare ends tonight," Ramirez said, his voice low but firm. Jensen nodded, snapping photos with a camera designed to capture evidence even in the darkest corners of their world.

Meanwhile, the sound of gunfire erupted, muffled but unmistakably close. Team Delta.

Major Reynolds crouched behind the remnants of a shattered wall, her breaths measured as she listened to the approach of Kozlov's elite guards. She signaled her team, and like the phantoms they were trained to be, they vanished into cover.

"Three... two..." she counted silently, waiting for the precise moment to unleash hell. The guards burst through the door, weapons at the ready, only to be met with a fury they couldn't have anticipated.

Team Delta moved as one, a symphony of controlled aggression. Bullets flew from their silenced pistols, each shot choreographed to incapacitate without needless death – a testament to their rigorous training and unwavering discipline.

Reynolds watched as her team advanced, exploiting every angle, using the environment to their advantage. They were relentless, pushing forward until the last of Kozlov's personal guard lay subdued or neutralized on the ground.

"Clear!" called out Specialist Carter, his voice steady despite the adrenaline that surged through them all. Reynolds surveyed the area with a critical eye. Every member of her team was accounted for, every threat contained.

"Delta, secure the perimeter," she commanded, her focus already shifting to the next stage of their operation. They had won the battle, but the war within these walls was far from over.

With the storage room secured and the checkpoint under control, both Team Charlie and Team Delta pushed deeper into the heart of darkness, knowing that every corner turned brought them closer to ending Kozlov's reign of terror.

"Regroup on me!" Captain Rodriguez's whisper sliced through the static of the comms, a beacon for Alpha, Bravo, and Charlie in the labyrinthine guts of the facility. The three teams converged like specters in the shadow-draped junction—a clutter of pipes and concrete that smelled of oil and cold sweat.

"Status?" Rodriguez demanded, his eyes darting between the faces illuminated by the faint glow of tactical displays.

"Security systems down," Sergeant Hawkins from Alpha reported, his hands still dancing across a tablet screen. "We own their eyes now."

"Lab secured," Lieutenant Thompson added, the weight of responsibility evident in her voice as she brandished a vial filled with an ominous liquid. "This is what we came for."

"Storage cleared," Ramirez chimed in, clipping a photo of the crates onto their secure channel. "No bioweapon, but plenty of evidence."

"Good work," Rodriguez nodded, processing the intel with the precision of a chess grandmaster envisioning the board several moves ahead. "Kozlov's command center is our next play. Move out."

The teams filtered into formation, ghosting down corridors marked by the echo of their silenced footsteps. They knew Kozlov's reputation for insidious traps all too well. Each member scanned the environment with hawk-like vigilance, searching for telltale signs of treachery.

"Tripwire," Specialist Jensen hissed, freezing a mere inch from a nearly invisible line stretched across the hallway. Rodriguez gestured, and two operatives moved forward, disarming the trap with steady hands—another potential disaster reduced to a harmless thread.

"Pressure plate," whispered Carter, pointing at a floor tile slightly raised above its neighbors. They bypassed it with balletic grace, each soldier stepping over the deadly square as if treading on sacred ground.

"Sniffers out," Reynolds ordered, and the team deployed their miniature drones, which buzzed ahead like mechanical hounds, sniffing out explosives. A soft chime sounded, and the group halted as one of the tiny machines hovered over a suspicious bulge in the wall.

"Explosive," confirmed Reynolds, reading the data stream from the drone. Ramirez stepped up, tools in hand, sweat beading on his brow despite the chill. The silence grew heavy as he worked, defusing the bomb with the meticulous care of a surgeon.

"Clear," he finally breathed, and a collective sigh whispered through the ranks.

Rodriguez led the way, each step a testament to their relentless training. They were close now; Kozlov's hubris palpable in the increasingly elaborate snares left in their path.

"Stay sharp," Rodriguez reminded them, but it was unnecessary. They were the sharpened edge of the spear, and as they navigated the traps with lethal caution, the inevitability of their success seemed almost preordained.

"Command center's just ahead," Rodriguez signaled, and the team tightened their formation, ready to face whatever hell awaited them beyond the next door. With General Kozlov's capture within their grasp, they pressed onward, undeterred by the specter of danger lurking in the shadows.

Team Delta stacked up against the command center's reinforced door, the silence palpable save for their steady breaths. Rodriguez gave a curt nod, and with a swift kick from Ramirez, the door burst open. They flooded in, weapons raised, eyes scanning.

The room erupted into chaos. Enemy soldiers, caught unawares, scrambled to retaliate as Delta's suppressed gunfire spat death across the room. Bullets tore through the air, ricocheting off metal surfaces with ear-piercing clangs. Rodriguez moved with practiced precision, each shot finding its mark.

"Kozlov!" he bellowed over the cacophony, his voice a commanding force amidst the pandemonium.

A figure detached from the shadows, the glint of medals on his uniform revealing General Kozlov's position. His eyes—cold, calculating—met Rodriguez's for a fleeting moment before the general turned and bolted.

"Rodriguez, pursuit!" Reynolds shouted, already engaging another wave of enemies.

Rodriguez broke rank, adrenaline surging as he chased Kozlov through the maze of corridors. The general was surprisingly agile, his uniform billowing behind him as he darted into a narrow passage hidden behind a sliding panel.

"Damn it," Rodriguez muttered, slamming his palm against the panel. It gave way, revealing the hidden tunnel—a dark maw waiting to swallow them whole.

"Come on," Rodriguez growled to himself, plunging into the darkness after Kozlov.

Their footsteps echoed in the tight space, a staccato rhythm that pulsed with the urgency of the chase. Rodriguez could see Kozlov's silhouette ahead, a ghostly apparition fleeing towards an uncertain freedom.

As they neared an intersection, Kozlov glanced back, his blue eyes flashing with defiance. He drew his sidearm, twisting around to fire. Rodriguez reacted instinctively, diving for cover as bullets whizzed by, chipping away at the concrete walls.

"Stop, Kozlov! It's over!" Rodriguez shouted, but his words were lost in another volley of gunfire.

Crouching low, Rodriguez returned fire, suppressing Kozlov long enough to edge forward. He needed to end this now, before Kozlov could disappear into the labyrinthine network of tunnels.

"Give it up, General," Rodriguez called out, his voice echoing ominously. "You've got nowhere to go!"

But Kozlov was a cornered beast, and cornered beasts were dangerous. As Rodriguez closed in, he knew the final confrontation was upon them—a dance with death in the bowels of the earth.

Rodriguez launched himself from the shadows, his body a missile of honed reflexes and disciplined strength. Kozlov was ready, his own combat training a dark mirror to Rodriguez's skill. They collided with the ferocity of a storm, fists and feet blurring in a lethal ballet.

The tunnel became their arena, echoes of grunts and the slap of flesh on flesh resounding off the walls. Rodriguez ducked a savage hook, countering with a swift uppercut that grazed Kozlov's chin, a promise of the strikes to follow.

"Is that all you have?" Kozlov taunted, spitting blood. His eyes held a war-hardened gleam, the burn of a man who had walked through fire and emerged unscathed.

"More than enough for you," Rodriguez shot back, driving a knee into Kozlov's midsection. Air whooshed from the General's lungs, his counter slower, but he managed to twist away, staying just out of reach.

Kozlov's hand snaked out, snagging Rodriguez's wrist, twisting. Pain shot up Rodriguez's arm, but he used the momentum, spinning into the lock and breaking free. He followed through, an elbow aiming for the temple. Kozlov dodged, barely.

"Your country will fall, Rodriguez," Kozlov hissed as they circled each other, predators seeking an advantage. "And you with it."

"Empty threats from a desperate man," Rodriguez replied, feigning left before striking right, a solid blow that rocked Kozlov's head back.

They traded blows, neither yielding, until with a guttural roar, Rodriguez feinted and landed a crushing blow to Kozlov's side. The General staggered, his form buckling, and Rodriguez seized the moment, tackling him to the ground.

On the gritty floor, they grappled, Kozlov fighting with the viciousness of a cornered animal, but Rodriguez's resolve was ironclad. With a final twist and a deft move learned in darker days, he locked Kozlov's arm behind his back and pressed his face into the dirt.

"Yield!" Rodriguez demanded, the weight of his duty anchoring him.

"Never..." Kozlov gasped, but the fight was gone from his voice.

"Then we do this the hard way," Rodriguez said, cuffing the General's wrists tightly. Standing, he hauled Kozlov to his feet, the general now a prisoner of war.

With Kozlov secured, Rodriguez keyed his comms, "Kozlov is in custody. Secure the facility and start the sweep for intel."

Acknowledgments crackled through his earpiece as teams Alpha through Delta confirmed, moving with practiced precision. They scoured rooms, confiscating documents, hard drives, anything that could shed light on the enemy's plans.

"Facility is secure, Captain," came the report. "We've got everything. Ready to exfil."

"Good work," Rodriguez replied, eyeing Kozlov with a steely gaze. "Let's get out of here."

As they moved towards the extraction point, Rodriguez felt the weight of the mission lifting. They had succeeded. They had neutralized the threat and captured one of the most dangerous men alive. And though the scars of battle would linger, the safety of countless lives was worth every drop of sweat and blood shed in these shadowed corridors.

The facility's stark lights flickered overhead as Captain Rodriguez led the way, a tight grip on Kozlov's bound arm. The echo of their boots against the cold concrete floor punctuated the silence left in the wake of chaos. Each step was a countdown to freedom, to the end of a mission that hung heavy on his shoulders.

"Move," he said curtly, his voice barely rising above a whisper, but it carried the weight of command.

Kozlov, his once imposing figure now diminished by defeat, moved with grudging compliance. Despite the restraints, there was something unnerving about the general's composure, a sense that even now, captured and cornered, he was analyzing every detail, plotting.

Behind them, teams Alpha, Bravo, and Charlie followed in formation, their movements synchronized. They carried with them the hard-won evidence of victory: drives filled with data, vials of deadly pathogens now rendered harmless, and documents that would unravel networks of terror.

Lieutenant Thompson cradled a secured case containing the neutralized bioweapon, its destructive potential sealed away forever. His eyes met Rodriguez's for a moment, an unspoken acknowledgment of the stakes they had faced.

"Watch those corners," Sergeant Ramirez called out, his gaze sweeping the shadows. Even in retreat, vigilance was their creed, the unseen enemy their constant adversary.

The distant hum of helicopter blades began to infiltrate the compound's oppressive silence, the sound growing louder with each step toward salvation. It was the beat of survival, of extraction so near Rodriguez could almost feel the wind from the rotors.

"Almost there, Captain," Major Reynolds said, his voice steady despite the adrenaline that still coursed through his veins. "Birds are spinning up."

"Roger that," Rodriguez replied, his focus unwavering as they approached the final stretch, the last doorway between them and the open air.

A sudden sharp crackle of debris underfoot caused heads to turn, hands to tighten on weapons. But it was only a stray pebble, a small reminder that even the most controlled escape was not immune to the whims of chance.

"Keep it tight," Rodriguez instructed, pushing through the door into the cool night, the stars burning overhead like silent witnesses to the night's events.

They emerged into the clearing where the extraction helicopters waited, their blades cutting through the darkness, the downdraft sending a spray of dust and leaves swirling around them.

"Load him up!" Rodriguez barked, nodding towards Kozlov. The General's blue eyes, cold and calculating, swept over the scene before him, taking in every face, every weapon. But there was no escape, not this time.

As the team secured Kozlov into the chopper, Rodriguez allowed himself one brief moment to watch the facility shrink below them, a monolith of secrets now laid bare. Then, with the roar of engines drowning out all else, he turned his gaze to the horizon, where dawn was just beginning to break.

"Mission complete," he murmured, as the first rays of sunlight pierced the darkness, heralding the end of the longest night.

CHAPTER 20

The darkness of the research facility enveloped Captain James Rodriguez like a heavy cloak as he led Team Alpha through the dimly lit corridors. The whispers of his footsteps were barely audible, even to his own ears. He glanced at the night vision goggles framing his piercing brown eyes, their green glow casting an eerie light on the walls around him.

"Keep it tight," he murmured into his mic, his voice low and steady. His team responded with soft clicks of acknowledgement, the sound making its way through the communication devices implanted into their ears.

A sudden movement caught Rodriguez's attention, and he immediately signaled for his team to halt. Through the shadows, he could make out a group of enemy guards patrolling the hallway ahead. Their weapons glinted menacingly in the scarce light.

"Bravo Two, this is Alpha One," he whispered into his mic. "We've got tangos up ahead. Preparing for silent takedown."

"Copy that, Alpha One," came the reply from Bravo Team's leader, Lieutenant Thompson. "Proceed with caution."

Rodriguez surveyed his surroundings, calculating the guards' positions and noting potential obstacles. He knew that if they didn't eliminate the threat quickly and quietly, the alarm would be raised, and their mission would be compromised. The weight of responsibility bore down on him, but he steeled himself against it.

"Alright, listen up," he said to his team. "Sergeant Mitchell, you take the one on the left. Corporal Ramirez, get the one by the door. I'll handle the other two. On my mark... Go!"

In perfect synchrony, the members of Team Alpha sprang into action. Captain Rodriguez lunged forward, his muscular frame propelled by sheer determination. With a swift, calculated strike, he took down one guard using hand-to-hand combat while simultaneously firing his suppressed weapon at another. The shots were barely audible, their quiet efficiency a testament to his years of experience.

"Targets neutralized," he reported, scanning the area for any sign of an alarm. "Proceeding with mission."

"Good work, Alpha One," Lieutenant Thompson replied. "Keep us updated on your progress."

As Captain Rodriguez continued to lead his team deeper into the research facility, he couldn't help but reflect on the stakes of this mission. The bioweapon they sought to destroy could claim countless lives if it fell into the wrong hands. It was up to them to ensure that nightmare never became a reality.

"Stay focused, everyone," he told his team, his tone laced with encouragement and camaraderie. "We're in this together. Let's make sure we all come out the other side."

With renewed determination, Team Alpha pressed onward, ever vigilant against the dangers lurking in the shadows.

Lieutenant Emily Thompson's heart pounded in her chest as she crouched behind a stack of crates, her piercing blue eyes scanning the dimly lit corridor for any sign of movement. Her mind raced with tactical calculations, assessing the best course of action to secure the main entrance of the research facility.

"Bravo Two," she whispered into her radio, "split off and provide cover fire. Bravo One, on me. We're securing the front."

"Copy that, Lieutenant," came the reply from one of her team members as they quickly moved into position.

As Team Bravo advanced, a deafening burst of gunfire erupted from the shadows. Enemy forces had been lying in wait, ready to ambush the approaching soldiers. Emily's years of training kicked in, and she instinctively dove for cover, narrowly avoiding a hail of bullets.

"Engage!" she shouted, her voice steady despite the chaos around her. She emerged from her hiding spot, her rifle raised and firing with deadly accuracy, picking off enemy combatants one by one.

"Thompson, watch your six!" yelled Sam Hayes, his strong voice cutting through the din. Hearing the warning, Emily whirled around just in time to see an enemy soldier aiming at her. Her reflexes took over, and she squeezed the trigger, dropping him before he could fire.

"Thanks, Sam," she said, her breath coming in short gasps. There was no time for fear or hesitation; every moment mattered.

"Anytime, Emily," he replied, his words colored by the bond forged during their previous missions together.

Meanwhile, Team Charlie navigated a minefield of booby traps, each member displaying impressive focus and precision. They scanned the floor for tripwires and walls for hidden explosive devices.

"Careful, Charlie Three," warned Lieutenant Hayes, spotting a barely visible wire stretched across their path. The soldiers moved with utmost caution, their expertise in disarming and bypassing traps shining through.

"Disarmed," Hayes reported, his voice a low whisper. "Pressing on."

Emily knew the importance of their mission weighed heavily on everyone's shoulders. Each team had its own obstacles to overcome, but they couldn't afford any missteps. The lives lost if the bioweapon fell into enemy hands would be unfathomable.

"Keep pushing, Bravo One," she urged her team, her determination stronger than ever. "We can't let these bastards win. We're doing this for all the people counting on us."

As Team Bravo continued their relentless firefight, Emily's thoughts briefly turned to the mountains she had climbed in her past. Though the circumstances were different, the same tenacity that had driven her to conquer those peaks now fueled her resolve to complete this mission successfully.

"Stay strong," she whispered to herself, her eyes locked on the enemy forces. "We will prevail."

Sweat dripped from Sergeant Baker's brow as Team Delta moved cautiously through the dimly lit corridor. The heavy breathing of his comrades echoed around him, all of them ready for an imminent encounter with General Kozlov's personal guard.

"Stay sharp, Delta," Captain Hawkins whispered, his voice barely audible. "We're about to face the best of the best."

As they turned a corner, the team came face-to-face with the heavily armed unit, their cold eyes meeting behind black masks. Without hesitation, they launched into a brutal close-quarters battle. Sergeant Baker felt the adrenaline coursing through his veins as he threw himself into hand-to-hand combat, his fists and feet connecting with bone.

"Take 'em down!" Captain Hawkins shouted, his pistol barking in the confined space. Simultaneously, the other team members unleashed a torrent of gunfire and explosives, the deafening cacophony punctuated by pained grunts and the sickening crunch of bodies hitting the floor.

"Die, you evil bastards!" Sergeant Baker growled through gritted teeth, delivering a crushing blow to an enemy soldier. He knew what was at stake – countless lives depended on their success, and failure was not an option.

"Delta Three, cover me!" Captain Hawkins called out, ducking behind a pillar to reload his weapon. Sergeant Baker quickly provided covering fire, his heart pounding in his chest as bullets zipped past him.

"Got your back, Cap!" he yelled, sharing a brief nod with his captain before diving back into the fray. In the heat of battle, Sergeant Baker's mind briefly wandered to his wife and daughter, their faces fueling his determination to see this mission through.

As the last of General Kozlov's guards fell, Team Delta regrouped and pressed on, their footsteps echoing in the now eerily quiet facility. They soon found themselves standing in the heart of the bioweapon's laboratory, the cold metallic hum of machinery surrounding them.

"Alright, Delta," Captain Hawkins said, his voice steady and determined. "Let's make sure this nightmare never sees the light of day."

"Roger that, Cap," Sergeant Baker replied, his heart swelling with pride for his team and their shared purpose. They moved swiftly, each member setting charges on the critical research and development equipment, ensuring the bioweapon could not be replicated.

"Charges set, Captain," Sergeant Baker confirmed, watching as the others did the same.

"Good work, Delta," Captain Hawkins praised, his eyes sweeping the room one last time before giving the order. "Let's get out of here and bring this place down."

With that, Team Delta retraced their steps, their minds racing with the knowledge that they had come one step closer to completing their mission. Sergeant Baker knew there was still a long road ahead, but he allowed himself a moment to feel the weight of their accomplishment, knowing that they had saved countless lives by preventing the bioweapon from falling into the wrong hands.

As Captain Rodriguez's boots splashed through the shallow puddles in the dimly lit corridor, his breaths came in tense, measured gasps. The silence was suddenly shattered by the sound of heavy, labored breathing and the distant echo of footsteps. General Kozlov emerged from the darkness, an eerie grin plastered on his face as he stepped into the faint light.

"Captain Rodriguez," he drawled, his voice cold and menacing. "I must commend you for making it this far. But you really should have known better than to think you could stop me."

Rodriguez clenched his jaw, his grip tightening around his weapon. "You won't get away with this, Kozlov. We've already destroyed your precious bioweapon."

"Ah, but you see, Captain," Kozlov sneered, "you underestimate my resources. I always have a contingency plan."

"Is that so?" Rodriguez asked, his heart pounding in his chest. He needed to keep Kozlov talking, try to buy some time for his team. "Your guards were no match for us. What makes you think you can stop us now?"

"Because I am not like them," Kozlov replied, his eyes narrowing dangerously. "I am the final obstacle standing between you and victory."

"Then let's settle this," Rodriguez challenged, tossing aside his weapon and raising his fists.

"Very well," Kozlov agreed, his lips twisting into a sinister smile. "Let's dance."

They circled each other warily, each man sizing up his opponent. Rodriguez knew Kozlov was a formidable foe, but he had faced countless dangers before, and he wasn't about to back down now. His team was counting on him.

Kozlov lunged first, his fist connecting with Rodriguez's side, sending a jolt of pain through him. Gritting his teeth, Rodriguez retaliated with a blow to Kozlov's jaw. The two men exchanged vicious strikes, neither giving an inch.

As they fought, Rodriguez's thoughts raced. He had to find a weakness, some way to gain the upper hand. He couldn't let his team down, not when they were so close to victory.

"Your arrogance will be your downfall, Captain," Kozlov taunted, landing another punch that sent Rodriguez stumbling back. "You cannot defeat me."

"Watch me," Rodriguez growled, wiping blood from his lip as he charged forward, his determination unwavering. This was for his country, for the lives that would be saved by stopping Kozlov's twisted plans.

The battle raged on, each man growing more exhausted but never surrendering. Rodriguez's body ached, but he refused to give in. He couldn't afford to fail now. And then, just as hope seemed to be slipping away, he saw it—a split second of vulnerability in Kozlov's defenses.

Rodriguez seized the opportunity, landing a devastating blow that sent Kozlov crashing to the ground, momentarily incapacitated. It was enough. The tide had turned, and as Rodriguez looked down at his fallen enemy, he knew that this final showdown had brought them one step closer to completing their mission.

As bullets whizzed past, Lieutenant Emily Thompson crouched behind a toppled metal cabinet, her heart pounding in her ears. She scanned the chaos around her, her sharp blue eyes darting between her comrades and the enemy forces that threatened them.

"Bravo team, suppressive fire!" she shouted into her headset, her voice steady despite the adrenaline coursing through her veins. "Hayes, cover our six!"

"Copy, Thompson," Lieutenant Samuel Hayes replied, his voice strained from the effort of providing cover fire. His recent torture had taken its toll, but his determination remained unshakable.

Emily focused on her breathing, steadying herself as she raised her sniper rifle, expertly picking off enemy soldiers who dared to venture too close to her comrades. Her fingers danced across the trigger with lethal precision, each shot finding its mark.

"Thompson, Rodriguez is still engaged with Kozlov!" Captain James Rodriguez's voice crackled through her earpiece, punctuated by the sounds of grunts and blows exchanged between the two powerful men. "We need to end this now!"

"Understood, Captain," Emily responded, her mind racing as she searched for an opening. She watched their struggle intently, waiting for the perfect moment to strike.

Kozlov laughed maniacally as he fought Rodriguez, taunting him with every blow. "Your efforts are futile, Captain! You will never defeat me!" His cold blue eyes locked onto Emily for a brief moment, sending a shiver down her spine.

"Rodriguez, keep him busy," she thought, taking aim at General Kozlov. As her hands steadied, she waited for the right moment, the exact instant when her intervention would tip the scales in their favor.

"Thompson, we can't hold them off much longer!" Hayes yelled, desperation creeping into his voice as enemy reinforcements continued to pour into the room.

"Almost there, just a few more seconds!" Emily replied, her heart pounding in her chest. Time seemed to slow as she focused her aim on Kozlov's exposed shoulder, knowing that a well-placed shot could disrupt his balance and provide Rodriguez with the opportunity he needed.

With a deep breath, she squeezed the trigger. The bullet sliced through the air, finding its mark and striking Kozlov with enough force to make him falter. Rodriguez seized the opportunity, landing a devastating blow that sent the enemy commander crumbling to the ground.

"Kozlov is down!" Emily shouted triumphantly, feeling a surge of relief wash over her. "Now's our chance, everyone move!"

"Excellent work, Thompson," Rodriguez panted, his voice filled with gratitude. "Let's finish this mission and get out of here."

As the team surged forward, Emily felt a sense of pride swell within her. They had faced countless challenges, but their unwavering resolve had brought them to the cusp of victory. And together, she knew they would complete their mission and save countless lives.

Captain Rodriguez stood over the defeated General Kozlov, his chest heaving with the exertion of their battle. He knew they had no time to waste. "Alpha, Bravo, Charlie, Delta! Regroup and move to the extraction point! We're getting out of here!" he ordered into his earpiece.

"Copy that, Captain," came the simultaneous replies, as the teams sprang into action. The facility was still swarming with enemy forces, but with their commander incapacitated, it was only a matter of time before their defenses crumbled.

"Thompson, provide cover fire while we move!" Rodriguez barked, as the team members began to push forward, picking off enemies and clearing a path toward the extraction point.

"Understood, Captain," Emily replied, her rifle at the ready. As she fired, she couldn't help but worry about what other surprises Kozlov might have in store for them. His cunning nature meant that they could never be too careful.

"Watch those corners!" Hayes shouted, as a well-aimed shot took down another enemy soldier. "Kozlov may be down, but his men won't give up without a fight."

The teams moved like a well-oiled machine, their training and experience evident in every precise movement. They covered each other's backs, efficiently eliminating any threats that stood in their way. Still, Emily couldn't shake the nagging feeling that something was amiss.

"Rodriguez," she called out, her voice tense. "We need to create a diversion. I've got a bad feeling we're walking into an ambush."

"Agreed," the captain replied, his eyes scanning their surroundings. "Set the charges; we'll detonate them when we reach the extraction point. It should buy us some time."

"Copy that." Emily quickly set to work planting explosives along their path, her fingers deftly connecting wires and securing timers. She knew that the slightest mistake could cost them their lives.

"Charges set, Captain," she reported, once her task was complete. "Ready to detonate on your command."

"Good work, Thompson. Let's move!" Rodriguez led his team through the last stretch of the facility, their boots pounding against the cold metal floor as they raced toward the extraction point.

"Captain, we're in position!" came Lieutenant Thompson's voice over the earpiece. "Ready to blow this place sky-high!"

"Detonate the charges," Rodriguez commanded, his heart racing with anticipation. "Let's give 'em a show they won't forget."

The explosion shook the entire facility, its deafening roar echoing through the halls as fire and debris filled the air. The enemy forces, caught off guard by the sudden chaos, scrambled to react, their attention drawn away from the fleeing teams.

"Go, go, go!" Rodriguez urged, as his team sprinted toward the extraction point, daring to hope that they might finally be free of Kozlov's deadly trap.

The night air swirled around them as the teams sprinted out of the facility, the smoke and fire from the explosions casting eerie shadows across their faces. Captain Rodriguez could feel the adrenaline surging through him, his senses heightened to their peak. He glanced back at Lieutenant Thompson, who nodded, her blue eyes alight with determination.

"Stay sharp," Rodriguez warned over the comms. "We've got a clear path to the rendezvous, but we're not out of the woods yet."

"Copy that, Captain," Sergeant Ramirez replied, his breaths measured as they continued running across the uneven terrain, their boots sinking into the soft earth. "Watch your footing, everyone."

Rodriguez's heart raced as he recalled the layout of the area, mentally plotting the obstacles they would need to overcome. A sudden gunfire erupted in the distance, forcing them to take cover behind a cluster of rocks. Major Reynolds peered around the corner, assessing the situation.

"Two enemy patrols ahead," he reported, his voice low and steady. "Seems like they were alerted by the explosions."

"Alright, let's do this quietly," Thompson whispered, taking out her suppressed weapon. "Ramirez, you and I will take the left flank; Reynolds and Hayes, the right. Captain, provide cover."

"Understood," Rodriguez acknowledged, watching as the team members split up, moving with precision and stealth, their training evident in every movement.

A series of muffled shots rang out, and within seconds, the enemy patrols lay motionless on the ground. The team regrouped, their hearts pounding in unison as they closed in on the extraction point.

"Captain, we're approaching a steep drop-off," Hayes alerted, his voice strained from the physical exertion. "We'll need to rappel down."

"Roger that," Rodriguez confirmed, pulling a compact grappling hook from his belt. "Secure the lines and let's get moving."

As they descended the cliff face, Rodriguez couldn't help but marvel at the sheer determination of his team. Even Hayes, who had endured unspeakable torture, showed no signs of faltering. The captain's thoughts wandered briefly to General Kozlov, the man responsible for all this pain and suffering. He clenched his jaw, vowing that justice would be served.

"Captain, there's a river up ahead," Ramirez reported, his voice cutting through Rodriguez's thoughts. "We'll need to cross it to reach the rendezvous point."

"Affirmative," Rodriguez replied, as the team pulled themselves out of the harnesses and trudged towards the river, their exhaustion beginning to show. "Let's make it quick; the extraction bird will be here soon."

The water was ice cold, biting at their skin as they waded across, careful not to lose their footing on the slippery rocks beneath the surface. As they emerged on the other side, soaked and shivering, a powerful gust of wind announced the arrival of the helicopter—its rotors slicing through the air with a deafening roar.

"Let's go, people!" Reynolds shouted, as they sprinted towards the waiting aircraft. One by one, they climbed aboard, their hands slick with sweat as they grabbed hold of the safety ropes.

"Everyone in?" Rodriguez called out, scanning the faces of his team members.

"Good to go, Captain," Thompson confirmed, her eyes meeting his with a mixture of relief and pride.

"Roger that," Rodriguez replied, signaling to the helicopter pilot to lift off. As they ascended into the night sky, leaving the burning facility and defeated enemy forces behind, he allowed himself a moment to take it all in—the mission was a success.

The helicopter's blades cut through the darkness, casting fragmented shadows on the weary faces of the team members inside. Captain Rodriguez leaned back in his seat, the tension slowly draining from his body as he allowed himself to savor their victory.

"Can't believe we pulled it off," Ramirez muttered, a rare smile crossing his face. He glanced at Rodriguez expectantly, waiting for a response.

"Neither can I, Sergeant," Rodriguez admitted, his fingers drumming against his thigh. "But we did it—we stopped that bioweapon before it could be unleashed." He couldn't help but feel a sense of pride swell within him, knowing they had saved countless lives.

"Damn right we did!" Major Reynolds chimed in, clapping Rodriguez on the shoulder. "You led us well, Captain. We're all still here because of you."

"Thank you, Major, but it took every last one of us working together to get this done," Rodriguez said, his gaze sweeping over the team. He caught Lieutenant Thompson's eye and offered a nod of gratitude. She gave a small smile in return, acknowledging his unspoken appreciation.

"Captain," Hayes spoke up, his voice barely audible over the roar of the rotors. "What about Kozlov? What's going to happen to him?"

"General Kozlov will face justice," Rodriguez replied firmly, his thoughts drifting back to their harrowing confrontation with the enemy commander. "He won't be hurting anyone else after this."

A solemn silence settled over the cabin as the weight of their actions sunk in. They had prevented a global catastrophe by the thinnest of margins, and yet, there was no time to dwell on it. Their next mission would come soon enough, another chance to protect those who couldn't protect themselves.

Just then, a burst of static erupted from the radio, followed by a familiar voice. "This is HQ—confirming your successful extraction. Well done, teams."

"Copy that, HQ," Rodriguez replied, his voice steady and confident. "Mission accomplished."

As the helicopter banked sharply, gaining altitude to avoid any potential pursuit, Rodriguez closed his eyes for a moment, allowing himself a brief respite from the relentless pace of their lives. The wind whipped through the open door, carrying with it the scent of victory and a promise of hope for the future.

"Alright, everyone," he finally said, his brown eyes reflecting the determination of a seasoned warrior. "Rest up while you can. We're going to need our strength for whatever comes next."

With that, the team members settled in, each lost in their own thoughts as they flew towards home—bruised, battered, but unbroken. They had faced the darkness together and emerged victorious, a living testament to the indomitable human spirit.

CHAPTER 21

The debriefing room was cold and sterile, the dim light casting harsh shadows on the faces of the military intelligence officers gathered around Lieutenant Samuel Hayes. Their eyes bored into him, hungry for the critical intel he held within his tortured mind.

"Let's start from the beginning, Lieutenant," one officer prompted, his voice low and urgent.

Hayes closed his eyes briefly, steeling himself to recount the experiences that had left their mark on his body and soul. He took a deep breath, feeling the tightness in his chest as memories came flooding back, clawing at his resolve.

"During my last recon mission, we discovered that the enemy is developing a new bioweapon," he began, his voice steady despite the tremor in his hands. "I managed to infiltrate their research facility, posing as a scientist."

As he spoke, the room seemed to transform before his eyes. The sterile walls faded into the dark corners of the clandestine laboratory he had infiltrated. He could almost smell the acrid odor of chemicals, hear the distant hum of machinery. But no matter how vivid the memories, Hayes refused to allow them to break him.

"The weapon they're working on... It's unlike anything we've seen before," he continued, his voice strained but resolute. "It has the potential to wipe out entire cities within hours. And they're close – very close – to completing it."

A collective shudder ran through the officers, the weight of his words sinking in like a stone cast into dark waters. They exchanged uneasy glances, fully aware of the urgency of their response.

"Where is this research facility, Lieutenant?" asked one of the officers, her voice tense with anticipation.

"Coordinates 36.1294, -115.1747," Hayes replied without hesitation. Now that he had started, the information poured forth like water from a broken dam. "It's hidden in plain sight, disguised as a civilian laboratory. But the horrors within it... They're very real."

For a moment, the room was silent, the air thick with the knowledge of the deadly threat they faced. The officers looked to one another, their expressions a mix of fear and determination. But Hayes could see it in their eyes: They would stop at nothing to prevent this bioweapon from being unleashed upon the world.

"Good work, Lieutenant," one of the officers finally said, breaking the silence. "Now we just need to act on this information – and fast."

The room seemed to shrink around them, a palpable pressure building as Lieutenant Hayes continued to divulge the chilling details of the enemy's plans. The intelligence officers leaned in closer, their pens furiously scribbling notes on the pads before them while their eyes remained locked onto Hayes, absorbing every word.

"Are there any weaknesses in the facility's security, Lieutenant?" asked a bespectacled officer, his eyes darting between Hayes and his notepad.

"Minimal," Hayes replied, exhaling slowly. "But it's not impenetrable. There's a ventilation system on the east side that could provide access. It won't be easy, but with the right team, it's doable."

The officers exchanged glances, their minds already racing with potential strategies. Hayes could sense their determination hardening like steel, forged by the urgency of their mission. He knew these men and women would stop at nothing to protect their country from the impending threat.

"Is there a timeframe we should be aware of, Lieutenant?" another officer inquired, her voice steady but laced with anxiety. "How much time do we have to act?"

"Days, if not hours," Hayes admitted, his heart heavy with the knowledge. "They are dangerously close to completing the bioweapon, and once it's ready, they will not hesitate to use it."

The tension in the room tightened like a coiled spring, the officers' resolve solidifying as the gravity of their task settled upon them. Their faces were etched with grim determination, each one quietly vowing to bring this nightmare to an end. They knew the consequences of failure were unthinkable, and so too did Hayes.

"Then we must act swiftly and decisively," declared the officer who had first broken the silence earlier. "We'll assemble our best teams and strike without warning. This bioweapon will never see the light of day."

"Agreed," chimed in the bespectacled officer. "Let's waste no time in planning our assault. We have lives to save and a nation to protect."

As their voices melded into a chorus of resolve, Hayes felt a flicker of hope ignite within him. These men and women would not falter, would not waver. They would stand against the darkness, united and unyielding.

"Thank you for everything, Lieutenant Hayes," the female officer said, reaching out to place a reassuring hand on his shoulder. "We'll take it from here."

"Thank you," Hayes replied, his voice thick with gratitude and pride. He had done his part, and now it was up to them to finish this fight. And as he looked into their eyes – those fierce, unwavering gazes – he knew that they would succeed. The future of their country depended on it.

The heavy door, its frame scarred by the passage of time, stood between the Special Forces teams and the information that could change everything. In the dimly lit room, their anxious breaths mingled with the distant hum of generators, creating an atmosphere thick with anticipation. Lieutenant Emily Thompson's blue eyes were fixed on the door, her fingers drumming an impatient rhythm against her thigh.

"Any moment now," she murmured, though whether to herself or her comrades was unclear. The other team members exchanged glances, their faces a tapestry of hope, anxiety, and readiness for the next mission.

"Hey, Thompson," called Sergeant Williams from across the room, his voice cutting through the tension. "You think Hayes made it through the debriefing all right?"

Emily hesitated for a moment before answering, her thoughts briefly drifting to the haunted look in Sam's eyes when they had rescued him. "He's strong," she replied with conviction. "If anyone can pull through this, it's him."

"Damn right," agreed Corporal Stevens, a steely determination entering her voice. "We didn't go through all that hell just for him to crack now."

"Quiet down, everyone," Captain Rodriguez interjected, his tone firm but understanding. "We'll know soon enough what happens next. Until then, let's stay focused and ready."

As they fell silent once more, Emily couldn't help but feel the weight of their shared experiences pressing down upon her. It was not simply their duty to their country that fueled their resolve, but also their bond as a team – forged in fire and tempered by adversity. They would face whatever lay ahead together, no matter the cost.

"Captain, you think we're gonna be the ones sent in?" asked Private Simmons, breaking the silence that had settled over the room.

"Wouldn't surprise me," Emily replied before Captain Rodriguez could respond. "We're the ones who got Sam out, after all."

"Right," Captain Rodriguez agreed, nodding thoughtfully. "And if it comes down to it, we'll give it everything we've got. Just like always."

"Damn straight," Emily whispered, her fingers curling into fists as an ember of determination ignited within her. The stakes had never been higher, but neither had their resolve.

"Remember," Captain Rodriguez continued, his eyes sweeping over the team, "whatever happens, we stick together. We trust each other, we support each other, and we get the job done."

A chorus of affirmations filled the room, each voice strong and resolute in the face of the unknown. Emily felt a surge of pride for her team and knew that, whatever lay beyond that door, they would face it head-on – together.

The door to the debriefing room creaked open, and Lieutenant Samuel Hayes stepped out, his face a tapestry of exhaustion interwoven with relief. The tense silence that had blanketed the waiting area shattered as the Special Forces team surged forward, their eyes trained on Hayes.

"Sam!" Emily called out, her voice a blend of concern and anticipation. She moved to his side, her piercing blue eyes scanning him for any signs of lingering pain from his ordeal. "Are you okay?"

Hayes met her gaze, his haunted eyes briefly softening. "I'm fine, Emily," he replied, his voice steady but weary. "Just glad it's over."

"Good job, Lieutenant," Captain Rodriguez said, clapping Sam on the shoulder. "We've all been waiting to hear what you learned."

As the rest of the team gathered around Hayes, each face reflecting varying degrees of hope, anxiety, and readiness, he nodded and took a deep breath. He looked at Emily and then turned his attention to Captain Rodriguez, who nodded in encouragement.

"Alright," Hayes began, his voice taking on the measured tone of one bearing vital intelligence. "The enemy is planning a large-scale attack using a bioweapon they've been developing in a hidden research facility. I managed to find out its location during my time in captivity."

"Where is it?" Private Simmons asked, his youthful face etched with determination.

"Northern Siberia," Hayes answered. "In a remote region where they've built an underground lab."

"Jesus," Simmons breathed, exchanging a glance with the others.

"Time is of the essence," Hayes continued, looking from one team member to another. "If we don't act now, the consequences could be catastrophic."

Emily felt the weight of his words settle upon her shoulders, the gravity of their mission now undeniable. Her thoughts immediately drifted to the treacherous terrain that awaited them, her mountaineering experience both an asset and a haunting reminder of the challenges they faced.

"Whatever it takes," she whispered, more to herself than anyone else. "We'll stop them."

"Damn right we will," Captain Rodriguez agreed, his dark eyes filled with resolve. "We've got your back, Sam. We're in this together."

Hayes nodded, his face displaying gratitude mixed with the shadows of his recent trauma. The room was charged with the energy of shared determination, each team member united in their commitment to protect their country from this imminent threat.

"Get some rest, Lieutenant," Emily urged softly, placing a hand on Hayes' arm. "We'll need you at your best for what's coming."

"Will do," he replied, offering a small smile that was tinged with exhaustion. "Thank you all."

As Hayes left the room, the team exchanged resolute glances, their thoughts focused on the mission ahead and the obstacles they would overcome. There was no time for hesitation or doubt – only action, unwavering courage, and the unity forged amongst them.

The dim light cast an eerie glow over the faces of the Special Forces team, gathered around Lieutenant Hayes in a tight circle. Emily Thompson's blue eyes flickered with concern as she studied Hayes' bruised visage, still haunted by his recent ordeal.

"Listen up, everyone," Hayes began, his voice low but firm. "This intel is vital. The enemy is developing a bioweapon that could cause unimaginable devastation. We're talking about millions of lives at stake if we don't act fast."

Emily felt her heart pounding in her chest, an icy thread of fear threatening to take hold. She pushed it back, focusing on Hayes' words and the mission at hand. Beside her, Captain Rodriguez clenched his fists, his knuckles turning white with tension.

"Where's the research facility?" Emily asked, her voice steady despite the turmoil roiling within her.

"Hidden deep in the mountains," Hayes replied, his gaze meeting hers with unwavering intensity. "I've given the coordinates to the intelligence officers. It'll be a treacherous climb, but that's where they're developing this weapon."

"Then that's where we're going," Emily declared, her mountaineering experience fueling her determination. Inside, she weighed the risks against the looming threat, knowing there was no room for error. Their success would be measured not only in the lives saved, but also the bonds forged amongst them as they faced the harrowing unknown.

"Time is of the essence," Hayes continued, his voice grave. "We need to dismantle their operation before it's too late."

"Understood, Lieutenant," replied Captain Rodriguez, the team following suit with murmurs of agreement. Together, they absorbed the magnitude of their task, their expressions hardening with resolve.

In the silence that followed, Emily's mind raced, already planning their route through the formidable terrain. Her thoughts were haunted by images of the potential carnage the bioweapon could unleash, fueling her determination to stop it at any cost.

"Let's gear up and move out," she said, her voice devoid of doubt. "We know what we have to do."

As the team dispersed to prepare for their mission, Emily caught Hayes' eye, offering a supportive nod. In that brief moment, they shared an understanding – a silent vow to confront the looming danger head-on, whatever the consequences.

They would not fail. Not with so much at stake.

The blinding sun glared down on the bustling city, casting a golden hue on the triumphant parade that wove its way through the throngs of cheering citizens. Captain Rodriguez stood atop a float decorated with banners and flags, his piercing brown eyes scanning the jubilant crowd as they hailed him and his team as heroes. The noise was deafening, yet he couldn't help but feel a sense of satisfaction for a job well done.

"Can you believe this?" Sergeant Ramirez shouted over the cacophony, a rare smile playing on his lips as he waved to the crowd. "After everything we've been through, it's hard to take it all in."

"Truthfully, I'm still processing," Rodriguez admitted, his voice tinged with both pride and exhaustion. Internally, he grappled with the whirlwind of emotions, from relief that the bioweapon had been destroyed to concern for the safety of his country moving forward.

"Captain!" A reporter called out to him from below, her microphone raised high. "How does it feel to be named the nation's saviors?"

"Grateful," he answered firmly, his eyes meeting hers with unwavering intensity. "But we cannot forget the sacrifices made to achieve this victory. It was a team effort, and we're honored to have played our part."

Around them, the other members of the Special Forces teams basked in the adulation, their faces reflecting a mix of exhilaration and somber remembrance. Lieutenant Thompson, standing just behind Rodriguez, smiled warmly at the ecstatic crowd, her blue eyes shimmering with unshed tears as she thought about those who hadn't made it back.

"Emily," Rodriguez said softly, leaning closer so only she could hear him amidst the clamor. "You did an incredible job out there. We wouldn't have made it without you."

"Thank you, James," she replied, her eyes meeting his with genuine appreciation. "But like you said, it was a team effort. We all played our part."

As the parade continued through the city streets, Rodriguez allowed himself a moment of introspection. He knew the fight wasn't over; there would always be new threats to face and missions to undertake.

But for now, he took solace in the fact that they had succeeded in averting disaster and saving countless lives.

"Captain," Major Reynolds interjected, his voice steady despite the surrounding chaos. "I just wanted to say it's been an honor serving with you."

"Likewise, David," Rodriguez responded sincerely, clapping him on the shoulder. "We've come a long way together, and I couldn't have asked for a better team."

As the float turned onto the final stretch of the parade route, Colonel Vasquez stepped forward, her sharp brown eyes alight with pride. "This is only the beginning, my friends," she declared, her tone inspiring confidence. "Let the world know that we will always be ready to defend our country, no matter the cost."

The cheers grew louder, and Rodriguez found himself swelling with renewed determination. Together, they had faced the unimaginable and emerged victorious. And as long as they stood united, there was nothing they couldn't conquer.

"Here's to us, and to the future," Emily whispered, her gaze locked on the horizon. "May we always rise to the challenge."

"Agreed," Rodriguez nodded, his heart filled with both humility and resolve. "Together, we are unstoppable."

The sun dipped low in the horizon, casting long shadows over the makeshift stage where the Special Forces teams stood, medals gleaming on their uniforms. Captain James Rodriguez looked out at the sea of faces gathered before them – the families they had saved, the citizens whose lives would continue undisturbed thanks to their efforts. He felt a swell of pride for his team and the sacrifices they'd made, but his mind was never far from the challenges that still lay ahead.

"Captain Rodriguez," a reporter called out, thrusting a microphone towards him. "What's next for your team after this incredible victory?"

Rodriguez met her gaze evenly, aware that every word carried weight. "We're grateful for the recognition, but our work is far from done," he replied, his voice firm and resolute. "Our focus remains on ensuring the safety of our nation and its people. We'll continue to train, adapt, and face any threats that come our way."

The crowd erupted in applause, and Rodriguez couldn't help but feel moved by their support. Turning to his team, he saw similar emotions reflected in their eyes. Lieutenant Emily Thompson stood tall, her posture radiating strength despite the lingering shadows of past missions. Sergeant Miguel Ramirez, ever stoic, gave a solemn nod from his place beside her.

"None of us do this for the glory or recognition," Emily said quietly, catching Rodriguez's eye. "But it does remind us why we fight – for these people, and the future they deserve."

"Couldn't have said it better myself," Rodriguez agreed, his thoughts drifting to the bonds they'd forged under fire. They were more than just a team; they were family, bound together by shared experiences and an unshakable dedication to their cause.

As the ceremony drew to a close, Major David Reynolds stepped forward, his piercing blue eyes locking onto each of his teammates in turn. "I've served alongside many in my time, but never have I been prouder than when fighting with all of you," he declared, his voice heavy with emotion. "We've faced the unimaginable together, and we've prevailed. Let's carry that strength with us into every mission, every challenge that lies ahead."

"Here, here!" Lieutenant Samuel Hayes agreed, clapping Reynolds on the shoulder. The ordeal he had endured still haunted him, but his determination to continue serving was now stronger than ever. "Let's make this victory just one of many."

"United we stand," Rodriguez said solemnly, his heart swelling with pride and conviction. "And together, we'll keep our nation safe, no matter what comes our way."

As the sun finally vanished beneath the horizon, casting the world into twilight, the team stood shoulder to shoulder, their expressions resolute. They were more than heroes; they were protectors, guardians of a future worth fighting for. And as long as they drew breath, they would face each new challenge head-on, united by unbreakable bonds and a shared purpose.

As the last echoes of applause faded into silence, Captain James Rodriguez's mind was already racing forward, his thoughts focused on their next mission. The weighty responsibility of leading his team into the unknown once more pressed down on him, but he knew they were up for the challenge.

"Alright, everyone," Rodriguez said, clapping his hands together to catch the attention of his teammates. "The celebration's over. It's time to get back to work."

Lieutenant Emily Thompson nodded in agreement, her blue eyes hardening with determination. "We've got a job to do, and we'll see it through to the end." She glanced at her comrades, her gaze unwavering. "No matter what it takes."

"Damn right," Sergeant Miguel Ramirez chimed in, his lean frame tensing with anticipation. He clenched his fists, his knuckles whitening under the pressure. "We've come this far. We won't let anything stand in our way now."

As they gathered around the briefing table, files and photographs scattered across its surface, Rodriguez couldn't help but feel a surge of pride in his team. They had been through hell and back, yet their resolve had never faltered. Together, they would face whatever dangers lay ahead – and they would triumph.

"Listen up," Major David Reynolds said, his voice steady and assured as he addressed the team. "Our intel indicates that the bioweapon is being developed in a remote research facility. We need to move fast and hit them hard before they can unleash this horror upon the world."

"Time is of the essence," Lieutenant Samuel Hayes added, his recent ordeal only serving to strengthen his commitment to the mission. "Every moment we delay puts more lives at risk."

As Rodriguez's eyes scanned the map before him, he couldn't shake the sense of urgency that gripped his chest. This was it. This was the moment they had been preparing for, the culmination of their efforts. Failure was not an option.

"Alright, team," he said, his voice carrying a steely resolve. "We've got our target. We know what's at stake. Let's make sure we put an end to this threat once and for all."

"Sir, yes sir!" came the resounding response, each member of the team standing tall and proud, their expressions reflecting both hope and determination.

As they huddled together, reviewing maps and discussing strategies, Rodriguez knew deep down that they were ready. The bond between them was stronger than ever, forged through shared experiences and an unshakable dedication to their cause.

"Remember," he reminded them, locking eyes with each in turn, "we're a team. We watch each other's backs, and we get this done – together."

"United we stand," Thompson echoed, her gaze unwavering as she met Rodriguez's stare.

"Divided we fall," Reynolds added, his words heavy with conviction.

"Let's do this," Ramirez said, his face set in an expression of fierce determination.

"Time to make history," Hayes agreed, his haunted eyes betraying no hint of fear or hesitation.

With renewed vigor, the team dispersed, each member moving swiftly to gather their gear and prepare for the mission ahead. As Rodriguez watched them, his heart swelled with pride and admiration. They were more than just soldiers; they were heroes, bound by a common purpose and a fierce loyalty to one another.

"Alright, let's move out," Rodriguez commanded, his voice ringing with authority.

And without a moment's hesitation, the team filed out of the room, their resolve unwavering and their determination to destroy the bioweapon stronger than ever.

CHAPTER 22

The sun pierced through the haze as the military transport plane's ramp lowered, casting a warm glow on the tarmac. Captain James Rodriguez was the first to descend, his eyes narrowing to adjust to the harsh daylight. He breathed in deeply, detecting the familiar scent of their homeland that lingered in the air - a mix of earth, diesel, and the faint aroma of local cuisine from nearby food stalls.

"Welcome home, sir," one of the crew members saluted as Rodriguez stepped off the ramp, his polished boots hitting the ground with an authoritative thud.

"Thank you, soldier," he replied, nodding briefly before turning to watch his team exit the aircraft.

As each member stepped onto the tarmac, their faces softened ever so slightly, the signs of exhaustion and tension momentarily replaced by relief. For Rodriguez, it was an unspoken reminder of the bond they shared, forged through adversity and countless harrowing missions.

"Look who's here to greet us, Captain," Sergeant Moreno said, nodding towards a small group of family members and loved ones waiting just beyond the runway. Their faces were etched with anticipation, tears threatening to spill over as they caught sight of the returning heroes.

"Let's go meet them," Rodriguez said, a rare smile gracing his lips. His heart swelled with pride for leading these brave men and women back home safely. The weight of their sacrifices still hung heavily on his mind, but he knew this reunion would offer a brief respite.

"Sir, yes, sir!" the team responded in unison, following their leader as they approached their emotional welcome party.

"Mommy!" a little girl cried out from the crowd, sprinting towards Sergeant Moreno with arms outstretched. Her tiny legs pumped furiously, closing the distance between them as fast as her small frame could manage.

"Hey there, little lightning bolt!" Moreno scooped her up in his arms, the joy in his voice unmistakable.

"Welcome back, brother," a woman embraced her sibling tightly, whispering words of gratitude that were barely audible amidst the heartfelt greetings.

"Captain, my family's right over there," Private Johnson said, her eyes shimmering with emotion. "I can't thank you enough for bringing us all home."

"Johnson, it was an honor to serve with you," Rodriguez replied earnestly, clapping her on the shoulder. "Now go enjoy this moment with your family."

"Thank you, sir." She nodded and rushed towards her waiting loved ones, the warmth of their embrace enveloping her like a protective shield.

As the team members reunited with their families, Captain Rodriguez took a moment to observe the scene, allowing himself to bask in the warmth of their happiness. The weight of their mission still lingered, but for now, he knew they had earned this brief respite from the dangers they faced together. And as the sun continued to break through the haze, the light seemed to symbolize the hope that always followed even the darkest of times.

The sun's rays danced on the tarmac, heatwaves rippling through the air like an invisible tide. Captain Rodriguez's breath hitched as his wife came into view, her face a mix of relief and joy. He could see the gleam in her eyes even from this distance, and it felt as though an anchor had been lifted from his chest.

"James!" she called out, her voice barely audible over the hum of the aircraft engines behind him. As they closed the gap between them, he marveled at how surreal this moment felt. The world around him blurred into insignificance as he wrapped his arms around her, their shared heartbeat drowning out all other sounds.

"God, I've missed you," Rodriguez whispered into her hair, his voice thick with emotion. His mind flickered to the mission's weight, but he pushed that aside for now.

"Me too, so much." She pulled back just enough to look him in the eye. "I'm so proud of you, James."

"Thank you, love," he replied, feeling a surge of warmth fill him. "It was one hell of a mission. But we made it, and we're home."

Around them, the team members were reuniting with their loved ones. Their voices were filled with equal parts exhaustion and gratitude, their smiles betraying the relief of survival.

"Captain Rodriguez," Corporal Thompson approached, a broad grin on his face. His mother stood beside him, tears streaming down her cheeks. "I'd like you to meet my mom."

"Ma'am," Rodriguez said, extending his hand. "I'm honored to meet you. Your son is an incredible soldier."

"Thank you, Captain," she managed to choke out, clasping his hand tightly. "Thank you for bringing him home."

"Mom, the captain kept us focused during those tough moments," Thompson added, pride evident in his voice.

"Family is what got us through," Rodriguez said, giving a small nod. "We fought to return to our loved ones."

"Your family must be so proud of you too, Captain," Thompson's mother said as she wiped her tears.

"Rodriguez!" Sergeant Mitchell shouted, his arms around his wife and daughter. "Come join us for a photo!"

"Be right there, Mitch!" he called back before gently extricating himself from his wife's embrace. "Let me introduce you to the team."

"Of course," she agreed, linking her arm with his. Together, they walked towards their brothers-in-arms, feeling the camaraderie that had been forged in the fires of adversity.

"Alright, everyone, squeeze in!" Mitchell's wife instructed, holding up her phone for the photo. With laughter and good-natured jostling, the soldiers arranged themselves alongside their families, their smiles bright and genuine.

"Welcome home!" she yelled, snapping the picture.

"Welcome home," Rodriguez echoed in his thoughts, allowing himself to savor this brief moment of peace before the weight of the mission returned. But for now, surrounded by love and support, he knew they could face whatever challenges lay ahead.

Through the bustling airport, Captain Rodriguez led his team and their families, his stride steady as his eyes scanned the surroundings. He had always been vigilant, a trait that had kept him alive through countless missions. But today, it was not just his life that he felt responsible for – every member of his team and their loved ones were under his watchful gaze.

"Captain," Mitchell whispered, standing close to Rodriguez's side. "Looks like we've got some reporters waiting up ahead."

Rodriguez glanced over and saw a group of cameras and microphones, the journalists behind them eagerly awaiting the chance to capture their first reactions and stories. He squared his shoulders and turned to address his team.

"Listen up, everyone. Reporters are waiting for us. It's your choice if you want to give an interview or not, but remember: our priority is getting home to our loved ones and finding some peace," he said, his voice firm yet understanding.

"Copy that, sir," Thompson replied, adjusting his grip on his daughter's hand.

"Let's keep moving," Rodriguez added, gesturing for the team to continue onward.

As they approached the reporters, the cameras began to flash, the journalists calling out questions to the team members, their voices eager and insistent. The soldiers remained stoic, their military uniforms still pristine despite the long journey home.

"Captain Rodriguez, can you tell us about your mission?" one reporter asked, thrusting her microphone toward him.

"Sorry, ma'am, no comment," he responded politely, guiding his wife past the throng of reporters.

"Specialist Thompson, how does it feel to be back with your family?" another journalist inquired, turning his attention to Thompson.

"Feels like I'm finally home," Thompson answered, smiling down at his daughter before firmly adding, "Excuse us, please." He guided his family away from the prying eyes and invasive questions, seeking solace in their embrace.

Rodriguez watched as his team members politely declined the interviews, their focus on reuniting with their loved ones and finding a moment of peace. He couldn't help but feel a swell of pride for the men and women who had stood by him through the most harrowing mission of their lives. They were more than just soldiers; they were family.

"Captain!" a voice called out from behind them. Rodriguez turned to see Colonel Vasquez approaching, her eyes shining with gratitude. "I wanted to congratulate you and your team on your successful mission."

"Thank you, ma'am," he replied, saluting her out of habit. "It wouldn't have been possible without the support and skill of my team."

"Your humility does you credit, Captain," she said, nodding her approval. "Now go enjoy some well-deserved rest with your family."

"Roger that, ma'am," Rodriguez responded, allowing himself a small smile. As they continued toward the exit, he felt the weight of responsibility lift ever so slightly from his shoulders. For now, it was time to focus on the people who mattered most.

A whirlwind of dust whipped up by the military transport vehicles swirled around Captain Rodriguez and his team. He squinted into the wind, shielding his eyes with one hand as he motioned for the others to board. The sight of the powerful Humvees brought forth a surge of adrenaline, a familiar sensation he had learned to embrace throughout his career.

"Alright, let's move it, soldiers!" Captain Rodriguez barked, clapping a firm hand on the shoulder of the nearest team member. "We've got debriefing and medical check-ups waiting for us back at base."

"Copy that, sir," replied one of the soldiers, who had just reunited with his wife and son. Together, they climbed into the vehicle, their faces etched with a mixture of exhaustion and relief.

As Rodriguez settled into his seat, the engine roared to life, drowning out the cacophony of the airport. He stared out the window, watching the familiar landscape of his home country blur past. Though the mission was over, its weight still bore down upon him like an invisible yoke.

"Captain Rodriguez, are you alright?" a voice asked, snapping him out of his reverie. Turning toward the source, he saw the concerned expression of Sergeant Thompson, a trusted confidante and invaluable member of his team.

"Nothing a little rest won't fix," Rodriguez replied, attempting a reassuring smile. "We'll be fine once we get through this debriefing."

"Understood, sir," Thompson nodded, accepting the explanation without further probing.

Upon arriving at the base, the team members were immediately escorted to the infirmary, where a team of medical personnel stood ready to examine their injuries and provide necessary treatment. The sterile smell of antiseptic filled Rodriguez's nostrils as he stepped inside, bringing back memories of previous missions and the wounds they had sustained.

"Captain, if you could just have a seat here," said a nurse, gesturing to an examination table. "We'll get started right away."

"Thank you," he replied, his voice betraying a hint of weariness. As the nurse began her assessment, Rodriguez couldn't help but let his thoughts drift to his family waiting at home. He longed for their warmth and comfort, a balm to soothe the scars left by the mission.

"Looks like your injuries are mostly superficial, Captain," the nurse announced, her tone professional yet empathetic. "Just some cuts and bruises, but we'll make sure they're cleaned and dressed properly."

"Appreciate it," Rodriguez responded, nodding his thanks as she applied a bandage to a particularly deep gash on his forearm.

"Alright, sir. You're all set," she said, stepping back with a smile. "Make sure you take it easy for a while and give those injuries some time to heal."

"Will do," he assured her, swinging his legs off the table and standing up. His body still ached from the ordeal, but he felt a renewed sense of purpose. They had survived, accomplished their mission, and now it was time to focus on healing – physically and emotionally.

With that thought in mind, Captain James Rodriguez led his team out of the infirmary, ready to face whatever challenges awaited them next.

Captain Rodriguez leaned against the cool metal wall, watching his team members huddled together as they waited their turn for medical attention. Their faces, bruised and dirt-streaked, still managed to carry expressions of relief and camaraderie. The air was filled with the faint rumble of aircraft engines nearby, but the sound seemed distant, swallowed by the stories being shared among the group.

"Hey Cap," Specialist Thompson called out, a grin spreading across his face despite the bandages on his cheek. "Remember when you had to wrestle that guard in the control room?"

A wave of laughter swept through the team, and Rodriguez couldn't help but chuckle, feeling the tension in his muscles ease slightly. "Yeah, I do," he replied, recalling the adrenaline-fueled struggle. "I wasn't sure who was going to win that fight for a moment."

"Bet that guy didn't know what hit him," Sergeant Davis chimed in, a glint of pride in her eyes. "You're one hell of a fighter, Captain."

Rodriguez's thoughts wandered to the moments leading up to that confrontation, the lives that were saved because of their actions. He let himself feel the weight of those memories, knowing it was a part of who he was – a soldier fighting for something greater than himself.

As the team continued sharing recollections, Rodriguez's phone buzzed in his pocket, snapping him back to the present. Pulling it out, he saw Colonel Vasquez's name flashing on the screen. Stepping away from the group, he pressed the phone to his ear, "Captain Rodriguez speaking."

"Captain, it's Colonel Vasquez," her voice was crisp and clear, cutting through the background noise. "I just wanted to congratulate you and your team on an outstanding mission. You've done your country proud, and we are all grateful for your service."

"Thank you, Colonel," Rodriguez replied, feeling a rush of pride and gratitude. "My team was instrumental in our success. I couldn't have asked for a better group of soldiers to fight alongside."

"Your leadership is a testament to that, Captain," Colonel Vasquez said, the warmth in her voice evident. "Take care of your team, and make sure you all get some well-deserved rest. We'll debrief when you're ready."

"Understood, Colonel. Thank you again." With a final nod, Rodriguez hung up the phone and returned to his team.

"Everything alright, sir?" asked Lieutenant Mitchell, concern etched on his face.

"Better than alright," Rodriguez answered, clapping Mitchell on the shoulder. "Colonel Vasquez congratulated us on our mission. We've made our country proud."

The news seemed to bolster the spirits of the already exhausted group, and smiles spread across their faces as they continued swapping stories, each one a reminder of the strength they found in each other during the darkest moments of their mission.

"Alright, team," Rodriguez finally announced, feeling the weight of responsibility settle back onto his shoulders. "Let's finish up here and then get some rest. Tomorrow, we start rebuilding and preparing for whatever comes next."

He knew the road ahead wouldn't be easy, but as he looked at the faces of his team, their camaraderie shining through the exhaustion and pain, he felt a surge of confidence. Together, they had faced incredible odds and emerged victorious – and whatever challenges awaited them, they would face them as one.

"Roger that, Captain," they chorused, their voices filled with determination and resolve. And as Rodriguez led them out of the waiting area, he knew they were more than just a team – they were a family, bound together by shared experiences and a commitment to protect their home, no matter the cost.

The sun dipped below the horizon, casting an array of vibrant oranges and reds across the sky. Captain Rodriguez looked out the window as his team filed out of the medical facility, their faces weary but relieved. The weight of their mission still hung heavy in the air, yet there was a sense of hope that pulsed through the group.

"Take it easy, Mitchell," Rodriguez advised, seeing the young soldier wince as he adjusted the sling around his arm. "You'll be back to full strength in no time."

"Thanks, Cap. I intend to," Mitchell replied with a grin before joining the others.

With the last of his team members leaving the room, Rodriguez found himself alone with his thoughts. He leaned against the windowsill, his eyes taking in the fading sunlight while his mind replayed moments from the harrowing mission they had just completed.

"Was it worth it?" he asked himself, images of fallen comrades flashing through his mind. His heart clenched at the thought of the sacrifices made, and he wondered if the cost had been too high.

"Captain Rodriguez," a familiar voice pulled him from his introspection. It was Lieutenant Harding, her own injuries freshly bandaged. "We're all set for some well-deserved rest. Are you alright?"

Rodriguez blinked, forcing a smile onto his face. "Yes, of course. Just... reflecting on everything."

"Understandable," she nodded, pausing for a moment before continuing. "Sir, I just wanted to say – thank you. You led us through hell and back, and we wouldn't have made it without you."

"Thank you, Lieutenant," he replied, touched by her words. "But it's not just my leadership; it's the resilience and dedication of this entire team. We got through this together."

"Absolutely, sir," she agreed, a small smile playing on her lips. "But you're the glue that holds us together. We trust you with our lives."

"Your faith in me means more than I can express," Rodriguez admitted, his voice heavy with emotion. "Now go get some rest, Harding. You deserve it."

"Roger that, Captain," she said, giving him a respectful nod before leaving the room.

As the door clicked shut behind her, Rodriguez turned back to the window. The sun had disappeared completely now, leaving the world in twilight. He took a deep breath, feeling the weight of responsibility settle once more on his shoulders.

"Whatever comes next," he whispered into the gathering darkness, "we'll face it together."

And with that resolute vow, Captain Rodriguez left the room to join his team members, ready to guide them through the challenges ahead and to honor the sacrifices they had all made.

The sun cast long shadows as Captain Rodriguez stood at the entrance of the military base, his team gathered around him. They had been granted leave, and the world outside beckoned with a newfound allure. He took a deep breath, filling his lungs with the crisp air that smelled of freedom.

"Alright, everyone," he addressed his team in a solemn tone, capturing their attention. "You've all earned your time off. Take care of yourselves, spend time with your loved ones, and remember – we'll always have each other's backs."

"Roger that, Captain," replied Lieutenant Harding, her eyes gleaming with gratitude. The others nodded in agreement, their faces reflecting a mix of exhaustion and anticipation for the days ahead.

"Dismissed," Rodriguez ordered, watching as they dispersed in different directions. As they did so, he couldn't help but feel an overwhelming pride in his team, and a renewed appreciation for life.

"Captain," called out Sergeant Thompson, walking over to Rodriguez with a slight limp – a lingering reminder of their recent mission. "Mind if I catch a ride with you? My place isn't too far from yours."

"Of course, Sergeant," he agreed, clapping Thompson on the back. "Let's go home."

As they drove through familiar streets, Rodriguez noticed every detail with heightened senses – the vibrant flowers blooming in neighborhood gardens, the laughter of children playing in the park, and the scent of freshly cut grass. It was a stark contrast to the high-stakes missions they had just left behind, and he felt a sense of gratitude wash over him.

Upon arriving at his house, Captain Rodriguez stepped out of the car and took a moment to appreciate the simple beauty of his home – the red brick facade, the well-tended lawn, and the porch swing where he'd spent countless evenings with his spouse. Inhaling deeply, he could almost taste the comfort of the routine that awaited him within.

"See you around, Captain," Thompson said, his voice weary but relieved. "Take care of yourself."

"Same to you, Sergeant," Rodriguez replied, watching as Thompson continued down the street to his own home.

As Captain Rodriguez stepped through the front door, he was enveloped by the familiar scent of home-cooked meals and the distant hum of a television somewhere inside. He felt a strange mix of emotions – relief, joy, and a lingering sense of responsibility for those who had not returned. But for now, he was home, and he would cherish every moment.

"James!" called out his spouse's warm voice from the kitchen, followed by the sound of hurried footsteps.

"Hey," he managed to say before being wrapped in a tight embrace, tears streaming down both their faces. As they stood there, tangled in each other's arms, Captain Rodriguez knew that no matter what challenges lay ahead, he would confront them head-on, with the unwavering support of his loved ones and the unbreakable bond he shared with his team.

Lieutenant Emily Thompson stood in her childhood bedroom, the late afternoon sun casting a warm glow through the open window. The walls were adorned with medals and certificates from her days as a star athlete, a testament to her fierce determination and discipline. She breathed in deeply, savoring the familiar scent of lavender and the faintest hint of her mother's perfume.

"Emmy, how are you feeling?" her mother asked, entering the room with a tray of tea and cookies.

"Better now that I'm home, Mom," Emily replied, forcing a smile. "It's good to be back."

"Your father and I are so proud of you," her mother said, tears filling her eyes as she sat on the edge of the bed. "We were so worried, but we never doubted your strength."

Emily took her mother's hand, squeezing it gently. "Thanks, Mom. Your support means everything to me."

Across town, Sergeant Miguel Ramirez found solace in his family's embrace, their laughter ringing through the air as they shared stories and memories over a home-cooked meal. His eyes flickered between his wife and children, a warmth spreading through him that he hadn't felt since before the mission.

"Tell us more about your team, Miguel," his wife, Rosa, prompted, her dark eyes filled with curiosity and concern.

Ramirez hesitated for a moment, considering what stories he could share without burdening them with the weight of their experiences. "Well," he began, "Captain Rodriguez is an incredible leader. We all trust him with our lives."

"Sounds like you've made some lifelong friends, then," Rosa said, smiling at him.

As the sun dipped below the horizon, Lieutenant Samuel Hayes sat on the porch of his family's farmhouse, his gaze fixed on the distant mountains that had once seemed so unattainable. He listened to the crickets singing their twilight symphony, their music transporting him back to simpler times.

"Sam," his sister, Hannah, said softly as she joined him on the porch steps. "I can't imagine what you've been through, but I want you to know that we're here for you, always."

"Thanks, Han," he replied, his voice cracking with emotion. "It's good to be home."

"Promise me one thing," Hannah said, looking into his eyes with a fierce determination. "Promise me that you'll let us help you heal."

"I promise," he whispered, and in the golden light of the setting sun, the weight of their mission seemed to lift ever so slightly as they found solace in the warmth of their relationships and the beauty of life's simplest moments.

CHAPTER 23

Captain James Rodriguez stood in the dimly lit armory, his piercing brown eyes scanning the room as his team meticulously geared up around him. The click-clack of magazines locking into place echoed through the air, punctuated by the low murmurs and grunts of his comrades. Tall and muscular, he moved with a fluid grace that belied his size, his cropped dark hair casting a shadow on his furrowed brow.

"Check your gear twice, people," Rodriguez barked, his voice authoritative yet laced with camaraderie. "We don't need any surprises when we're in the lion's den."

The soldiers exchanged determined glances, their faces a mixture of focus and resolve. They knew the stakes couldn't be higher; they had a chance to eliminate an unprecedented threat to national security.

"Captain," called out Sergeant Thompson, a longtime friend and confidant, "what's the intel on this new mission?"

Rodriguez strode over, clasping Thompson's shoulder firmly. "The enemy's most secure research facility," he said, his voice steady and even. "Our mission is to infiltrate it and destroy their bioweapon before it can be unleashed on the world."

A hushed silence fell over the room as the gravity of their task sank in. Each soldier understood the magnitude of their responsibility, and the consequences of failure were too dire to entertain.

"Are we clear on our objectives?" Rodriguez asked, his eyes sweeping across the faces of his team, seeking confirmation of their commitment.

"Sir, yes, sir!" came the chorus of resolute replies.

"Good," Rodriguez nodded, satisfied. "Stay sharp, stay focused, and trust in your training. We've faced tough odds before, but we always come out on top. This time will be no different."

As he watched his team members strapping on their body armor and checking their weapons one last time, Rodriguez allowed himself a moment of introspection. He knew that every mission carried the weight of lives lost, and the memories of fallen comrades haunted him. But the same unyielding commitment to safeguard national security pushed him forward, the unwavering resolve that had earned him the respect of his team and superiors alike.

"Captain," Thompson said, breaking into his thoughts, "we've got your back. Whatever it takes, we'll get this done."

Rodriguez locked eyes with his sergeant, his gaze steady and resolute. "I know you will," he replied solemnly, the shared history between them unspoken yet palpable. "Now let's move out."

With their weapons at the ready and determination etched upon their faces, Captain Rodriguez and his team set forth on a mission that could change the course of history. Their objective was clear: infiltrate the enemy stronghold, destroy the bioweapon, and return home as heroes. Failure, as always, was not an option.

The fluorescent lights in the briefing room flickered overhead, casting an eerie glow on the faces of Captain Rodriguez and his team as they filed in. Colonel Maria Vasquez stood at the front, a laser pointer in hand, her sharp brown eyes scanning each soldier with practiced scrutiny. They'd been through hell together, but there was no time for sentimentality; the stakes were too high.

"Listen up," she began, her voice calm yet commanding. "We've received intel on the enemy's most secure research facility. It houses a bioweapon that could cause catastrophic damage if unleashed. Our mission is to infiltrate the facility, destroy the weapon, and get out alive." Her gaze hardened, leaving no doubt as to the gravity of their task. "Failure is not an option."

Rodriguez felt a shiver run down his spine, but he met the colonel's gaze with unwavering determination. He knew his team would follow him into the depths of hell if necessary, and he would do everything in his power to bring them back safely.

Colonel Vasquez turned her attention to the screen behind her, revealing satellite images of the research facility. "This place is a fortress, heavily guarded and under constant surveillance," she explained, pointing out the various security checkpoints and defense systems. "However, we've identified several weak points in their defenses that we can exploit. We'll split into three teams, each with a specific objective."

As she outlined the plan, Rodriguez focused intently on every detail. He mentally reviewed the strengths and weaknesses of each member of his team, strategizing how best to utilize their skills. There was no room for error or hesitation.

"Remember," Colonel Vasquez concluded, "the enemy will show us no mercy, so we must be relentless in our pursuit. Trust your instincts, watch each other's backs, and complete the mission. Dismissed."

The teams dispersed, the tension in the air palpable. Rodriguez watched as his soldiers went through last-minute equipment checks and whispered reassurances to one another. He could see the nerves in their hands as they gripped their weapons tighter, but also the steely resolve that shone in their eyes.

"Captain," Thompson murmured, sidling up beside him. "I know it's not my place to say, but... be careful out there, alright?"

Rodriguez clapped a hand on his sergeant's shoulder, offering a tight smile. "You too, Thompson. We'll get this done."

As they made their final preparations, Rodriguez couldn't shake the nagging feeling that something was amiss. But he pushed the thought aside, focusing instead on the mission at hand. They'd faced impossible odds before, and they'd do it again. For their country, for their comrades, and for the countless lives that hung in the balance.

With a deep breath, Captain Rodriguez and his team braced themselves for the dangerous mission ahead, steeling their minds and bodies for the trials to come. Failure was not an option, and they would face whatever challenges awaited them with courage and determination.

The roaring engines of the helicopters and transport vehicles cut through the silence of the night, casting long shadows across the faces of Captain Rodriguez and his team as they prepared to depart. The scent of fuel hung heavy in the air, a harsh reminder of the dangerous mission that lay ahead. Rodriguez took stock of his soldiers, each face etched with determination and focus, their eyes locked on the horizon.

"Alright, everyone!" he called over the din of the engines. "This is it! Stay sharp, stick to the plan, and we'll make it out of this alive!"

Lieutenant Thompson nodded firmly, her blonde hair whipping around her face in the wind. "You heard the Captain, let's move out!" she shouted, gesturing for her team to follow her into one of the helicopters.

Rodriguez watched as Major Reynolds and Sergeant Ramirez led their respective teams towards the waiting transport vehicles. Their movements were swift and precise, betraying no hint of hesitation or doubt. As Lieutenant Hayes boarded the helicopter alongside Rodriguez, the haunted look in his eyes did little to hide his fierce determination.

"Captain," Hayes said, gripping Rodriguez's arm briefly. "We can do this. We have to."

"Damn right, we can," Rodriguez replied, clapping him on the back before boarding the helicopter. "And we will."

As the helicopters and transport vehicles surged forward, the soldiers exchanged tense glances, their fingers twitching on triggers and their minds racing with thoughts of the challenges to come. They were a united front, each individual driven by their duty, loyalty, and an unyielding commitment to protect their country from the deadly bioweapon that threatened countless lives.

Hours later, under the cover of darkness, the teams arrived at the enemy research facility. From a distance, they could see the heavily guarded perimeter, with watchtowers looming like silent sentinels and spotlights sweeping across the dark landscape. The very air seemed charged with danger, and each soldier felt the weight of their mission pressing down upon them.

"Captain Rodriguez," whispered Ramirez through the comms, his voice barely audible over the rustling of leaves as they navigated the treacherous terrain. "We've got eyes on the target. Two guards patrolling the eastern entrance, another pair by the western gate."

"Copy that, Sergeant," Rodriguez replied, his own voice equally hushed. "Proceed with caution, and remember: stealth is our ally tonight. We can't afford to be detected."

As they inched closer to the research facility, Rodriguez could feel the adrenaline coursing through his veins, sharpening his senses and steeling his resolve. Every muscle in his body was coiled like a spring, ready to leap into action at a moment's notice.

"Alright, team," he muttered under his breath, knowing that the lives of millions hung in the balance. "Let's do what we came here for."

With those words, Captain Rodriguez led his team forward, each step bringing them closer to danger, but also closer to victory. And as they vanished into the shadows, they knew that there was no turning back.

"Split up and proceed as planned," Captain Rodriguez whispered into his earpiece, his eyes scanning the dimly lit interior of the research facility. The teams, now inside the compound, moved like shadows, their determination evident in every silent step they took.

"Roger that, Captain," Lieutenant Thompson's voice crackled through the comms, her tone calm but focused. She led her team down a narrow corridor, her keen intellect analyzing each security measure they encountered. With nimble fingers, she disabled a keypad lock, granting them access to a restricted area.

"Emily," Rodriguez thought, impressed by her proficiency, "always knows how to get the job done."

Meanwhile, Sergeant Ramirez and his team crept along an air vent, their breathing shallow in the confined space. Ramirez, with his extensive desert warfare experience, was no stranger to navigating treacherous terrain. He signaled his team to halt, peering through the vent's grate at two guards below, unaware of their presence.

"Samuels, on my mark," Ramirez whispered, his dark brown eyes never leaving the guards. "Three, two, one...now!" In perfect synchrony, they dropped from the vent, swiftly neutralizing the guards before they could react.

"Situation under control, Captain," Ramirez reported, his voice steady.

"Good work, Sergeant," Rodriguez replied, feeling a swell of pride for his skilled team members.

Major Reynolds, with his covert operative expertise, guided his own team through the labyrinthine facility. His sharp blue eyes scanned every corner, his mind working overtime to predict potential dangers. They came across a security checkpoint, where a cluster of armed guards stood watch.

"Stay low and follow my lead," Reynolds murmured. His team nodded, their trust in him absolute. He crept forward, expertly using cover and timing to slip past the guards undetected.

"Captain Rodriguez," Reynolds' voice came through the comms, "checkpoint cleared. Proceeding to the next objective."

"Copy that, Major," Rodriguez acknowledged, his muscles tense as he led his own team deeper into the facility.

"Emily, Miguel, David," Rodriguez thought, mentally assessing their progress. "We must stay focused and remain undetected."

Suddenly, an intense firefight erupted in a nearby hallway. Thompson's team had been ambushed. Rodriguez tensed, every nerve screaming for him to rush to their aid. But he knew they needed to stick to the plan.

"Thompson, we're pinned down," one of her team members called out.

"Stay calm," she ordered, her mind racing to find a solution. "Cover me, I'm going for that control panel."

"Roger, Lieutenant," came the reply, as her teammates provided cover fire.

"Captain," Thompson's voice was strained but determined, "we've got this. Keep moving."

"Understood," Rodriguez replied, his heart pounding in his chest. He trusted her capabilities, but couldn't shake the concern for her safety. "Stay safe, Emily," he thought, pushing forward with renewed determination. The mission depended on them all.

The sound of heavy boots echoed through the dimly-lit corridor as Captain James Rodriguez and his team made their way deeper into the enemy's research facility. Beads of sweat formed on his forehead as he gripped his weapon, his senses heightened by the tension in the air.

"Captain," Lieutenant Emily Thompson's voice crackled through the comms, "we've reached the central command center. Initiating system shutdown."

"Copy that, Lieutenant," Rodriguez replied, his focus unwavering. He knew they had to act fast, or all their efforts would be for naught.

Suddenly, a shrill alarm pierced the silence, causing his heart to race. The facility was now on high alert, and enemy forces would soon converge upon them. Ramirez cursed under his breath, having inadvertently triggered the alarm while attempting to disable a security camera.

"Everyone, regroup at the rendezvous point!" Major David Reynolds ordered, his voice calm yet urgent. "We'll have to fight our way out."

"Roger that," Rodriguez acknowledged, his determined gaze meeting those of his teammates. They knew what lay ahead - a gauntlet of heavily armed guards - but they also understood the stakes. Failure was not an option.

As they rushed towards the rendezvous point, waves of enemy forces emerged from every corner, their weapons blazing. Rodriguez led the charge, expertly taking down one guard after another with lethal precision. His mind raced, calculating their next move even as bullets whizzed past them.

"Emily, how's it going with the system shutdown?" he asked, ducking behind cover and returning fire.

"Almost there, Captain," Thompson responded, her fingers flying over the control panel. "Just need a few more seconds."

"Make it quick," Rodriguez urged, feeling the relentless pressure of the advancing enemy forces. He could see the strain on his team's faces, but their determination never wavered.

"Got it!" Thompson exclaimed, the facility's lights flickering as she disabled the power grid. "The bioweapon is now vulnerable."

"Good work, Lieutenant," Rodriguez praised, his heart swelling with pride. "Now let's finish this."

With renewed resolve, the teams pushed forward, eliminating all resistance in their path. The deafening roar of gunfire filled the air, but the soldiers' focus never wavered. Inch by inch, they fought their way towards the heart of the research facility, where the deadly bioweapon awaited.

"Captain, we've reached the containment chamber," Reynolds reported, his voice hoarse from the intensity of the battle. "Setting charges now."

"Copy that," Rodriguez responded, gunning down another enemy soldier. "Prepare for extraction."

As the last charge was set, the teams made a desperate final push towards the exit, cutting down wave after wave of enemy forces. They knew that every second mattered, and their relentless determination shone through as they fought their way to freedom.

"Charges set, Captain," Reynolds confirmed, breathing heavily. "We're ready to blow this place to hell."

"Roger that, Major," Rodriguez replied, his gaze sweeping across the battlefield one last time. "Let's get out of here."

"Three... two... one..." The countdown echoed in his ears as he sprinted towards the exit, his teammates at his side. With a thunderous explosion, the research facility crumbled behind them, the deadly bioweapon destroyed once and for all.

"Mission accomplished," Rodriguez whispered, his voice barely audible above the chaos around him. The weight of their success heavy on his shoulders, he couldn't help but feel a rush of relief and gratitude for the brave men and women who had stood by his side. They had done the impossible, and their actions would echo throughout history.

The containment chamber loomed before them, a hulking mass of steel and glass that housed the deadly bioweapon. Captain Rodriguez could feel his heart pounding in his chest as they approached, knowing that they were just moments away from either victory or oblivion.

"Reynolds, set the charges," he ordered, his voice steady despite the adrenaline coursing through his veins. "We've got three minutes to get out of here."

"Roger that, Captain," Reynolds replied, working quickly and efficiently to attach the explosives to the chamber's weak points.

"Captain, we've got company!" shouted Vasquez, his eyes widening at the sight of the approaching enemy forces, led by none other than General Viktor Kozlov himself.

"Everyone, get ready for a fight!" Rodriguez barked, his eyes locked on Kozlov's cold blue gaze. This was it – the final showdown.

"Rodriguez," Kozlov sneered, his voice dripping with disdain. "I'm impressed you made it this far. But your luck has run out."

"Time will tell, General. I wouldn't underestimate us," Rodriguez retorted, gripping his rifle tightly.

"Enough talk," Kozlov snarled, raising his weapon. "Kill them all!"

"Charges set, Captain!" Reynolds shouted over the gunfire, his hands now free to help fend off the enemy onslaught.

"Good work, now let's get out of here!" Rodriguez commanded, firing at the waves of enemy soldiers trying to block their escape.

"Two minutes left!" Reynolds warned, his eyes darting back and forth between the timer and the relentless assault.

As they fought their way through the corridors, every step felt like an eternity. Each bullet fired, every fallen enemy soldier, brought them closer to their goal, but also to the ticking clock that threatened to turn the entire facility into a fiery tomb.

"Captain, Kozlov's on our tail!" Vasquez shouted, his voice tense and urgent.

"Keep moving!" Rodriguez ordered, trying to ignore the fear that threatened to paralyze him. "We can't let him stop us!"

"Thirty seconds!" Reynolds yelled, his voice strained as they neared the exit.

"Almost there!" Rodriguez reassured his team, his eyes locked on the rapidly approaching exit door.

Just as they were about to make their escape, Kozlov appeared in front of them, blocking their path with a twisted grin.

"Going somewhere?" he taunted, leveling his weapon at Rodriguez's chest.

"Damn it," Rodriguez cursed inwardly, knowing they couldn't afford any more delays. He took a deep breath, focusing all his strength and determination into this final confrontation. "If you want to stop us, you'll have to go through me."

"Always happy to oblige," Kozlov sneered, pulling the trigger.

"NOW!" Rodriguez roared, his team launching themselves at Kozlov with deadly precision. The intensity of their teamwork caught Kozlov off guard, allowing Rodriguez to disarm him and deliver a crushing blow to his skull.

"Five seconds! GO!" Rodriguez screamed, shoving Kozlov's unconscious body aside as they sprinted for the exit.

As they burst through the doors and into the night, the facility exploded behind them, sending a massive fireball into the sky. They had done it – the bioweapon was destroyed, and General Kozlov was defeated.

"Mission accomplished," Rodriguez whispered, his heart still racing from their narrow escape. Emotions swirled within him - relief, pride, and determination to continue fighting for their country. Together, they had faced the most dangerous mission of their lives and emerged victorious.

The thundering blast of the exploding research facility filled the air, casting an ominous red glow on the faces of Captain Rodriguez and his team as they sprinted from the collapsing structure. The ground shook beneath their feet, fragments of debris raining down around them like a deadly hailstorm. Rodriguez could feel the heat of the explosion singeing the hairs on the back of his neck, urging him to push himself faster, harder.

"Keep moving!" he barked, desperation lacing his voice. He could see the exit up ahead, a narrow sliver of hope amid the chaos and destruction. The countdown clock in his head was ticking down to zero, each passing second a reminder that there would be no second chances here.

"Captain, look out!" Specialist Martinez cried out, sweeping Rodriguez's legs out from under him just as a large chunk of concrete crashed down where he had been standing moments ago. The sudden impact left him gasping for breath, but he didn't have time to waste on pain.

"Thanks," Rodriguez muttered, hauling himself back to his feet with Martinez's help. With one last burst of speed, the team dove through the exit, leaving the fiery hellstorm behind them.

As they collapsed on the ground outside the facility, panting and covered in sweat, dirt, and blood, Rodriguez took a moment to assess the condition of his team. Specialist Thompson was clutching her side, a dark stain spreading across her uniform from a wound she had sustained during the firefight with Kozlov. Corporal Diaz was helping her, his own face bruised and battered – but alive.

"Is everyone okay?" Rodriguez asked, his voice hoarse from smoke and exhaustion.

"Could be worse, sir," Thompson replied through gritted teeth, trying to hide the pain radiating through her body. "We did it, right?"

Rodriguez nodded, gazing at the smoldering ruins of the facility. "We did it," he confirmed, relief washing over him like a tidal wave. But as he surveyed his battered and bruised team, he knew that their victory had come at a cost – one they would all carry with them for the rest of their lives.

"Kozlov?" Diaz inquired, his eyes flicking back to the entrance they had just escaped from.

"Down," Rodriguez said grimly. "But let's not celebrate just yet. We've got wounded to tend to, and we need to get out of here before reinforcements arrive."

"Copy that," Martinez agreed, already moving to help Thompson to her feet. The once-proud research facility was now nothing more than a smoldering pile of rubble, but the danger wasn't over yet. They were still deep in enemy territory, and every second they lingered was another second their enemies had to regroup and retaliate.

As they helped each other to their feet and began the long trek back to their extraction point, Rodriguez couldn't help but reflect on the mission they had just completed. The bioweapon was destroyed, and a dangerous threat had been neutralized – but at what cost? What kind of world awaited them when they returned home?

"Let's move out," he commanded, pushing aside his doubts and focusing on the task at hand. They had survived against all odds, and now it was time to return to friendly soil and prepare for whatever challenges lay ahead.

The sun crept over the horizon, casting a warm glow on the weary soldiers as they trudged away from the charred remains of the research facility. The adrenaline that had fueled their desperate escape now began to dissipate, leaving behind only exhaustion and the aches of injuries sustained in battle.

"Damn, I could use a vacation," Diaz muttered between labored breaths, his voice laced with fatigue.

"Where would you even go?" Martinez asked, his attempt at humor evident despite the pain etched on his face.

"Somewhere with a beach and no bioweapons," Diaz replied, eliciting a weak chuckle from the others.

Captain Rodriguez glanced around at his team, each member bearing the physical and emotional scars of their mission. He knew that despite their victory, the gravity of their actions weighed heavily on them all. They had destroyed a deadly weapon, but how many more lurked in the shadows?

"Listen up," Rodriguez said, gathering their attention. "We did what we came here to do. That bioweapon is gone, and we've put a serious dent in our enemy's plans. But there's still work to be done."

"Work we'll do together, sir," Lieutenant Thompson interjected, her eyes reflecting a quiet determination despite her injuries.

"Damn right," Sergeant Ramirez agreed, nodding his head in solidarity.

"Remember," Major Reynolds added, his voice steady and reassuring, "we're a team. We've got each other's backs, no matter what comes next."

Rodriguez allowed himself a small smile, grateful for the unwavering loyalty and dedication of his comrades. As they continued their journey back to friendly soil, he found solace in the thought that they would face whatever challenges lay ahead united in their commitment to protecting their country.

"Let's keep moving," he ordered, his mind already turning to future missions and potential threats. "We'll rest and regroup once we're safely home."

"Copy that, Captain," Lieutenant Hayes responded, his voice steady despite the lingering shadows of his recent ordeal.

As the sun rose higher in the sky, casting its golden light on the battered but unbroken team, their resolve to continue serving their country and defending it from future dangers grew stronger with each step. They had accomplished the impossible and would carry that victory, along with the lessons learned and memories forged, into battles yet to come.

CHAPTER 24

Captain James Rodriguez sat alone in a dimly lit room, the flickering shadows casting an eerie glow on his weary face. The weight of their recent mission bore down on him like a crushing burden, causing him to clench his fists so tightly that his knuckles turned white. His mind raced through memories of the battles fought and sacrifices made – moments that now haunted him.

"Sir?" Lieutenant Emily Thompson's voice pierced through his thoughts as she stood in the doorway, her eyes filled with concern. "Are you alright?"

"Come in, Emily," he said, releasing his grip and rubbing his temples.

As she took a seat opposite him, Captain Rodriguez couldn't help but remember a pivotal moment during their mission when they had shared a rare, heartfelt conversation amidst the chaos of war.

"Remember that night on the mountain ridge, Emily? When we talked about our fears and hopes for the future?" he asked, his voice tinged with melancholy.

Lieutenant Thompson nodded, her piercing blue eyes clouding over. "How could I forget, sir? It was the first time we let our guard down and really opened up to each other."

"Everyone thinks I'm this unbreakable force," Captain Rodriguez confided, his voice barely a whisper. "But that night, I felt vulnerable. And I think you did too."

Emily's lips quivered as she nodded, conceding to his words. "I've never been more scared in my life, sir. But at the same time, talking to you gave me hope. Hope that maybe we could make it out alive... and make a difference."

"Even in the midst of horror, there's always hope," Captain Rodriguez murmured, his brown eyes brimming with emotion. "We may not be able to control the outcome of every battle, but we can choose how we face them – together."

"Always together, sir." Emily reached across the small table, her hand brushing against his. "We've come so far, and we'll continue to fight for our future – no matter what it takes."

"Indeed," he agreed, his voice firm and resolute. "For all those who have fallen, and for all those who still stand beside us. We owe it to them – and to ourselves."

As they sat in silence, the weight of their shared memories and unspoken fears hung heavy in the air. Yet beneath the shadows of war, a deep connection had been forged – one that would endure through the darkest days and into the uncertain future. Together, they would face whatever challenges lay ahead, steadfast in their duty and unwavering in their belief in each other.

The sun dipped low in the sky, casting long shadows across the quiet courtyard. Lieutenant Emily Thompson sat alone on a worn wooden bench, her piercing blue eyes fixed on the horizon. A gentle breeze played with her blonde hair as she traced her fingers over the jagged scars crisscrossing her arm – each one a testament to the battles they had fought and the sacrifices that had been made.

"Hey, Em," Samuel Hayes called out softly, approaching her from behind. "You alright?"

She looked up at him, her expression somber. "Just... remembering."

"Me too." He sat down beside her, his own gaze distant. "We lost some good people out there."

Emily nodded, swallowing hard. "I know. I can't help but wonder if we could have done more to save them."

"War has its price," Sam said gently, placing a reassuring hand on her shoulder. "We did our best, Emily. We can't save everyone."

"I know," she whispered, her voice cracking. "But it doesn't make it hurt any less."

As their thoughts turned to the fallen, Sergeant Miguel Ramirez sought solace within the hallowed walls of a small chapel. The muted glow of flickering candles cast ethereal shadows upon his tanned face, his dark brown eyes closed in prayer. His shoulders sagged under the weight of responsibility he bore for his team – every life lost was another burden upon his heart.

"Forgive me, Father," he murmured, his hands clasped tightly together. "For all the lives I couldn't save, and for all the sins I have committed in the name of duty."

"God knows your heart, my son," came a soft voice from behind him. Startled, Miguel looked up to see an elderly priest standing by the door. "He knows the burden you carry."

"Does He?" Miguel asked, his voice strained. "Sometimes, I wonder if He's even listening."

"God is always listening," the priest replied, a gentle smile gracing his wrinkled face. "It's up to us to find the strength to go on, in spite of our pain."

"Thank you, Father," Miguel said, his eyes filling with renewed determination. "I will do my best to honor the memory of those who have fallen, and to lead my team through whatever battles may come."

"May God be with you, Sergeant Ramirez," the priest whispered, making the sign of the cross as the soldier stood and left the chapel.

As Emily and Sam sat together on the bench, their shared sorrow slowly giving way to quiet resolve, Miguel rejoined them, his posture strong and unwavering. The sun sank below the horizon, bathing them in twilight's embrace, but they knew that this darkness would not last forever.

"Tomorrow," Emily whispered, her voice filled with determination, "we'll pick up the pieces and keep moving forward."

"Always forward," Sam agreed, squeezing her shoulder gently.

"Juntos," Miguel added, his voice steady and sure. "We'll face whatever comes, together."

Major Reynolds stood on the edge of a cliff, the ocean sprawling out before him like an endless expanse of blue. The wind whipped through his hair as he gazed out at the horizon, his fists clenched tightly at his sides. Memories of battles fought and lives saved surged through him, fueling the determination that burned within. He knew, more than ever, that his unwavering commitment to his duty was what drove him forward.

"Major Reynolds," Captain Rodriguez's voice cut through the roaring wind. "It's time."

"Of course, Captain," David replied, turning to face James. They exchanged a brief nod, acknowledging the weight of responsibility they both carried.

In the small meeting room, the team gathered around a makeshift table, their faces etched with exhaustion and determination. Captain Rodriguez looked at each of them in turn, his piercing brown eyes filled with gratitude for their sacrifices and unbreakable trust in one another.

"Alright, everyone," James began, his voice firm yet laced with camaraderie. "We've been through hell and back together. We faced challenges that would've broken lesser teams, but we came out stronger. I want to give each of you the floor to share your thoughts and reflections on this mission."

As the team members spoke, they shared stories of courage under fire, the bonds they'd formed and the lessons they'd learned. Major

Reynolds listened intently, his eyes flicking between his teammates as they recounted their experiences.

"During the firefight in the warehouse," Emily started, "I was pinned down and running low on ammo. Sam risked his life to get me the supplies I needed." She turned to Sam with gratitude in her eyes. "Thank you."

"Anytime, Thompson," Sam replied, a small smile tugging at the corner of his mouth.

Miguel chimed in, his voice steady but tinged with emotion. "There were moments when I felt overwhelmed by the weight of my decisions, but I found strength in knowing I had all of you by my side."

"Juntos," James agreed, his gaze sweeping across the room. "Together, we are more than just a team. We're a family."

As the meeting continued, the air in the room seemed to lighten, as if the shared reflections helped to ease the burden they each carried. It was evident that their camaraderie and trust in one another were unshakeable.

"Before we conclude," Captain Rodriguez said, his voice filled with pride, "I want you all to know how honored I am to lead this team. Each of you has shown exceptional bravery and dedication in the face of adversity. Remember, our duty is greater than any one of us, and the impact we have on the world is immeasurable."

The team members exchanged nods and small smiles, their spirits lifted by their shared reflections and renewed sense of purpose. They stood together, ready to face whatever challenges lay ahead, knowing that they had each other's backs.

"Dismissed," James commanded, watching as his team left the room, heads held high, determination shining in their eyes. He knew they were prepared for the next mission, together and stronger than ever before.

As Lieutenant Thompson replayed the recent mission in her mind, her thoughts drifted to a moment when their team faced insurmountable odds. They had been pinned down by enemy gunfire, their backs against a crumbling stone wall. The air was thick with dust and the acrid smell of burnt gunpowder.

"Emily!" Lieutenant Hayes shouted over the deafening sound of battle. "I need you on the roof! Take out that sniper!"

Thompson's heart raced as she nodded, knowing the immense responsibility placed upon her shoulders. She mustered every ounce of her strength and agility, scaling the wall with practiced precision. Her fingers found purchase on jagged rocks, adrenaline coursing through her veins.

"Cover me!" she yelled, hoisting herself onto the roof. Her piercing blue eyes scanned the horizon, quickly locating the enemy sniper. With unwavering focus, she took aim and fired, eliminating the threat in one swift motion.

"Sniper down!" she called out, relief washing over her as her team advanced forward, their determination unyielding in the face of danger.

Back in the meeting room, Thompson hesitated before finally opening up about her fears and doubts. "I never thought I'd say this, but there were times during the mission when I wasn't sure if I could go on," she admitted, her voice barely more than a whisper.

"Emily," Captain Rodriguez reassured her, "we all have moments of doubt, but what sets us apart is our ability to push past those fears and continue moving forward. You've proven time and again that you're a vital part of this team."

"Your resilience has always been an inspiration to us all," added Lieutenant Hayes, his words carrying the weight of their shared experiences. "You should be proud of everything you've accomplished."

Thompson felt her chest tighten with emotion as her teammates' words sunk in. She knew they were right; it was her unwavering determination and the support of her team that had carried her through their harrowing mission.

"Thank you," she said quietly, touched by their faith in her. "I wouldn't be here without all of you."

"None of us would, Emily," Captain Rodriguez replied, his eyes meeting hers with a blend of understanding and camaraderie. "We're stronger together, and there's nothing we can't face as long as we have each other's backs."

As the room filled with murmurs of agreement and quiet resolve, Thompson felt a renewed sense of purpose take root within her. They were a unit bound by trust, forged in the heat of battle and tempered by shared sacrifice. Together, they would face whatever challenges lay ahead, united and unbreakable.

The light from the setting sun streamed through the blinds, casting long shadows across the room as Sergeant Miguel Ramirez stared at his hands. The rugged lines and callouses spoke volumes about the battles he had fought, the lives saved, and the comrades lost. His dark brown eyes seemed to see beyond the confines of the room, reflecting on the emotional scars that went far deeper than those visible on his body.

"Another tough mission, huh?" Major David Reynolds sat down opposite him, his voice steady and calm as always.

Miguel nodded slowly, his gaze never leaving his hands. "Every time we go out there, it feels like we lose a little more of ourselves."

"War does that," David replied. "But what's important is that we remember why we're fighting and who we're fighting for. Our sacrifices have meaning, even if it's hard to see sometimes."

"Si," Miguel agreed, finally looking up to meet David's piercing blue eyes. "I am grateful for our team's resilience. We face so much adversity together, yet we still come back stronger each time."

David leaned back in his chair, the muscles in his arms tensing beneath his rolled-up sleeves as he crossed them over his chest. "It's not just about our physical strength, though. It's the bond we share, the trust and understanding that can only come from facing life and death together. That's what gets us through these missions."

Miguel's lips curved into a small, wistful smile. "Yes, the bond we share... It is a rare gift, one that I will always cherish."

"Which is why it's crucial that we take care of ourselves and each other," David said, leaning forward with an intensity that matched his words. "We all bear the weight of these missions in different ways. Some days are harder than others, but we must never forget that we're not alone in our struggles."

"True," Miguel sighed. "I know how easy it is to become consumed by our own pain, but when I see the strength and determination of my brothers and sisters in arms, it reminds me that we are all in this together."

They sat in silence for a moment, the shadows in the room lengthening as the sun dipped below the horizon. The unspoken promise hung heavy in the air – a commitment to support one another through every battle, every loss, and every victory.

"Come on," David said finally, standing up and extending a hand to help Miguel to his feet. "Let's go join the others. We've got more challenges ahead of us, but as long as we stand together, there's nothing we can't overcome."

Miguel clasped David's hand, feeling the strength and solidarity in their grip. With a renewed sense of purpose, he rose and followed

David out of the room, ready to face whatever lay ahead – together with his team, bound by an unbreakable bond forged in the fires of adversity.

The dim light overhead flickered, casting a somber glow over the worn faces of the team members that filled the small meeting room. Captain James Rodriguez stood at the front, his piercing brown eyes scanning the room as he took in the lingering signs of fatigue and pain etched across the faces of his comrades. He knew they had each faced their own demons during this mission, and the weight of those memories threatened to engulf them all.

"Listen up, everyone," Captain Rodriguez began, his voice strong and steady despite the exhaustion that clawed at him. "I know we've all been through hell and back. We've faced insurmountable odds, fought tooth and nail for every inch of progress, and ultimately achieved our objective."

His gaze held each of theirs in turn, ensuring they understood the gravity of his words. "But I want you all to remember something. While it's easy to focus on the losses we've suffered and the scars we bear, we must also recognize the impact our actions have had on the world. The sacrifices we've made, the lives we've saved... it all matters."

As he spoke, the room seemed to grow warmer, the shadows receding under the force of his conviction. He could see the change rippling through his team, the weight of their burdens lifting ever so slightly with each word.

"Each and every one of you has shown an unwavering dedication to our mission and to one another. It's that commitment that has brought us this far, and it's that same commitment that will carry us forward."

Captain Rodriguez paused, taking a deep breath as he locked eyes with Lieutenant Thompson. "We may be bruised, battered, and scarred, but we are not broken. So long as we stand together, there is no challenge too great, no enemy too fierce. We are a family, bound by blood, sweat, and tears - and nothing can ever break that bond."

He let his words sink in, the silence in the room pregnant with emotion. And then, slowly, as if by some unspoken signal, the team members began to nod and exchange small smiles. Their spirits were lifted, and they found solace in their shared reflections and renewed sense of purpose.

"Whatever challenges lie ahead," Captain Rodriguez continued, "we'll face them together. Side by side, we'll continue to fight for our country, our comrades, and for all those who depend on us. We owe it to ourselves, to each other, and to those who have given their lives so that we might stand here today."

With that, he offered a firm nod to his team, and one by one, they rose to their feet, determination etched into their features. They stood together, united in purpose, ready to face whatever lay ahead - knowing that they had each other's backs, come what may.

As the team filed out of the meeting room, they found themselves standing side by side in the dimly lit corridor. Their shadows, cast by the faint glow of overhead lights, stretched out before them like ethereal echoes of the bond that united them. The darkness seemed to envelop their silhouettes, but their unwavering determination shone through, casting a light that could never be extinguished.

"Alright, team," Captain Rodriguez began, his voice steady and authoritative, "we've got work to do. Time to gear up and get ready for our next mission."

"Roger that, Captain," Lieutenant Thompson replied, her piercing blue eyes reflecting the fire within her. As she clenched her fists, her thoughts turned briefly to the fallen comrades they'd left behind - but the memory of their sacrifices only fueled her resolve.

Sergeant Ramirez studied the faces of his teammates, each scar and bruise a testament to the battles they'd fought together. He knew that the weight of their losses would never truly leave them, but it was the bonds they'd forged that gave him strength. "We'll make them proud, Captain," he said quietly, his voice firm with conviction.

"Damn right we will," Major Reynolds added, his gaze steady and intense as he surveyed the horizon, already planning their approach. The wind whipped through his hair, mirroring the turbulence of his thoughts as he contemplated the challenges ahead. He knew the stakes were higher than ever before, but there was not a shred of doubt in his mind that they would rise to meet them.

"Captain," Lieutenant Hayes spoke up, his voice measured despite the haunted look in his eyes, "I'm ready to do whatever it takes. We all are."

"Good," Captain Rodriguez nodded, appreciating the steadfastness of his team. "We don't know what lies ahead, but I have faith in every single one of you. Together, there's nothing we can't overcome."

As the team began to move, their synchronized steps echoing through the otherwise silent base, they carried with them a sense of anticipation and determination. They knew that the road ahead would be treacherous, fraught with danger at every turn - but with each step, they also felt the unbreakable bond that had been forged in the fires of adversity.

"Let's do this," Captain Rodriguez said, his voice barely more than a whisper, yet it carried the weight of absolute certainty. The team responded with nods and steely gazes, knowing that no matter what lay ahead, they would face it as one.

Their shadows melded into a single inky mass on the frigid, unforgiving concrete below as they advanced, a fierce and determined army of two. The next chapter of their saga loomed ahead, rife with peril and unknown trials - but they were resolute, driven to carve out a legacy that would endure for eons to come.

About the Author

Brian Leslie is a Nationally Recognized Coercive Interrogation Expert, Commercial Fiction Writer and Best Selling Author. He is regularly retained by Federal, State, and Military Courts on high-profile murder cases throughout the United States. www.brianlesliemedia.com

Read more at https://www.brianlesliemedia.com.

TRUE
AMERICAN
PUBLISHING

About the Publisher

As a boutique book publisher, we take on only a few new authors per year. We focus on building an author's brand, thereby directing more resources towards their overall success. Authors accepted by True American Publishing become creative partners, therefore, participating in their own success.

Milton Keynes UK
Ingram Content Group UK Ltd.
UKHW040838160724
445389UK00001B/53

9 798227 518217